The Pray-ers

Novel 1, Troubles

The Pray-ers

Novel 1, Troubles

A Novel by Mark S Mirza
C: (404) 606-2322
E: mark@ctmprayer.org
W: www.ThePray-ers.com
© 2016, CTM Publishing, Inc.
850 Piedmont Ave NE #1506
Atlanta GA 30308

PREFACE

WHY WRITE THIS BOOK?

As I write this book the desired outcome is very specific and very simple. First, admittedly I want you to learn prayer. I don't just want you to learn ABOUT prayer, but I want to hear of prayer becoming who you are, how you breathe Christianity, if you will. So to reach that aim you will see much repetition by various characters in various situations, but handling the problems the same way. Secondly, and this is very important to me: I want you to enjoy yourself.

There are a few comments that need to be made first regarding some of the characters and the writing style adopted herein.

ANGELS AND DEMONS

Another issue that needs to be mentioned is the interaction in the book with angels and demons. My concern has been that the character of the demons would not be viewed ghoulishly, giving them more power than they actually have, but I did not want to jokingly have them dressed in red, with pitchforks, where they would not be taken seriously. I believe that the book reaches a healthy balance. The book will speak for itself, but I hope that you will walk away with a healthy respect for what I believe are very real demons that are constantly trying to influence us. So let me state a few things up front, to help you keep a healthy, orthodox, Christian worldview regarding these nemeses of ours:

- I am taking *great* liberty as a writer, speaking about demons and assigning characteristics to them that we have no clue about. This is being done of course, for the sole purpose of showing the victory that we already have in Christ through prayer.

- This book is not written for you to develop a focus upon demons or draw unbiblically supported conclusions about demons.

- That there is a hierarchy seems clear by certain passages in the Old and New Testaments,[1] but that a demon's "overlord" does the things that they do in this book is completely fictitious, so please, Please, PLEASE, do not make me wish I had NOT included them.

If you find yourself with an over-focus on demons, I have not implored you strongly enough above. The reality is that because of what we already have in Christ, we are already victorious.[2] Let the focus not be on outwitting demons, but rather reexamine your prayer life and let scripture direct your prayers, based on promises and truth already[3] in scripture. Scripture is clear, our struggle is not against flesh and blood[4] and our praying in this regard is from victory, which in part means we trust God's already clearly stated Word. Instead of trying to attain victory by doing battle against a demon, our role in spiritual warfare is to allow the, *already victorious Jesus* to live through us.

I hope that you notice that these characters are not focused on "besting" a demon; they are simply trusting God by faith. As you wander through this book you will see the truth of 1 John

---

[1] Daniel 10:13, Ephesians 1:21, 3:10, 6:12b
[2] Colossians 2:15
[3] *Already* is being overused here for a reason. As Christians, when we find ourselves in a spiritual battle, we often let our emotions run away with us and forget what we already have in Christ, when really, our battle-stance should be *because of* what we already have as Christians.
[4] Ephesians 6:12a

5:4, which tells us faith is that which overcomes the world. The demon is not overcome by the strength of our speaking to it.

Regarding angels, I don't want to give anything away, so again just recognize that I purposely used some liberty—okay, a lot of liberty—as a writer.

Enough of the theology lesson, please, just watch these men and women's lives in this book and have fun learning prayer.

CAPITALIZATION OF DEMON'S NAMES

Additionally, on this subject of demons, you will see that the pronouns for the demons, including satan are not capitalized. This is a personal preference of mine, the author. It is not the publisher's. They may in fact struggle with my decision. It is a very strong conviction on my part, though, and is a condition I have placed on myself even in my personal devotions for a number of years. I hope that you will not think poorly of the publisher or me for so blatantly disregarding an important writing rule.

FOOTNOTES

I did not add footnotes in an effort to turn this book into a scholarly piece of work; far from it. I want you to enjoy your reading, but there will come a time when you want to duplicate what the characters are doing or praying. When you do, I want you to have at your fingertips the scriptures or reasons why they believe what they believe[1].

---

[1] 1 Peter 3:15

AT THE BACK OF THE BOOK

There is a complete list of characters and the pronunciation of their names, in order by era, as well as a discussion on the use of references, the three eras' time frames and the *Wesley Family Prayers Book.*

DEDICATION

Finally, I'd like to dedicate this book to the members of every church where I speak. When I leave them, I promise to pray for them each Sunday. When I pray, I pray from Colossians 4:2-4: that they will be devoted to prayer, watchful, and thankful, and that periodically they will remember to pray for me, that God will open doors so that I may speak this message and speak it boldly, as I know that I should.

Enjoy,

Mark S Mirza
December 28, 2015

1

Angels & Demons

He sat slouched over on a mossy green stump of stone. He looked down in shame, and his eyes darted back and forth, looking from one demon's ugly feet to another. Shame overcame him, shame and anger!

Their meeting took place in what looked like a rundown castle. The stone floor where his eyes were facing showed scratches caused by age. The cold-looking granite, dark and slimy had few speckles of white, and every one that should be seen had lost their luster years earlier. They were hidden by dirt and grime that no one would ever wipe up. The darkness that enveloped the scene completely eclipsed any type of light, yet in the shadowy glow one could see others in the room, not clearly, of course, not at all like when one is outside in the light. No, this scene appeared more like the dense fog that comes at night and is so thick that it feels gritty.

The putrid air remained thick with smells that always seemed to linger and were never gone. If you described the smells, you would describe them as ugly. You would describe them as the smells of rot. And he would not be able to describe them at all since the smells seemed natural to him. The air, so thick that he had to take deep breaths, caused his distorted and crooked body, whose limbs normally looked like toothpicks with skin over them, to inflate to a grotesque image.

If one scanned the crowd in the room of his coworkers and put aside their appearance, one could be looking at a group of deacons, where discord ruled the meeting. The crowd could be a Wednesday night board meeting called for the whole church to attend, where one group wants to get its point across, whatever the cost. The crowd could also have been one's home, where neither Mom nor Dad willingly submitted to one another,[1] and as a result there would be much contention, in the deacon's meeting, the church meeting, the home, or in this case, where demons gathered.

Periodic puffs of foul-smelling odor rose above the crowd, and the proverbial spotlight illuminated katepa. Everyone focused upon him, sneering at him, and some were just outright laughing at him. His crooked jaw set and he seethed with anger, and at the same time, he experienced a healthy dose of fear. His anger came because his inept overlord chose to mock, lecture and threaten him. Everyone knew that the only reason joln got his position had to do with political connections. But the very real fear that katepa experienced came because he knew that at any moment joln could send him to a place in the universe that would be eternal torment before his time,[2] so katepa continued to listen meekly as joln's inflated ego acted even more arrogantly, if that were possible, than everyone but he knew he had a right to act.

A few human centuries earlier joln had become the overseer in what the humans now called North America. His fat rippled, upside down "V" body shape and style so differed from katepa's

---

[1] Ephesians 5:21
[2] Matthew 8:29

2

bones with skin on them that you would think joln had been created in a different world. While katepa clearly had defined limbs, albeit very skinny. His whole body, including his torso looked like toothpicks with skin over them. On the other hand, joln's torso and limbs were fat folds. He had a fat face that angled out from the top of a rounded head. As his face angled out, it also began to ripple, so that the folds were larger and larger in circumference as you looked down his body. As the folds went down his body they seemed to absorb his limbs. He seemed to have no limbs at all, and yet as he singled out katepa, joln took his right as an overlord, slapping his underling.

The master, satan himself, had sent a new directive, and joln singled out katepa to express this new directive's emphasis and meaning. "But to call it a new directive didn't accurately explain it either," thought katepa as he kept his head down, and this too angered him. He had been in the business of deceiving humankind for the last 6,000 years. He knew what to do. He knew his expectation. That this sloppy, ignorant, unqualified overlord leaned down, bent over him, slapped him around, and spit on him every time he emphasized a word become more and more than katepa could handle. He wanted to reach up and grab joln by his bulging rippled throat, when joln brought up katepa's Achilles heel, his past failures.

As katepa shriveled even more under the gaze of everyone else in the meeting, joln brought up Thales, the first-century nephew of Epaphras. And then, just to rub salt in the wound, joln brought up Alexander Rich, the nineteenth-century itinerant preacher in the United States.

"Two failures! Add it up, joln, you good-for-nothing blowhard. I've had two failures in the last two thousand years. With these mortals having a life span of seventy years, do you know how many successes I've had?" All of this katepa merely thought, for he would never say it out loud. He knew the expectation of this group. And the expectation would never change. Perfection, no failures, ever ... and he had failed, twice.

Others in this room had failed that many times and more. He knew that, and so did everyone else, but the rule in this putrid underworld had always been the same, "Take care of yourself and yourself only." When others were under fire from an overlord, be glad that you were not, and add to the insults as best you can. The humans called it "looking out for number one."

"Those idiots," snarled katepa to no one in particular. "Don't the humans know that looking out for number-one originated with us?"

But right now the spotlight of fumes and spittle rained down on katepa and it sickened him. Everyone got to focus on his failures.

He hated the memory of his first failure. This came at the hands of Thales, the charge given him by haodtie, the Colossae overlord, shortly after Thales moved to Colossae to be with his uncle Epaphras, who led this new church. "This failure," remembered katepa, as joln made clear to everybody else in the room just then, "shouldn't be assigned to me. Don't they remember the incredibly difficult task related to this assignment? Epaphras and Paul were traveling companions, the great apostle Paul! And to make matters even more difficult, what did Epaphras excel in? That's right he focused on and he excelled in ..." He hated to say the word or even think the word, because it devastated so much of their domain. All of his comrades hated the word. "Epaphras excelled in prayer."

Oh, he hated prayer. He hated prayer more than he hated joln, and right now katepa would risk his eternal future by tearing joln apart. He also hated, and this he could voice, the Holy One's angel, Hael, who had been there serving and ministering[1] to the Holy Enemies' saint, causing katepa to be bested by both Thales and Rich. "Blast him! BLAST him!" thought katepa.

"This moron of an overlord," continued katepa with his hatred of joln exploding. "He doesn't even know why we are scared of prayer. I've heard him. The moron! It isn't because the Holy Enemy moves. Well, okay, slightly that, the real reason is because of the way prayer moves the Christians. They end up more deeply knowing our Enemy, the Enemy! The more these Christians that pray know scripture, the better they know the Enemy, and the more faith they pray with. Oh, it's just a disaster." And then katepa remembered something that he had learned many centuries before, "Deceive the Christians into letting them know ABOUT God without intimately KNOWING God."

He became angrier and angrier with joln for being so ignorant and for being so arrogant. As katepa worked up the courage to reach out and tear joln apart, joln started to needle him about Alexander Rich.

"Another of my failures that shouldn't be considered my fault either. Rich and that rebel D. L. Moody were boyhood friends ... and then he became beloved by all those crazy Georgia Baptists, even though his roots were from the North. I had no control over what those other demon's pray-ers did. My charge preached and circuit rode during the time the Baptists, ugh, that word again ... prayed. They prayed, and their prayers worked!"

As much as he hated to admit it, joln's assessment needed no correction, katepa registered his second failure.

"Even with the great war between the states, katepa failed to bring down the slave-loving circuit rider." So joln continued to rub katepa's crooked face into his failure.

---

[1] Hebrews 1:14

But he wouldn't fail again. How could he? His latest charge, Dr. Dale, a university track coach at a secular university would be putty in his hands. "At a secular university," thought katepa. "It's not even a Christian university."

In katepa's mind and in his experience no difference existed between the secular and the Christian universities today. "Advantage katepa!" he said to himself, ignoring joln.

Droning on about katepa's ineptness, joln said, "and so he should *not* be an example to you."

Continuing to ignore joln as best he could, katepa thought about his new responsibility. He would take this charge and expose every one of his weaknesses, exploit his wifey-poo, exploit those he coached, and prove to this imbecilic overlord joln that he, katepa, would handle any challenge that their master might throw out.

He realized that there were bound to be a few challenges, of course. After all, this track coach, the so-called Dr. Dale, involved himself in a small group of men that prayed together periodically, but this group hadn't shown up on anybody's radar down here. So katepa expected this prayer group to go the way of most prayer groups ... nowhere. "They can pray their eyeballs out." katepa smiled to himself. "We will just listen and laugh."

"They are the typical prayer group, katepa. They barely register down here, so see if you can control your charge." Now joln brought his lips to within inches of katepa's ears and whispered to him. "Do you think that you can get this one right, you weasel of a demon?"

Thinking to himself, katepa said, "Of course, you selfish, lying, deceptive bungler, joln. You won't tell everyone the potential problems, will you? There are two of them, Dr. Dale is the member of a church where the pastor *is known* down here, and precisely because of that most disgusting of words, of actions ... he prays and is known as a pray-er.

"But there might be another problem," but it shouldn't be a big deal, katepa thought. "This idiot track coach is trying to take on the responsibility of mentoring young athletes in prayer." He knew that if not handled properly, his efforts could get out of hand very quickly, "Causing us major problems and the Enemy victories that should never be allowed."

But katepa knew how to fix that. He would just keep these young, inexperienced pray-ers ignorant of the Holy Enemy's Holy Book, and he'd keep them focused on the wrong motivation, so that they *never* saw answers in their prayer lives.

So long as these young people only think they know whom they're praying to, they would fail. "I don't care if they know about God; I do not want them to know their God, the Enemy, and in the USA today," katepa thought, "what these foolish Christians don't know, is how often we laugh at them. They think they know prayer, they are only ignorant and do not know what they do not know."

Yep, it would be the Seven Sons of Sceva[1] all over again. "What a great time of laughing we had during that human fiasco," thought katepa. "Those 'holy men' were simply praying nonsense, as I will deceive Dr. Dale's people to do. Who knows? Maybe it'll become the new story down here, 'The seven or eight or however many, sons of Dale' that I get to beat up and cause their prayer life to be ineffective. So many of them are already loud and powerful of voice but completely ineffective where it counts, in the spiritual realm. This'll be fun."

Turning, joln yelled, "Are you listening to me, katepa?"

It wouldn't be long before joln started cursing and swearing at him, but katepa knew the expectations that were on him. The

---

[1] Acts 19:13-16

master had decided there would be a new emphasis in two areas, so-called Christian contentment and so-called Christian salvation.

"With this charge, and in this era of withering Christianity, in this location, *no longer* the Bible Belt, I won't fail."

In fact, after he excelled, he would petition the senior demons to promote him into the overlord position over joln. "It could happen. Yes, it could happen. I will make it happen." katepa seethed with anger.

"You're going down, joln! And I, katepa, I'm gonna make it happen. You are toast, you blathering idiot."

Standing smartly at attention, in a completely different realm, Hael beamed in the light that surrounded him. The light filled him with peace and confidence. He excitedly listened to his direct supervisor because he had been given a rare opportunity. In the past, this assignment would be given almost exclusively to the archangels, Michael and Gabriel. Hael could hardly believe it, but today he had the honor of being selected by the Almighty to make actual contact with his charge.

Hael stood nine feet tall with a massive chest and a rippled gut that on earth would be called a twelve-pack, except that it would always be covered by a white robe. The only hint to the strongly built angel, if you looked close enough would be the tightly wrapped belt, a cloth sash, really, tied about his waist, and it displayed the "V" body cut that went from his broad shoulders down to his waist.

As his supervisor took a message from another part of the glorious kingdom, he stepped back from Hael for some privacy. As Hael stood there, awaiting further instructions, he daydreamed.

Hael would make personal, unmistakable, and ongoing contact with a mortal for the initial purpose of simply developing a relationship with him. "How exciting this is going to be!" Hael thought.

Typical in this realm is to never know where the relationship would go or why it would go the directions it did, but he knew, as all of the Holy One's angels knew, God took full and complete responsibility for it, making the future not his concern. "My responsibility is to be obedient, for God demonstrates time and time again who He is and that He can be trusted," acknowledged Hael. "He is the Alpha and the Omega, the Beginning and the End."[1]

Hael had been the guardian angel for Thales and Alexander Rich, and because of their obedience to whom they knew God to be, they were spiritually successful in their earthly life, regardless of whether or not katepa stuck to them to afflict them. It would be katepa that he would be guarding Dr. Dale Riley against, and while he pondered the enemy's demon, Hael didn't worry about it. He learned a long time ago to not worry about tomorrow, for tomorrow always takes care of itself, and besides, today has enough issues of its own.[2]

Hael's supervisor spoke to him again. "Hael, the rules of engagement are very specific, though. You will ONLY engage as you have permission. And when it is deemed by the Lord that He wants to allow difficulties into Dale's life, or even bring them into his life,[3] we will NOT stop them or warn Dr. Dale, okay?"

"Of course, sir," Hael replied, acknowledging this well known requirement. It had been the standard order, ever since his

---

[1] Revelation 1:8
[2] Matthew 6:34
[3] 2 Chronicles 7:13

9

promotion to guardian angel right before the New Testament earthquake[1] at Christ's death.

Furrowing his brow, Hael tilted his head a bit and, interrupted for a moment, he said, "It will probably be a bit more difficult now, though, don't you think? I mean, since I will be in actual contact with Dr. Dale, he could conceivably ask me why I didn't step in."

"True enough, Hael," came the reply. "We'll handle each instance on a case-by-case basis, but you know as well as I do, my friend, those will be the times that the Almighty uses to prepare your charge."

"Prepare him for what?" Hael asked, trying to coax a response.

Hael, whose wingspan reached eighteen feet, realized as soon as the words were out of his mouth that he had gone too far. He slowly bowed his head, his wings lifting slightly off his back and fluttered out of embarrassment.

"Hael, my good friend, you know the rules here. We obey and leave the details to our God."

"Of course. My apologies."

"None needed. The truth is, Hael, I wish I had the assignment. Blessings, big guy!"

As his supervisor went his way, Hael again took stock of his responsibilities. He knew the Word, and that it said that he would be a ministering spirit,[2] "Hael smiled. "And I'll be able to minister in a personal way that few of the humans ever know that they are experiencing.[3] Hmm," he continued, "and few of us get to experience, either."

He wanted to let out a holy shout ... but he didn't.

---

[1] Matthew 27:51m
[2] Hebrews 1:14
[3] Hebrews 13:2

2

First Century

Epaphras had just stood up from being on his knees. While he might still be young in age, he had to get up slowly for his knees hurt after being on them for so long. Of course he wouldn't admit this to anyone, but often he had to go from his knees to a chair, just to rub the top of his legs and sometimes the knees, when he had been prostrate before God. When he laid on them a long time and they were up against the hard ground is when he moved the slowest and rubbed his legs the longest. He could see why some of his older brothers and sisters preferred to pray sitting down. But, Epaphras loved to pray on his knees. He knew that scripture never dictated a person's particular body position during prayer, rather, God's interest always centered around the position of the pray-er's heart.

And today would be no exception, starting his prayers on his knees just a few feet from his writing desk Epaphras liked to move his wooden stool away from his desk and set it under the lone window in his room. Early in the afternoon, the sun would shine in onto him and when there were clouds, as there were today he often saw the rays coming through on the edges of the clouds. The rays made him feel like God's presence filled the sky, and he loved God's presence.

Today Epaphras had started on his knees letting the sun beat straight down upon his back since he prayed today in the middle of the day he said, "oh Father, I love the warmth of the sun that You provided for us. Thank You for the healing,[1] the spiritual healing that comes from those rays, hitting my back as I spend time with You. I know that the healing comes from Your presence, but oh Father, I so enjoy the beautiful picture that I get to see. Praise You, Lord."

Sitting on his bench now, his time of prayers over, Epaphras thought about his early life. He grew up in a Christian home and remembered that prayer always seemed to be something that eluded him. "Difficult to constantly do," he would say. He struggled to embrace prayer. He knew its importance, but, frankly, it bored him.

Still rubbing his knees and watching the orange glow of the setting sun he said, "Father, I remember when prayer encompassed nothing more than simply asking You about this, talking to You about that, and saying amen. My prayers were simple and then they were over. Thank You for being so patient with me and drawing me into an intimate relationship with You."

Epaphras remembered hearing people in his church talk about 'Intimacy with God' which sounded good to him, but as a fairly new Christian he didn't understand what they were talking about. "God," he would say, "I don't understand intimacy with You. It doesn't make any sense to me. Please teach me intimacy with You." He prayed this over and over again. In fact, at one point, he stopped praying for intimacy, because it seemed like God had decided to not answer this request of his.

---

[1] Malachi 4:2

The truth, he realized later, is that God *refused to speak to him* about this subject, and He hadn't spoken for over three years. Then one day, Epaphras realized that the love he had grown to have for prayer related perfectly to his desire to understand intimacy. Three plus years later, God had answered his prayer for intimacy. And when he began to relate the two, prayer and intimacy he began to see that intimacy with God had to do with his relationship to God, and that relationship supported the real basis of prayer. "Oh Lord," he would say, "You are more interested in my relationship to You. The purpose of prayer is intimacy and relationship, not, forgive me, using You as a magical talisman. No, that misses the point of prayer. You are interested in a relationship.

"Just like I cannot be intimate with anyone," he remembered thinking, "that I do not have a sincere relationship with, I cannot have intimacy with You, Lord, unless there is true relationship. Oh, I get it Lord. Please, continue to teach me about this wonderful thing called prayer. Teach me how my communication with You is critical in this relationship."

And then his prayer life changed. His focus in prayer changed from being 'Epaphras-centered' to 'God-centered.' He found that his real joy came when he simply sat in his quiet place of prayer, and just enjoyed God's company, whether they spoke or not.[1]

Now he found himself in a situation that he had been in many times before. Sitting in the quietness of where he had just prayed, rubbing his legs and thinking about his time in prayer. He might say that he meditated on his time with the Lord. Actually he still remained in prayer, technically, he supposed. And he could tell

---

[1] The inspiration for this line comes from Leonard Ravenhill who says, "I have some of the greatest times of prayer when I say nothing."

that God had started to stir something in his spirit. Epaphras would need to continue to seek the Lord.

Epaphras enjoyed this sense that he had. It caused a sense of great awe in his life, great awe and great responsibility. He knew that he would be hearing from God soon. He could tell this, because deep in his spirit an unmistakable uncomfortableness that he could not shake had settled upon him. He didn't know why, but he knew the gnawing, somewhere deep in his gut. He had an odd peace, a sure expectation ... yes, an expectation that he should seek the Lord all the more. He would continue to seek God and Epaphras knew that God would make Himself known[1] as He always did.

There had been a time early in his Christian life when he would've looked at those feelings and thought that something terrible would be on its way. But he had matured in his praying, praise the Lord. He now realized that the Lord used this way to get his attention and prepare him, usually by prompting Epaphras to spend more time reading in his parchments. This is what God would use to get him wrestling in prayer. He would read a passage, sometimes only a single sentence and then in his brain look over the words, consider them together and consider them individually. And as he "chewed-on" and laid quiet before portions of scripture Epaphras would talk to God.

"Or, more rightly Lord, You would talk to me," said Epaphras barely above a whisper.

He loved the way the Lord communicated with him. Sometimes through the old parchments, other times through impressions upon his spirit. And sometimes through something as simple as an unmistakable peace. But he had learned that critically important to prayer would be to continue to pray, even though he had already heard God's voice, for often God merely

---

[1] Jeremiah 29:13

began a conversation with Epaphras, and over time, God would mold Epaphras's heart to His plan, to God's plan.

"You are fooling yourself, you are actually demonstrating that you don't trust God Epaphras," countered haodtie. "At the very least, you are demonstrating that you doubt what God originally said," whispered haodtie, not giving up on trying to influence this man of prayer, Epaphras.

The well respected demon overlord haodtie enjoyed his peers, as best one enjoys another in this abode. Hard working, this overlord put in his time alongside his other demon comrades. Everyone liked how his mind worked and how he always had an answer, although often they had to pry his ideas out of him. No one in the underworld could figure this out, for haodtie hadn't always been this way. In fact, the change in him only recently occurred, only over the last twenty-five or so human years.

His fellow demons didn't know why he no longer spoke unless necessary. It had begun when he took a sabbatical from the Colossae area, where he had been leader for a number of centuries. Playing in one of the cities that the humans now called the Decapolis, causing his share of havoc with men's lives and otherwise staying out of trouble, a very strong, very domineering, very pushy demon blindsided him. This demon gathered up haodtie and a number of other demons and they were forced to harass a man in the area of the Gerasenes.

When haodtie would think about it, he began by smiling thinking of the incredible trouble they caused one man, and then two, and then the entire town. A few times the townspeople bound the man, both his hands and feet with chains, but through the supernatural power of these demons the man would break the chains. After that the towns people refused to try and hold him down. But then it happened. The Son of their Enemy came on the scene. How bizarre of an experience would this be for the remainder of haodtie's days. One moment he and his friends were tormenting this man, the next moment this lead demon made them all shut up and the next moment haodtie found himself in a filthy four legged pig running down a hillside into the water. As the pigs drowned haodtie saw his chance to escape back to Colossae and he did.

The scary part though came when he read the reports of this man that they had possessed. He remembered that the man asked the Son of their Enemy to let him go with them and He refused, telling him to return to his town and tell everyone what He had done for him. And he did … and that scared haodtie. He knew the Son of their Enemy had power, after all haodtie watched the Second Person of the Godhead speak the fish and birds and animals and man into existence on what would be known as day five and six of creation.[1] But not until that experience, with the pigs, did haodtie realize just how much his comrades were under the Holy Enemy's authority and sovereignty.

And then later this account had been written into their holy books[2] only to remind humans forever of the relatively simple victory Jesus had over an entire legion of them. No, haodtie saw something from a perspective he did not like. He would continue to do his job and do it to the best of his ability but he knew that when their Enemy wanted them gone, they were gone and they would have no choice but to obey. The Son of their Enemy truly is sovereign. So he would do his best to deceive Epaphras.

Epaphras saw the very same principle of God molding his heart when he would prepare his sermons for his church there at

---

[1] Genesis 1:20ff
[2] Mark 5:1-20

Colossae. He would hear from the Lord and write down what he believed he heard. And yet even though he knew he clearly heard from the Lord, the more he walked through his message, the more he wrote notes, and the more he studied Scripture, the more the Lord tweaked the message. And the message would become something far from where it started. Peace would come and intensify when he continued to pray over areas that he believed God had clearly spoken. Why? He realized that God molded men's hearts this way. He molded his own heart like this, causing Epaphras to desire what God desired. "Thank You for the reality that my life is a process, Lord, and that which You began, You will finish."[1]

He loved that about the comforting, encouraging Holy Spirit.[2] And yet he knew that so many of his brothers and sisters in Christ were ignorant about this Holy Spirit. In fact, he constantly desired to pray, as Paul said, "in the Holy Spirit." This meant that Epaphras clearly sensed the leading of the Spirit, and he prayed in concert with, in accordance with, according to, and in the power of the Holy Spirit. Effective praying came from this kind of God focused praying. His congregation demonstrated great immaturity in this part of their Christian life, and he realized that his role, among other things would, for the rest of his life, be to build their prayer foundation[3] for things in this life were only going to get worse,[4] as Paul constantly told his disciples when they traveled and he taught them.

Epaphras seemed to always get into trouble with his congregation every time he talked about whether their prayers were effective or not.

---

[1] Philippians 1:6
[2] John 14:16, and John 16:7
[3] The mission statement for Common Thread Ministries is to rebuild the foundations of prayer which comes from Psalm 11:3
[4] 2 Timothy 3:13

It seemed like he saw a phenomenon among his people that he did not like. They were saying that God hears EVERY prayer of followers of The Way. Epaphras understood this error. He knew that they were merely encouraging the weak hearted and the hurting, but in truth, since he corrected them he would get into trouble. He had to constantly explain to his folks the reality that God didn't always hear their prayers. And so he would say,

"There are circumstances under which God will NOT hear your prayers."

And then he would enumerate them.

"Please do not forget these:

- Motive, the new letter from Jesus brother says that our selfish motives keeps God from hearing our prayers[1]
- Doubt, the same letter talks about doubt when we pray instead of confidence that God IS GOING to answer[2] keeping us from answered prayer
- Unforgiveness. This is something that Jesus talked about a number of times and Mark, Peter's associate wrote it in his letter[3]
- Bad marriage relationships, this time from Peter's own lips, would hinder ones prayers[4]
- And then there were other things like stinginess[5] and Idols of the heart.[6]

"But the one that concerns me the most for you," he often told them, "is unconfessed sin. This is the one that you ignore the most." Epaphras got angry just thinking about it.

---

[1] James 4:3
[2] James 1:6-7
[3] Mark 11:25
[4] 1 Peter 3:7
[5] Proverbs 21:13
[6] Ezekiel 14:3

"You know that sometimes the anxiety you have is because of sin. The Psalmist David made that clear, twice.[1] And the son of David, Solomon wrote about sin being something that makes your prayers detestable to God.[2]

"Oh my friends," he would plead with them, "I am sure that all of you remember reading about the prophet Isaiah telling us that sin causes a barrier between us and God."[3] This congregation of his frustrated him. But not just him, his people were frustrated too.

He knew that God had given him insights into prayer, not because he deserved it but far from that. Epaphras had no clue why God used him, but He did. And he knew that he needed to, in as loving a way as he could, help encourage the brothers and sisters to be more effective at prayer and to be more effective pray-ers.

Something that he didn't find in Scripture anywhere, but he couldn't help think that it occurred, had to do with the demons that are listening to his congregations' prayers. He thought, "They are probably laughing at my congregation. Oh Father, give me wisdom[4] about how to lead my folks into a personal and intimate prayer life."

He had been thinking about those laughing demons when he saw and listened to dear Sister Hagne pray. He felt so bad for her, but as a part of his congregation he felt compelled to help her understand her praying better. And then he would get embarrassed when he tried to correct her. "Agathon, you are her husband, and my senior deacon," Epaphras had begun to think to himself lately, "Surely you see this."

---

[1] Psalm 38:18, 40:12
[2] Proverbs 28:9
[3] Isaiah 59:2
[4] James 1:5

But as he always tried to do, he corrected privately, corrected lovingly, and, hopefully, corrected humbly. And to her credit she seemed okay with that.

"Did she get it?" he thought to himself. "Will her praying change? I guess what bothers me the most, Lord, is that none of my deacons correct her, and I can only wonder Lord, if Agathon does at home. I doubt it …. Do my deacons even see her praying as a distraction that needs to be corrected, for her sake, and for the sake of the flock? I fear that she is greatly distracting them Lord. Oh Lord, give me wisdom in teaching on prayer.

"Thank You, Lord that she prays, but Father, open the spiritual eyes and ears of my congregation that when they hear her praying, their focus would be on the hope of Your Son's calling in their life. Lord, help them focus on the riches of His glory, that they have here on earth, not just when they get to heaven. And Father, in spite of Sister Hagne, let my congregation experience the greatness of Your power in them, simply because they are believers.[1] Thank You, Lord for hearing my prayer, and bringing me peace about Sister Hagne."

Sister Hagne never used to be a bother when she prayed until recently. "In fact," thought Epaphras, "These problems started when Epaphras promoted her husband to the position of senior deacon. Hmm, Lord, that's when it started, didn't it?"

What Epaphras struggled with, and what had started once Agathon became the senior deacon is that Hagne seemed to wait to pray until everyone could hear and silence filled the prayer room. She then slowly raised her voice to drown out everyone who would begin to pray around her. And then, as if she knew that she now had everyone's attention, she started to use words she never uses. She wanted to impress everyone around her, rather than simply and humbly taking the time to address God.

---

[1] Ephesians 1:18-19a

Epaphras got the feeling that she had moved from crying out to God for His will and direction and wisdom, to giving God advice about what she wanted.

"But aren't you the one, Epaphras who has told us that we often do not have because we do not ask?"[1] In a continuing defense of her prayers Sister Hagne went on, "I remember when you told us that Epaphras. You had just told us about a letter that Jesus's brother had written. I'm just praying the way that you said we should pray if we were to seek God."

Sister Hagne, well into her middle ages, past child bearing years and a plump little woman with rosy cheeks who waddled about from conversation to conversation as if she had to make sure she did not miss a conversation. Even when Epaphras had sat her down at the last house meeting her eyes were darting about, probably trying to remember which conversations she needed to invest in, all the while that he talked to her.

Epaphras chuckled pulling her attention back to him and said, "Okay, you're right Hagne." He had to agree, those were words he had used. He had been with Paul when he had the great blessing of hearing a copy of the letter written by Jesus's brother James, read by Paul.

Rubbing his knees less now, but watching just a sliver of the sun left on the horizon, Epaphras still needed to challenge Hagne, "But why? Why?" Epaphras continued to reflect upon his problem with her. "Why did she seem to understand when he told her that her prayers still needed to be predicated on God's will? Something else is in my spirit bothering me about her praying? What, Lord? What is it?

"I praise You, Lord that she understands when I tell her that Your will is preeminent, not hers, and she gets that. But there is something else Father. What is it?"

---

[1] James 4:2e

21

Dropping back to his knees he prayed simply a question, "Is it her pride Lord?"

And then after a long period of silence, where Epaphras just waited on the Lord in His presence he said, "That is it! Her pride!" Epaphras knew that he could no longer laugh at the errors in her praying but that he had to gently and lovingly deal with her...and soon.

"There is no way Epaphras, that I am giving her up." The demon overlord haodtie grumbled into Epaphras's ear.

"Father," Epaphras began, "You have clearly said that pride goes before a fall,[1] and yet, Solomon also said, and this is my concern for Hagne Lord, 'when pride comes, soon disgrace will follow.'[2] Father, I do not want to see this happen to my friends. I covenant with You, Lord, to continue praying for them. Let me not sin by ceasing to pray for them.[3]

"Father, I do not know what to do. I need wisdom about this too. Wisdom Lord and faith. Oh Father, give me the faith and the confidence to know that when I speak to my friend's wife that I am speaking what You want said and not simply what is expedient for me.

"Father, give me wisdom...

"Father, I need You...

"Father, You are sovereign...[4]

---

[1] Proverbs 16:18
[2] Proverbs 11:2
[3] 1 Samuel 12:23a
[4] Psalm 103:19

"Father, the prophet said that You use our world as a footstool, and in the very next sentence he said that You are close to the lowly.[1] I feel like the lowly one here and so I need Your closeness as I work this out with Hagne."

With that, Epaphras got off of his knees, again, and this time he looked out and the beautiful Colossae sunset had gone and darkness had settled in.

"Epaphras, I'll take every advantage of her that I can." said haodtie to no one in particular.

As the lead demon in the area that the mortals called Colossae, haodtie loved seeing the earthlings' situations. He would then analyze them and imagine how he might spiritually impact each and every one of them. Speaking into the spiritual ears of humans could be a delicate matter as he had to always apply two issues to everything he did.

First, he knew that his master, satan himself, had a directive, a plan that needed to be adhered to. But then he also needed to consider the Holy Enemy and his "latitude," if you will, that haodtie, and all of the demon hoard had to be cognizant of. And that last part really challenged haodtie, for though he didn't work for the Enemy, and really, haodtie didn't seem to care what the Enemy said. But somehow, and this frustrated him to no end, somehow, every time haodtie had a plan, the Holy Enemy seemed to already be aware of how far he would go, what the outcome would be, and that it would be used for the glory of Him, the Holy Enemy! It seemed that He used everything for the better to His so called children, whom He said He loved, and who it appeared He called for HIS purposes.[2] It frustrated him and the

---

[1] Isaiah 66:1-2
[2] Romans 8:28

entire hoard of demons. But since his experience with the pigs it seemed disturbingly frustrating to haodtie. This Holy Enemy's sovereignty knew no bounds or limitations. He shuddered when he thought of it.

And yet, while it frustrated haodtie, he gained some relief since it seemed that the people assigned to him appeared to be completely oblivious to the Holy Enemy's plans for their lives. He believed that he would lose this edge if these humans, whom he spoke deception into, ever decided to trust their God rather than to worry. This would be something that haodtie would work at exploiting. "And with Hagne, she is so insecure that she'd rather be angry and think that she is in control than trust your God Epaphras. No Epaphras, you will be the way that I destroy Paul, through you and this little so called house church."

At that thought haodtie smiled and chuckled. "Hagne will be a problem for you, Epaphras," whispered haodtie, close enough so that Epaphras's spiritual ears could pick up the words which were meant to cause fear.

Epaphras decided to stop by this week and make sure Hagne accepted his gentle rebuke. She would, he thought. Since his congregation continued to grow there were numerous problem pray-ers besides Hagne. But they were his people. Sitting on his bench now, hearing the night sounds overtake his small room he quieted his heart and tried to listen to the Lord again. Instead he heard the evening birds singing and some wild animals in the distance. Epaphras, still quiet, then heard the sounds of the city coming to life and thinking of his people who had to live in that world every day he exclaimed, "Oh Lord, how I long to see them mature in the faith.[1] I trust You Father to fill me with the

---

[1] Colossians 4:12m

knowledge of Your will, giving me all wisdom and spiritual understanding so that I walk worthy of You, especially as I correct my people, and grow in the knowledge of You."[1]

As Epaphras lit the lamp on his table he opened the parchment that currently occupied his study time. He remembered the slight uneasiness in his spirit (which he knew had nothing to do with Sister Hagne), and he trusted God to reveal to him whatever He wanted to whenever He wanted to. And then, Epaphras would know why he felt the way he did.

Trying to put the distraction behind him so that he could read he simply mouthed quietly, "Lord, why is there an uneasiness in my spirit? What are You trying to tell me?"

---

[1] Colossians 1:9b-10

3

Nineteenth Century

Early in the War Between the States, the South made sure that a parson would be assigned to each company. General Lee, a true fundamentalist in every sense of the word, believed in the fundamentals of "Holy Writ," as he liked to call the Bible. He also knew that since the Bible always did him good, and helped him as he lived his life, he would make available to every one of his troops the same blessing. As such, he required that spiritual leaders should accompany as many of his soldiers as he could get his hands on.

Brother Alexander Rich, in his mid-twenties had been an itinerant preacher in central Georgia for only a few years when the war broke out. And so, he sought God's counsel, as he always did, before he made a decision.

Often his decision making process centered around the foundation of 1 Corinthians 14:33 where Paul had made clear that God is not the author of confusion. He never ceased to be amazed that his congregation would quote that part of the verse but not the rest, "For the rest of the verse Almighty Jehovah is what keeps me trusting You to lead me. You tell me that not only are You not the author of confusion but that You are the author of peace. Praise You, Lord!"

And with that foundational comfort, he and God spent time talking about what he should do. God didn't speak to him audibly of course, but by impressions on his heart, and conformation in the Holy Book, Alexander Rich would usually have clear direction from God.

"Oh Lord, should I go back home to the North," he wondered? "I have no peace Lord, Oh I don't have any peace when I think about doing that, Lord."

Alexander Rich had grown up in Massachusetts his whole life. He had visited Georgia one summer when he turned fifteen years old, and that convinced him of the merits of the South. The South had crawled under his skin. He loved how wooded and green the entire state seemed to be. Even when the train went through the great and, later he found out, the dreadful city of Atlanta, the foliage had a lushness to it that screamed, "green trees and plants." He loved that too about where he lived in Northfield, Massachusetts. But in Georgia it felt more like a wilderness. In Northfield, the towns were too organized, too "established," too much like an English city. He realized that he had felt a draw to Georgia way before God called him to be a preacher there.

Brother Rich would reflect on his experience to move to Georgia often, and tell folks, when they were asking for direction, "Sometimes, God draws you in numerous ways to His will. The key, when you are praying for direction, is first to have no unconfessed sins in your life, and then trust God to give you no peace until you find His will."

Though he had only been an itinerant preacher for a few years, he had learned this truth, and even shared it with his younger friend Dwight, that he grew up with. His friend, who also taught God's Word, and, even though they lived hundreds of miles apart, Alex in central Georgia and his friend Dwight in Chicago, where he had just moved and served God by teaching young boys. They both were living out Proverbs 27:17: two men, acting as iron in one another's lives, sharpening one another, as well as others.

"Dwight," Alexander Rich had recently written to his friend, Dwight L. Moody, "this is why we do not move, until we have peace. Because when the storms of life come and things look like they are heading for disaster, we can always remember that God had clearly said, 'Go here,' or 'Go there.' Being obedient and submitting to God is the key Dwight.

Alexander Rich prayed before he finished his letter, and then asked his friend to pray for him, that he would make the right decision, God's decision, regarding what to do about entering the war for the decision time would soon be upon him.

Dwight had written back and his letter prompted Alexander to again get onto his knees and cry out to God for direction. His letter encouraged Rich, "Al, I never looked at this story of Jesus's disciples in this way, but go back and look up Luke 8:22-25. It is the story of Jesus calming the storm. I have always focused on the fact that Jesus slept when the disciples were worried, but look at verse 22. It is Jesus giving his men direction. And now look at Matthew 14:22, where Jesus walks on the water. Jesus commanded the disciples to get into the boat and head across water.

"Here's my point Al, the disciples were in harm's way, *precisely because* they were obedient.

"I confess Al, I cannot join the Union effort, not because I disagree with the cause, I do not. I agree with the cause, on many levels. You remember me telling you about the first time I met Abe Lincoln. You laugh at my butchering of the English language, you would not believe how the President had to skip so many words, trying to read the story of the prodigal son because he could not pronounce them. I believe, for that reason and for so many serious ones, I am on his side, but, I cannot take up arms. So, no matter what storms come my way, I have to hold to my Quaker-like beliefs and not join the Union army."

And with that word from his friend, Alexander Rich again petitioned the Lord, "Father, even with this coming war I have no doubt, when I remember Your call on my life that You called me here to these Georgians."

Alexander Rich sensed a need to pause, and meditate on that fact, the fact that God had called him to the numerous Georgian congregations.

After a few more minutes of being in silence before the Lord, he mused, "Hmm, You called me here." He now laid prostrate, desiring to hear a clear word from the Lord. Periodically he would lift his head from the ground and turn to passages in the Scripture that he felt impressed upon his heart. As he explored the Word, he kept his Bible open when he prayed. He found an old verse that had become his friend many times. 1 Corinthians 14:33 told him that God is not a God of confusion, but rather is a God of peace. When people in his flock ask him to pray for direction Alexander would say, "I'll pray for you, but you may not like the way I pray." And then he would pray, "Father, because Your Word says that You are a God of peace and not confusion, I trust You to give my friend NO PEACE whatsoever, until he finds exactly what You want him to do."

And with that reminder, he felt like his God called him to remain with his flock, wherever they may go, and whomever it may be. And so, he enlisted in the Southern Confederacy as a noncombatant chaplain, or parson. Like his friend Dwight Lyman Moody, Rich had no plans to take up arms against another human being, but he clearly felt the sense of responsibility that he had for his congregations. There, with his congregation, is where he had his peace. And so, he would stay with the males of his congregations. Wherever they went, he would accompany them as a confederate.

Shortly after he and most of his congregations joined the Southern efforts, and the company they were in moved north. There began, what would later become an infamous battle. This battle, in September of 1862, became known as The Battle of Antietam.

Before the battle, Brother Rich traveled from tent to tent encouraging the men. He had done this many times before this battle, often in the rain so he had to keep his Bible under his slicker. Brother Rich would read Scripture and pray with the men. He never ceased to be amazed at how the simple act of praying with someone would be such an encouragement. The more he thought about it, the more he remembered that the Lord's words do not return void,[1] so it made sense to him that the reading of the Word would bring encouragement. But prayer became another way to handle the Word of God. The Word, couched in prayers, brought great encouragement also, maybe more so. And what a great encouragement to the men. That always humbled him. The Lord used him, Alexander Rich, to encourage these men.

When he took the time to think about it he found himself admiring the decisions made by General Lee, including his desire to be a godly man in the midst of a war. While he may not have agreed with the war effort, from General Lee's perspective, he couldn't fault the man's character. It even carried forward in this engagement, the Battle of Antietam, when before the

---

[1] Isaiah 55:11

engagement started General Lee insisted upon asking the Marylanders to join the Confederates.

But when they refused the conflict began. To call this a bloody conflict would not be accurate enough. To call it awful would not be big enough. Alexander Rich saw men blown apart when a cannon ball would hit them, or blown partially apart when the explosive would land near them. Brother Rich couldn't pray for the all of the wounded, because the sheer number of casualties were so overwhelming. There were too many on the battle field. He had to get up off of his knees and help triage as many of them as he could. He couldn't believe the incredible waste in war.

The first day, the losses were 12,000 casualties for the Union and 13,000 casualties for the Confederates. Later Brother Rich learned that that the overall casualties exceeded 27,000.

Here, at the Battle of Antietam, Brother Rich and his few remaining company were captured. The battle became infamous for more deaths suffered in that one day, than the deaths of all Americans in the American Revolution, War of 1812, and the Mexican-American War combined.

As the prisoners were being moved into the stockade, a young teenage Union corporal, not ten years his junior asked, "Parson, what is your name and where is your gun?"

"Son, I don't have a gun. God did not call me to fire upon another human being. Instead, He called me to serve Him as these men's pastor." replied Brother Alexander Rich.

As he listened to the pastor's response, he cocked his head, frowned, and said, "You don't sound like you're from the South Parson. Where are you from?"

"Well, by the sound of your accent, I can tell you that I'm from just a little bit south of you. Massachusetts, actually."

"Then why are you with these rebels, parson?"

"Because this is where God has called me, son."

And with that, Alexander Rich entered into captivity with his southern parishioners. He earned the admiration and trust of every captured Confederate imprisoned with him. Even the Union soldiers recognized that the parson could leave their prison anytime. He gained their admiration by staying with those God had called him to shepherd.

Things were very difficult during many of those days, "But this war wouldn't last forever," he thought. "And when it is over I'll return to my congregations, back to the real world, back to where life would be easier and problems would be fewer."

"I don't think so Rich," croaked a passing demon who knew humankind and especially church leaders. "I've been working with your kind a long time, and if there is one thing I know about parishioners, is how glad I am that they are human. Because they are parson, I can influence them with just a whisper."

And now, twenty some odd years later he still lived in the South. While he could no longer be called a slender young preacher he certainly wouldn't be called fat. He carried a barrel of a torso, a small barrel and there may be a few more pounds that had latched onto his body, BUT he enjoyed some real good Georgia cooking nearly every Sunday, so that made the extra weight okay, right?

4

Current Era

Dale Riley, head track and cross country coach at Macon Poly Technic University (MPTU) had again awakened at 3:30 in the morning. This happened pretty often lately. He'd wake up, stressed over his wife's and his childlessness and have to spend time with the Lord to get some peace about his concerns. Often the peace came right away, simply submitting to the Lord, recognizing that what God had already forgiven, God had also forgotten.[1]

Going to the bathroom and coming back to bed without getting back into bed, he knelt down beside his bed, his wife still fast asleep. Silent, not letting distractions enter his mind he paused to say, "Oh Father..." and then he rested in more silence.

A few moments later he began again, "Oh Lord..." and then he continued with, "Lord, I need to talk to Margie about this, don't I?" And immediately a peace started to come as he found himself having this same conversation over the last few early mornings.

---

[1] Hebrews 8:12

"Thank You Father for allowing me to experience this anxiety, not because I like it, but because it causes me to draw closer to You. And oh Lord, I want as much of Your presence as I can get. Thank You for loving me Lord, and forgiving me. I know that when I am reminded of my past, it is either from the evil one, or my flesh, but not from You. Praise You, Lord."

And so became his custom that when he awakened like this, Dale would pray completely through the item laid on his heart and then set there in silence awaiting the God of the universe, the One who allowed him to be awakened to lay something else on his heart to pray for.

Before long he found himself praying for his colleagues. He had enjoyed many good relationships at MPTU and looked forward to what God would do through his praying for his friends.

"Oh Lord, let me see the answers to some of these prayers while I am still here on earth. Allow me Lord, only as it pleases You and gives You glory, to see You work in the lives of the men and women that I work with. Lord, You are not willing that any should perish. Save the most godless among them Father, for Your glory."

Still on his knees and praying without a sound, Dale paused again for the Lord to lay something else on his heart…and He did.

"Thank You Father for a wife who also has an influence on campus. Oh Lord, I trust You to move on our campus, and as I come before You, allow me to bear fruit, because of Your Son Jesus, the stem of Jesse, and I, a branch from his roots bearing fruit. Allow for the Spirit of the LORD to rest upon Margie and I. Allow the spirit of wisdom and understanding, allow the spirit of counsel and strength, and the spirit of knowledge and the fear of the LORD. And Lord, as I delight in reverencing You, let me not judge by what I see or make decisions by what I hear,[1] for I want to do Your will and watch You work among my colleagues. Praise You, Lord, for this burden, and thank You for what You intend to do, using, I trust, Margie and me.

Later that same day Professor Gonzalez left the Peyton Anderson Cancer Center on First Street in her new hometown of Macon, Georgia. She realized, as she walked out of the new medical building which had just opened up, that she trembled to the point that she slowed down to steady herself. She stopped alongside the red brick wall outside of the entrance. Before she walked up the stairs she grabbed the silver handrail and steadied herself. How could this be the news Dr. Kuykendall had for her?

Professor Isabela Gonzalez, a strikingly beautiful 30-ish psych professor at MPTU had a hatred for Christians that defied even her own senses, when she really stopped to think about it. Her striking features of long, naturally dark brown hair, so dark that at times it looked black went well below her shoulders to the middle of her back. While she stood a petite 5' 6" in height the way she walked spoke volumes of her self-assurance, and, if necessary, her willingness to do battle with anyone's ideology that challenged hers. She had a bold and at times harsh persona, "If the situation called for it," she always seemed to decide.

She also had a distinguishing feature that helped to soften her intenseness. Her eyes. Isabela Gonzalez, born in Guadalajara Mexico and emigrated, "Legally I might add," she would say and then add, "But I'm for as much illegal immigration as can be had. Her almond shaped eyes and her Central Mexican background spoke of something else and it angered her more than she could say. Somewhere in her genealogy were Japanese slaves.

---

[1] Isaiah 11:1-3

35

"White, rich, Europeans and Americans were going to pay some day for the way they treated humankind." This became her mantra at cocktail parties, and once when a visiting professor tried to suggest that the people groups in the countries the slaves came from had to be culpable too, Professor Isabela Gonzalez backed this poor man into a corner speaking to him with a palpable venom that filled the room the moment she opened her mouth. And as soon as she started, a friend of hers who had seen Isabela respond like this before came up to her, gently grabbing her by the arm and pulled her aside, much to the gratefulness of the visiting professor and the party's host.

This is the anger that started to boil in her again as she thought more and more about the news she had just been given. Although she tried to not point her anger at anyone in particular she found herself wanting to point her anger somewhere, so she chose to be angry at her doctor. "Kuykendall asks if I'm okay to drive home by myself? Misogynistic baloney! All men act like this. Especially the religious ones. Can he pray for me? Who does he think he is asking such a personal question?"

But now that she reached the top of the stairs and headed into the parking lot, she approached her car and began to cry.

Leaning in behind her, joln reminded her that, "life is turning out to be hopeless, and all of your plans and expectations are turning to nothing. All of the money you've been saving has been for nothing."

"Oh God," she started to say.

"God?" remarked joln so forcefully that had she been able to feel it, she would have felt the spittle that left the demon's mouth. And then he continued, but he continued both forcefully and kindly, "He has no interest in being there for you. And He's not here for you now. In fact you know that He doesn't exist except in the minds of those foolish Christians like Julienne."

"How could that foolish Julienne give the kind of cold, unloving, 'Christianese answer,' she did on my test? That isn't the way to help people even if they are as misguided as her. All of them," she murmured, "all of those misguided fools are following an equally misguided Jewish Carpenter."

Being a good multitasker, Professor Gonzalez had taken tests into the waiting room to review and score while she waited for Dr. Kuykendall.

All of her anger now pointed toward Julienne. No longer did her doctor enter her cross-hairs but Julienne did. "I suppose it's fortuitous," she continued, "that I read her answer while awaiting Dr. Kuykendall in his waiting room. If I had any doubts about giving her a zero then, those doubts are gone now."

Coming up alongside joln, katepa said, "The last thing I ever want to do is give you a compliment, but," he continued grudgingly, "you did good joln. I now have a huge advantage over Dr. Dale."

The heavily wrinkled, A-framed hulk of a demon joln had no idea how to respond to a compliment. In fact, here in this realm they were practically unheard of, and as he turned to see the toothpick wide katepa, joln merely felt rage.

As katepa looked at joln's reaction, he could tell that it would only result in another insult giving this imbecilic demon a compliment.

"You're a loser katepa," slowly oozed out of joln's lips.

She got into her car and tried to compose herself. She wiped her tears, reapplied some makeup and took a deep breath. "Need to get a second opinion," she thought. "And need to do my best at ridding the world of one more 'do-gooder' self-righteous psychologist wannabe, that misguided Julienne.

Speaking to herself as she applied some color to her face, "You have a class in 45 minutes, get your act together girl."

Driving to Macon Poly Technic University (MPTU) she started to think about the "do-gooders" on campus that she has met. She had only been there for a year, but already they had annoyed her more than she could bear.

Isabela wondered to herself, "Hadn't she come here to make a difference in these 'Bible-belt' people?

"Of course I have," she said, now getting stronger and stronger the more she realized the stupidity of these backward thinking people who call themselves Christians. And then as if she were speaking directly to the university she said, "After all MPTU, this is why I came to you." She couldn't help but be so proud of her university roots. She graduated from an Ivy League school, from the much more advanced, and she proudly added as she now thought out loud, "the much more progressive northeast."

"This will make them think twice about spreading their worthless religion to the students, won't it Ms. Gonzalez?" as joln, the demon assigned to her, took advantage of the anger she felt.

He knew that a main plank in the evil one's plans not only focused much attention on destroying Christianity, but to cause as many people as possible to never turn toward it.

Recalling a major directive handed down by his master satan, joln reminded himself, "One of the major reasons we have success with you foolish people, is because we use your anger about one thing, and redirect it to anger against the Holy Enemy."

Now back into the ear of Professor Gonzalez joln whispered, "You get to do a great service for the world and MPTU. You and everyone else get to watch one of their precious 'Bible-study' students fail, Professor Gonzalez, simply because they chose to answer your test question with a Bible principle, instead of what you have taught them … They are so foolish. And Prof, they will think twice next time, won't they?"

"How stupid are these people?" She now got angrier and angrier. "Especially that husband and wife team. Well, failing their star sprinter will speak volumes to them."

As she entered the faculty parking lot she went back to the doctor's prognosis. She better seek a second opinion.

"Baby," Dale said to his wife when she got up, "I need to share something with you when we spend our Bible reading time together on the porch, okay?"

"Of course Dale," Margie responded, getting her coffee that Dale had prepared.

Every morning for the last few years he and his wife would spend 10 minutes each morning in the Word together. It didn't seem like much time, but it had turned into a very sweet time together.

Margie had always been a major workaholic, a perfectionist really, and so squeezing time out of her day, especially in the morning would, "never happen," as she saw it. She listened to the Christian radio every day while she got ready, usually two full radio shows. "That is a lot of Bible study every day," she convinced herself.

As she poured her coffee, she remembered that day, a few years ago. Dale had said to her, "Baby, what is 10 minutes out of your day of 10 to 12 hours spent at work? If I watch the time, will you read Scripture with me today?"

More feeling sorry for him than anything else, she agreed. They read a Proverb, the chapter for whatever day of the month they were on, and then a short passage in a devotional of hers and then her devotional verse of the day. Usually they would also pray, based on that devotional verse, so that they were praying Scripture back to God. Dale had watched the time and right at 10 minutes after they started, he got up.

"Baby, it's been ten minutes. We need to get up."

And what amazed her, what she still remembered, she said to Dale when she got out of the shower, "You know honey, I'm sure glad we put a time limit on it. I think this will work." And it had.

Arriving at their rendezvous location to read scripture she asked, "What did you want to talk about Dale? Is it your un-fitful night sleep these last few nights?"

"How did you know about that?" he responded.

Giving a slight chuckle, she put her arm inside his arm that held his coffee, and then reaching up and kissing him on the cheek she said, "I sleep with you, silly. I know when you get up."

Sitting down on their wicker sofa, sipping on their coffee, Dale looked at Margie with an intensity that caused her to put her coffee down. "Talk to me Dale."

Dale and Margie were healthy and yet, if he were honest, he'd have said that while he could stand to lose fifteen or twenty pounds, Margie had always been very conscientious about her weight, and as such, always looked great. And this morning like all of the others, even though she didn't have her face painted on yet, he thought his wife looked gorgeous.

"I've just been wondering baby. I mean, well, you know, we both work around these kids all day long and well, I've been wondering." He paused again, this time for a long time, and Margie knew just to wait him out. "I've been waking up honey with an anxiety in the pit of my stomach, over us," he paused again and then continued, "not having kids."

When he paused this time there were tears in his eyes. Margie saw them and just looked down. She didn't cry very often, but this time she had to fight back a tear.

They didn't say anything, and they didn't read scripture today. They just sat there, holding each other's hand. After a couple of minutes Dale turned to their verse of the day, to read it and pray it back to God. It happened to be Margie's favorite passage, Proverbs 3:5-6. Dale prayed, "Father, I trust You with my whole heart. I can ONLY trust You, for I cannot trust in myself. I cannot lean on my own understanding. I need You! I acknowledge Lord that there are consequences to sin, and so I trust You to direct my path."

And then Margie prayed, "Oh Father, You gave me this passage immediately after our mistake those many years ago. I thank You for this verse, and the special place that it has had in my heart. We acknowledge You, Lord, so direct our paths, bringing my husband a special reminder that he is Your servant, and has found favor in Your eyes.[1] Cause him now to again not be plagued by our mistake."

They both hugged for a few minutes, not saying a word, and when they got up, Margie to finish putting on her face, and Dale to go for a run, they connected differently. They both sensed that this problem would no longer wake either of them up again … at least for a time.

As Dale went out for his five mile run, he thanked the Lord for the anxiety. He thanked the Lord for the past, including their gargantuan mistake. He praised the Lord for being so forgiving, "and for loving me in spite of me, Lord."

All the while enjoying the beautiful creation that his Creator had made, Dale knew that the One he prayed to held him and his wife in the palm of His hand. And with that thought Dale remembered a recent verse that he had prayed to the Lord, "Father, You not only hold me in the palm of Your hands, Your Word says that You have inscribed Margie and me, in the palm of Your hands.[2] Praise You, Lord."

And as he turned back toward home, he had a peace, a peace that he knew came because he trusted in his God, stayed steadfast in what he knew to be true, namely that his sins were forgiven. "And what came Lord? As always, perfect peace came.[3] Oh praise You, Father."

Dale returned home, showered and felt better than he had for days.

---

[1] 1 Samuel 1:18
[2] Isaiah 49:16
[3] Isaiah 26:3

5

Nineteenth Century

Georgia cooking! Brother Alexander Rich still enjoyed the Central Georgia cooking even though he had now been in Georgia more than half his life. Actually, Georgia cooking, after a strong Sunday morning service. "Wow, ain't nothin better" thought the itinerant preacher. The McCreedy home had fed him some thick ham, black eyed peas, cornbread and such a huge mess of collards that the day could have been January 1st. But more than all that, he loved the pot licker. Everyone in his congregations knew that he loved the pot licker, and they often bottled it so that he could warm it up later and drink down that incredible soup.

And today Mrs. McCreedy had outdone herself. She had taken the time to smoke a turkey and then used smoked turkey in the collards, rather than her typical ham hock. Had he heard her right? Did she sarcastically blame her daughter? Did she say that, "If this isn't good it is Gretchen's fault, she is the one who suggested that they not use the ham-hock."

Hmm, Gretchen isn't here. He wanted to say good-bye to her. Oh well, next time.

"What a meal. What a meal," thought Alexander Rich to himself.

The long-time itinerant preacher to central Georgia had traveled the state for thirty-two years, enjoying every bit of the traveling in his circuit. He loved being on the trail. The year, 1885 put The War Between the States over for 20 years. He had a chest length grey beard and a slightly sagging face. It sagged just enough to, sometimes, give him a tired look. Taller than most men of his day at six feet tall, his weight, depending upon whose houses he had been eating at, ranged from 220 pounds to 230 pounds. His weight made him very glad that his horse, a taller than normal Appaloosa, at 17+ hands, carried him better than other horses and other Appaloosas in particular would carry a man his size. He needed a stronger horse, "Because of all this food my people make me eat."

The preacher walked outside in his new softer ankle-high boots, no longer wearing the hard leather, pointy-toed boots that ran up over his calf. They had a steel toe, in case he and Sterling collided, but they were a bit wider and softer for his riding. He could no longer use spurs, but he didn't need them with Sterling. After all, Sterling knew his job and, it seemed to the preacher, Sterling enjoyed doing his part. The soft wool trousers stood up well to the elements and his jacket he folded nicely and put into a saddle bag. The preacher would pull it out before Wednesday service and let it air out before he put it on again. He had two ties, a grey one and a blue one, and he would wear one for the entire week before he alternated to the next one.

The only problem with his ensemble, he conceded, seemed to be his dress shirts. He liked to dress up, and could never get a dress shirt to be as snowy white clean as the day he purchased it. No matter what he did, after they were worn, they never seemed to be as bright white. Alexander, when looking at his, less than

44

white shirts would sometimes console himself with, "I'm sure God doesn't have that problem in heaven, does He?"

The preacher, known both here on earth and in heaven as a man of prayer would never cease to pray.[1] He and God would talk about everything and anything at any time.

He got ready to mount Sterling and thought about his meal, his horse and where he'd be praying shortly when, as he said goodbye to the McCreedys, Brother Alex (as his friends called him) had a nagging hesitation in his spirit. Where did this nagging come from? Different from what will come to him when God is getting ready to speak to him, this nagging would need to be explored.

"Where did it come from?" He continued to think about it. "Lord, I know what it is like to be moved by Your Holy Spirit, to seek You. Is this what You are calling me to, to seek You?"

How often had he mounted his horse Sterling, given him the reins, and sought God for direction? But today, this prompted his spirit differently. "What am I experiencing God?" He thought to himself. "Perhaps the dinner conversation caused my spirit to stir?"

"What did she say," Brother Alex continued to ponder? "What did she try to imply? She seemed to be concerned about his health? And why would my health seem to bother her? Surely God would speak to him if he wanted to communicate, wouldn't He?" And yet, Alexander Rich knew that God used others at times. "No, this seemed different to me. In fact," he wondered, "this may not even be from the Lord.

"Oh, Father, what am I missing?"

And then it hit him, fear.

---

[1] 1 Thessalonians 5:17

"Fear? Where did that come from?" He wondered. "Lord, I have been Your servant for too long to let fear be an issue in my life."

He remembered his naiveté, twenty-plus years earlier when he longed for the war to get over, so he could go back to his so called "easier life" of being a parson and a preacher for his churches, here in middle Georgia, actually for several churches that he ministered to. At least during the Civil War Brother Alex knew where the bullets were coming from. Now as a pastor there were too many bullets that came at him, and he didn't know it until they hit him, truly the fiery darts of the evil one.[1] And yet, Brother Rich had decided long ago of the truth in the Apostle Paul's assessment of the Christian's struggle, to never be against flesh and blood[2] even though flesh and blood did battle against him. The evil one used whom he chose. Alexander Rich would battle him, not the people. And battling the evil one, Jesus had already done, and won.[3]

"Father," Brother Rich continued, "I am letting something said to me bother me. I know this is not from You. By faith Father, I trust You to do something different with my brain than where it wants to go normally. Thank You for Your shield Lord. By faith[4] I trust You to straighten out my thinking by stopping the evil one's fiery darts. And Father, thank You for emphasizing this part of the armor. You knew Lord, how important it would be when we face difficulties. You said, 'Above all...'[5] meaning, to me anyway, 'More important than anything else I do, *anything* else,' I am, by faith, to trust You to overcome where my brain wants to go, namely this fear. Father, in the midst of this warfare

---

[1] Ephesians 6:16e
[2] Ephesians 6:12a
[3] John 16:33
[4] Ephesians 6:16m
[5] Ephesians 6:16a

I come to Your Son, my Truth, and I enter Your throne room by His righteousness, not mine, praise You, and oh Lord, even now, You are already giving me peace.[1] Thank You, Lord, that John reiterates this, but in a different way, showing me that what overcomes the world is my faith.[2] Praise You, Lord!

"Amazing Lord, how these prayers are able to go from my heart to Your thrown room, just in this short walk from the McCreedy's to Sterling. Lord I so love being in relationship with You. Lord I need no other relationship since I have You. Praise You, Lord. Praise You."

Putting his saddle on Sterling, Mr. and Mrs. McCreedy following him and Brother Rich remembered a passage that reassured him why he needed no other relationship that the one he had with the Lord. He quoted it silently, personalizing it to himself:

When I pass through the waters, You will be with me, Lord; And through the rivers, they will not overflow Sterling or me. When I walk through the fiery trials, I am confident that I will not be scorched, nor will the flame burn me. For You are the LORD my God, The Holy One of Israel, my Savior.[3]

---

[1] Ephesians 6:14-15
[2] 1 John 5:4b
[3] Isaiah 43:2-3a

47

6

The Underworld

As he quoted scripture, and unbeknown to Brother Alexander Rich, in the lair of the evil one, katepa had been giving his final report on Thais. She had just died, and so, participating in the standard procedure, a final report needed to be given to his overlord, haodtie, before katepa learned his new assignment. For nearly 2000 years, and nearly 40 charges, katepa had been answering to haodtie in the land now called Turkey by the humans. He loved what this part of the world had become. Especially now, since the Turks had been warring recently and causing great havoc in the location of the ancient Babylonians by persecuting Christians, and it looked like there would possibly be wars in the near future with the Europeans. He looked forward to the upcoming horrific time, the kind of atrocious, dreadful and grisly times that any demon would hope for.

But what did katepa see? It appeared that he would no longer be in this part of the world. "Nooooo!" He screamed, and as he screamed he could see his spittle landing on djaod, haodtie and joln. Then he could see his head being grabbed by djaod whose position in these principalities put him one step below satan himself. The entire carcass formerly known as katepa would be thrown into the endless fire. He could see it all, as if in slow motion, and so he remained, grateful he had only thought this direct and strongly felt rejection. And so katepa stood there and he thought, rather than spoke. Yet the word still filled his mind as a scream ... "Nooooo."

Reflecting on his 2000 years under haodtie, he remembered his first charge, the charge that haodtie recruited him to harass. "Oh how dismally their relationship had started," thought katepa. He would never forget his first charge under haodtie, that young rebel Thales, the nephew of Epaphras whom Epaphras brought in to groom him to "take over the family business," thought katepa sarcastically.

But in reality, katepa realized all too late, that Epaphras, who ended up being a fellow prisoner with Paul[1] and teacher of the Colossae church, would prove to be an irritation to katepa as he did his best to influence Thales. What no one in the underworld expected or realized about Epaphras had to do with the constant distraction he would be to katepa and his comrades, even now 2000 years after his death.

"Praise our glorious evil father that at least Epaphras is dead," inclined katepa.

No one realized that Epaphras would become the great teacher of that, ugly painful discipline, he hated to even think the word, prayer, but he did. Epaphras starred in this discipline of theirs. And then, simply because Paul included the praying efforts of Epaphras in one of his letters,[2] Epaphras taught the Christ followers, even now, 2000 years later, in the discipline of, "ugh," prayer.

---

[1] Philemon 23
[2] Colossians 4:12

As katepa mulled this unexpected and unforeseen reminder over in his mind he had to admit, to himself of course, that "Epaphras remained, 2000 years later, an excellent teacher...but a rebel teacher."

Thales, the nephew of Epaphras, had been katepa's first and only real failure, and as circumstances would have it, this failure occurred as katepa and haodtie were just getting acquainted, just learning each other.

"What a way to start a relationship," katepa realized. "Not that we really have relationships in the underworld anyway."

Demons didn't have caring and pathetically loving relationships with one another, as he saw that the foolish Enemy did. Mostly demons exuded toward one another, in word and body language, what they expected their charges to do and feel toward their fellow humans, except for one thing - loyalty. The master, satan, unwaveringly expected loyalty. We must be loyal to our goal, and haodtie, after working with katepa a bit, had figured out how to motivate him to excel. It had taken a few centuries, after the failure of Thales, but katepa and haodtie had a good working relationship.

And so it startled and disappointed katepa to see the upper echelon overlord djaod, and some brand new overlord, not one he knew, but one he'd heard about. This new overlord, joln, entered the room with djaod as katepa gave his report.

So startled he had a hard time keeping his mind on his report, he did the best he could in this, what he knew would be, a difficult thing to do, for, he knew that a change would be coming. This greatly disappointed katepa because he knew about this new overlord. Apparently this new overlord had picked up a new assignment, because of politics, not because of ability. Every single demon that knew joln, every one, remarked about his incompetency, about his conniving, and about him being a lying scoundrel that would tear your head off if you embarrassed him in any way.

Apparently he had convinced the group of upper echelon demons that this "new land," as it had been called for nearly a hundred earthling years, would make a serious name for itself, since it had just won its freedom. "Oh the loveliness of the death of warring humans," katepa digressed. Apparently joln had convinced them that this land would grow way beyond the current, periodic group of "Americans." That this stupid idea caught traction at all amazed katepa, after all this "new land" would always be a land of idolatrous tribes. It had been for nearly 5000 years since Noah's flood. No European would head to this new land, at least not permanently, and the ones who were there now would go home when they missed their families.

"Noah's flood," katepa digressed again, "Whew, what a scary time." All of katepa's comrades were afraid that the flood, once it began, would be a trick of their Holy Enemy, a trick to put them out of business, permanently, katepa, bringing his thoughts back to the present time came back to the nineteenth century.

But to think that this new land required its own overlord, well, crazier things had probably been done, but katepa could not recall any. Anyway, joln had won the day and now, everyone agreed, you didn't want to work with him because his inflated ego burst at the seams of propriety, even for this unholy group of demons. No one, not here in the underworld or on earth had a right to have the unmerited ego joln had.

So why were they here? What did they have up their sleeve?

Although katepa didn't know exactly why they were there, he decided that he could handle and control the political and pathetic joln.

51

Instead of beginning his relationship with joln by "man-handling" him, katepa received an immediate and "not-so surprising" rude awakening.

After he had given his report to haodtie, he heard the usual, "well done, but." Even though there were more "buts" than usual, katepa knew that with djaod present, haodtie would be expected to be more critical than usual.

What katepa did not expect though, came next. It appeared that his concerns about a new assignment, and about this new overlord were validated. He would be heading out to the new land, the so called Americas. After so long in the Colossae area, nearly 2000 mortal years, he would be leaving. And djaod began the conversation.

When djaod stood, he stood three times as tall as katepa making him nearly twelve feet tall, and all muscle. His huge wings when spread out had to have been thirty feet from tip to tip. Only once had katepa seen djaod's wings spread out. He remembered it because this odd flying upper echelon demon had to have had a broken wing that did not heal properly. When katepa saw him fly he flew crookedly. It seemed like for every thrust forward that djaod made his crooked wing caused him to go to the side, so he had to stroke extra harder with the good wing. Anyway, it looked odd, so odd, that katepa would never forget it.

"We are making a change katepa, and we want you to play an important part in it. We have decided that we need to add more of your level of comrades in the new land and we are giving you a charge that is already old and ready to die. But first, this is joln, you'll answer to him from now on."

As joln sidled up to katepa, his face contorted and his voice came out with a hateful, mocking hiss. So close that katepa smelled his foul odor, joln said, "You are not someone I want on my team katepa. I have looked over your history and it is an embarrassment. As soon as I can replace you I will." With that last word he sprayed katepa with spittle.

"I have a project for you katepa," backing away so that everyone could hear, joln continued, "a gospel preacher who is old and needs to be broken, and broken in a way that will impact his churches for generations to come. This is an area of the new world where they are …" He didn't want to use the "P" word in front of djaod. So joln said, "They have started communicating with our Enemy in a way that is changing the influence we have enjoyed, and we have traced it back to this old decrepit preacher. It's not a very difficult job, but I personally think you'll fail. I'm being forced, however, to give you this project."

With his project explained to him, katepa left the room. But he didn't leave the room excited about his new project, no, he now seethed with contempt, contempt for this new overlord of his. He would have to take out as much anger as he could, or as he would be allowed, on a human.

The project to destroy the growing central Georgia church prayer movement, through the life of Alexander Rich would be his focus, and clearly this made sense. He is a very well-known and liked pastor who practices what he preaches, especially when it comes to prayer. And not only does he pray with people everywhere he goes, he bridges the denominations smoothly too. As an older itinerant, who has been in the same area for over 30 years, his downfall would break the hearts of central Georgians, most of which he had blessed at their birth, married, and would end up burying. And if this part of the new land were going to grow (which katepa doubted) then this failure would impact Christianity and thwart the Holy Enemies' plans for years to come, "and maybe," thought katepa, "let me get back to the real world, greater Europe."

7

Nineteenth Century

While this went on in the evil lair katepa finished his unwelcome transfer to Alexander Rich and saw his new charge on a very tall Appaloosa. "Well," thought katepa, "tall for your standards, you ignorant humans, but not ours."

Brother Alexander Rich considered the fear that hampered him. Fear hadn't ever been something that weighed upon Brother Alex. "What could be different now?" He thought.

Looking at mounting his 17.2h Appaloosa, Brother Alex realized that while he loved his taller than normal horse, "this horse is getting tougher and tougher to mount." He thought to himself. He finally mounted Sterling with a grunt and then grabbed the reins and laid them with one hand over Sterling's neck so that the horse turned allowing him to give a waving arch goodbye to Geraldine and Hatch McCreedy.

The hosts were on their porch waving goodbye to Brother Rich with as much loving enthusiasm as he had ever seen.

Overwhelmed by their hospitality, he remembered the wonderful and scrumptious food.

"How come Geraldine and Hatch never seem to gain weight with all of that great food they cook?" They were in their fifties, about his age, but they seemed to be as skinny as a rail, both of them.

"Maybe it's their nervous energy? That must be it," he thought as he started to ride off. "Come to think of it," he continued to ponder, "Gretchen also is small in stature.

"In fact," he thought, "I still don't see Gretchen?" And with no more thought than that of Gretchen, he headed off into the woods to the sounds of the birds that he had grown to love.

Straining to listen to which bird he would hear first, his ears fell upon an entire cacophony of sounds. He heard the White-Throated Sparrow, the Brown Thrasher, a Yellow Rumped Warbler and he even thought he heard a Carolina Wren. And then, as usual, right here at the beginning of the forest he heard the unmistakable sound of a hardworking woodpecker. It seemed close, and before long it would drown out the other birds ... and so it did.

As Brother Rich moved pass the town and into the woods he imagined that the woodpecker he listened to had to be a hard working woodpecker, and yet, even though he could hear it so clearly, he rarely saw it. He heard it often, but rarely saw it. And today remained the same. He never saw it.

He could tell by the pecking sound that he listened to the Downy Woodpecker. Usually distinctive because it did not have much, if any red on its feathers, compared to the Red-Bellied Woodpecker that, didn't have much red on his belly but had it on the plume of his head.

On his trail toward Dry Branch, where he hoped to arrive late tonight or tomorrow depending upon what the Lord had in store for him, he began to pray. The sounds of the birds began to fade away as he focused his mind upon the Lord and Brother Rich began to think to himself, "I have always had a strong trust in You, God. A trust that *everything* that entered my life came, only after You have filtered it through Your sovereign will. I'm in an area of America that I love, the outdoors. The outdoors and pioneering. What is going on in my spirit Lord?"

And then, as he led Sterling up the path to the west to Dry Branch rather than on the east trail toward Savannah he continued his prayer, Father of all, Prince of Peace, great Comforter, please share with me what you are trying to say to me?" And with that he fell silent, seeking the Lord.

Far from where he started, born in Northfield Massachusetts, he relocated to Georgia at a time when tempers were beginning to flair regarding the owning of slaves.

At the request of his lifelong friend Dwight Moody, Al (as only Dwight called him) went to the very center of Georgia, to lovingly share Christ, in the area opened up 75 years earlier by John Wesley. "John Wesley, what a praying Christian man," Brother Alex let his mind get sidetracked for a few minutes.

Brother Alex had decided many years earlier that John Wesley helped him appreciate the "finer-things," though you wouldn't know it to look at him. Many called him a modern day John the Baptist, which he took as a great compliment, but he knew those who said that were talking about his garments, not what Jesus meant when He called The Baptist the greatest of all the prophets.

His Georgian church members weren't making fun of him, it's not like they were saying, "Oh bless your heart, you foolish Northerner." No, even though they sometimes didn't trust his "Northern thinking," they all still loved and respected him. Of that, Brother Alex had no doubt whatsoever.

He returned to the bothersome thing in the back of his mind, "What could it be? What could be weighing so heavily back there?"

And then his mind again started to wander. He thought about earlier times…

"And during the war," Brother Alex went on analyzing, "hadn't he proven himself? He may have been from the North, but being called by God to the South, he committed himself to being their chaplain, and when the North caught them, he remained with his southern troops," he continued to digress.

"Father, the finer things I've enjoyed have always come from what I read and then turn into prayer," he thought to himself, "Much like the Wesleys did in all of their writing, especially those wonderful hymns, spiritual poetry really, and of course their teaching on prayer.

"Oh Lord, thank You for this wonderful gift of prayer. I don't understand it, but I am so grateful for it. You have brought me the ultimate in the 'finer-things,' namely, an intimacy that I could never have had any other way, and certainly not with any other person."

As Brother Alex crested the first hill that leaves Jeffersonville and the McCreedy place, he decided to pull out the prayer book that had taught him that prayer, when done right, would be so much more than asking God for what he wanted for himself. Prayer, he had learned, real prayer, sought the heart of God for what He wanted, for him, Alexander. The *Wesley Family Prayers Book* had been such a great teacher of prayer to him. Oh, what a great book he had found! And what a great adventure in finding it.

He would never forget the adventure. In 1850, at the age of seventeen years old he and his family traveled to the state of Georgia where his maternal grandparents lived. Because he had no brothers or sisters, Alexander's parents allowed him to take a friend with him. His parents knew whom he would ask, Dwight.

They had been close friends since poor Dwight had come and worked for Howard Rich, Alexander's father. Dwight, about eight years old at the time, had a small job on the farm, cutting broom corn. He and his older brother had crossed the Connecticut River with "that old drunk ferryman." They were lucky they made it across the river at night. Something in young Dwight's character appealed to Howard and Edwina Rich. They liked him. He may have been a bit too feisty though, a practical joker, which sometimes got their own son in trouble, like the trouble they got into every time they would harass old "Squire" Alexander and his home. But in disciplining the boys, they were very sensitive to not break Dwight's will. Dwight's father had died at a young age and it left the four-year-old without a father. The Rich's knew that Dwight would need all the courage he could muster up, to live a successful life as a poverty stricken fellow. And so they were very happy to have Dwight join them on their trip to Georgia.

Thinking about that book he had carried with him for thirty years, the Wesley book with the amazing prayers in it, Brother Alex remembered with a chuckle where and how he got it. He and Moody were on the train from Boston, Massachusetts to Georgia to visit Al's grandparents. He'd never forget. Dwight, as stir crazy as ever decided that when the train stopped in New York City he and Al should jump out of the train and look around. By the time they got back to the train station, the train had gone. Boy did he get in trouble for that.

But the next day, huddled together in the train station, waiting for another train to continue their trip, Al saw it … a dry goods market.

The huge store seemed to be bigger than most houses in Northfield, and printed on the plate glass window he saw a sign that read, "Books-Cheap." Alexander loved to read and Dwight knew it and often made fun of Al. "Al, you're just too learned for me," Dwight would sarcastically say, making an obvious two syllables out of the word "learn-ed."

"Dwight, come with me. Hurry! I want to find a new book to read. And this is just the place to get it, New York City. Here everything they have is the newest and greatest."

The boys ran across the street, nearly being run over by a railroad car being pulled by horses. This strange carriage would never be seen in Northfield. The red painted car appeared to be nearly as long as the rail car they had been on from Boston to New York. But instead of being pulled by a locomotive, two hard working horses pulled it. Thankfully, for the horses, the carriage ran on tracks, railroad tracks that were imbedded in the ground, but the scariest part of what they saw, besides the fact that it wouldn't stop for them to cross, came when they realized how many people were on it.

The car came clanking by them and Al and Dwight could see that there must have been at least ten windows on each side, and each window had men standing in front of it, hanging on as if standing on a step outside of the car. The boys were surprised that no one had fallen off. As the boys looked at the car passing them, and then looked back to one another they saw the back of the car. It had what they could only call a "porch" with men crammed onto it.

They both looked at each other and without saying a word just shook their heads. They weren't in the little town of Northfield, Massachusetts anymore. In their minds, the entire townspeople of Northfield could have fit into that car. Brushing off the dust they continued toward the store, refocusing on what nearly got them run over.

As they ran into the store Al followed Dwight to the books, where they found an adventure book, *The Personal History, Adventures, Experiences and Observation of David Copperfield, The Younger of Blunderstone Rookery*. Both boys were now excited, for they had just started reading the series of David Copperfield in school that year. Al reached into his pocket to pull out his wallet and the scary realization of "no wallet" set in. He didn't have his wallet and now there would be no way to get it. He and Dwight were lucky he had their train tickets in his shirt pocket, but he didn't have his wallet. He only had a nickel in his pocket. Disappointed the two boys started to walk out.

"Hey Al," Dwight said with a sarcastic smirk, "Why don't you look over there, at those old ones they're selling for 5 cents each."

And with that, the seventeen-year-old Alexander Rich had found a book, written in 1790, that he would read often, second only to his trusty Bible. Dwight may have been sarcastic, but Al had found a lifelong friend in the *Wesley Family Prayers Book*.

Now, about a mile from the McCreedy's home, and well into the woods, Brother Rich came back to his thoughts about his nagging fear. "Father," Brother Rich began, "Your Word says that when I need wisdom You will give me what I need, and in abundance.[1] Oh Lord, I do need Your wisdom now. To understand how You want me to pray about this nagging concern that I have."

As he prayed, still on the back of his horse, he reached his special place in the woods to pray. He dismounted Sterling and got straight to his knees. The place had an old stone, somewhat square, that often had moss on it. This had been his special place

[1] James 1:6

of prayer every time he left Jeffersonville. He liked to stop here and pray for those to whom he had just ministered. But this time he would talk to the Lord about himself, and this fear he knew that he needed to shake.

He rarely prayed for himself first, in fact, maybe never, but he sensed that he needed to deal with his fear, or fears (he didn't know yet), before he could pray for his people. He sensed that he might be on his knees for a while so he immediately got back up, took the bridle and the saddle off of Sterling and let him graze.

Coming back to his stone, he silently approached the throne of grace with confidence, looking for mercy and grace to help him in his time of need.[1] He knelt there, remained silent, not saying a word...

When katepa saw the concern on the face of Alexander he snickered to himself. "Preacher," he said to himself, "I don't have to read your thoughts, I know what is going on in there." Chuckling to himself, katepa continued, "But preacher," laughing now, "I know something you don't know. I have just started a new battle against you. The Holy Enemy has allowed you into my crosshairs, and you are going down to the grave an embarrassed old man." With this katepa howled a shrill cackle, and slipped into the darkness of the trees, emerging at the same moment in the kitchen at the McCreedy place.

Mrs. McCreedy had finished washing the napkins used at dinner. Early every Sunday evening Mr. McCreedy went downstairs to look at his mercantile store. He had just come back up from downstairs where he always liked to make sure that

---

[1] Hebrews 4:16

everything would be ready for Monday morning. He didn't consider it work, after all, that wouldn't be right since he didn't believe in working on the Sabbath. But, surely it would be okay to just make sure the store needed no dusting, new product boxes were opened, displays moved around so that people would walk around his shop. The mouse traps were reset, the counter wiped down and many other miscellaneous things that he could do, he did.

"Papa," Mrs. McCreedy said to her husband when he entered, "I wonder if our preacher is getting too old."

Mr. McCreedy didn't think it odd that she said something that bizarre. After all, he knew her, and knew that she could come out with the oddest statements. What caught Mr. McCreedy's ears were her inflections. She stated a fact, to her. She didn't ask a question. She had already made up her mind, so he did what he normally did. He ignored her statement.

He responded with, "Sure Mama, sure, but tell Gretchen that I want her to change the hat display tomorrow. She always does such a nice job with them. I think it's because she likes them so much. By the way Mama," turning serious now, "can you see your way fit to give Gretchen that hat that she has been enjoying so much lately?"

"Yes Hatch, yes I will," Mrs. McCreedy answered. "But see here now. We need a new younger pastor."

Only the demons could contort their faces into such an ugly sight and just then, with his cheshire grin bulging out beyond the sides of his face causing his cheeks to widen grotesquely, katepa knew a battle had begun, and "the sainted Brother Rich" would be in for the battle of his life. "In fact," thought katepa, "if enough anxiety occurred, perhaps this battle could cost him his life, naturally of course, because the Holy Enemy had not given permission to touch his body." He started to laugh a sinister belly laugh that made him think of other sainted Christians he had brought down the same way. "Finish well?[1] Huh! Not on your life, and not on my watch, preacher. Neither will you fight a good fight or finish well. And you will certainly not appear to keep the faith."[2]

"Lord," Hael caught himself thinking, "I want to help Pastor Rich in a very tangible way. Please Lord, give me some freedom here."

"Eventually Hael. I know you want to help him," Hael heard the Lord say to him. "Eventually. Bide your time though. There are things that cannot happen in our preacher's life without them coming to him painfully."

"Lord," Hael now addressed the Lord directly, "I know that You use all things for the better,[3] and I know that You are completely trustworthy.[4] I just hate to see the handwriting on the wall,[5] pun intended sir, and it's easy to see that this poor guy is in for pain before it gets better."

"Hael," the Lord continued, "You, of all of my angels, know how much I love these people, and how because I know them, I know what I need to let occur in their lives. I'm proud of you for looking at katepa's plans the way you do though, for what katepa does not realize is that I am using him to work blessings into Pastor Rich's life, *and* his progeny for generations to come. It has to happen this way, my precious friend, for a future charge of yours to have the tools that he'll need. You'll see, just be patient."

---

[1] Acts 20:24
[2] 2 Timothy 4:7
[3] Romans 8:28
[4] Psalm 31:14
[5] Daniel 5:5a

"Thank You, Lord God Almighty. You are so amazing," Hael thought, "Even though we are very different from the mortals, Lord God, You know what I need to hear to have peace in Your plans."

After some more reflection, Hael thought of his charges throughout the last six millennia. "Oh how wonderful it is to see these mortals stopping and listening, REALLY listening, to their Lord." And with that Hael received reassurance.

8

Current Era

"Dr. Dale," someone yelled out from the parking lot as Dale headed for his car. The sun shone as Dale approached his small economical car. The temperature warm, it just felt great to be out of doors, but, as wonderful as the heat from the sunlight felt on his body, he couldn't help but feel the overflow, in his spirit, from what a great time of prayer he had just finished.

It always amazed Dale that he actually enjoyed the time he spent doing what he, for so long, thought of as a boring Christian discipline. Far from boring, he always experienced an intimacy with the Lord that he knew he could never experience with anyone else. And yet when he thought about it, he had to admit that while he enjoyed it, he had to work at it. Prayer never came easily to Dale. Praying with other men, as he had just done, had such a different intensity than when he prayed by himself. Something about people praying together always filled him with an awe, as if touching that request, that somehow God honored differently … differently, but not better than when he prayed on his own.[1]

What an unlikely thing for him to do on his Saturdays even if it only took up two Saturdays per month. He remembered the first time he went to this men's prayer group, three years earlier. He only went to this men's prayer meeting because his Bible study teacher kept insisting. In fact, he went to shut the guy up. He knew that John would continue to ask him until he finally went. John told him what time it started, 8:00 am, what time it ended, 10:00 am, and that they were very particular about ending *exactly* on time. John said that they wanted the men's families to know that their dad, husband, etc. were on their way home at 10:01 am. That appealed to Dale, Doc, as his friends called him. Doc knew what time it started and knew what time it ended. He could go, once…maybe twice…but *not* to pray.

Doc remembered arriving that first Saturday at *"The Issachar Men Prayer Group,"* as they called themselves. He learned that in 1 Chronicles 12:32 the Issachar Men were men who knew the times, and knew what they must do, which, by application to the twenty-first century, meant "to pray."

There were tables of coffee and donuts, really disgusting donuts, so bad that he almost had a third one. At 8:30 they were in the sanctuary singing, and while he couldn't carry a tune, he thought the men sounded pretty good. One of the leaders gave a couple of announcements and then another layman spoke, or more accurately, taught a ten-minute Bible lesson on prayer. "Interesting," Doc thought, "Even though Dr. Bob, his senior pastor sat in the audience, a layman spoke. Hmm, that seemed odd. Odd, or intriguing?" He knew that his pastor exhibited a sincerely humble attitude, and this seemed to be another example

---

[1] Matthew 18:19

of that humility. "He didn't have to always speak, interesting," Doc thought.

Then the speaker ended with, "Pray for an hour, until you hear the music."

At this John directed Dale to a group of seven or eight men who would pray for the next hour. "What?" he remembered thinking, "Pray for an hour? You've got to be kidding!" And then the men started to pray. Some prayed short prayers, some long prayers, some used "Thee and Thou" and some just talked like regular guys.

But what most impressed Doc that day came from one of the men who had brought his eight-year-old son. The son, not the dad had impressed Doc, in fact, he found himself envying this boy, the eight-year-old son. As he listened to his incredibly, childlike prayers, they seemed, to him anyway, to have as much or more power as the older men whom Doc knew were solid pray-ers.

Doc remembered that three years earlier, he had left that first time intrigued, and thought, "Well, I might return, one more time, maybe." He laughed at himself for now he couldn't imagine doing anything else, and truly wondered where his Christian life would be without this group of men that had become his family. Psalm 133:1 had come to life in him. We were brothers, dwelling together in a unity that he would never have understood any other way.

"Dr. Dale," said the voice again, and Doc jerked back to reality, leaving his memory as someone still called his name.

Turning to the direction of the sound Dale saw Dean heading his way. "Dean, it's Doc or Dale, not Dr. Dale, unless you're in one of my classes at the university. I've told you that before my friend. How are you doing?"

67

Dean, a 50-ish year old man that Doc didn't known real well, but had enjoyed getting to know. He liked Dean since Dean exhibited an energy that made no sense for his years, or his weight. Dean, a good 40-pounds overweight, didn't seem slowed by it at all. The few times he and Dean had talked he could tell that Dean had an excitement for being saved that reminded Dale of some of his young athletes that had their early Christian training in the Navigators. So many of these young athletes expressed a joy in the Lord that completely overwhelmed them, not because of their superior knowledge, but because of their superior relationship with the Lord.

As Dean huffed and puffed getting closer to Dale, he admitted to himself that he didn't know much about Dean, besides Dean's anger toward God a few times recently. But his anger toward God when his son-in-law lost his job, and then when his mother passed away actually caused Dean to be drawn closer to this God he struggled with. While Dale wouldn't admit this to anyone, he enjoyed watching Dean begin angry with God, submit to his sovereignty and then grow in Christ. It thrilled Dale to have him as a part of the men's prayer group.

"Dale, I have been attending now for over a year, and, forgive me, I know you don't know me very well, but I'd like to help out." Dean had hustled to Dale's car where he showed a little of his weight by perspiring and breathing a bit deeply, but he had his infectious and completely sincere smile on his face.

"You are a real organized leader and so I'm sure you don't need much help, but I'd like to do something. This has been such a blessing to me, Dale. The relationships I'm developing, not only with the men, but with God too. I don't know why, but each time I'm here, I feel like I need to do more. I'll do anything: hand out the prayer sheets, clean up afterwards, anything, just use me."

"I will Dean," said Dale smiling with thoughtful eyes that would have told Dean more, had he known what Dale had already been praying about. "Let me pray about it, and let's get together for breakfast one day the week after next. I don't know what your schedule is but mine at the university is pretty hectic. I do try to leave Tuesday mornings open though. I have an early workout group that I'm responsible for, but then I'm available at 9:00 am. Are you up for that?"

"Sure," said Dean. "I'm in business for myself, so I can be pretty creative with my time. Where at on Tuesday?"

"There's a great old pancake house just off I-16 at 2nd Street. It's called The Original Pancake House, and it looks like it could have been there since before IHOP opened its doors. Meet you there at 9:00, a week from this Tuesday."

"Great!" Dean responded with a huge grin on his face and turned to head toward his car.

He had only made it a couple of steps when Dale said, "Let me pray for you Dean before I let you go."

And with that Dean returned to Dale. Clasping each other by the right hand as if shaking hands, Dale pulled Dean closer to him and placed his left hand on Dean's shoulder. "Father, fill Dean and I with the knowledge of Your will. Give us wisdom and spiritual understanding that we walk worthy of You, are fully pleasing to You, and bear fruit in every good work that we do, as we grow in the knowledge of You."[1]

Dale finished his prayer and then, still holding onto Dean's right hand he said, "I need you to be praying about this, okay Dean?"

"Of course!" Dean answered excitedly.

"Love you man." Dale said.

"Love you too Dale … Doc."

---

[1] Colossians 1:9b-10

69

Dale chuckled and turned back to his car.

As Dale got into his car he wondered if this might be that answer to prayer that he had been talking to the Lord about for a few weeks. It seemed like the Lord had been silent. Actually, when Dale admitted it, God had been silent. But Dale got used to that. In fact, he had taught the men this morning on that very subject. The title of his message being, "Silence, God and Praying," which came from Jeremiah 29:13. He told the men that, "This became one of the few 'uplifting' passages that Jeremiah shared with the Israelite captives.

"In the context of this passage God told the deported, captive, carried away Israelites, not just that they'd be rescued, but when they would be leaving their captivity, namely 70 years from the time captivity started. God told them to build houses, marry, plant gardens, and to pray for the peace of the cities where they lived. This part of the message must have been a challenge for the Israelites. I mean just imagine, God said to pray for good of ... the people who had made you slaves. How bizarre that must have sounded."

Nearly half the men in the Issachar Men Prayer Group were African-American, so having this conversation about slavery always made Dale uncomfortable, and clearly some of the men were also uncomfortable. Because of that Dale took it slow, walking through God's love for mankind, all mankind, even vile sinners, "Which," Dale reminded them, "Such were you and I."[1]

"I think that verses eight and nine imply that the supposed Israelite spiritual leaders in Babylon considered Jeremiah crazy, and 'The last thing we should do is pray for peace for our captors.' But this is the way God works," Dale went on, "So often, what we want is contrary to what God wants, which is why verse 10 goes on. God reminds the Israelites that He knows what He is

---

[1] 1 Corinthians 6:11

doing, His plans for them, and it is good, and it is peaceful, *even in* the midst of suffering.

"Does that remind you of a few passages I mention to you often? How about Psalm 103:19 where God says that His throne is above the heavens and that He is sovereign over all. I would hope that when I mentioned, 'peace in the midst of suffering' you thought of Philippians 4:6-7, because that peace that He gives you that will completely transcend your own understanding. And then 2 Corinthians 1:4 where God tells us that He gives us comfort that we can then comfort others in the self-same way.

"Back to Jeremiah 29, around verse 12, I think, God says, 'Then (meaning, I believe, when the 70 years are up) you'll pray to me, I'll hear it, and I'll answer.' We don't have time to look it up, but that is exactly what Daniel did. He saw the prophecy, this passage, in the scroll of Jeremiah,[1] and he calculated the years, realized that the 70 years were nearly up, and started praying to God. And what did Daniel pray? Look at it this week in Daniel chapter nine. Note that Daniel, even though he knew clearly God's will, did something FAR from what we do today. Instead of demanding from God what he wanted, what he knew God's will to be, Daniel pleaded with God with, we could say, his whole heart, and soul and mind.

As Dale saw the men beginning to grasp what he taught, some of them nodding, some of them still looking a bit quizzical, Dale took the message to where he wanted to go, namely the practical side of "silently seeking God."

Dale continued, "Now this is just from me, Dale, Doc to some of you, but I share this from my experiences in prayer. In Holy Writ, in this passage, we have Daniel's prayer, but I cannot help but think that much of Daniel's prayer time saw him silently seeking God. We think, here in the twenty-first century, that

---

[1] Daniel 9:2

71

silence needs to be filled with words. NO! My friends, we have lost the art of seeking God in silence, and letting God be silent back at us.

"Now let's look at the verse I wanted to share with you, verse 13. Look at it in the ESV, it says:

And ye shall seek me, and find me,
when ye shall search for me with all your heart.

"Here's the point that I want to make, something I want you to practice when you are praying, perhaps here, but certainly when you get home. Don't miss this, okay? Sometimes when you seek the Lord, He is silent, right? Well sometimes, *you need to seek Him in silence.* That's right, sometimes in silence. Sometimes, just by being in His presence and being silent, is how your 'seeking Him' needs to start. Here's what will happen, and this is why I hope you are led to practice it in our corporate prayer settings in a few minutes, the silence will drive you crazy."

Dale then paused and a number of the men chuckled. But some of them were thinking about Dale's words and Dale could see them thinking and knew they'd try it. He smiled watching his men get it.

"It will, at first, feel crazy, but then you will begin to see that this is how God often begins to speak to your spirit. Don't miss the challenge…I don't understand what it is, but we like to fill silence with words, and I think that God wants us to just sit there, in His presence, waiting on Him. I have quoted for you, many times, Leonard Ravenhill. He once said, 'I have some of the greatest times of prayer when I say nothing.'

"So let me encourage you when you seek the Lord, do not be afraid to seek the Lord in silence." As Dale saw his men thinking, he began to wonder if they were being challenged by the same thing he deals with, when he seeks God in silence. He added some advice on dealing with the distractions that the evil one sends.

"Sometimes the evil one will come upon you and you will have things impact your brain, like, 'I need to take out the garbage.' Well do what I do, write it down on a piece of paper. There is something amazing about taking that thing in your brain and letting it roll down to your shoulder, along your arm, out your fingertips and through a pencil onto a piece of paper that somehow 'magically,' in quotes, of course, takes it off of your brain. The evil one meant it to distract you, so deal with it. Write it down.

"I need to close and we need to pray guys, so let me end with this. I have been seeking God about something I want to do on these Saturday mornings. I've been seeking the Lord on this for a few months, and this week I thought I should pull the trigger and move forward, but all that I have had in my spirit, has been an uneasiness. Often this uneasiness, you might even call it 'a troubled spirit,' is how the Lord gets me ready to hear from Him. So, since I haven't heard from Him yet, and since He is silent, I just continue in kind with Him. He already knows what I am petitioning Him for, so I have found great peace all week, not in reminding Him of my need (to hear direction from Him) but just sitting in silence, sometimes opening scripture, but knowing that when He is ready, He will share with me His will, and in the meantime, I'm content to sit in His presence, waiting."

After his message he closed in prayer and then told the men to "pray until you hear the music."

Finally getting into his car, Dale knew that God spoke to him through the voice of Dean. He didn't know for sure what that looked like or what that meant, but he could tell that the dimness he had been experiencing just began to clear up.

"And as usual Lord, Your silence forced me to trust You, or more accurately, for You to strengthen my faith muscle on this subject. Thank You, Lord, that You brought Dean to talk to me today, and after my message to the men, that, as usual became a message to me, not just them. Praise You, Lord! Oh Lord, You are so great."

He would look forward to what the Lord would say, as Dale continued to seek the Lord, and, it would be interesting to see if the Lord chose to break His silence … and something told him God would break the silence. In fact, he believed that God already had. Dale would pray for Dean between now and next Tuesday, and together they would see what would happen.

As he drove home, Dale smiled a knowing smile of confirmation. He didn't have time this morning to get into the first half of verse 14[1] with the men. It says: *"And I will be found of you, saith the Lord ... "* But he knew that the Lord had just let Himself be found by Dale. Amazingly his uneasiness over this subject disappeared.

"Oh Lord, You are too much. You are so interested in every little thing in our life. I shared with the men my uneasiness to pull the trigger on this new project, and Father, through Dean you are beginning to answer it. Thank You, Father. Prepare Dean and myself for what You have planned in our lives, Father."

Sitting comfortably in the back of Dale's car, nine-foot tall Hael sat with his body adjusting naturally so that it fit into the space given, which in this case happened to be a little gas saver.

"It is amazing," Hael thought, "How God Almighty made our angelic bodies. Without any pain, they shrunk to whatever size he needed to fit into. But," Hael thought and laughed to

---

[1] Jeremiah 29:14

himself, "it would be kind of fun to have the top off of this car and then my full height could stick out in the rushing air." He laughed again wondering what would happen if the roof were gone, his full torso extended above the car, and his wings with an eighteen-foot wingspan were outstretched.

He laughed again then came back to his charge, "Good man, Dale. This will be an exciting time." Hael spoke in a low voice. "Soon," he thought, "soon I will be making contact with Dale, just not yet, and not from the back of his car."

"Is there something in the back of my car?" wondered Dale. He thought he saw some movement but, "Nah, probably just my imagination."

"You idiot Doc, there *is* something in the back of your car," spat katepa. And as katepa pondered what might be happening, realizing that the angel from the Holy Enemy named Hael allowed Dale to see him, katepa realized that something on the horizon might be going terribly wrong.

"New rules," he said in a low rumble. But his real thoughts were, "I might be in *big* trouble."

9

First Century

Hagne and the way she prayed would have to wait. Epaphras could not let the distractions that Hagne could be to others, while she prayed out loud, be an issue with him as he actively waited on the Lord.

"And why doesn't her husband Agathon deal with it. He's my senior…" Epaphras didn't even finish the thought in his mind for he knew what just happened came from the evil one sidetracking his focus from the Word.

"Father, I thank You for all things[1] so I thank You that Hagne, her constant praying to impress others, and her husband Agathon not dealing with it is on my heart, not because I want to spend time thinking about them and how I will deal with it, but because I believe that You are using this to cause me to focus upon You. Thank You, Lord.

"Jesus's brother James reminded us that when we need wisdom we need only seek You, and You will give us wisdom.[2] As I wait upon You, in Your Word I trust You to fill me with all

---

[1] Ephesians 5:20
[2] James 1:5

wisdom and understanding which is so much more important than gold and silver,[1] as King Solomon teaches us in his great book of Proverbs."

Epaphras needed to spend time in the Word. The apostle Paul had taught Epaphras, very early in their friendship, this important discipline for every preacher of the Gospel of Christ. He said that Barnabas, Paul's mentor[2] after his Damascus Road conversion,[3] taught Paul about something the early disciples did. (Barnabas had been around from the very beginning of this sect now being called Christian)[4]. Barnabas said that the early disciples had a meeting with all of their followers and said basically, "Look, we cannot keep on waiting on tables. We have *got to* spend time in the Word and in prayer."[5]

"The point," said Paul to Epaphras, "is not to let anything get in the way of your studying the Word and your praying, not even troubles with your people that you know you will eventually need to handle. As long as you are spending time with the Lord, He will show you how and when to deal with them, but *do not* get sidetracked."

From that day on Epaphras had guarded his study and prayer time. And now his focus became his time for study. Something else had come from this though, and it seemed to surprise even Paul, when Epaphras prayed he noticed that Epaphras had the parchments opened, and they, the parchments *"directed"* Epaphras's praying.

He loved the discipline he had fallen into guided by his Helper and Guide,[6] the Holy Spirit. He liked to come to the Lord

---

[1] Proverbs 16:16
[2] Acts 4:36; 9:27a; 11:25-26a
[3] Acts 9:1ff
[4] Acts 11:26e
[5] Acts 6:2
[6] John 16:13a

without his prayer list, open the parchment and let the Holy Spirit take a passage and weave it into a situation that he desired to lift up to the Lord. He loved to pray like this ...

Today, as he prepared himself for studying the parchment of Deuteronomy, he first talking to the Lord and reminded the Lord that he still had no idea what this uneasiness in his spirit meant.

So as Epaphras read his parchment he started to praise the Lord. He found that praising the Lord, for who He is, and not for what He does became a great way for him to get his mind focused upon the Lord. He sat praising the Lord for the opportunity to be in ministry. He praised and thanked the Lord for his congregation (including Hagne). He thought of their faithful work, their loving deeds, and their endearing hope that they had because of the Lord Jesus Christ.[1] He loved these folks, even the challenging ones, and so he started to thank the Lord for all of the difficult ones.

As he sat silently for a moment, he remembered a meeting he and Paul had some three years earlier, where Paul talked about the Philippians and said something about being thankful for that which makes one anxious.[2] Epaphras remembered thinking, "Paul, this is getting too close to my exact situation." Epaphras already had the letter to the Thessalonians where Paul had said that they were to give thanks in everything,[3] but then when Paul talked about the Ephesians he said something similar, but one word became different. Instead of saying be thankful *IN* everything, Paul had said be thankful *FOR* everything.

At the time this really bothered Epaphras because he had to experience a particularly difficult member of his congregation. Brother Agathon had just been promoted to a senior leadership

---

[1] 1 Thessalonians 1:2-3
[2] Philippians 4:6
[3] 1 Thessalonians 5:18a

position of deacon, and not soon afterwards, due to his pride, Agathon had started to change the way he made decisions.

Epaphras learned a quick lesson about something that he saw as completely counter intuitive.

"My dear brother in Christ, Agathon," Epaphras muttered out loud, smiling, thinking of this *formerly*, difficult member. "Oh Agathon, you put me in a position to be taught so much by our Lord. Thank you my dear friend. Agathon," he thought again. And then laughing out loud, and saying quite loudly, "Agathon!" Epaphras laughed again, and then lowered his voice, "Agathon, I love you my friend. You taught me so much. Lord, I praise You and I love You. For You use even difficulties for the better.[1] Thank You, Lord!"

Somewhere in the crevices, the foul air that stirred up in the unseen, lower heavenlies, the part of existence that lies between what the mortal humans see and what is in the demonic world, a thwarted overlord spat out curses just at the mention of the name Agathon. This demon, haodtie, thought that he had found a quiet part of the world to work. And most of the time quietness reigned. He experienced quietness and ease for a very long time. He loved the area. To him the area appeared beautiful. Over the previous few hundred years, he had even had a few volcanoes churning up this desolate part of the world where he worked. When they occurred, a number of times by the way, they destroyed the city, they destroyed lives ... Beautiful, he loved it!

He loved the Colossae resident's pride in their dark red wool called Colossinum, which had exceptional quality. And as a good demon haodtie wove treachery into the lives of these proud people. And where he had the opportunity, he wove more pride

---

[1] Romans 8:28

79

into the already proud. "Ahh, such job satisfaction," he often mused.

As the commercial focus increased and money entered the town so did other businesses and soon Colossae became a booming metropolis. After a time haodtie shifted the business owners' focus onto their own pleasures. So while they had money, and others were working all day long for their masters, the rich would have all night banquets. Before long they were spending their days lounging in beautiful gardens and their nights in drunken revelry.

"Oh, praise our great satan!" He had to do something to keep his own pride in check. And then when Laodicea started to eclipse Colossae in the region, haodtie turned their pride into anger and bitterness. "Ohh, I am sooooo good," quipped haodtie more than once.

When Laodicea grew the town quickly became a major center of commercial activity. And of course, unhealthy competition between the cities began to occur.

Smiling as wide as only his kind could do, he rolled his eyes to the top of his sockets and closed them and said, "Oh how glorious to see hate for one another build up." He paused and his cheshire grin bulged out beyond the sides of his face, causing his cheeks to widen grotesquely as he cherished his work.

Then Epaphras showed up. The few minor challenges to his domain changed when Epaphras came on the scene and haodtie would be bested for the first time, because Epaphras prayed. "Ohhh," he snorted, "So many things were different now that the Son of our Enemy, the One they called the Almighty God, Jehovah, the Jews called Him, had been raised from the dead. He made spectacles of us, and defeated us, putting us under his foot.[1]

---

[1] 1 Corinthians 15:27; Ephesians 1:22a; Colossians 2:15

but," haodtie snickered with a crooked smile, "through healthy deception, we could still win battles."

"But Epaphras," thought haodtie. "No, his zeal made him more than just a mere rebel; a zealous rebel would be a better name for him, zealous for Jesus, zealous for his areas of responsibility, and zealous for prayer."

Speaking to no one in particular, haodtie snarled, "I spent months preparing Agathon and his wife to be your downfall, Epaphras. And you started to fall for it, you zealous praying fool. You chose to be deceived by 'your wisdom' as you saw the good in Agathon that I wanted you to see. You fool Epaphras, you started to completely ignore his shortcomings. I had you! You fool, you heard him pray, and you let his holy words fool you into thinking he had a more righteous heart than he did. Curse you, Epaphras. Curse you! What I meant for evil ended up being for your good.[1]

"Stop praying to that Enemy of mine Epaphras. STOP!"

While haodtie got more and more worked up, spitting out of his crooked mouth, every few words … In the same proximity as haodtie, but in a realm as different as light and darkness, a smartly standing, handsome and nine-foot (2M) tall angel, Hael, allowed the beginnings of a barely perceptible smile.

Observing this realm that haodtie lived in and that Hael lived in never ceased to be a vision of incredible paradox. Both of these angels (the guardian angel and the demonic angel) lived in completely different surroundings and yet they both lived in what Paul called "the heavenlies."[2] The paradox became even more unknowable and incredible when the truth of Ephesians

---

[1] Genesis 50:20 (cf Genesis 45:5-8)
[2] Ephesians 3:10 and 6:12

1:3, 20, and 2:6 were added into the mix. For Christians, *still* living on the earth are given spiritual blessings in the heavenlies,[1] Christ is sitting at the right hand of God in the heavenlies,[2] and Christians sit together with Christ in the heavenlies.[3]

Even to Hael it didn't quite make sense, and yet it did, for he could see in all of God's creation a simple principle prevailed. When the focus became ungodliness, death (of many sorts) soon followed, and where the focus became godliness there both life and peace prevailed.[4]

And yet when looking into the world of the demons, it is darkness and foul odors, ugliness and grotesque images, hate and jealousy. But when looking into the world that Hael operates, though they are both in the heavenlies, there exists light and incense, beauty and majesty, love and peace.

Hael contemplated all of this when he remembered something that the Son had said when He inhabited earth. Hael personally observed when Jesus healed the man blind from birth.[5] Hael thought about all that occurred during that day and couldn't help himself. He let his smile from a moment earlier turn to a chuckle, then he laughed and then this nine-foot tall buffed warrior lost his self-control. He laughed so deeply that haodtie couldn't help but look at Hael.

Hael saw haodtie looking with great contempt toward him and continued to laugh, now doubling over in a godly pride for his Master. Hael didn't feel sorry for haodtie at all. Four thousand years earlier haodtie had chosen who his master would be.

Hael's Master, Jesus, the Son of God, perfectly described the contrast between Hael's realm and the demon's realm every time

---

[1] Ephesians 1:3
[2] Ephesians 1:20
[3] Ephesians 2:6
[4] Romans 8:6
[5] John 9:1-10:21

He focused on His Father being glorified. This contrast would then carry over into the world that these humans had to live in. Jesus, after healing the man born blind taught his arrogant disciples that God's glory, should be the focus of this man's healing, not sin.[1] And then, in addition to His sometimes arrogant disciples, Jesus had to deal with elitist Pharisees.[2] He then brought the entire comparison together, the life lived in the heavenlies, as well as the life lived on earth when He said, "The evil one comes only to kill and to steal and to destroy, but take heart, I have come that you may live life abundantly."[3]

Hael regained his composure and stood smartly near his charge, Epaphras, who had chosen to trust the Lord in the midst of his difficulties with Agathon, rather than to let the evil one deceive him and take him into a living death of disappointment, anger, and human contempt toward another human being.

As he continued, haodtie's emphasis changed, "Epaphras, you have become as infamous as that multi-color jacketed self-righteous son, Joseph."

Joseph had caused the disgusting learning experience that now became, all demons' biggest prayer nemesis. Moses recorded it in their historical account which they called he Book of the Beginnings. Again, haodtie couldn't contain himself and he blurted out, "We did everything to him that we could think of, outside of taking his life." As incredible foul odors came out of his mouth, spittle dribbled down his mouth, and with that haodtie started to calm down. "And even after all that we did, Joseph stands up to his brothers, out of anger and hate? No! Out of this

---

[1] John 9:3
[2] John 9:30-34
[3] John 10:10

disgusting, sickening, love. Out of love, he told them, 'what they meant for evil, God used for great good.'[1]

"Sickening!" continued haodtie, continuing to again get more and more worked up.

And in the same way, the faith Epaphras had in God's sovereignty, thwarted haodtie, forcing him to seek help from another demon. He had to admit it, he needed help in this part of the world.

"Epaphras is teaching people about prayer," murmured a sputtering haodtie, and not just any prayer, but efficacious, wrestling prayer."

The domain that haodtie had as his assignment had begun to change, and NOT for the better. These crazy Christians were beginning to trust their God, rather than to listen to the intimations placed in their head by the world, their flesh, and haodtie. Deceiving these people became more and more of a problem, "all because these people were seeing and learning of all that they have in Christ.[2] "I *hate* this," cried haodtie. "I have got to break it. And I will, but I need some help."

And with that, haodtie thought about a new hardworking demon he had heard about, katepa. He would be assigned to the next helper that the church leader Epaphras would call for he knew that Epaphras would be calling someone soon. "Epaphras you don't know it yet, you disgusting fervent pray-er, but I've been at this long enough to know that your God Jehovah, is moving in your heart and mind, and that a helper for you is on the way. But we'll not lose to you again."

---

[1] Genesis 50:20
[2] Ephesians 2:1-10

As Hael stood back and watched and listened to haodtie, he wondered as he often did, "Do you guys just not get it? God Jehovah is sovereign. Other than some skirmishes, you cannot ever win. The account of satan and Job should have made that clear to you."

And as quickly as the thought came, it left him. For Hael's bigger concern always needed to be human kind, and especially the Christians. Hael usually got assigned to *Christian Pray-ers* and he saw the various ways in which people went about praying. It never ceased to amaze him how he could see a pray-er, solidly taught by Godly parents to trust God, and then when they prayed, they sounded like they needed to plead and plead and plead with God, rather than to merely trust Him for whom He is and what He has said He will do.

That's why the account of Job refreshed him so, and why satan's minions, not learning from it, were so frustrated. Hael couldn't help but smile a small smile at their frustration.

Thinking again about the enemy that mankind faced Hael thought, "Didn't satan realize that God used him and his fellow demons to accomplish His will? These crazy demons, nearly all of which (except those covering Job's three friends) were standing there watching this Job event. We all were. God's use of satan became so obvious to all of us."

Hael continued to contemplate that event. "Incredible, just incredible. Every time Job lost something, the demons roared with odorous glee, and we," he remembered, "just patiently stood by, waiting for God to be seen in Job's life."

How glad Hael always admitted, for as he remembered it, he never even considered joining satan's angels.

"How could I?" Hael, so filled with joy as he thought about that first week of creation when the Lord God Jehovah chose to create them. "He created us. He wanted us to serve Him," Hael joyfully considered. "Oh great God, what a wonderful time we had, watching the garden get tilled by Adam, watching him live in that great and beautiful place, and I admit, serving with lucifer, that great and beautiful angel...until wickedness[1] and violence[2] and pride[3] were found in him."

Hael's thoughts trailed off and he stood at attention, taking in everything, both in the demonic world and the human world, while all the time listening for instructions from God.

---

[1] Ezekiel 28:15
[2] Ezekiel 28:16
[3] Ezekiel 28:17

10

Nineteenth Century

Quietly on his knees at his stone prayer bench Brother Alexander's thoughts drifted to the Civil War from twenty years earlier. Creeping into his mind seemed to be his naïveté that he experienced as the war ended. "Why did I think that unity would follow the war?" This thought always plagued him. Being from the North, he thought that everyone had a similar mindset, or at least soon would have.

"We have just been through an incredible war. A unified spirit is what makes sense. How could it be any different? In fact," he remembered thinking, "I'm looking forward to getting back to my different and varied congregations. This will be a fun time of ministry."

But unification eluded his churches. He came home (to central Georgia), to more and stronger racism than he had ever experienced. Not only racism, but he came home to stronger and stronger church individualism.

If you were not a Baptist, then the Baptists didn't want to worship with you, and if you were not a Methodist, then the Methodists didn't want to worship with you. And if you were a black parishioner who used to worship in the balcony when the white folks worshipped on the ground floor, maybe the time had come that the black and the white folks of the same denomination worshipped at different times, and maybe even in different buildings.

"Pride!" That dirty issue is what Alexander Rich saw, and it made him sick. "Lord, how can I deal with this? How do You want me to deal with this? Father, so many of these men, the ones who are pastoring churches are hurting, and their congregations seem to want to inflict more pain on them. Please give me direction Lord."

For months Brother Rich prayed about this every time he left a church to head to the next congregation. It became, if you will, a habit, that he would seek the Lord for what to do about this incredible disconnect that only got worse.

And then one day, leaving Jeffersonville for Dry Branch, just like now, he remembered what Jesus said in the gospel: "Where two or three are gathered, there I am in your midst, and whatsoever things you may ask in My name, my Father will do for you, that He may be glorified.[1]

"And what Father, would bring You more glory, than us being unified. Your Son said that it would be by our unity that people would know that He came from heaven.[2] Forgive us Lord for our disunity.

"Hmmm." Alexander Rich remembered thinking, "Maybe these hurting pastors would like to get together as a group to pray?" And with that, the idea of a monthly pastors' prayer meeting began.

It took a while at first to bring all of the pastors together, and then once they were together their praying styles were a huge

---

[1] Matthew 18:19
[2] John 17:21

challenge, not so much because people were offended by one another, but just because they prayed so differently. And the "differences" caused distractions. The distractions caused frustration, and the frustration nearly broke up the groups, but they hung together, giving liberty to one another as they were there to meet God, instead of influencing their peers about God.

Alexander laughed thinking about the first few times. He remembered opening his eyes to see the Baptist pastor from the Mt Zion Baptist Church, who had just finished praying a short (forty-five second), loving, soft-spoken prayer. He started to chuckle remembering that the Mt Zion pastor looked, with his eyes wide opened, at the Methodist preacher who had just started and already reached a very loud volume. He sounded like it must be Sunday preaching time, or, it may have sounded like he wanted to wake up God. Then, about fifteen minutes later, Rich opened his eyes again for it sounded like the Methodist had finally wound down, getting ready to end. And sure enough, the Mt Zion pastor looked scared to death. Even now, nearly twenty years later Brother Rich smiled at that memory.

"Oh, what a challenge, those early days, but what fruit!" Rich happily reminisced, and then remembered the traveling pastor who came with a large group of well-behaved, and seemingly well-dressed black "helpers."

All of the pastors who came to those once per month prayer meetings would break bread together the first night and then pray all day the next day, fasting until the mid-afternoon when they would break their fast together, go back to praying, and then leave on the morning of the third day. Halfway through the second day one of the brothers came to Rich privately and said that the traveling preacher, one none of them knew and had a large retinue of helpers, tried to secretly sell them.

Rich became infuriated, pulled out a bull-whip and nearly throttled the preacher to within an inch of his life, right then and there in front of everyone.

Shortly after this incident Rich met with the pastors near Savannah. He didn't get there often, but tried to reach out to the pastors a couple of times a year. Their prayer time this day occurred in the little community off the Ogeechee River, where the old Bethel Baptist Church stood. It had been around since 1797 and stood between Richmond Hill and Port Wentworth. It's location, far enough out of Savannah for the brothers to feel like they were away from their responsibilities, and yet close enough to other towns that they could draw from numerous church pastors would be the ideal location.

Rich stayed with the Baptist pastor who would be described, and self-described as a jump-up-and-down, get-excited, very high energy, "Methodist-Wannabe." Pastor Deas always joked about becoming a Methodist. "Just can't accept the baptismal method," Deas would always say.

On this particular trip there were, as always, a large group of first time pastors. One of them, a young seminarian, pastoring his first flock seemed to Rich to be a pastor who struggled with race issues. Rich noticed him visibly troubled by the "variety" of the pastors. And so, as Rich always did, he pulled this new pastor aside to help him deal with the prejudice in his heart.

Rich learned that this pastor, twenty-one-year-old Ebenezer Watson and his wife had one child.

"What do you mean you don't see this brother?" Wailed Alexander Rich in frustration.

"I'm just not comfortable praying with these, how do I say it, these "dark-colored people."

"My poor misguided friend," Rich said, getting his temper back in line with his desire to be a man that edifies. "Let me try this. Look up Paul the apostle in Galatians the third chapter, and read the twenty-eighth verse. Do you see where Paul says that there is neither Jew nor Greek, slave nor free, etc.?"

"Of course I see that, and know it Brother Alexander!" Exasperated, this young pastor then said, a bit louder than he wanted, "They're *not* like me."

"Let me give you one more argument, then I need to get these pastors together to pray, okay?" Growing more and more tired, Alexander Rich continued. "You believe in the flood right?"

"Oh yes!" The preacher responded, "Worldwide disaster, worldwide flood."

"Then," Rich interrupted, glad at least that this young pastor had not caved to the growing debate about the age of the earth and the truth of the first eleven chapters of Genesis. "Then, my friend, if we all came from the same parents, do you know what that means?"

Brother Rich had the young man's complete attention. He leaned forward, intrigued, eyes widening, and awaiting a deep truth.

"What that means my young racist friend is that you have a little black guy inside of you somewhere."

Remembering that story always brought a smile to his face, for this young pastor, a young man that Brother Rich has been honored to mentor, is still in the same church in Savannah and has had a fifteen-year ministry to the former slaves, and much to Brother Ebenezer's surprise, his congregation fully supported this local mission enterprise.

"Well," Rich thought to himself, "not all of these prayer meeting beginnings were funny, but they have been a blessing to these pastors. Praise You, Lord, praise You."

Smiling the proud smile of a father who watched his young son moving into manhood, Hael stood at attention in the background, observing a number of things at once. Hael observed the frustration of the evil one's emissary, katepa, bellowing odious clouds of cursing that took the form of spittle being breathed out and smoke rising from his nostrils.

It always seemed a curious thing to Hael, that where incense, prayer, is pleasing to the Lord,[1] the demons, who don't pray, would talk to themselves. Since they don't pray to satan, what comes out of their mouth is nothing like praying. Their words still had an odor, but instead of it being a lovely sensation to the nose, the sensation is better defined as foul and disgusting, hence when Hael got too close for his liking, he not only saw and heard the demons cursing, but he smelled them cursing too, and he could only describe the smell as ugly.

Just as katepa expected, he saw other demons converge on him. Alexander Rich now prayed, thanking God, "for the nearly twenty years of prayer meetings, and the good that it had brought." As Rich prayed, somehow, katepa still didn't know how this happened, all of the demons associated with the results of previous year's prayers, wound up in his vicinity, and each of them would strike katepa mercilessly.

"I will take you apart you ignorant preacher and follower of a carpenter." And as katepa said these words, between angry blows from demons, he saw Hael and glared at him. And then *katepa* saw Hael's smile turn into a chuckle.

---

[1] Psalm 141:2

11

Current era

At the end of the day for the mortals katepa made his rounds checking on his charges. As he came upon Dr. Dale, katepa noticed that Dale had his Bible open to and had been studying and meditating on John 17:21.

"What are you doing? You stupid Christ follower," snorted katepa.

"He's preparing to defeat you katepa, you good for nothing little toad," spit joln just behind the ear of katepa and then continued, "This prayer group may not be known to us yet, but look at them you less than scum demon whom I never wanted on my team. Look at them!" joln now bellowed. "They are becoming a prayer force to reckon with and it is all your fault katepa."

"Father," Dale prayed, seeking God for clarity and direction. "I understand the meaning of the verse Lord. I just don't understand why You are burdening me with this? Father, I get it, that unity among the brethren is critical for people to know that

Your Son came to us from You. But why Lord, are You laying this on my heart? I have not been able to go any further than this verse, even though I started studying this passage a few days ago. Father, I trust You, for Your direction, for Your guidance. Lord, when I need wisdom I am to come to You,[1] and so here I am, seeking wisdom from You. I trust You Father, to give me that wisdom in Your timing."

At that instant, Dale remembered being in college in California, many years earlier and hearing a special speaker at a church. Dale hadn't thought of Dr. C. M. Ward for a long time. Pastor Ward, back then a very old man, hadn't entered Dale's mind for a long time. Hmm, I wonder what he is doing in my brain now?

After C. M. Ward spoke and sat down, the audience left their seats for the door but Dale felt compelled to go up and speak to Mr. Ward. Even before he heard him speak, Dale had known of Dr. C. M. Ward because of some books (really booklets) that he had purchased that were written by him. Dale had never heard him on the radio, and while he didn't completely agree with all of his theology he had read his books and found his writing engaging and challenging. So Dale went to where Dr. Ward sat and began to talk to him about his recent activities which, besides school, amounted to only one other thing, and that which took his time, apologetics, Dale loved to do. Dale spent hours every week teaching apologetics and then taking his protégés out into the streets to share the real Jesus to folks who were caught up in the cults.

"But so what Lord? That meeting, although great motivated me years ago, what does that have to do with now with this verse. Lord, I am grateful for my memory of C. M. Ward, but I need

---

[1] James 1:5

94

clarity on John 17:21. Why can I not get this off my heart?" Dale pleaded.

And then he got it, unity, unity in the body.

"Noooooo!" yelled katepa at the top of his lungs.

"Soon I'll be able to replace you katepa," snickered joln as he slithered by and slapped him behind the ears. And as katepa turned to look at his nemesis, his overlord joln he saw it, somehow, the other demons who had charges that were being, and would be impacted by Coach Dale Riley were making their way by katepa in a single file line. Each one pummeled him to one extent or another. The last thing katepa remembered, a giant demon raised a fist. His fist alone looked to be twice the size katepa. The fist swung toward katepa, and he blacked out. He woke up with bruises that were a message to him. They signified what would occur if Dr. Dale became successful in teaching his men to be effective in their praying.

"Oh Father," started Dale, "You have laid on my heart to pray for the historic Macon churches and now I think that I am seeing the reason. Oh Lord, I soooo remember that night that C. M. Ward spoke. Afterwards, after we spoke, I will never forget that shaking, bony finger pointing to the congregation that had started to leave, and him saying, 'There they go.' Father, he simply affirmed, what You have made clear to me, that my ministry is to the church."

"How can I get them together Father?" asked Dale. "How can I bring …" Then he tailed off because he sensed the Holy Spirit prodding his spirit.

"Hmm," said Dale reflectively, out loud and to no one in particular. "I think it's time for a new prayer group, but this time a prayer group made up of a bunch of pastors."

As joln went by katepa and noticed that he had regained consciousness he spit out the words, "You are a loser, katepa."

12

First Century

Epaphras still recalled his challenging learning experience with Paul three years earlier, about being thankful, when he remembered some more of Paul's conversation. His memory made him feel like Paul and he were back in their meeting room. Paul had just told Epaphras, for what seemed like the "umpteenth" time, "Epaphras, wait, you do not get to be thankful *in*[1] a difficult situation and not be thankful *for*[2] the situation. That is just illogical, and I might add, selfish on your part."

"Why Paul?" Epaphras began to get a bit angry with Paul, "Surely God understands that there are just difficult circumstances that He has allowed into my life through which I would learn endurance. I can learn in it and not be thankful for it."

Paul lowered his face and his eyes into his lap, gave a short chuckle and Epaphras knew that his argument would be cast aside, with love, of course. How long would Paul take? Two sentences, maybe three?

---

[1] 1 Thessalonians 5:18
[2] Ephesians 5:20

"My friend," Paul said, "because God is sovereign. *nothing* is in your life that God did not plan for and approve. He chooses to use these circumstances by His good graces and Your faith in Him for the better. In everything or for everything isn't the point Epaphras. The point is that we are to be thankful *about* everything ... because God is sovereign[1] and He works all things out for the better for those who love Him and are called according to His promises."[2]

"Three sentences," thought Epaphras sarcastically. "But the first sentence had so many words in it that it could have been counted as two, making Paul's explanation four sentences long, not three.

"Alright Paul, I get it. I'll start asking the Lord what things there are in my life that I can be thankful for, *because of the problems Agathon has brought into my life ...*"

Thinking to himself, Eaphras continued, "Agathon is bound to still be a real challenge to me even after I thank God *for* him."

As usual, Paul's wisdom paid great benefits, not only for the spiritual benefit of Epaphras but also for his personal comfort and ultimately for his congregation as he began to comfort them the selfsame way the Lord comforted him.[3] It turned out that the burden Epaphras felt for Agathon caused him to seek the Lord much more than normal. He realized that because of the burden of Agathon, Epaphras spent a lot more time with the Lord. Epaphras also found much more peace with the Lord. Before Agathon Epaphras didn't have to "work for peace," but with the Agathon problem, Epaphras relied more upon God.

"Amazing," Epaphras remembered thinking, "Completely, in fact totally counter intuitive. Because I couldn't get the peace on

---

[1] Psalm 103:19
[2] Romans 8:28
[3] 2 Corinthians 1:4

my own, the peace came as I trusted God. Amazing! And incredible!"

"God also taught you about faith Epaphras," Hael had said to no one in particular, "Through your faith, Epaphras, peace came." Hael knew that Paul had already taught about faith by using the armor of a shield, as an allegorical way to explain to folks that faith would be as one uses a shield, that "by faith," Epaphras would stop the fiery darts.[1] Hael knew that God has always been the shield,[2] but Paul clearly explained, the fiery darts would hit the shield and stop because of the faith of the one "lifting" the shield.

"Oh these humans," Hael thought, "Why do they not realize what they have in Christ. Victory! They have victory."

"Epaphras, you will be very excited to learn about how God uses your faith to stop the fiery darts, but one's faith is in our Sovereign God, Epaphras, the One who has brought and allowed these difficult people into your life. So for right now, learn the concept of thanking God Jehovah in and for everything."

"Because the time that Epaphras spent with the Lord grew, his intimacy with the Lord grew. More than that his desire to pray for his congregation intensified. Epaphras would spend hours in prayer for his congregation … and wonder where the time went. When he walked from town to town, the entire time would be spent in prayer. And miss prayer? When he had company arrive early in the morning, he so missed his time that would usually be set aside for praying.

---

[1] Ephesians 6:16
[2] Psalm 28:7

God showed Epaphras that he could truly be called a God of endurance and encouragement. His Father gave him great joy and great peace, simply because Epaphras knew God as a believer.[1] "God gave me joy and peace, in spite of me, and in spite of Agathon. Huh," Epaphras continued, slower and more thoughtfully, "Perhaps God gave me that joy and peace *because of* Agathon. Oh Lord," Epaphras chuckled again to himself, "Thank You for Agathon."

Epaphras then remembered the next day, three years ago, when Paul looked curiously at Epaphras and asked, "Who is this new Epaphras I see?"

"Well," Epaphras started, a little sheepishly, "Well, I took what you said yesterday for gospel truth. I thought about looking up in my parchments to prove you wrong, but I could sense in my spirit … you were right. So I started to ask God what all of the reasons were, or if there were any, that I could be thankful for Agathon …"

"And?" Paul asked.

"Oh, Paul, amazing. All I can say is, 'amazing.' When I considered all the changes and challenges in my ministry and my life, and then I imagined how God used these things in my life for the good of my people, I then thought of all of the things that my people were doing in other's lives and sure enough, there were, to my great surprise, actually, to my great comfort. Paul," Epaphras continued, "there were a thousand things for which to thank Him.[2] I am so grateful that God brought Agathon into my life."

---

[1] Romans 15:13

[2] Mama Miriam, in a little village in Kenya, had this same testimony to me. On the 2nd day of my visit in May 2014 she argued with me saying, "Mark, you don't know what you're talking about! Why should I thank God for my leg that hurts so much I can't sleep. But I knew God's Word

"Brilliant, what else Epaphras?" asked Paul.

Epaphras continued, "Do you remember in the book of the Chronicles where it is written that the Lord said that all of us who are called by His name are to humbly come before Him, seeking His face…?"[1]

"Yes, of course I do Epaphras. I love that passage. I pray it often for my nation."

"Me too, Paul. I used to love praying that for your people, but I am reconsidering that."

"What, 'used to?' What are you saying?" Paul responded, trying to understand Epaphras's meaning.

"Yes, I looked it up last night. Do you remember the sentence before that passage Paul?"

Looking into his memory Paul replied, "No…no Epaphras, I don't. What does it say?"

"Well God is speaking," Epaphras went on, "and He says, 'If I, meaning, when I bring the natural disasters, and if I, meaning when I bring the things that effect your income, and if I, meaning when I bring the pestilences.'[2] Do you see it Paul? Jehovah is saying *that He brings these things to us.* That made me stop and think about Agathon, and your advice about being thankful. It made me realize that God brought Agathon into my life for a purpose. I'm that purpose Paul. God brought Agathon to me because He knew that there are things in my life that I would not deal with if Agathon were not in my life.

"In fact, it went further than that my friend, I realized that God has Agathon's address. He knows how to get ahold of Agathon if He wants. Isn't that amazing?"

---

said that, so I asked Him what I could give thanks for." And then, tearing up she said, "There were a thousand things for which to thank Him."

[1] 2 Chronicles 7:14

[2] 2 Chronicles 7:13

"Yes, of course Epaphras, but I still don't see how that applies to you *no longer praying* that passage for our nation."

"Paul, I believe that God is judging the Israelites for their rejection of the Messiah. I know that you believe that too …"

"Yes, so what?"

"Well, I believe that God is not wanting the Israelites to run to him for some miraculous peace, but rather He is wanting them to do what the passage really says: humble themselves before Him, seek His face, forget about seeking His arm. He is able to care for all of their needs. I believe Paul, that when your countrymen, not just yours but mine too - when our countrymen seek His face, they will want to deal with personal sin and will choose to keep short accounts with God. They will seek forgiveness, and then our God will heal land, but not their entire country. That time is probably past. I believe the better application for us today is that God will heal the land where they walk, where they work, where they live. Then, and this is the great part, and then … Paul, do you recall the next sentence, after humbling ourselves, etc.?"

"Yes, Epaphras. Yes, I see where you are going. God said that after the Israelites humble themselves, seek His face and turn from their wicked ways, He says, 'Now I will listen to you.'[1] You know what Epaphras, I think that I have always missed that. I have always considered the praying about humbling and seeking and asking for forgiveness *to be the prayer.* But the reality is, that it is only after 'humbling ourselves' by focusing upon God and then praying for forgiveness because we are seeking His face, is the time when God is ready to hear our prayers."

Epaphras just sat there, proud of himself for the insight that the Lord had given him, and yet he also realized that his feelings were really feelings of gratefulness, not pride. A grateful

---

[1] 2 Chronicles 7:15

Epaphras realized that God considered him worthy enough to experience a suffering for His Son Christ, that as usual meant to strengthen him.

"Oh Epaphras," Paul continued, "Your congregation is so fortunate to have you praying for them. I love you, my friend."

If Epaphras and Paul could see into the demonic horde that surrounded them they would have first seen a large odorous being step over to haodtie and smack him seemingly across the universe. This, haodtie would *never* live down. Far from destroying this man Paul through whom he mentored, Paul would now mentor many, many more and haodtie would be responsible for a whole focus on teaching that would encourage faith, faith in their Enemy, the Son of God.

"You idiot haodtie!" roared djaod. "Couldn't you keep Epaphras deceived long enough to think his pride should be the focus? Where did you get your training? You are a stupid fool. I can see this having incredibly destructive ramifications to us down the road ... and it did."

Not able to control his anger, again djaod, haodtie's upper echelon overlord went over to haodtie and smacked him. This time haodtie's grotesque head snapped backwards, nearly coming off at the shoulder wings.

"Oh Great and Almighty God," began Hael. "While I laugh at these demons' calamity,[1] I love my work, watching You move in the life of Epaphras as he accepts the crosses You ask him to bear.[2] Thank You, Lord, for this assignment."

---

[1] Proverbs 1:26
[2] John 16:24

Epaphras learned how to pray fervently for people, and this learning experience came by way of a "problem person" three years ago, named Agathon.

Epaphras opened up the parchment he had chosen to study, the Deuteronomy scroll. He had just started restudying this yesterday and in the early part of the parchment where Moses tells the children of Israel that because of them he would not be able to enter the promised land. Then, to add salt into the wounds, Jehovah told Moses that he had to not only command Joshua, but also encourage and strengthen him too.[1]

"Hmm, that is odd," he thought. "Why does this resonate with me? I'm not sarcastic with my congregation as it seemed Moses constantly put upon the Israelites ... what is it?" Moses's dad resonated in Epaphras's mind. "Why his dad?" Epaphras continued to ponder. "Lord, is it his father-in-law that is resonating with me? What connection did either father have to this passage that I'm reading? None, of course."

Epaphras had spent many minutes contemplating all of this, rolling over each sentence in the parchment over and over again, meditating on them really, when he realized that it didn't have anything to do with Moses, but with him, Epaphras, and his troubled spirit. That's it! His spirit, *"un-troubled"* itself.

"Thales, is that it Lord?"

Thales, his nephew, by marriage, kind-of, came from a family known for their faith. This nephew, as Epaphras began to surmise, would soon be on his way to a new focus in life. He'd need all the faith he could muster.

---

[1] Deuteronomy 3:23-28

Epaphras's brother, Basileios, and his wife Myrrine had raised Thales from birth. While he never knew his birth mother, Thales had been born of a great heritage. And he knew that he had been very lucky to be raised by the God-fearing Basileios, and his birth mother's sister, Myrrine. But the great heritage that Thales found such pride in came from his grandmother.

Thales' mother, the daughter whom Jesus healed, would forever be known as the child healed when Jesus confronted the Syrophoenician woman.[1] His father died in Tyre well before Thales' birth. As the time of Thales' birth drew near his mother left Tyre with all of her family, including her mother, the Syrophoenician woman. The family left escaping persecution, heading to Colossae where her brother-in-law, Basileios had a brother named Epaphras.

Epaphras had just started a church for The Way, but Euanthe died giving birth to him, near Hierapolis, while still on the road from Tyre to Colossae. Due to the sudden death of the mother outside of Hierapolis, the family stayed there and never made it to Colossae.

Thales grew up with his uncle Basileios and "Uncle" Epaphras visited often as Hierapolis and Colossae were only seven miles apart.

Epaphras and Thales grew close, but he only saw Thales when Thales' behavior excelled. "Epaphras," Basileios said when Epaphras visited for dinner a few months earlier, "Thales is prone to fantasizing about adventures. You never see it Epaphras," said a frustrated Basileios, "He always has been and it makes me wonder if he will trust God for his future, or give God advice, when it comes to his future."

But Epaphras saw more in Thales than his brother Basileios did. Epaphras saw in Thales a young man who greatly hungered

---

[1] Mark 7:24-30

for "something" even though Thales himself did not know what yet. Now perhaps Epaphras knew what that would soon be.

Epaphras had often talked to Thales about the adventures Paul and those who were with him were experiencing and so he knew of his obsession with adventure. So, as a good shepherd, who had learned a long time ago to be a good listener, he let Basileios, his brother, go on talking about Thales.

"We don't know what to do with him Epaphras. Myrrine and I are so frustrated with him. We're trying to raise him as our own son. He claims to love the Messiah. He acknowledges his grandmother's witness, and he claims to want to do God's will. He has always been given top marks in his study of the parchments, but something isn't right."

Basileios and Epaphras had just had this conversation a few months earlier at dinner.

"Would Thales make a good understudy?" Epaphras thought to himself at that moment.

And now, today, he thought it again. "Is this the opportunity that would allow me to spend more time with Paul?"

Inexplicably pausing for a few moments Epaphras continued, this time in a reverent prayer, "Oh Lord, thank You, my troubled spirit is gone …

"Oh, Father, You are always good. As I begin to pray for Thales and whether or not I should commit to pouring myself into him, I trust you to make clear to me, Thales, Basileios and Myrrine if this is Your will. Lord I trust you to take the desire off of my heart,[1] if this not be Your will, and I trust You, Lord, to give us perfect peace.[2] But Father, where we move in directions

---

[1] Proverbs 21:1 (cf Psalm 37:4, When we delight ourselves in Him, he gives us the desires of our heart, but, because He can move the heart of a king, He can move our heart, in fact, He takes desires off of our heart, like He moves the hearts of kings)
[2] 1 Corinthians 14:33

that are not where You want us to go, I trust you for no peace whatsoever. And Father, give me complete peace about when I should reach out to them … if I should. Thank You, Father."

After praying this Epaphras's uneasiness left.

Then haodtie's uneasiness started. A new earthling, Thales. What do I not know about him? He had been around in the Colossae and Hierapolis area for a while but seemed to be nothing more than an impudent young person. Oh, how he hated these young Christ followers. They were so unpredictable. And this one, with his family history could be a problem. Who should we get to take responsibility for him. With Epaphras thinking that this will allow him to get away, much could be ruined in Colossae … with the right deception.

Within a few minutes, in the upper echelons of the evil one's lair, the name of Thales began being bandied about.

"Is this the one that we can manipulate, so as to begin the process of bringing down Paul's efforts?" barked djaod.

The evil lair's report on Thales arrived and haodtie read it as did djaod.

"Thales is a young good looking man (by human standards) and he has not known a woman yet. He is a strong athletic man who likes to … oh, look at this … it appears that Thales likes to dream about being a world traveler."

"That's it haodtie, we want Thales to feel trapped in Colossae," djaod said, with an arrogant laugh.

"Uhm, that's … okay, overlord djaod," haodtie said with a scared expression on his face, like he might share a thought that, if he were not careful could possibly get his head ripped off.

Starting off simply annoyed at haodtie, and then raising his voice in intensity, djaod said, "what, haodtie, are you getting ready to disagree with me? Have you lost your mind? Where is your excitement for my idea?" djaod now bellowed.

"Well sir, I'm just thinking," haodtie murmured.

"Speak up, haodtie! What's on your mind?"

"Well sir," haodtie began again, "I'm just wondering if another variation on that would be to deceive him into thinking that every day in Colossae *is his* adventure, now that he works with his Uncle Epaphras. He has been living in the Colossae area for some time already. Let's play to his pride. Let's convince him that what he is doing is so important that seeking direction from the Holy Enemy is a waste of his time. He would spend so much time stuck on himself that he would do his 'holy-work' out of his own strength, rather than in faith and out of the strength of you know who."

"Hmm, haodtie, that idea has some merit," said djaod thoughtfully, "and I think that I have just the young demon to put under you to help you accomplish this. His name is katepa and he comes very well recommended." With his expression hardening djaod ordered, "Put him on observation for now, and have him report to you regularly," and then, softening a bit sarcastically haodtie thought, djaod said, "As you and katepa get to know each other, haodtie."

13

Current Era

"Strength workouts guys. You should be working on the weights, not sitting on your tails." Doc, as his athletes liked to call him, had just walked into the weight room to find most of his athletes talking instead of working. Thursday during the season his team hit the weights. In fact, they did this every Tuesday and Thursday.

"Check-out, Doc," Julienne, his 800 meter star stood up and came to him, starting her sentence the way she always did, with her South-Central Los Angles flair. She said, "Check-out," ending the word "out" with a lower pitch than the previous word. It always sounded like a high pitched screech that ended abruptly, but you knew who spoke for the unmistakable Julienne had her own style.

Doc loved these guys, men and women, whom the Lord had entrusted into his hands. They all had a great relationship with him, and he took seriously what he had learned years earlier, namely that at college, or in this case university, there would be things learned, disciplines started, and mistakes made that would stay with them their whole life. And Doc knowing this, felt it to be his responsibility to mold these men and women as much as he could.

Doc had gone to Stanislaus State College, at the time a small college in the California state system. Now it had university status in a little town called Turlock, located 90 miles south of Sacramento in the central valley. The central valley became prominent to Dale's generation by the old cowboy TV program, *The Big Valley,* where the matron Barbara Stanwyck ran her ranch. The San Joaquin Valley where the TV program took place is part of the "Great Central Valley" which is made up of The San Joaquin Valley in the south and The Sacramento Valley in the north. Together this "Great Central Valley" is hundreds of miles long from north to south.

So when people would ask him where they could find Turlock on the map, and why he went to school there he would say, "Turlock and San Francisco and Sacramento make a perfect ninety-mile triangle, ninety miles south of Sacramento and ninety miles south east of San Francisco. Why did I go? Just by accident I read a bio on the new track coach out there. I read that as a Kenyan long distance runner he used to train in the Lake Nakuru National Park. I worked there in the Turlock area the year before, on a senior high church mission trip and fell in love with the town. It's small-ish size appealed to me even though it had a good sized population. It had a small town 'feel' even though it housed a state college.

"After I had been there for a few years I realized that I could write my Doctorate under this coach consistent with my passion: long distance running. And who'd of thought that my doctorate would be *Jumping the Steeplechase Water-Jump.*"

He would then add, looking around as if to tell a secret, "I ate at a fast food restaurant that I had never seen before: Jack-In-The-Box. It had greasy tacos that the more I ate, the more I wanted. Margie thinks they're disgusting … but I love them. We don't get out there very much, but every time we go to San Francisco I take her for a romantic dinner at Jack-In-The-Box. Two tacos for ninety cents. It's the most inexpensive romantic dinner in San Francisco."

Once when he told that story in front of Margie she chimed in, "The only reason he calls it romantic is because that's his justification. Believe me there is *nothing* romantic about it."

"Check-out, Doc," Julienne had said again, "my psych prof gave me a zero for my answer to her question about dealing with adversity." As Julienne got up from among the group and walked over toward him, he blew his whistle. "All right team, go to work," he tossed out as he reached for Julienne's paper.

The test, a short one question test read: *Faced with a client who has had a stable life, but is now facing a situation that threatens his stability and is causing him to despair, in what direction would you help him proceed? (Make whatever simple assumptions you would like to make to help 'flesh-out' your answer)*

Doc perused her answer. Looking up after a couple of moments he said, "Great answer! Margie's Bible study has had an impact hasn't it?" Margie, his wife of 23 years, has held a Bible study with the girls on the track team for a number of years, and Julienne, thanks in part to her grandmother that she lived with, has been in it all four years of her university life.

"But I can see why Professor Gonzalez didn't like it, Julienne, not enough psychobabble."

"Check-out, not enough psychobabble? How about *no* psychobabble, Doc."

"That's my point, kiddo." Doc's wheels were already turning with how he might help Julienne, but he couldn't tell her and possibly raise expectations. But another reason he wouldn't share what he thought about how he might help her had to do with, what to Coach Dale seemed to be even more important, and that issue had to do with not violating an important principle his students needed to learn, and that had to do with authority. Doc had a strong belief in standing up with those that are in authority, like a prof, and not taking his athlete's side, in front of the athlete.

"Check-out, Doc," Julienne's voice started to shake, "I need this class to graduate in my major."

"A psych major, right Julienne?"

"Major psych job," yelled Antoine, one of the athletes on the weights and a number of the athletes laughed.

"Focus on your work Antoine," yelled back Doc.

"Julienne, let's pray about this." As she bowed her head, Doc laid his hand on her shoulder. He made it a point to always do this in front of others and with his hand obviously on a shoulder nearest whomever else happened to be in the room. That way no question ever arose about his actions. "Lord," he began, "Your Word says that when we need wisdom we are to ask of You, who gives wisdom to us generously.[1] Father, Julienne needs wisdom in what to do. We trust You to make plain Your will for her. In Your Son's name we pray, Amen."

"Amen," said Julienne softly, wiping away a tear.

"Amen," muffled Antoine under the last rep of a particularly heavy bench set.

"Amen," said everyone else, following Antoine's lead.

"Get at it you guys," snickered Doc.

"Guess I need to just trust the Lord to handle this for me, don't I?" Julienne said rhetorically, so coach didn't respond. She continued, looking up at Dale. "I need to put my money where my mouth is and take my own advice."

---

[1] James 1:5

Smiling at his star track athlete Coach Dale just smiled and said, "Amen Julienne, Amen."

And then Antoine said, "Amen."

The other athletes responded with "Amen."

And everyone laughed, even Coach.

Not to miss a single opportunity, katepa, sitting in the corner of the weight room, where only he could smell his foul odor started to wonder if he could use this situation to his own evil desires. An idea began to form. He'd have to get approval from his idiotic overlord joln, but this plan had good potential.

"Hmm," he started to imagine, "I can see Julienne not graduating with her major, because she focused on a principle from the Holy Enemy. This would cause her to think twice about using their Holy Book to live by, or discuss in front of those who did not view their Book as truth."

The more he thought about this the more pride he experienced and the larger he would allow his head to grow. He kept inhaling deeper and deeper without exhaling until his head grew to three times larger than its normal size. Looking like a giant beach ball on toothpicks, katepa felt very proud of himself.

He began to explore where else this would impact Julienne. "It would more easily draw her away from the Holy Enemy when future difficult decisions came up. And then there's Antoine. I can see his sarcasm turning into lust, getting his mind off of the focus this mortal Coach Dale wants his mind on. And then there is the coach … What do I do with that rebel? Ms. Gonzalez, yes. If he holds to his ways, he will at some time reach out to Gonzalez, Professor Gonzalez, or as she likes to say, *Ms. Gonzalez*. Yes, I think that it is time for her and Coach to come to blows. Who knows, maybe he'll be his typical 'nice' (pathetically nice) self and reach out to touch her arm, or her shoulder and she can call it rape, or maybe, at the very least look at it as a misogynist, aggressive male's attempt to invade her space." He saw all kinds of ways to use this for his unholy direction.

"Yes," katepa continued, "This should cause Doc to think twice before he is his pathetically nice, Holy Enemy-like self. I don't know," rubbing what would be his hands together, he added, "There are lots of options to cause failure, lots of options."

That evening when Dale had reached home his wife waited for him so that they could go to the grocery store together.

"Hey baby, before we go to the store, we need to pray for Julienne," Dale said.

"Yah, she called me, Dale. Did she tell you her answer?"

"Yes," he responded. "I am so proud of her. She said it just like I teach the guys at our Issachar Men Prayer Group. She said that she would tell her client, who would be a Christian because that is the type of psychology she wants to practice, Christian Psychology, to get a clearer perspective of the problem by doing a very simple task. Take a piece of paper and ask God to reveal all of the things that they can give thanks for in their situation. Tell them not fret if some of the things have seemingly nothing to do with the situation, let God lead them into the various reasons they can give thanks. Instead of fretting, it'll change their perspective."

"Great answer," Margie said, "But I can see why her professor didn't like it. What are you going to do?"

"I don't know yet babe. Let's pray." And with that, he and Margie held hands, and he lifted his voice to the Lord ...

"Noooo! Go to the grocery store you fools, go to the grocery store," groaned katepa.

Hael smiled.

"Father," Dale began, "as Margie and I come boldly into Your throne room,[1] we recognize that we are not entering in arrogantly, but rather confidently. We are confident that while thousands of angels are worshipping You,[2] You incline Your ear to hear what we have to say.[3] That never ceases to excite, amaze and humble me when I think of that Lord. Thank You for hearing Margie and I Lord. We lift up to You our sister in Christ, Julienne, who from our perspective is getting a raw deal, and yet Lord, we recognize that You are completely sovereign, and so because of that, we do not ask You to keep Julienne *out* of the problems of the world,[4] but Father, comfort her ...

"Not the Holy Enemy's book," katepa yelled.

... while she is in this worldly system. And Father, because You are the God of hope, fill her with great joy and great peace simply because she is a believer, and as you do that Father, we trust You to give her a hope that overflows, from the power of

---

[1] Hebrews 4:16a
[2] Revelation 5:11b
[3] Psalm 40:1b
[4] John 17:15a (cf 2 Corinthians 1:4a recognizing that God comforts us IN our afflictions)

the Holy Spirit living inside of her.[1] And Father, because this is Your Word and Your will, I don't pray this as if you can do it or that You will do it, but rather that You are already in the process of doing it, as Mark 11:24 prompts us to pray. We love You, Lord, and we trust You. Amen." And with that, Dale gently squeezed Margie's hand twice, which they worked out years earlier as her cue to pray, if she wanted to pray.

"Father," she started, "I simply want to add, from Philippians 4:6 and 7, that Julienne would take her own advice, and come to You with all of the things that she can give thanks for in this. And as she does that Father, I trust that You will give her a peace that transcends every single bit of her understanding. Father, when Dale and I next talk to her, we trust You to cause her to be so at peace that it blesses us also. And Father, I too end this prayer with the understanding that I am praying Your Word, and as such, I know that it is Your will, so I trust You to already be in the process of doing this in Julienne's life."

And with that, she kissed him full on the lips and said, "Amen. I love you honey."

"Thanks babe," were the only words he could get out. That kiss made him want to kiss her back, longer and more passionately.

"I hate you guys," katepa spit out.

On the way to the store, something seemed to be behind Dale. Well, not exactly … What he saw seemed to fill up the backseat, but no, nothing is even in the backseat except some

---

[1] Romans 15:13

running clothes. "I must be imagining things," he thought to himself. And then he chuckled, "Big things."

"What's that honey," Margie asked.

"Nothing baby, nothing," said Dale, and then he continued. "I know that this sounds weird, but lately, when I get into the car I feel like I am seeing something in the backseat. When I look, nothing is there."

He looked over at Margie whose mind had already moved on to something else and he ended with, "It's nothing babe, probably just my imagination."

Hael raised his eyebrows, looking forward to the time, real soon, when he would be able to make himself known to Dale. "I still like the idea of Dale taking down the top and me sitting fully erect in the back seat," Hael thought to himself. "Hmm," he continued, "I better not let my wings out." And then Hael paused and raised his eyebrows thinking about those people that wear counterfeit wings, are attached to a speed boat by a rope, and the wings pull them off the water into the sky. "Yep, I better keep my wings in when Dale takes the top down."

Getting home after the grocery store, Dale started to open the door, "Hmm, there it is again. Did you see that baby?

"What Dale?"

"Oh nothing, let's get the groceries."

As Dale brought in the last bags, Margie made dinner and then they would pray. Dale and Margie found that at dinner time they did their most fervent praying … sometimes the food would get cold, but that never bothered them. Just the two of them were at home, so they could take their time and eat at their leisure.

They had tried praying together in the morning, at bedtime, on the weekends, but nothing seemed to work like dinnertime. In the morning they were often on two different schedules, even though they had one car and rode to work together (they both worked at the university). Then at night, after dinner they'd read together and often Margie would fall asleep on Dale's lap while reading. Praying that late didn't work either. They found that dinnertime worked best as then they would both be the freshest. And so with the food served hot in front of them they would pray … for all of the things that the Lord laid on their hearts. That night they had prayed for Dean, that Dean would have perfect peace about what Dale suspected he would ask him to do, and that Dale would have *no peace* whatsoever if this Tuesday would not be the time to ask Dean to be his lead in this endeavor.

14

Current Era

The next day Dale and Margie were driving home from work when Margie asked, "When did you say you were meeting with Dean, babe?"

Dale had shared with her that he thought Dean might be the answer to his prayer request that he had been wrestling with God about lately. And Margie had been praying for their meeting since he told her.

"So do you like him, Dale?" she asked.

"Oh yeah! I like his excitement. It seems so genuine to me. He reminds me of Chuck, my friend in college who went into the Navy after high school and had the opportunity to be discipled by some guys that were part of The Navigators. When he came to college he had such an excitement for God ... a genuine excitement about being a Christian, like what I see in Dean. I'm looking forward to having breakfast with Dean on Tuesday. We need to pray for his and my meeting each night between now and then, okay?"

Margie rolled her eyes, not so that Dale would see, but just because she knew her role and had already been praying for their meeting. "Good idea baby," she said, "Let's start tonight."

"Great idea," he said, not anymore the wiser. "But you know, I've known Dean for a while and interacted with him before. There have been a couple of incidents in his life over the last few months that he and I have talked about, and somewhere he has talked to the other guys who have asked me for advice. Dean has had times where he has been very angry at God for allowing difficulties into the lives of various family members. So I've seen him hurting, and frankly I like his honesty, before men and before God."

As they went to bed Dale's limbs were unusually restless, so he got up to spend some time in the Word. He shut their bedroom door, went into their living room and grabbed his Bible. But staring at his Bible he didn't have a sense of where he should turn to or where he should begin.

"That's kind of weird," he murmured, and then to the Lord he asked, "Father, where would You have me look just now?" As Dale waited quietly before the Lord, *Angels Unawares*[1] came to his mind.

"What?"

"Dale, aren't you ready to go to bed ... it's late ... good night Dale," katepa tried to coax him with this distraction. But even that, he felt like he needed to say carefully, since a nine-foot tall angel stood nearby. He hated these angels. They were his enemy. They worked for the Holy Enemy. "What is Hael doing here, of all places?" As katepa mulled this over in his mind he could tell

---

[1] Hebrews 13:2b

that this angel, Hael, also understood their proximity to one another. The difference in the attitude of the angel is that the angel didn't seem to care. And then katepa saw something flicker across the face of Hael. "What? No, he's up to no good," thought katepa to himself. "I can feel it. This ugly hulk of a being is up to no good."

Dale looked in his concordance and said, "No good. There's nothing here. Lots of verses on angels, too many, and nothing with the word 'unawares.' Lord, I don't…" And then he remembered, "That might be King James. Where's my King James Bible?" he said more than asked.

After finding it, he realized that he didn't have a concordance for the KJV, "But never fear," and he pulled out his smart phone, going to the internet he searched for *Angels Unawares* and saw that the phone forwarded im to Hebrews 13:2 and here he found a number of versions of this verse. The King James and the English Standard Version were good, but the one he liked, and the one he started to meditate on he found in the 1560 edition of the Geneva Bible:

> *Be not forgetful to lodge strangers for thereby some have received angels into their houses unawares*

"Hmm," Dale thought to himself, "I wonder if I have ever met an angel and didn't realize it?"

Then katepa saw it, "No! No, this can't be happening." His voice trailed off as he just stood there, his mouth agape.

"You're in big trouble katepa," said joln with obvious joy in his hateful voice.

Dale went to get his modern copy of the 1560 Geneva Bible that his wife had bought him one Christmas. He wanted to see if there were any special footnotes when he heard, "Hello Dale."

Dale stopped dead in his tracks, "That's weird," he thought. And just then, gently and slowly materializing on his sofa he saw a huge hulk of a man facing him. Dale, who never startled, stepped back a few steps rather quickly.

"Dale, don't be scared," Hael said gently, and also melodically, Dale thought.

"Wait, no, his words were not merely melodical, they sounded, chordal. Dale heard three or four notes, all at the same time, with each word. He had never heard that beautiful of speech before."

They were both motionless, just staring at each other for a few moments, and as Dale's facial expressions relaxed, Hael stood up and extended his hand toward Dale … actually, down to Dale.

"Good evening," the nine-foot giant said, "My name is Hael."

As Dale looked at Hael's hand he took in the sight. This hulk of a man had to stand nearly nine feet tall. His huge muscular frame leaned down a bit to not hit the ceiling, much like people do when they are walking underneath helicopter blades.

With his eyes wide and looking up out of the top of his eyes to this giant, Dale started thinking to himself, "Wait a minute, this man can't be a man … nine feet tall … that voice … and his clothes, it's a robe, what is that behind him? Wings?" With that Dale retreated again.

"Dale,"

There again were the chords mingled with the simple words he used. Again, this sound made his words beautiful and wonderful.

"Dale, it's okay. I'm a friend. Don't be alarmed."

A dumfounded Dr. Dale tried to slow his brain down. A gazillion things were traveling through it, and as he slowed, he remembered that he had read about this before, yes, yes. "Gabriel?" he asked.

Chuckling, Hael said, "No Dale, that Gabriel spoke to Zacharias and Mary,[1] and a few more that haven't been recorded in God's Holy Book. I'm Hael, and I'm pleased to meet you." He held out his hand again.

This time Dale took it but he could barely get his hand and fingers around the breadth of the palm of Hael's hand.

Grabbing it with both hands Dale turned it over and looked at it in amazement. Dale said, "I'm sure glad Margie and I don't use your hand when we calculate Coração's height. He's 15.3 hands." Dale laughed nervously at his own joke.

"Yah, but Margie would win all of the jumping courses," Hael retorted, knowing full well that Dale's comment had to do with horse height measurement. He continued, "Besides, since her horse is 15.3h if you did use my hand she'd need a ladder to get on top of it." Then Hael laughed, as well as Dale, although Dale hadn't lost all of his nervousness.

"Wait until you and Margie get to heaven Dale, you're going to be impressed with our horses. You may even start riding again."

"Hmm, you seem to know a few things about me. Hael. Why is that?" Dale asked.

"Well, you might say that I'm your guardian angel, Dale and that's why I know a few things about you."

[1] Luke 1:19a

123

"Hmm, not like the guardian angels I've ever seen."

Chuckling a little louder now, Hael responded, "You've seen guardian angels?"

"Oh yes," Dale said, wondering how informal he could be, "His name is Clarence."

"Ah yes, I thought that you meant him. Well, when Jimmy Stewart arrived in heaven, he learned a couple of things, like that we get our wings differently than did his guardian angel, that we're not formerly human as Clarence played, and that we're a bit taller. There might have been one or two other things he learned, but listen, you're going to need your beauty rest so I don't want to keep you up all night."

Dale started warming to Hael. He seemed a bit witty and personable. "And I'm not afraid of him. When he told me not to worry, I didn't. Interesting," he thought, rather questionably. "So…

"…What am I doing here?" Hael completed the sentence.

And with that Dale nodded.

"I'm here to build a relationship with you, and that's all I know so far."

When he saw the questioning brow on Dale, Hael continued, "I don't know the future Dale, I'm not God. I'm just a servant like you … except that I'm a little bit taller, and I've been around a tad longer than you … Oh, and I have wings."

And with that, there appeared two huge wings that fluttered a bit before they disappeared. Dale leaned around and looked behind Hael. "Nothing broken. How did those wings flutter and not break my floor lamp behind you?"

"Good eye, Dale. We'll talk about that stuff later. There are a few things you need to know. First, I'm gonna be with you for a while."

"A while?" Dale questioned, "But you don't know how long?"

"Correct. Secondly, while I may be a guardian angel, and you'll know I'm here, do not rely upon me for anything. I'm not God, and I only step into time when my Master and yours bids me to do so. You're a man of prayer, when you need to pray, ALL of your prayers are to the throne room. That's when you have to pretend like I am not here."

"Hmm, that makes sense, but why are you here?"

"I don't know. And that brings up the third thing. I don't know the future. God will reveal to me what He wants to, when He wants to. Like you, Dale, I know God well enough to trust Him in everything. I don't have to know why something is happening the way it is to trust Him. He's sovereign, His throne is above the heavens and He is sovereign over all."

"Psalm 103:19," Dale blurted out, watching Hael smile. "Hmm, so you may not know the future, but surely you know scripture better than we do down here. There are huge arguments down here about various things, like the age of the earth, the proper view of Jesus's return, whether it'll be pre-trib, mid-trib or post-trib. And the issue of predestination versus free will. Can you help me with any of those?"

Hael smiled, and then pausing for a moment he said, "You remember the late Dr. Walter Martin, right? I know that you do because you have all of his works.

"Anyway Dale, at one point Dr. Martin spoke to a church, and he said to them, 'Pre-trib, mid-trib, or post-trib, it's all just a bunch of tribulation anyway. Men and women are dying and going to hell, and you're arguing about nothin.' I can't give you any direction on the return of the Christ, but accept Dr. Martin's words. Even though he preferred Eschatology from a post-

125

tribulationist view, he never let it be a bone of contention between him and anyone else.

"And as for the age of the earth, you know that he believed in an old earth, right? Well, when he got to heaven, he learned that the earth is only six-thousand-ish years old."

Dale smiled, "Yes, I knew he would." Dale felt himself getting tired, but the next statement woke him right up.

"And Dale, let me quote you," Hael continued. "You often say, 'The issue is not *when* He is coming again, but *that* He is coming again,' and I always love the way you add, 'in bodily form.'"

Dale got ready to speak when Hael continued, "Yes, I know why you add that, because the Jehovah's Witnesses talk about Christ already returning to earth, just NOT in bodily form."

The two men, well, Dale and Hael, the two servants looked at each other for a long moment, and then Dale cocked his head to the side, looking up at him. "You've been in my car haven't you?

Hael chuckled, and Dale smiled. And then a serious look came over Dale. Furrowing his brow he asked, "How did you fit back there?"

"Long story, Dale," responded Hael, but continuing he added, "Maybe you and I could drive with the top down."

Hael smiled broadly and Dale now chuckled, just imagining five feet of torso sticking out above the top of his car.

Dale liked this guy, this angel, and then thinking of Margie he asked, "Hey, can I tell my wife?" But Hael faded out and didn't respond.

After making some notes in his journal to look up *everything* he could find in scripture on angels, he pulled down Billy Graham's simple and outstanding work on angels. He opened it to read a bit and then realized he needed to sleep. His tiredness set in immediately.

Making his way to his bed and gently slipping inside the covers, Margie, with eyes closed asked, is everything all right Dale, I thought I heard you making noise?"

"No baby, just praying," and then he added, "And listening to, umm, listening to some music. Goodnight honey."

By this time joln had joined katepa watching the interchange. Both were wide-eyed and frightened. Uncharacteristically thinking out loud joln said, "This is a strange occurrence."

And then remembering that katepa could hear him, he turned on katepa, and with angry shouts he blubbered, "You idiot katepa. Couldn't you see this coming? You are such a failure! I want and expect nightly reports." He walked away from katepa and said, "Finally, finally katepa, I'll be able to get you out of my domain, you worthless piece of scum. Evolution isn't true katepa, but I'd bet that I can make a case for it, using you as proof of it. You never evolved! You're still pond scum!"

Secretly though, joln had no clue what this meant, whose fault it could be, and who would take the blame. All joln did know had to do with the intensity of his fear. This meant serious business would soon be at hand.

15

First Century

In the world of demons there is an organizational system which is a cause of great pride for them. They will keep track of who is unfaithful in a family, who is not. They will look at how problems are dealt with, both good and bad. And they have found that they can keep generation after generation in bondage, just by working the things found in parents and grandparents into the children.

The evil one's abilities to be deceptive had always been a cause for deep pain in Hael's heart. Especially since he saw his role as one who guards these mortals. After all, these, his charges were being prepared by God for heaven. But before the preparation, came the call, the call by God to salvation. "After all," thought Hael, "God has never been willing that any should perish."[1]

And so as good as the evil one's system is, it has never been a match for when God calls an unsaved person to salvation. Bonds were broken as easily as the snapping of a twig. An

---

[1] 1 Timothy 2:4a

example of a faithful family, the evil ones hated. There were great examples of families who dealt with problems well. Hael never ceased to be amazed by the Christians who struggled with praying about problems in their families. Hael realized, as he hoped the Christians also did, that they *should* go through problems, if for no other reason than they, the Christians, are the only ones on the earth equipped to deal with problems. Being indwelt by the Holy Spirit makes the Christians the ones who can show the world how to deal with problems. It only followed, in Hael's mind, that Christians should go through difficulties.

"What a great way to witness to the unbelieving world," he said to no one in particular.

Hael loved his work, and he loved the opportunities that he had to have "successes." He especially enjoyed participating recently in the life of a family that had become more and more important to the Apostle Paul and his teaching. The faith that Eunice and Lois had and the way they were imparting it into their son, and grandson, Timothy[1] gave Hael much reason for pride … holy pride, of course.

Hael finally began to see that the reason the Lord had assigned him to help with this family had to do with what he would eventually help Thales realize. Hael had heard the stories of the great faith of the Syrophoenician woman that Jesus encountered, and now he would have the opportunity to impact her grandson.

Grateful for this honor, Hael thought of Eunice and Lois and wondered if there would ever be a time when mothers were honored. God's Holy Word overflowed with so many examples of Godly women. "They should be honored," he wished.

And off the top of his head, Hael recited passages that had to do with Sarah, Jochebed, and Hannah. When he stopped he

---

[1] 2 Timothy 1:5

recited portions of King Lemuel's writings, the writings that Lemuel had learned from his mother. And then there were portions of Solomon's writings on intimacy that the humans considered a book of poetry. Hael also recalled the grand memory he had of watching the prophetess Anna when the Son of God made his earthly debut, being presented in Jerusalem just a few earth years earlier.

"Oh there are so many wonderful women made mention of in scripture, Lord." Shame filled him when he saw the way God's chosen people, the Jews, and then also the people of those times, treated women. And he wondered if the new sect, The Way, or The Christians would do the same thing too, or in love treat them differently?

"Show me what to do Lord. I am Your servant and desire to serve You as I work with Thales." And then Hael bowed low, in reverence to the God of the universe, whom he served by serving humanity.

As haodtie stood by in shock, his eyes began to bulge, and his head seemed to expand to grotesque proportions. Realizing that Hael now invaded his usually quiet realm, haodtie knew he would soon have trouble also but he couldn't say anything. He couldn't believe that this wonderful area of his would … and then he understood. This would become a battleground.

"Noooooo!" He bellowed at the top of his lungs. "No! Battle somewhere else!"

Epaphras had met with Thales's parents (guardians really) again, and they decided that Thales would join Epaphras soon from their home in Hierapolis, six miles outside of Colossae. So with Epaphras present, Basileios and Myrrine shared with Thales what they and Epaphras had decided, Thales could hardly contain his excitement. He saw it as a great big new adventure. But before Thales could get very worked up, Basileios and Myrrine, who were his guardians, and had raised him from birth, took the time to remind Thales of his real mother, Euanthe.

As they started to talk of Euanthe, Myrrine started to cry. These twenty some years later, she still missed her sister. And she remembered, too vividly, Basileios thought, of the sacred promise Euanthe made Myrrine swear, the night she died.

She had given birth to her son, and while Euanthe's mother, the Syrophoenician woman cleaned off little Thales, Myrrine held her dying sister's hand.

And although she had become very weak, Euanthe said, "Our mother has always been a woman of faith, Myrrine. She will help you."

Indeed, their mother would, for she listened from the same room to Euanthe speaking to Myrrine. Just then, having finished cleaning the baby, she handed Thales to the weakening Euanthe. All three of the ladies shared a tear filled few moments before he started to whimper.

"Euanthe," the Syrophoenician woman said, still wiping away tears, "I will make sure your son always remembers the story that I have told you and Myrrine since you were both young."

After a few more minutes of holding Thales, Euanthe could no longer hold him. She just got weaker and weaker, and speaking in a hushed voice that could barely be heard. With her mother holding Thales, Euanthe started to speak again, but Myrrine could not hear, and so she leaned her ear down to her sister's moving mouth. And then, as strongly as ever, Euanthe said, "I am counting on you Myrrine. You were watching me

131

when mother went to the Galilean Rabbi. You remember how mother said that He ignored her, but standing in front of the One they called Jesus, she insisted that He hear her[1] and my son must never forget that."

Euanthe stopped speaking. She faded fast now. Their mother, in the background holding Thales prayed and Myrrine dabbed Euanthe's head with a damp cloth.

Saying Amen, the sister's mother, Thales grandmother came up to them both again, and still holding Thales, Myrrine and the Syrophoenician woman, silently cried.

What seemed like hours later, but in reality only eclipsed a few minutes, Myrrine and her mother saw Euanthe smile, her shoulders relaxed and they could tell that she now had peace. Euanthe had seen Jesus, standing at the Throne of God, and Euanthe's husband stood there too, right alongside Jesus.

Euanthe took her last breath soon afterwards and the two women's crying continued, but they did not wail a cry that spoke of no hope. Rather, they thought precisely the opposite. They knew that they too would see her in the resurrection.[2]

Retelling the story to Thales had taken only a few moments and they spent more time discussing the interaction that his grandmother had with Jesus, but then they were all quiet, in reflection of Euanthe. After a few long moments, Myrrine, sitting there with her husband Basileios, their son Thales, her mother, and Epaphras, they recognized that beyond the feelings of missing her sister, they did not experience the sting of death.[3]

Of course Myrrine would never let Thales forget the story of great faith. Myrrine got the point, she would raise Thales with an

---

[1] Matthew 15:21-28
[2] John 11:24
[3] 1 Corinthians 15:55

appreciation of the faith of a mountain moving mustard seed.[1] In fact, for years after his birth, she would secretly think of him as a mustard seed, knowing the special meaning between her and her sister, that Thales would be a mountain of faith.

Epaphras nodded to Myrrine, as if he were telling her, "Please, keep speaking. Retell this story Myrrine."

And so she continued, "Thales, do you remember when, just a few years ago, a parchment came through that completely embarrassed your grandmother?"

Thales turned to look at his aging grandmother. She may be old, but she looked as smart and as sharp as he could ever remember. Admittedly, age had taken its toll. But through age, and through wrinkles a woman full of fun stood there, a woman truly fun to be around. Thales thought that when he got older he'd want to be just like her. She let him do whatever he wanted. Where his mom and dad were cautious grandma showed no concern. He decided that getting older didn't mean you were more cautious, it meant that you had seen everything, so why worry?

Watching his grandmother sit there he could tell that she not only heard and understood every word, she smirked from a place of mischievousness, hearing the story retold.

"The parchment had been written in the Hebrew tongue, Thales," continued Euanthe, "And it made mention of her, the interchange with Jesus, and the result. Your grandmother swore us, Basileios and I, to secrecy, but it turned out to be a wonderful teaching tool for you, as it gave us the opportunity to teach you the complete story."

"I seem to remember," Thales cut in, "that you said something like, 'Look, Thales!'" I think you were trying to settle me down long enough to read and then hear the story.

---

[1] Cf Mark 11:23 and Matthew 17:20

133

All of them laughed and Basileios remembered that night, "You need to see and understand this son."

And so Basileios took over the story, "Your grandmother is and has always been a woman of great faith in the Jewish God Jehovah."

And with that Thales's grandmother took over the story. "My son," she began in long drawn out words, as if she were measuring each syllable, "I want you to hear from my own lips why I have faith in the Jewish God. I had heard the stories of Jesus. Living in Tyre we were able to receive much news from the Galilean area." She stopped and reflected for a moment and then continued on, "I believe that Jehovah, the God of our Jewish friends, gave me a measure of faith,[1] for I would not have had it on my own. Then when I saw Him, Thales, I knew, I had no doubt that He would be able to heal your mother. Basileios called it my 'verbal banter' with Jesus, but no, I just chose to be stubborn and to not give up.[2] So my son, I knew that Jesus would hear my request, and if He willed it, I just knew that I would have my request from Him.[3] He did, and your mother's healing occurred immediately."

"I don't know a lot my son," she paused and everyone in the room chuckled because of this old woman's great wit. And then she continued. "My story and the story of the Leper that Jesus healed has taught me the same thing about prayer, and never forget this, okay?"

"Of course grandma, what is it?" Thales asked leaning toward her.

In fact everyone leaned toward her to here this wise woman.

---

[1] Romans 12:3e
[2] Matthew 7:7
[3] 1 John 5:14-15

"These are precious times, and will be gone one day if they are not all recorded," thought Epaphras. "I need to re-remind my friend Luke to get this story written like he has talked about."

The old woman continued, "Thales, the two things I learned is first, always trust that God is able to do anything; and second, approach him to find out if it is His will. If it is, it is as sure as completed."

"Great principle!" Epaphras thought while she went on.

"Thales, Our God spoke the words and this world leapt into existence, so whether or not God 'can' do something is *never* the question, is it?" She paused.

Before Thales could respond she went on, leaning closer to Thales now, "Son, when you pray, if you *ever* use the word 'can' I want you to be embarrassed."

Now sitting back up and looking at everybody she said, "You never have a reason to talk to God about whether or not He can do something…"

"Quiet you old woman," said a demon in the back of the room. "You are old and stupid," he tried to influence the listeners.

"… so never use that phrase my son. It is the way the demons will try to get you compromised and deceived. They want you to focus on doubting whether or not God 'can' when the only question is whether or not it's God's will."

"Amen," said Epaphras in a hushed tone.

And then Thales asked, "Grandma, can we know God's will though?" And as soon as he asked the question and saw the disappointed look on his grandmother's face he bowed his head ashamed of himself.

"Thales, I know you remember the letter James, Jesus's brother wrote," continuing she asked, "What did he say about doubting when we pray?"

"Yes grandmother, I remember," he said, very embarrassed.

"Well, then, tell me," the old woman insisted. Now she sat up, getting stronger and actually sounding angry at her grandson.

"He said not to doubt, grandmother. He said that whoever doubts is like someone being tossed to and fro in the wind."

"Yes, like I'm getting ready to do to you," she said and they all laughed.

After a few moments of silence Myrrine said, "I miss Euanthe."

"She is in heaven waiting for you auntie." said Thales confidently, and a new group of tears were shed by everyone.

Myrrine turned to her mother. "I remember when you went out to find Jesus mother. He had come to Tyre." She had to slow down as she felt her throat tighten and she began to choke up again, "You went out to find Him. He had hidden in a house of friends, for it seems he didn't want anyone to know His location in town."[1]

Myrrine and her mother now waffled back and forth from laughing to crying. "Oh, there may have been some stubbornness in my actions," the old woman said.

"She didn't give up Thales. An aunt stayed with your mother and me while momma went out to find Jesus." Looking at her mother now, Myrrine continued, "And you didn't take 'No' for an answer."

"But grandmother," Thales interjected, "why did Jesus put you through this?"

---

[1] Mark 7:24b

Basileios picked up the story now, and with the two women looking on he said, "Thales, we know now of course the character of our Savior, that He knew her faith even before the interchange began. I think son that He just wanted her to state it in front of everyone. And we have been told that the fisherman Simon, called Peter, has always been very moved by our mother's faith. In fact, he shares about her every time we have heard him speak, and we're told his scribe, John Mark, wrote another letter based on Peter's messages, expanding the early parchment we saw to include this story of your grandmother again."

"Thales," Basileios continued, "I thank God that I had the opportunity to raise you as my own son. If I ever let you think you were less than that then forgive me. I never wanted to communicate that to you. I'm very proud of you and call you my son just as much as ..." Myrrine, not so quietly now, continued to shed tears, but Thales kept his focus on Basileios, "... as much as anyone else in my family. I remember you in my prayers night and day Thales, and I will continue to, that I may be filled with joy son," Myrrine sobbed now, and after a pause they all laughed, Basileios, Thales, and Epaphras. Even Myrrine interrupted her crying and allowed a smile.

Epaphras sat back in his chair. While he had no children of his own he sat in silence and couldn't help but realize that he had just watched a father bless his son. A Godly man gave his son a blessing, a blessing that Thales would remember his entire life.

"Thales," Basileios continued, "When I remember the strong and genuine faith your mother had and the faith of your grandmother, I tell you here and now son, I am persuaded that it is in you too."[1]

Myrrine went back to sobbing.

---

[1] 2 Timothy 1:5

Ignoring his wife Basileios continued, "Thales, under Epaphras's leadership, you will have your spiritual gift that I see is in you stirred up. There will be times when you think you cannot do what you are asked to, but that is just the deception of satan. I am always here for you. Myrrine is always here for you, your grandmother is here for you, and of course, the Savior we serve is always here for you. Thales, He knows you personally, so do not *ever* think that you have a spirit of fear.[1] Rather, my son, my friend, my brother in Christ," Myrrine finally left the room to get another handkerchief, "you have been given power, love, and a sound mind."[2] He leaned closer to Thales now, "That same sound mind that is in your grandmother."

"Oh Lord," Hael said, "I am honored to be responsible for this boy."

"Oh underlord," haodtie could barely get the words out, "I need help."

---

[1] 2 Timothy 1:7a
[2] 2 Timothy 1:7b

16

Current Era

Dean waited in his car in front of the restaurant as Dale drove up. Getting out together they greeted each other with a handshake and a hug. "Just as two old Christian friends," thought Dale. "This is going to work."

Dean had a real estate broker's license, but with the economy sagging right now he made more money staying home and watching his grandkids ... which he would do for free, but his girls said, "Pop, we've got to pay a babysitter if you don't watch them, so let us pay you."

"Okay ladies, but I'm getting the better part of the deal here. I love being with these kids."

"They love you too, daddy," responded both girls in unison.

In the restaurant, Dean and Dale talked sports. Dale confessed to Dean that even though he grew up in the South, when he went to California to go to college he became a San Francisco Giants fan. He even told Dean that he covets a special shirt he bought, and when the Giants are in Atlanta, he will wear it to the ballgames. It says, "Barry Bonds Baseball." And with that Dean choked and almost spit out his coffee.

"I always enjoy wearing it, Dean. Well, except for one time," he said more thoughtfully. "I had taken a pastor and his wife to the game. The Giants were ahead and in the bottom of the ninth they sent in their closer, The Beard ..."

"Brian Wilson, Fear the Beard?" Dean shot in, "Three years ago?"

"Yes, how'd you know?"

"I sat there in the stadium and loved that last half of the inning."

"Oh Dean, this isn't going to work, this relationship between you and I, I can tell already," Dale trailed off, jokingly.

Dean picked up the story, "I stood up giving The Chop to the Giants, and..."

"Yes," Dale then took the story over, "The Beard, Brian Wilson choked, we lost the game, and the pastor's wife kept giving me 'The Chop' all the way out to the car. I've never invited her or her husband back to a game."

They both laughed and ate their breakfast, which had just arrived.

"Dean, let me tell you what I have in mind," Dale began, as he washed down his heart healthy omelet with some fresh orange juice. "You know that I have written a few books on praying scripture back to God. One is for children..."[1]

"Yah," Dean interrupted. "I love that book. I read a few pages to my grandkids every day. They are getting it, Dale. They are associating prayer with the Word of God. Yesterday I told them I would be gone when they arrived at Cynthia and my house today. Of course they asked me why and I told them that I would

---

[1] This is a real book that is available from www.ThePray-ers.com. It is a merging of a book from 1887, a book of verses written for children, and in "children-ese" with the addition of prayers, based on those verses. The idea is that children associate prayer with the Word of God. Grandparents are reading it to their kids getting as much from it as the kids.

be getting together with the man who wrote that book, and I wanted them to pray for us. They said okay and I didn't think anything of it again until at naptime we prayed, as we usually do before their nap. The verse in the book talked about the Lord coming to take home His believers, and Jeannie, the oldest one said, "Nope grandpa, this won't work."

"What do you mean honey, don't you want to go to heaven with Jesus when He returns for us?

"Of course grandpa," she said as incredulously as a four-year-old could. "But for you and the man you're meeting tomorrow, this won't do. Is there another Bible verse that we can pray for you two?"

"It so excited me, Dale." And with that Dean sat back and jumped back into his not so heart healthy pancakes.

"Wait! Don't leave me hanging Dean," cried Dale. "What did you tell them about what to pray for us?"

"Oddly enough Dale, not something I would have prayed normally. I usually pray something like 'Lord, open the eyes of my heart,' or 'Father, make your way clear.' But, and this is really bizarre Dale, I found myself quoting 1 Corinthians 14:33 to my grandkids, *'God is not a God of confusion, but is a God of peace...'* and then Dale," Dean chuckled, "I started explaining the verse. I said, 'grandpa needs to have peace about helping Mr. Dale so that I know I'm doing what God wants me to do, and not what I want to do just because I'm being selfish.'"

Dale smiled a satisfied smile, and Dean went on.

"Now here's the most bizarre part. They got it. Dale they understood! Jeannie said, 'I know grandpa, it's like when I want Shushu's toy, I feel bad when I take it and he cries. Mommie says I'm just being selfish.' And then, Dale she prayed, 'Dear God, please help grandpa not be selfish tomorrow, let him only take what You want him to, in Jesus Name, Amen.' Dale, they've got it."

Putting down his coffee, Dale felt a lump growing in his throat. He wiped his eyes. "Why is God using me?" he thought. "I am so unworthy, and yet God, You are doing just that, using me."

Dale often said, "God I know me, I wouldn't use me, but You are. Oh I praise You for that. And this became another example. Thank You, Lord."

After a few quiet moments Dale began again, "Dean, there is another book, to say that I've written it isn't accurate but let me tell you about it. It isn't published yet, and I think that it would make a wonderful group Bible study."

"Cool, how can I help?" said an excited Dean.

"Let me tell you about this book by telling you about a book written by R. A. Torrey. It's a little different than most. The copy I have is from 1966, but the author originally wrote the book in 1906. It's called *Studies in the Life and Teachings of Our Lord.* R. A. Torrey became a friend of D. L. Moody's. In fact, he became the president of Moody Bible Institute when Moody died. This book is a unique study of the gospels because, while the book is some 340+ pages long, nearly *every* sentence is a question."

Dean gave out a long low whistle.

"So here's what I've done Dean. My great-great-grandfather had a book written by the Wesleys and in the back of it is a group of prayers called, *A Collection of Prayers for Families.* Well what my great-great-grandfather did is that he wrote questions in his journal. Did I tell you that he lived as an itinerant preacher in Central Georgia?"

"Yes, you've mentioned that before at Issachar Men. You need to know, Dale, he'd be ashamed of you not being a Braves fan."

"He hailed from the North Dean," shot back Dale. Continuing on, "so what I've done is taken great-great-grandpa Alexander's notes and merged them together with the original *Wesley Family Prayers Book*, as questions, so that the questions will cause us to dive super deep into those prayers. Kind of like what Torrey did for the study of the gospels."

"Hmm," Dean responded, somewhat unimpressed. "May I speak frankly, Dale?

"Of course, Dean," replied a confused Dale.

"Well, the Wesleys were great men of course, but wouldn't it be better if we were digging into the Word, and not some men's prayers?"

Laughing a bit, for he now understood Dean's lack of enthusiasm, Dale said, "Great response Dean, great response. You are absolutely right my friend. Let me tell you the part I left out. These prayers by the Wesleys, are not just all about the Word of God, they *are* the Word of God. Every line! Just like what you are reading to your grandkids. You can go through all of the prayers and find Scripture for every line, for the whole thing. In studying these prayers, our study will actually be about how the Wesleys used Scripture to be their *prayer director.*"

Another long low whistle came from Dean. "Ohhh, I get it. That sounds very cool. So when do you want to teach it? Will it become a series at our Saturday prayer times, you know, just before we pray?

"Not exactly Dean," said Dale. "You see, we have 150 men show up for each prayer time. If they are there at 8:00 am, why shouldn't we start a 7:30 am Bible study over in the chapel?

"Ohhh, got it, got it." Dean said convinced he knew where Dale wanted to go, and how Dale wanted to use him. "Your giving us this teaching in small 10 minute portions would be too little. Cool! How can I help? I'm your man. I am excited and honored to do whatever you need. Can I sign men up? How about handouts, will you have handouts each week for them? You know, I'm pretty good on the computer too. Whatever you need done, I can do it."

"Good Dean," said Dale with a sly smile because he knew something that Dean did not, "because I want you to lead the Bible study."

Dean nearly choked, and Dale laughed, and smiled, and then laughed again.

After taking too big a gulp of very hot coffee with Dale laughing, Dean said, "Dale, you're crazy. I can't do that. I'm not ready."

"I know you're not Dean," Dale responded like it didn't matter to Dale. "Dean, I've managed a lot of people over the years, and do you know what I have found? When it comes to promoting them, you promote them a little bit beyond where they are at, so they have to reach for it.

"Here's the issue with me, actually two issues. And they both go back to the verse you quoted, 1 Corinthians 14:33. First Dean, do I have peace about asking you to lead this study … with my help of course, with my periodic guidance? And then, do you have peace about doing it? Well Dean, I do have peace about asking you. So the only question is, do you have peace about accepting the responsibility?"

The two men were silent for a few minutes and katepa tried to sort out how he could use this to his advantage. "There are lots of things I can do with this," were katepa's thoughts. "You guys are toast. There is something that we suspect of Dean that you guys don't know about. But it'll come out. And when it does I will fill his mind with so much anger and doubt and vitriol toward your God that he will blow his testimony. You guys can't win."

After eating the last few bites of his very syrup soaked pancakes, Dean looked up and said, "You set me up Dale, didn't you? You knew I just wanted to help, and you just played along with me, didn't you?"

"Well, let's just say that when I knew the punch line would be upon us, and you were taking that gulp of coffee, it did cross my mind that what might be upon me would be part of that coffee, I did slow down. So will you do it?" asked Dale.

"As weird as this sounds, to my own ears anyway, yes. Yes, I have peace about it, and I'm humbled to serve you in this way Dale."

They were both quiet for a moment and then Dean added, "Dale, I am feeling both humbled and excited at the same time. Is that normal?"

"Very much so my friend, very much so."

Hael stood by with another angel, Tephillah, Dean's guardian angel. "Bitter sweet, eh Teph?"

"Yes," Tephillah responded, "I'm both excited for Dean and concerned for him and his family."

"I know," replied Hael, "But we trust a risen Savior, right?"

As Dale headed back to the university he couldn't help but remember the look of shock that registered on Dean's face when he told him what he really wanted from Dean. And then the laugh the two had. Dean may be a little rough, but only a little, and Dale would be a good manager. He'd keep Dean under his wings until he could handle the responsibility without him. He really liked Dean, really liked him. So would the men. Dean's enthusiasm would be contagious.

"It might be dangerous," surmised Dale, speaking in his car to himself, "but I think I need to invite Dean to a Giants Game."

"I'd like to go too," came the tune from the back of the car.

Dale jumped and yanked the steering wheel causing his car to swerve, "We've got to work on your entry, Hael."

17

Nineteenth Century

Coming back to the present from his thoughts of the early ministry years, Alexander remembered how much he loved praying on this rock. He had a special location outside of every town he served, where he stopped and used that area as his special place to pray for each local flock before he completely left the town.

Often he would prepare for this place by pulling out his Bible immediately upon leaving town. He'd give Sterling the reins, open his Word and begin to meditate on who God revealed Himself to be in the passage as he read. He loved this style of reading the Word. He carefully kept himself from preparing a sermon, even though the distraction that the evil one threw out so often became, "how can I use this in a sermon?" He developed a long time ago a discipline of not studying when the focus should be preparing to spend time in prayer. Another of his disciplines would be to *not pull out* his prayer list, but rather trust the Holy Spirit to guide his mind while he read scripture. He would let the passages in scripture direct how to pray for the things that he sensed the Lord, by way of the Holy Spirit, had laid upon his heart.

He had always read that the men and women of old would pray with their Bibles open, and now he understood the peace that came with that. Amazingly, he not only loved to pray with the Bible leading him, but he couldn't imagine praying any other way. He knew that he didn't need to let his own priorities lead him.

But this afternoon became different. Today something impacted his heart and mind. As he thought about it he could only refer to it as spiritual warfare, and so wanting to understand the wiles of the evil one,[1] and knowing that greater is He that is in Brother Alex than he which is in the world,[2] Brother Alex did not pull out his Bible, he talked to God.

"Lord, Your word says that when I need wisdom I should ask of You and You will give it to me generously.[3] Oh Father, I need Your wisdom today."

Deep in silence and waiting upon God, he fidgeted thinking about pulling out his *Wesley Family Prayers Book*, as he had come to call the book that he found when he and Dwight were stuck overnight in New York City, those many years ago. As he started to reminisce about that trip, he had an immediate sense that the evil one wanted to distract him.

"Your Word also says that I am to be thankful regarding everything.[4] So I thank You, Lord, for this heaviness on my heart. I don't know why it is there, but I trust You to unfold for me what I can give thanks for."

---

[1] Ephesians 6:11e
[2] 1 John 4:4b
[3] James 1:5a
[4] Ephesians 5:20; 1 Thessalonians 5:18

As he steadied himself he stood up in silence next to his prayer rock for a few minutes, not saying a word, just being in the presence of the Lord.

After suggesting his thoughts into Mrs. McCreedy, katepa went back with Brother Alexander, just in time to hear him. "Blast!" katepa yelled. "Why are you thanking the Holy Enemy for heaviness on your heart? That doesn't make any sense, you ignorant preacher. Now is the time for you to remember the great adventure that you and Dwight had together as you found that book. Remember the overnight ... Blast you, you old stubborn preacher. How can a good memory like that be a distraction? Don't you take this thought of mine captive.[1]"

"Lord," Alexander continued, "I know that it makes no sense to thank You for difficulties, but you have shown me that You are sovereign, that Your throne is above all of the heavens.[2] You are my light and my salvation, whom do I have to fear?"[3] Chuckling to himself he went on, "You, oh Lord, are awesome! You have given me a peace that transcends every bit of my understanding,[4] a peace that I did not have a few minutes ago. Oh Lord, forgive me for the times I come to You with prayers and petitions and fail to also be thankful."

---

[1] 2 Corinthians 10:5
[2] Psalm 103:19
[3] Psalm 27:1a
[4] Philippians 4:7

149

Exhaling spittle and the deepest sarcasm katepa had heard in a long time, joln hovered over him, his foul scent bothering even katepa. "This is how you failed before," said joln maiciously. "You are an insignificant minion and I hate having you on my team. I knew this would happen with you."

If there were ever a time when he wanted to tout his success ratio it would be now, but he knew that joln would only scorn katepa's focus on the past.

"I know what I'm doing," growled katepa, "I'll get him. He won't keep on thanking our enemy."

"We'll see," joln spit out, just before he disappeared.

Privately katepa knew he had reason to be scared. This Alexander would not be easy, but rather, he would be difficult to deal with, if he kept thanking God in the midst of difficulties. This, he remembered is what caused his failure with Thales 2000 years earlier in Colossae. He would never forget that loss. Thanking the Holy Enemy for difficulties, how imbecilic, even for the Christ followers. But that is what they did, and that is what had happened when Paul taught Epaphras, when Epaphras had taught Thales, and when the Holy Enemy had, somehow, "inspired" Paul to twice record it after he had done us damage by writing it in the Thessalonian's letter.

"Yuk, this is bad enough," thought katepa, "That he told the Thessalonians." And so katepa did all that he could do to distract people enough to miss that part of the passage. And when that didn't work he would encourage them to be too selfishly wanting their own will, rather than to recognizing God's plan, which included giving thanks for things they did not want.

"But then Paul wrote nearly the same thing to the Ephesians," thought katepa, "Oh, this is going to be more than I can bear. Especially since this new letter is a letter that centered on what they now have in Christ…"

"Blast." katepa cried when he thought of the letter to the Philippians. For it made it clear that the things katepa and his fellow demons were working so hard to get men to be anxious about were what Paul had told them to be thankful for.

"Fortunately," katepa thought, and smiled, "Fortunately people are *not* prone to give thanks for it, and I can win that battle pretty easily ... *if their minds stay off thanking God."*

And then the second reason that secretly scared katepa also had similarities to Thales. Alexander has a similar spirit of adventurism that should have caused Thales' downfall. But instead the Holy Enemy, who claims to use "everything for the better,"[1] used that perfect weapon against katepa, strengthening Thales by humbling him, of all things, and this Brother Alex had the same spiritual experience.

"This could be a problem," worried katepa.

Appearing to do nothing but stand near his charge, the Guardian Angel Hael comforted Alexander Rich. As the servant of the living God, Hael ministered to his charge.[2]

Honored to serve the living God, Hael acted deliberately every time the Lord gave him approval to participate in the preacher's life. This afternoon and tonight would be no exception. There were going to be purposeful distractions that Hael would not be able to stop but he would be there, to the glory of God.

---

[1] Romans 8:28
[2] Hebrews 1:14

On his knees in the presence of God, he rested. It would not be long before Brother Alex had the sweet sensation that he had in fact heard from God.

"Alexander," God lovingly called to his heart. "You can thank Me, because I intend to use these times of heaviness to draw you to Me."

Normally Brother Alex would be praying for his flock by now, but right now he enjoyed the sweet time with the Lord. As he knelt there, eyes open, he often prayed with his eyes open in the forest, he could tell that someone else had been there recently. "Did they pray here too?" He wondered. "Oh Lord," he found himself praying, "is there another? Oh I miss corporate prayer with someone who wants to pray. I don't mean to complain. I hope I'm not complaining, but I so miss real corporate prayer. I so often have to pray with church members who are only there because they've been embarrassed into attending prayer service."

And the moment he said that, he felt the embarrassment, the chastisement, that came from the convicting Holy Spirit. "Father forgive me." he now pleaded with God, "I know that my struggle is not with flesh and blood.[1] You have given me more men and women of prayer than most circuit riding preachers have."

"You, You Christ follower! Can't you stay discouraged for a moment?" katepa wailed at Alexander.

With great maliciousness and the typical spittle that katepa had begun to get used to, "You'll lose another one katepa, you loser." added joln who had snuck up behind him.

And just then joln and katepa saw Hael. And they both, joln and katepa, immediately registered fear.

---

[1] Ephesians 6:12

Regaining his composure as quickly as he could joln said, "I have another comrade I need to visit. I like him more than I like you katepa, so I'll leave you with your charge, and your new friend." Nodding his wrinkled, triangular head toward Hael, joln laughed at katepa and then left.

Getting back onto his knees without saying a word, it could have been a few minutes or many minutes he didn't know, he just knew that he didn't deserve this blessing. The birds were wonderfully singing as they always do, especially in the early evening. In the midst of problems, Alexander Rich experienced rich, indeed, very rich blessings. In fact, he realized that his blessings came *because of* the problems he felt honored to experience, and just then he remembered a passage in Holy Writ … Colossians 3:23. "I am to work as if I am working unto You, Lord, for You are the One who has called me to this occupation. Amen Lord, Amen."

Bombarded by what experience told him were distractions from the evil one, he took each distraction one at a time. Sterling needed to be shod at his next stopover. (He wrote that down in his journal.) The Tharpes were having another baby in Dry Creek. He would need to talk to them about a baby dedication. Next month they could do it, the baby's due date seemed to be a ways away yet. He also wrote that down in his journal and vowed to talk to them later in the week.

The noises in his brain started to slow down when he recorded the "distractions" in his journal, and he rested again in the presence of the Lord. Presently he remembered that he had the *Wesley Family Prayers Book* within reach and opening it up to Sunday morning, looking only at the first paragraph he read:

ALMIGHTY and eternal GOD, we desire to praise thy holy name, for so graciously raising us up, in soundness of body and mind, to see the light of this day. We bless thee in behalf of all thy creatures; for "the eyes of all look unto thee, and you givest them their meat in due season." But above all we acknowledge thine inestimable benefits bestowed upon mankind in CHRIST JESUS. We thank thee for his miraculous birth, his most holy life, his bitter agony, his bloody death, his glorious resurrection on this day, his ascension into heaven, his triumph over all the powers of darkness, and his sitting at thy right hand for evermore.

And then as he had done for the last few decades, he pulled out his notes specifically written for this book. They were questions really that he had written going through each paragraph of these prayers. The questions helped him focus on what God would be saying to him through the Wesleys scriptural prayers. They had simply used God's Word to write these prayers. Often the Wesleys prayers prompted his prayers, applying them to his situations.

Brother Alex had been kneeling at the mossy stone for a few minutes, studying. "This stone isn't too terribly wet," he thought, "in fact, it felt cool and comfortable."

While reading the prayers he heard some twigs break in the background, but being in the forest that made sense to him. "Probably just a curious little animal," he thought. But then he heard it again, and this time, "It didn't sound like a curious animal," he thought. "This sounds too heavy to be a footfall … it's not Sterling. He's in the other direction."

"Is someone there?" he called out, "Come on out, I'm just kneeling here doing my devotions. Come sit with me and we will examine our souls together."

Some more twigs cracked and then after a pause, out came a surprisingly high pitched voice. Surprising Alexander Rich for he did not expect what he heard.

"Brother Rich?"

And he thought he recognized the voice. So with some trepidation, with some surprise, and a slight gladness in his heart that he could not understand, he lifted himself off his knees, turned to the voice and asked, "Gretchen? Gretchen McCreedy is that you?"

"Yes, Brother Rich, it's me, Gretchen," came the voice that seemed both embarrassed and relieved at the same time.

"What are you doing out here Gretchen?" asked Brother Rich as the younger folks out of respect called him.

Gretchen, the thirty-one-year-old daughter of the McCreedy's whom he had just had dinner with had always been a very pretty woman, and so his parishioners seemed to agree. Her husband had died some eight years earlier of Yellow Fever, after a business trip to New Orleans that the McCreedy family had taken. And by God's sovereignty, no one else had been infected.

Gretchen had never remarried, which he found interesting, because as he noticed again, she seemed to be quite attractive even to his fifty-year-old eyes.

Her thirty-one-year-old frame had some meat to her bones without being overweight. She would not be considered a skinny broomstick of a person like her parents. Her dark, thick, long brown hair which he didn't see down very often reached the small of her back, like it did tonight.

As she walked toward him all of these thoughts entered his brain but the thought about her looks that he enjoyed the most had to do with the smile on her face. She had a way of smiling that showed elegance beyond her years and betrayed mischievousness that he hoped she would never lose.

He guessed that the elegance in her smile came with maturing through her husband's death, but the mischievous smile came from her younger years. He remembered of a group of six and seven year olds that after church one day did a recital for the church and one of the girls, back then, had the same smile that she did now. He smiled too and then smiled at Gretchen.

"I thought that I would stop here and study, and then spend some time praying," he said.

"I know," she responded, not quite apologetically, but, well, mischievously.

With an eyebrow raised, he cocked his head to one side and said, "You know?"

"Umm, yes," she expressed sheepishly. "I have followed you out here a number of times in the past few years Brother Rich. I'm sorry for being so deceptive." She paused, waiting for him to get angry with her like her father would.

"But he wouldn't do that. It's not his way," she thought to herself and then smiled. In fact, those ways of his caused her to like him, maybe a lot. She liked this godly servant who always had everyone else's needs on his heart, instead of his own."

She continued speaking to him, "Brother Rich, when you pray I stay in the back praying with you." She started to relax, "I so enjoy it when you pray out loud, because I can then agree with you in prayer."

"So that means you have heard what I've said or prayed to God about some in your town?"

"And my own parents," she responded with a knowing smile, but she quickly added, "Don't worry. Your prayers will never go beyond me, never. In fact, when you leave to go on to Dry Branch I kneel down at your rock and pray for all of the things you just prayed. I want your prayers to be answered. And I remember you telling us that there is something even more efficacious about two people praying and agreeing together that God honors.[1] But," she continued, now picking up steam, "when I pray for some of them, I use a lot stronger words than you do, after all, I live with them every day, and you're absolutely right about every one of them." With this she knew that she had gone too far. "I'm sorry, I'm probably speaking a bit out of turn Brother Rich."

"It's okay Gretchen, thank you for your honesty and your modesty, but I will be more careful when I pray out loud," he chuckled, putting her at ease. "Speaking of modesty, it isn't wise for us to be out here like this together without an escort, wouldn't you agree?"

Without waiting for an answer, he motioned for her to sit on a log opposite his square stone. "I want you to go back to your folks home right away," he said like a preacher, but a preacher with a soft side to him, a true shepherd, she had come to realize. "Let me pray for you first, okay?"

"Oh, I'd love that Brother Rich."

As they bowed their heads and closed their eyes Gretchen looked up and said, "You know, I already feel like I pray with you, when I watch you pray."

And with that they both closed their eyes, "Father, the apostle Paul at the end of his brilliant Epistle to the Romans, verse 13 of chapter 15, wrote that You are the God of Hope, and I pray this for Gretchen now, that You are already in the process of filling her with great joy and great peace, simply because she is a believer. And as You do that Father, I am confident that when Gretchen returns home Mr. and Mrs. McCreedy will see a joy that is overflowing out of her, and they will see that it comes

---

[1] Matthew 18:19

157

from the Holy Spirit living inside of her. We pray this in the magnificent Name of the Son You sent to earth to save us. Amen."

Close enough to hear the prayer, the Jeffersonville town drunk Carrolton Faith heard everything. And in the prayer he heard come from the preacher a distant memory begged to come forward in his brain.

"What is it?" he thought to himself. Being slightly inebriated he couldn't place the memory. "Does it have something to do with my long dead parents? What is it?"

Gretchen left the woods, almost skipping, smiling to herself, and Brother Alex got back to his *Wesley Family Prayers Book* along with his special "questions" that he used.

Carrolton's father had been a preacher in Georgia's very early history. The state took up only half the acreage then that it did now.

Forcing his inebriated brain to return to the prayer he seemed to think that the prayer had something to do with his mother ...

"What is it?" he thought to himself again. He couldn't remember.

Looking at the thought merely as a distraction, he thought, a bit loudly, "What are you doing with my girlfriend preacher?" He thought he spoke in a low voice to himself, but it would not be as low as he thought.

Brother Rich came up off his stony stump faster than Carrolton, often called Carrol, would have expected him to move. Brother Rich yelled out for the intruder to show himself. And with that Carrol did so.

"Carrolton, what are you doing out here?" Feeling defensive for Gretchen, and seeing that Carrolton wanted to leave, Brother Rich pointed to the log Gretchen had sat on, "Sit there, Carrolton!"

"What were you doing here, Preacher?" Carrol tried to say, as soberly as he could.

"Carrol, did you say something about a girlfriend?"

Now confused and scared he hiccupped out, "I recognized that prayer you prayed with," another hiccup, "Sister Gretchen. Where'd you get it from, the Bible?"

"This would be great," thought katepa. "Get angry, you goody two shoes, the 'so-called' Brother Alex. You have the Enemy's angel," now katepa snickered and snarled, "but I have gossip. I will win. And you, old-man, you will go to your grave a disgraced preacher. Yes!"

Being a bit frustrated, and with some anger building up Brother Alex made a decision he would regret, "Until you are sober, Carrolton I will not talk to you about things of the Lord." Even as it came out of his mouth he realized that this man didn't deserve to be spoken to that way.

"My struggle isn't with flesh and blood," thought Rich, "I know that." And then Carrolton hiccupped again and Rich wanted to reach over and throttle him. "What would have happened to Gretchen if he had not been here to protect her? I will have to warn Gretchen the next time I am in town. But that won't be for at least a month. Perhaps I can write to her parents."

The newly placed demon katepa saw his plan work out even better than he had anticipated. Whispering in the ear of Carrol, he said, "I wonder what Mrs. McCreedy would think of her poor lonely daughter out here with the unmarried preacher … and, she had been out here with him many times."

"You're toast Sainted Brother Alexander," said katepa, "You are toast!"

After a half hour of Carrolton Faith sitting quietly and sheepishly with Brother Alexander, he turned to him saying, "Get out of here Carrolton," with more anger than he had spoken to anyone in a long while. "And don't let me catch you sneaking up on me, or anyone again."

With that Carrolton got up to leave, but when the two men's eyes met Carrolton's were not the same. He no longer looked sheepishly at Brother Alex, he now squinted with the wheels in his head turning. He schemed behind those bloodshot eyes.

Brother Alex didn't think twice about it, but he should have.

"I'm going to make so much trouble for you preacher. You're going to wish you never talked to me that way," thought an angry and seriously offended Carrolton Faith.

Getting back to his studying he realized that he would be spending the night out here, so he groomed his horse, built a fire and sat down to re-read the Wesley prayer that he had planned to study. He read again:

ALMIGHTY and eternal GOD, we desire to praise thy holy name, for so graciously raising us up, in soundness of body and mind, to see the light of this day. We bless thee in behalf of all thy creatures; for "the eyes of all look unto thee, and you givest them their meat in due season." But above all we acknowledge thine inestimable benefits bestowed upon mankind in CHRIST JESUS. We thank thee for his miraculous birth, his most holy life, his bitter agony, his bloody death, his glorious resurrection on this day, his ascension into heaven, his triumph over all the powers of darkness, and his sitting at thy right hand for evermore.

His study custom and discipline being to pull out his questions that he had written over time, he did so and let those questions, along with the prayers, deepen his prayer life and study the Word at the same time.

Gretchen's lovely smile crept back into his mind. "What? Where did that come from?" he moaned. "Lord, I don't need that kind of a distraction entering my brain right now. I submit to You, Lord,[1] I desire to focus on You, and so, by faith, I lift the shield of faith,[2] trusting you to do something different in my brain, which is always the result when You stop those fiery darts. I don't need to think about her when I want to spend time with you…via the Wesleys."

"You may take the thought of her captive right now,"[3] sneered katepa, "But there is coming soon, so much trouble into your life preacher that you will not be able to take anything

---

[1] James 4:7a
[2] Ephesians 6:16
[3] 2 Corinthians 10:5e

captive, because you will be captive to me and my thoughts in your brain."

Brother Rich pulled out his questions that go with the *Wesley Family Prayers Book* and quickly perused them. "Oh Lord I so enjoy praising You,"

- Which words and phrases give consideration to praising God?
- How does the above paragraph of praising compare to the way you praise?
- If "thanking" God is not "praising" God, when you praise the Lord, for how long do you praise Him (one or two sentences, ten minutes, how long)?
- Spend a moment right now praising the Lord. How quickly did it turn to you thanking the Lord?
- Which praises above do you recall praising God with?
- Have you ever praised the Lord for "raising," or waking you up?
- When is the last time you praised God for "all thy creatures," all of His animals?
- What verse is referenced about the way the Lord takes care of the animals?
- When you praise God for Christ, how specific are you?
- Do you thank the Father for the Son's "miraculous birth," or "His most holy life," or "His perfect life?"
- How about "the bitter agony" or "the bloody death … glorious resurrection," etc.?
- What words do you use when you pray?
- Do your words have to be as "large" as theirs? Why or why not?

- What are some of the "inestimable benefits" to us, 2000 years removed, because of Christ?
- How many verses in the paragraph above are referenced? Do you know which ones they are?

An hour later Brother Alex read the second paragraph of the *Wesley Family Prayers Book*, and going through the next set of questions. He had already written many notes in his journal and looked forward to another fire lit evening, studying the Word.

"Father, it is always amazing to me how you bring just the right Bible study to me when I need it. In this case, *Looking at Sinners with Love!* Oh, Father, forgive me for treating Carrolton the way I did. Give me the opportunity to ask his forgiveness when I return to Jeffersonville next month."

And then he began to read the next paragraph of prayers, and their corresponding questions.

> *O GOD, how great is thy love to the sinful sons of men, to give thy "only-begotten Son, that whosoever believeth on him might not perish, but have everlasting life!" How great is that love, which has committed our souls to one so "mighty to save;" and which has chosen us to be thy sons, and heirs together with CHRIST JESUS, and set such an High-Priest over thy house and family to make intercession for us, to pour thy blessings upon us, and to send forth his angels to "minister unto them who shall be heirs of salvation!" O the riches of thy grace, in sending the HOLY GHOST, to make us abound in hope that we shall one day rise from the dead, and, after our short labors here, rest with thee in thy eternal glory.*

- Do you see any "thanking God" yet?

- What do you think of, out of *your* eyes, not God's, when you see, "sinful sons of men?"
- Do you have love for them, or condemn them?
- Your answer should be that His love is mighty to, what?
- So, if you are praying for their salvation, do you expect God to save them?
- When's the last time you thanked God for "angels to minister" to you?
- To whom of the three persons of the trinity are we praying to in this paragraph?
- As used in this paragraph, what is the role of each person of the trinity?
- Who, above, is the beneficiary of "thy blessings"?
- If we are the beneficiary, why aren't we thanking the Father?
- Are you offended or uneasy about the discussion of "rising from the dead," participating in "short labors here," or resting "with thee?" Why or why not?
- Where do the progression of blessings for us begin and end in this paragraph?
- Why do you think the Wesleys could talk of death so easily and encouragingly?
- How many verses in the paragraph above are referenced? Do you know which ones they are?

After another hour he knew he needed to sleep, his fire would go out soon, and the thought of praying … the thought of praying with Gretchen, became a sweet memory of the day. "Hmm," he mumbled and smiled, "A sweet aroma unto You, Lord.[1] Goodnight, Father."

---

[1] Cf Revelation 5:8e and Psalm 141:2a

18

Current Era

The Saturday after Dean and Dale met at the pancake house the next Saturday men's prayer time came around again. The Issachar Men had finished singing and John, Dale's small group men's Bible study teacher gave the announcements before Dale came up to speak to the men. "Starting the next time we get together," John began, "in two weeks, Brother Dale intends to start a new Bible study before we start praying. Since we start at 8:00 am, this Bible study will begin at 7:30 am and run for half an hour."

There were a couple of "Amens" while John made a cursory look over at Dr. Bob the senior pastor. With upraised eyebrows, and possibly partially surprised, Dr. Bob acknowledged this with an "Amen" of his own. John encouraged the men to attend at 7:30 am, reassuring them that the Bible study would end with plenty of time for them to get coffee, Krispy Kreme donuts, and Chik-fil-A breakfast sandwiches before the prayer time started. And to that were many more, and much louder "Amens."

Dale, halfway up the steps to speak to the men when this second set of louder "Amens" erupted, stopped dead in his tracks.

Turning to look at, and pan across all one hundred forty-five or fifty men, they chuckled and he turned to keep going up the alter steps to the pulpit.

"Dean, would you stand up please?" Dale knew that Dean would be dreading this. Dean's sincere humility had become a trait that Dale loved in Dean.

Dale knew that humble Dean got excited about being entrusted with this responsibility, and yet Dean showed no outstanding pride about it. He had a humility that Dale suspected came from a man broken of all of his previous earthly successes, and loved by a God who had made it clear that He would take care of all of his needs … "But it's more than that," Dale wondered, "What is it?"

The previous Saturday, Dale had wondered when they met in his office after his home track meet. "What is it that he saw in Dean?"

After their breakfast, Dale suggested they meet to review the new Bible study and they did a couple of days later. Since this unique Bible study about prayer that Dale had prepared with the help of his great-great-grandfather and the Wesleys would be a challenge, he wanted to help Dean get his arms around it, and so they met in Dale's track office.

"Dale, we need to pray," a slightly uneasy Dean said almost as soon as they got into his office.

Dale shut the door and turned to Dean, "I agree my friend, let's pray, but Dean, I want us to be a bit deliberate about our praying, okay?"

"What do you mean Dale?"

"I have taught on this before, Dean," continued Dale. "Do you remember when I spoke recently about good deacons?" He lifted his hands to make quote marks around "good deacons." "I said, 'Here's what good deacons do. They come into their business meeting praying first.'" He again made quote marks with his fingers. "Because they are good deacons, end quote. They say 'Amen,' but then *they* figure out what God wants them to do.

"I've tried to demonstrate, Dean, that this is a problem today that we have let creep into our homes too."

"Oh, I'm with you Dale," Dean interrupted. "I remember when you taught us that. I remembered your words," Dean began to get a bit embarrassed." You said, '… what we need to do when we're making decisions is come to the Lord, put our agenda in the middle of the table, get on our bellies, and then talk to God about each agenda item.' You said that 'when we got off our bellies we'd know what God wanted us to do.' Well I remember that because of the size of my belly and because later that day my wife and I needed to make a decision about where we were living. Without getting into the details let me tell you what I did. She had a sheet of five or six questions that she had decided were questions we needed to answer to make a decision.

"I love her, she is so organized and analytical. Anyway, she had taken the time to boil down our decision making to these questions. Again, I don't want to get into all the details at this time, so let me just say that she had done an excellent job bringing our decision down to a few issues.

"But here's where the problem came in. She wanted to determine the answer to each decision with her wonderfully analytical brain …"

Just then joln appeared from the shadows. He stood stiff and tense, looking around like an angry animal poising to fight for his territory. Then he spotted a smirking katepa, "Not a word from you, katepa," joln growled.

"Oh, not at all, your over-lordship," replied katepa, barely able to hold back his contempt for this inept overlord.

Dean's wife Cynthia had been completely prepared by joln the way he wanted her set up, and joln had bragged that a potential prayer leader's family would soon have serious problems when this "discussion" began. Cynthia had an accounting degree and a fair bit of well-deserved pride. All joln did to Cynthia's memory of the last time they had to make a financial decision, included reminding her how it resulted in them losing a great deal of money, and who made the final decision 'because he chose his decision over her recommendation.'

And joln, with the well-equipped memory consistent with his hierarchical status, nudged her memory enough to develop anger and resentment.

What joln had not prepared for, and couldn't even if he knew it would happen, had to do with Dean's actions in the car before he pulled onto his street. Dean had stopped at the park, got out of his car, started to walk, and, joln hated even thinking about this, he, ugh, p-r-a-y-e-d.

As joln saw what happened, he immediately jumped into action, bombarding Dean's mind with what those mortals called, "noise." "It is nothing of the sort," he had roared.

And then Dean did what he had just recently started doing, he pulled out his smart phone and turning it on he went to the OneNote page for his journal for that day, and wrote down the things that were bombarding his brain:
- Take out the garbage

- Cynthia needs her shoes shined before church tomorrow
- Turn the grill on for barbeque as the girls' families are coming over for lunch

"I hate these Christ followers who actually listen and put into practice what their teachers teach them."

And with the "noise" gone, Dean petitioned the Lord with each area that joln had thought he had sewn up for ultimate family dissention, untrustworthiness, and ultimately, financially related unforgiveness, the marriage killer in his experience.

"Then this ignorant mortal had started his prayer," joln said to himself, remembering every one of Dean's words, "As I read Your word, I am reminded that 2 Thessalonians 1:11-12 accurately deals with the burden on my heart. I pray for Cynthia Lord, that since You consider her worthy of her calling, that by Your power you would fulfill every good purpose of hers, and every act that is prompted by her faith …" and then he added this, "but not a single one prompted by her flesh, unto Your glory"

"What? You bumbling, foolish …" and then profane expletives came from joln's mouth. "Where did that prayer come from? Where did you learn to apply the Holy Enemy's Word to your life? And then he finished by praying the next verse, that the Holy Enemy's Son would be glorified in him and in his wife."

By now joln fumed and could hardly contain his anxiety. And in a smelly, misty shadow, closer to joln than katepa wanted to be, a smiling katepa enjoyed himself. He watched his "overlord" fail.

"You are the loser, joln," whispered katepa so no one could hear but joln.

"Ugh, Ugh-ugh-ugh," joln responded, unable to say anything else.

And then katepa couldn't contain himself. Dripping with condescension he said, "You look like these mortals' children, joln. I don't like you, that isn't a secret, but you are such an inept moron. Quit jumping up and down like that. It's embarrassing."

Thinking he would experience this alone, and now knowing that katepa saw it all, a mortified joln slipped into another location away from katepa. And the rest, as joln knew, would be history.

"So after I prayed at the park," Dean continued to explain, "I went home and Cynthia met me at the door … with a piece of paper in hand.

"Dean, you are a little late today," a sincerely concerned wife asked, "Is everything okay?"

"Yah baby, I just felt like I needed to stop over at the park and pray.

And with that, I took her lovingly by the hands and said, "Let's pray about these decisions the way Brother Dale taught us today."

"What do you mean," a frowning Cynthia said. "I mean, of course, okay, no problem, I think we should pray first too."

"Umm, honey, let me share with you what I mean." Dean consoled, "I'd like us to put your points in the middle of the table, and then let's get on our knees and begin to talk to God about each item, slowly, completely, and only go to the next item when you and I both think that it is time. It's okay if we revisit the item a few times." He chuckled and went on, "This isn't a 'one-and-done' prayer. If you want to pray about an agenda item a few times, that's okay, alright babe?"

I noticed that she seemed a bit put off and disappointed, which surprisingly left her as quickly as she blinked. Before I knew it she said, "Okay sweetheart, that's a good idea."

"Now that ain't Cynthia, Dale. I don't know what happened, because she is usually a bit more, well, obstinate about financial decisions, especially after some of the bonehead decisions I have made. Anyway, we went to the sofa, got on our knees, put her sheet of paper in the middle and started to talk to God deliberately about each item. And guess what?

"You knew what to do?" finished Dale, with a question.

"Yes. Amazingly, when we were done we knew what to do."

"What is it about Dean?" Dale wondered again from his office. Dean sat across from him, telling Dale of his interaction with his Cynthia, when Dale realized what it is that he so liked about Dean, "Faith! That's it. Dean had faith, childlike, trusting faith. Dean just trusted that if God said it then that settled it."

Recalling bits and pieces of the conversation while Dale walked to the podium, he smiled admiringly at Dean, and with that in his mind, Dale had Dean stand in front of the men. "You may not know Dean, but as I spend time with him I believe that he is just the right man to lead our next discipleship direction, namely a Bible study. It will be in the chapel, so join us there, next time we meet, at 7:30 am.

19

Current Era

It would be another late night for Dale. He could tell by the uneasiness in his spirit. After talking and laughing with Margie, catching up and talking about the next day, he rolled out of bed. "I need to open my Bible, baby."

"Why don't you read here Dale, turn on the light and I'll turn the other way."

"Thanks baby, but I'm going to want to make notes and study I think." And with that Dale left the room.

He had been in the living room only a few minutes when Hael started to appear. "And started to appear is the exact way to describe it," he thought. "Why don't you just 'poof' appear Hael?"

"Let me say it the way that you in the south would understand it … Because all y'all would be too startled."

"Fair enough," Dale conceded.

The two began talking as if they were best friends who saw each other nearly every day. Hael nearly immediately said, "Dale, go slow with Julienne's situation. There are things going on with Professor Gonzalez that you aren't privy to, and for that matter may never be. You need to take your own advice from 1 Corinthians 14:33, okay?"

"Sure," Dale acknowledged, and then finished his sentence with his own advice, "Seek the Lord. No peace, no move, right?"

"Right on Dale."

And Dale raised his eyebrows at the slang employed by Hael.

"Hael, I have a bunch of questions for you and well, I guess I need to take them slowly but can I ask you just one?"

Warily Hael conceded, "You ask and then I'll either answer you or I won't, okay?"

"Fair enough. I wanted to ask you, whom have you 'guarded' in the past? Are you able to tell me?"

Chuckling Hael said, "as a matter of fact Dale, I have been told, just today, that I can tell you about two of them that …"

"Wait, wait Hael, how did you know that I'd be asking …"

"Me that question Dale?"

"Well, yes, I mean …"

"Dale," Hael continued deliberately, "where do you think the idea to ask me about this came from? Do you remember Proverbs 21:1?"

"Of course I do, I describe the verse all of the time when I tell people why they do not need to question praying for the things that the Lord lays on their heart." Speaking more thoughtfully Dale continued, "Just like God moves the hearts of kings, He moves my heart."

"Yes, but don't forget," Hael broke in, "there is also the Word, and the promptings that come from reading and digesting it, as the Holy Spirit moves you. So, when you abide in Jesus and He abides in you, you bear the fruit that the Lord wants you to bear."[1]

---

[1] John 15:5

"Hmm, okay, that makes sense. So tell me, who are the two you have been given permission to tell me about?"

"Well," started Hael, "you realize that the ones I give you, and their information, as I'm allowed to give it, is for the purpose of building your prayer life."

"Sure, that makes sense Hael. But let me tell you why I ask the question. I'm just curious, if we trust God for things, for everything, then what does the angel do? I'm just wondering if there are things in the past that I can research and see better how you do what you do."

"Fair question Dale, and the answer is from scripture. We are, what Hebrews 1:14 calls, ministering spirits that are sent to serve all y'all." Dale still looked thoughtfully and missed Hael's attempt at southern humor so Hael continued, "We are carrying out what God wants done. Let me give you an example from your own life.

"Do you remember," Hael asked, "when you were young and went to Whispering Pines Christian Camp? You were nine or ten years old and you were on the Teeter Totter. Do you remember the other person jumping off and you fell down flat, sharp and hard?"

"Yes I do remember that Hael. My hand got caught underneath the wooden seat I sat on. I remember that I believed myself to be so fortunate because I had a ring of some sort on that hand, and the wild thing is that the fall bent the ring, and did not hurt my hand."

"Good memory Dale. That happened like that because of me."

"What? Are you trying to tell me you're the one that jumped off the other end of the Teeter Totter?"

"No Dale, I put your hand with the ring under the seat so that you wouldn't hurt your back, and put the hand positioned in such a way that the fall would bend the ring but not hurt your hand.

Hael sat silently and Dale, thoughtfully, started to speak again, "Hael I don't know if you can read my mind but the other day I thought about that very incident on the playground at Whispering Pines Christian Camp."

Hael chuckled and said, "That doesn't surprise me Dale. You see the Holy Spirit knew that we would be talking tonight and prepared you with that memory."

Dale continued, "Hael, I remember when I thought about that. Right then and there I stopped and thanked the Lord for the many ways in which He protects me."

"Dale, that's one of the things we love about you. You do not plead and plead with God for protection, you merely trust Him to be the Protector He has said that He is. And we noticed that you do the same thing with money, don't you?"

Humbly Dale responded, "Yes, when Margie's and my checking account gets very, very low, we never say, 'Oh no Lord, what are you gonna do or how are you going to …? Or what's gonna happen?"

"Your prayer is almost exactly the same each time," Hael now took over the conversation, "you say to the Lord: 'Thank you for another opportunity for You to strengthen our faith muscles and we get to watch You do it.'"

Hael let Dale reflect a little and then said, "Dale, do you remember when you were driving late one night, turning from I-75 onto I-16. You were getting off at exit 1A, where you always get off to go home, and some young girl came barreling down behind you …"

"Yes, I remember Hael, I didn't think she saw anything ahead of her and so I braced for an impact."

"That's right, and do you remember her looking up?"

"Yes I do, and she immediately hit the brakes and slid around me."

"Yes she did, Dale, bless her heart," said Hael with a healthy dose of sarcasm.

"It's getting late Dale, but let me just tell you quickly that we will talk about a young man I guarded back at the beginning of the Christian era named Thales. He's the nephew of a Bible character named Epaphras."

"What?" cried Dale, louder than he wanted to. "You can tell me about Epaphras?"

"Slow down Dale. I can tell you about the things Thales learned under Epaphras, but Epaphras is off limits."

"Honey," came a concerned question from their bedroom, "is everything okay?"

"Yah baby," Dale responded, "just a little excited out here." He knew that Margie would be back to sleep in minutes.

"You'll not find anything on Thales, but I have been given permission to share with you some pretty interesting anecdotes from his life. And I think you'll find it exciting as well." Hael hesitated, "As well as a confirmation to some of the things that you practice and teach regarding prayer."

"What kind of things Hale?"

"Well, over time Dale, we'll talk about spiritual warfare, decision making, dealing with troubles, etc. As I know that you realize Dale, because I've heard you teach on it, things are going to get a lot worse down here on earth, before they get better, if they get better … before the Lord comes of course. But, here's the point Dale. The Christians on earth have got to rebuild their prayer foundations, or else they will cave in the way they live and reject the God of the Bible in their heart."

"Wow! That sounds exciting. When will we go over these things?"

"In time, Dale, in time."

They both sat there for a moment, Dale thinking and Hael watching Dale think. He couldn't read Dale's mind, but he knew mortals well enough to almost see the wheels turning in Dale's head.

After a moment Dale went on, "You said there were two mortals, Hael that you guarded that you could tell me about. Tell me a little about the second one?"

Slowly, but deliberately, Hael said, "He happened to be an itinerant preacher ..."

Hael saw Dale perk up and his eyes widen.

"His circuit included middle Georgia, Dale," continued Hael, "a few generations ago."

Dale now moved to the front of his chair.

"His name is Pastor Alexander Rich, Dale." Hael, not quite finished, let the words hang in the air.

Dales eyes began to tear up.

"Yes, your great-great-grandfather Dale."

Hael allowed a few moments for that to sink in, and then he told him, "I have to be very careful what I tell you about him, okay?"

Dale nodded his understanding, and with that, Hael faded back out for the next time they would get together.

Numb and excited, overwhelmed and honored, Dale went to the book of Hebrews, to continue his study of angels.

20

First Century

Two months after he had begun his new job, Thales, had been getting used to his responsibilities. Having some downtime he relaxed among the parchments owned by Epaphras.

The parchments that Epaphras had at his home were amazing. Previous to this adventure, Thales experience with parchments were the weekly parchment his house-church leader reviewed, if he had one at all. To have so many parchments at his fingertips became a huge encouragement and motivation to Thales's spiritual life.

One of the first thing that Thales noticed when he started studying the parchments had to do with how sturdy they were. Thales had seen a few Papyrus letters that came to his grandmother, but these soon became brittle and as such didn't last long. "Interesting," thought Thales, "the papyrus when woven together makes durable rugs, tents, baskets, boats, etc., but when dried and used as a simple letter it had a significantly reduced life. These parchments, on the other hand are incredible in their durability, which makes sense because they are made from the skins of calves or baby goats."

Being the understudy to his Uncle Epaphras began as a huge challenge and a huge disappointment. Two months earlier Thales' imagination had his future *very* different. After all, Thales's view of his future centered around him wanting to be an adventurer. So when his mother and father told him that he would be working with his Uncle Epaphras, he had visions of traveling with Epaphras, perhaps even being his bodyguard. But being the understudy to Epaphras, which he soon found out, this shocked his thoughts about his future. This station in life, two months ago, would be the furthest thing from what he had assumed would be his lot, his future.

His Uncle Epaphras shared with him his first day there, about a prayer request that he felt had been answered in the person of Thales. "Wow," Thales remembered thinking when his uncle shared that with him, "God talked to my uncle about me. Wow!" Thales moved his meager things from Hierapolis to downtown Colossae where Epaphras lived. He would have liked to have needed a cart to make the move, but he didn't need one, he had so few things. He merely filled a rucksack and then threw it over his back, and traveled the six miles along the Lycus River from Hierapolis to Colossae.

As he walked along the river he had visions of taking this tributary to the Maeander River. "What an exciting trip that could be!" he thought.

"'That *will be*,' is what you really mean, Thales," sneered katepa who did a bit more than merely observing.

"Actually, Paul and his entourage probably already have travel dates and tickets for Uncle Epaphras and myself," concluded Thales. "Oh what a trip this will be!" The Lycus River, really just a tributary of the Maeander River would be their route that they would have to travel, for a full one hundred miles before they reached the Maeander and then they would go by Ephesus. "Yes!" Thales threw up his hand in exultation. "I will finally get to be an adventurer."

Walking along the Lycus River to his new home, he started to think of the last time he got to visit Colossae. He had come to visit his uncle and help him organize his parchments. He enjoyed opening many of them up, but as he did, he found himself getting tired. And so, on the second day of his visit he left Epaphras's house about noon and went for a walk into the town center. As he walked through the meat market and then on to the fruit stands, he started to smell something lovely. It's aroma caught him completely off guard because it smelled completely different from the smells his senses were taking in. As he came around a stand full of apples and pomegranates, he saw where the aroma came from. There, only a few feet away stood a flower stand, between the weavers and the sandal makers.

At the flower stand he saw a beautiful Jewish girl working there. Thales strode up and chose a handful of flowers. Going up to the teenage girl, he guessed that her age would be near his. She held herself like an elegant young woman. The closer he got to her the more his hands started to sweat and then his throat became dry so he could barely speak.

Also at the flower stand sat a woman who looked like she could be the girl's mother. Thales started off like a young proud peacock, but the closer he got to the girl the more nervous he became. By the time he needed to pay the girl he couldn't work up the courage to ask her name, fortunately he heard her mother referred to the girl as Mary.

Getting nearer to Colossae, his knapsack heavier over his shoulder than he would have imagined, his mind drifted to Mary. "I'll need to keep fresh flowers in Uncle Epaphras's home," he decided.

"The fool, Thales, is on his way," katepa reported to haodtie.

"Good," haodtie said, nearly rubbing his claws together. "Is he still deceived into thinking he will be a great adventurer?"

"I helped him think that way while he traveled to Colossae," confessed katepa.

"Very good, katepa. You will find that I am an easy overlord, if you think ahead, use our master's wisdom, and are a team player," confided haodtie. "Oh," he added, "And *don't* fail."

Thales got closer to Colossae where his new adventure would begin when the wonderful aromas he had just savored, from his memory of Mary and the flower stand changed. He realized that he had entered the city behind a caravan of camels. The caravan clanked and squeaked and Thales could barely contain himself as he thought of all of the unique artifacts that would be for sale. He looked at this caravan where stacks were so high that the stack of goods on each camel had started to lean over. Thales laughed, thinking about how he might be just like those goods, leaning over as the traveling took on many days. "Oh Lord, this is so exciting. I thank You for giving me this opened door to travel with Paul and Uncle Epaphras."

"Curious," came a thought to Thales from somewhere that he could not put a finger on, "Why am I not as excited as a few days ago?" The thought simply ran through his brain and then left him as he reached the outskirts of the town.

When Thales arrived and settled into his room, Epaphras gave Thales his first lesson on prayer. "Thales," Epaphras began, "there will be times when you pray to God and you have an uncertain feeling in your spirit, not quite a sense of dread, but similar to that. You will find an uncomfortableness that is not quenched quickly. Every time this occurs Thales, slow down, and spend some time seeking the Father[1] for direction and for his still small voice.[2] His direction will come in peace that He gives you, but more often the knowledge that you need to seek the Lord will come because you have a lack of peace."

"Yes, I think I understand," said Thales, with a bit more self-assured understanding than Epaphras felt comfortable with. "I believe that the Lord has been speaking to me for a long time, Uncle Epaphras. I am confident that this assignment with you is God's will for my life."

Epaphras knew what Thales did not, that he would soon experience a great disappointment. He knew his nephew's real desires. The question would be, "How do I tell Thales he is not going to travel with us, and motivate him at the same time?"

"Thales, tell me, what is it that you are seeing as God's will for your life?"

"Oh, that's easy! I think God wants me to travel with you, maybe as your bodyguard, or Paul's. After all, it has been my heart's desire for a long time to do that, and I have never forgotten the words of the writer of the Psalm who said, "When I delight myself in Him, He will give me the desires of my heart.[3] Don't you agree with that passage Uncle Epaphras?"

Epaphras looked down at the tale for a moment. "This would be harder than I had originally expected," thought Epaphras.

---

[1] Jeremiah 29:13-14a
[2] 1 Kings 19:12b
[3] Psalm 37:4

"Just put him out of his misery Epaphras," whispered haodtie.

"Push him Thales," screamed katepa, and then after seeing a snarling look from haodtie, katepa said a little quieter, "Thales, ask him how soon you get to start traveling."

Standing tall and at attention, the Guardian Angel Hael stood behind Thales. "I have your back Thales," whispered Hael as he looked over at katepa.

"When did he show up?" snarled katepa while throwing his head toward Hael.

"I don't know," responded haodtie who still shuddered[1] in awe of the Holy Enemy's abilities now that Jesus came to earth and defeated the demons on the cross. Continuing, haodtie said, "but katepa, be careful."

"Thales, I love that passage too," Epaphras continued, seeing that Thales wanted to keep talking. "Let's examine this a bit, okay?"

"Oh, umm, okay Uncle."

"Thales, give me that parchment over there." Epaphras pointed to a cubby hole that said poetry."

---

[1] James 2:19

Demonic groanings could be heard all through the cavernous lair as both haodtie and katepa could see that this overgrown angel in white standing guard over these mortals, stood, but not alone. He ... "No," they both cried. No!"

Their Holy Enemy, the Holy Spirit, in this case, had just given some insight to Epaphras that would cause joln and katepa to lose their power of deception over Thales, that they had been whispering into his ear.

Smiling in the background. A background of light and glory, that would always be very different from the lair of haodtie and katepa, a solidly standing, reverent and respectable Hael just smiled. "It is so peaceful," he thought, "that when I serve the King, I don't have to manipulate and coerce the humans. God is in control. God is sovereign." Hael continued to reflect, "It is interesting that the demons say we are weak for following Jehovah, because in a sense they are right. We do not take advantage of situations these mortals find themselves in. But that is where the demons' understanding falls apart, for it is in our supposed weakness where strength finds itself."[1] Hael smiled again, "God Almighty, Your ways are so far above all others' ways.[2] We are so fortunate that You are our God. I am honored to serve You."

"I will win this battle," katepa thought to himself, "and rub your squeaky clean face in it you overgrown do-gooder and adventurer wannabe Thales."

---

[1] 2 Corinthians 12:10e
[2] Isaiah 55:8

"Thales, what is meant by the writer when he said, 'Delight yourself in the Lord?'"

"Enjoy the Lord," Thales said, a little incredulously.

"So you mean, like play marbles with Him, exercise with Him? What do you mean?"

"Well, he's clearly saying that you should make sure that what you are getting delight in is centered around the Lord."

"Okay, can you elaborate a bit more? Can you be more specific?"

"Hmm," Thales now sat back and crumpled his brow as he looked up through the window and into the heavens, without looking at anything in particular. "Well, I guess that the writer is wanting us to make sure that what delights us, is what the Lord wants us to get delight in."

"Okay," responded Epaphras cautiously. "So, what if I have any unconfessed and unforsaken sin in my life, how will that impact 'delighting myself in the Lord.'"

As Thales mulled that over in his brain he began to feel uneasy, not sure why, but he shrugged it off. "As I think about your question Uncle, I am reminded of other passages like the Proverbs of Solomon where he says that if we do not obey the Word, our prayers are detestable to God.[1] And then there is the prophet Isaiah, who near the end of his parchment writes that sin separates us from God.[2] Hmm, Uncle, I am also reminded of Solomon's Lamentation where he writes that sin in our life causes, sort of, a cloud. I remember the words 'that our prayers will not penetrate,'[3] which I think is like saying, 'my prayers will

---

[1] Proverbs 28:9
[2] Isaiah 59:2
[3] Lamentations 3:44

185

not even go through the ceiling above us.' Is that the right way to look at that passage Uncle?"

"Yes Thales," responded an encouraged Uncle Epaphras. "This boy is very smart," thought the proud uncle. "His brother and sister-in-law taught him well."

"So think about this Thales," started up Epaphras again, "Would selfishness be God's will? Why, or why not?"

"Well no, of course not Uncle, and I suppose that it would not be God's will because selfishness is a sin."

"This seemed pretty obvious," thought Thales. "Is this how remedial my training is going to be? Huh, this will be boring."

"Thales," Epaphras interrupted Thales thoughts, "I want you to hang in there with me, I'm bringing this up this way for a reason. Have you ever considered getting a blank parchment and at the top of it writing God's Will For My Life, and then at the bottom of it, signing it, with nothing in the middle?"

Thales thought for a moment, another sense of uneasiness had come his way. "That's kind of scary Uncle," stated Thales, rather awkwardly.

Epaphras smiled, "My son," Epaphras said as lovingly as he could, "You have answered honestly, and that is more important than you realize. Have you ever asked God what He wants for your life? Or have you always assumed that you already knew what God wanted you to do?"

"Hmm, Uncle, that lack of peace that you talked about earlier is what has just gripped my spirit. Can you tell me what you think I should do with my life?"

"Thales, I cannot tell you what you should do with your life. My ideas and my thoughts are not what you need to hear. You need to spend time seeking the face of God. I like to call that 'wrestling' with God. Will you take some time and wrestle with God for His will and direction for your life?"

"Yes Uncle, I will. I think I'll go back to my room and spend time with the Lord. I have a parchment and a quill that I use to make notes about things, often daily. I find that it helps me to write down some of the things that the Father and I talk about."

"Where would you focus your activity haodtie?" asked a genuinely concerned katepa.

Breathing deeply in and out, haodtie began to see the unraveling of a demonic plan before it even got off of the ground. He and katepa had planned for every contingency except this one, Thales studying the Enemy's Holy Book. With defeat beginning to show in haodtie's features he said, "Don't challenge his understanding, he seems to be quite comfortable in his understanding of the words. Instead, remind him of how tired he is and how sleepy he should be." Although haodtie got ready to fly off to another part of this underworld, he thought of something else and turned back to katepa. "Encourage him to lie down on his cot, while he 'meditates' on that infernal book."

"Good idea haodtie," responded katepa.

"I'll be back when Thales wakes up," laughed haodtie, and then he disappeared.

Two hours later Thales emerged from his room, his personal parchment in hand.

"Uncle, have you ever fallen asleep for a few minutes when you are praying, or reading or studying?"

Epaphras laughed, "Yes, and I heard you snoring Thales."

Thales's face reddened, and his eyes grew large out of embarrassment and then, trying to salvage the situation Thales said, "I'm so sorry, Uncle, but I ..." Before he could finish, Epaphras cut in.

"You don't need to be embarrassed. I used to be embarrassed when that happened to me too, Thales, and then I found in the Psalms where David says ..."

Epaphras looked at the scroll in Thales's hands.

"Thales, it is in the same parchment that you are looking at. Let me see it, and I'll find it."

Epaphras then turned back toward the beginning of this scroll commonly considered the first scroll of five, of the Psalms and found the place he wanted and then said, "David wrote this one too Thales, and note here where he says 'I will bless the Lord who is my counsel and even at night my heart counsels, or instructs me.'[1] Thales, I used to be embarrassed when I fell asleep too, especially during prayer, but then I found this verse and realized that when I woke up my mind usually seemed much clearer on the subject that, before I slept seemed to perplex me."

And then looking back down at the parchment he reread, "even at night my mind instructs me."

Looking up to his relieved nephew he smiled at Thales, "Don't worry, son; it's okay to fall asleep in prayer or during study ... just not when I am speaking, okay?"

"Okay," came the reply from Thales, breathing much easier now, and then they both laughed together.

Standing at attention, ramrod straight and every bit of nine feet tall, Hael smiled a proud smile. In that other realm, the realm of darkness and foul odors, he heard cursing coming from two demons who had no choice but to acknowledge to themselves where the rest of this conversation would be going.

---

[1] Psalm 16:7

"As I talked to God Uncle, after I woke up," he said a bit sheepishly, to which Epaphras did not respond. "I remembered the beginning of Isaiah and the beginning of Jeremiah, where the prophets were challenged by God to do what He wanted them to do, even though it may be different from what they wanted. I also remembered, and very clearly, the words of Isaiah, where he said, talking of God that 'His ways are not our ways, and our ways are not His ways.'[1] It sobered me Uncle, but strangely, it also comforted me."

"Interesting, Thales," remarked Epaphras, "Why do you think that it comforted you?"

Thales thought for a moment and then said, "Clearly, it's comforting because of what the Psalmist writes in the last scroll of the Psalms, when he says that the Father is sovereign overall and that His throne is above the heavens.[2] When I felt comforted, the comfort existed, not because of me, but because I knew that I could trust God with whatever He wanted for me in my life, and strangely I'm comfortable with that."

Thales spent a few quiet moments thinking to himself, with Epaphras just observing him, and then he continued and said thoughtfully, "I guess what it means Uncle, is that nothing catches God by surprise, so again I can trust Him."

Another groan, deep in the underbelly of the satanic lair came gurgling out of katepa. If you were there with him, you would be able to see, and probably hear the spittle squeezing through his teeth as he pursed his crooked lips so hard that he

---

[1] Isaiah 55:8
[2] Psalm 103:19

didn't know whether to spit, to scream, or to try and suck in all the oxygen in the room.

Growling as he said it, "Your assignment is going to be tougher to influence than we all thought, katepa," went a headshaking haodtie, as he passed by.

Epaphras then told Thales about his seeking God recently that resulted in him talking to Thales parents about Thales moving to Colossae with him. "I believe that what the Lord laid on my heart Thales, has to do with taking your training to another level. And I will do that by pouring myself into you." Epaphras paused, "I think, Thales, that God wants you to be my understudy, which would eventually allow me to travel with Paul, while you take care of the Colossae flock."

Thales felt like he had been kicked in the belly … but he didn't want to look disappointed. In fact, he concerned himself with wondering if his disappointment showed on his face, when he realized something else, surprisingly, he also had an unaccountable peace, a peace that certainly had to do with Thales's mind focused on the Lord.[1]

"Interesting," he thought. "This peace is a strange feeling …"

Watching Thales's facial expressions change from slight shock to a struggled peace, to what he saw as resignation and nearly perfect peace, Epaphras said, "Thales, Paul speaks about what I think I am seeing in you. What I think I see, son, is where he talks about a peace that God gives you that transcends every single bit of your understanding."[2]

---

[1] Isaiah 26:3
[2] Philippians 4:7

And here Thales sat, two months later, but still clearly awed by the greatness of God's peace, being trained to shepherd the flock while his Uncle Epaphras would travel with Paul.

"Peace to do that which sat way outside of my plans two months ago. What a great God," Thales thought. "A great God that has great plans, whatever they may be.

"You, Oh Lord work out Your plans in my life, because of and through Your faithful love. I know that Your love is unfailing and that You will never abandon me.[1] Your hands have shaped me and have made me.[2] I trust Your future plans for me Lord."

Thales continued to study for another thirty minutes before putting the parchments away. As he did so his thoughts went to this pretty Jewish girl whom he didn't really know. Thinking to himself he said, "Hmm, I wonder if she plays a part in God's plans for me?"

---

[1] Psalm 138:8
[2] Job 10:8a

21

Current Era

"I'm just not up to it," Isabela Gonzalez told a fellow psych professor. She continued, "Now that I'm home Neil, I'm not feeling well."

"I hope it's nothing serious Isabela," replied Neil.

"If you only knew," thought Isabela.

"See you Monday Neil."

"Alright, goodbye."

And the two hung up, but Isabela felt overwhelmed, she had just returned from a second opinion. This one from an oncologist in the Southeastern Surgical Oncology building. The problem with this report is that it appeared to be worse than the first one.

"And what's with all of these ignorant, religious people wanting to pray with me?"

She knew that she just crossed a line she did not want to cross, one where she would take her anger out on another, but she didn't care. In fact, she would get wound up and really let it fly ...

"That's it Isabela," joln consoled her, "These Christians are ignorant. They have no truth, and certainly no brains."

Isabela continued, "How stupid can these people be. They don't know spit about people's feelings and they have no regard for what people normally prefer to keep private. I do not understand why these mean arrogant ..." And then she stopped her ranting and observed something that she did not expect to hear coming out of her mouth, "how do I account for the strange peace that I saw in them?"

"It's fake Isabela," joln continued, "They think if they can pray with you, it'll add a notch in their spiritual gun belt."

"It can't be real," she concluded. "It can't be real."

Grateful, thinking that he brought her back to focusing on her anger joln realized that far from getting angry, she instead began to wonder, she became curious, she ..., "Noooo! No! No! Not that," came the words spitting out of joln's mouth.

And then from somewhere in the bright heavenlies, the Spirit began to move. There came a whirlwind from the north, a great cloud with fire flashing back and forth and brilliant light all around it.[1]

"No! This isn't going to be good," an angry joln thought.

---

[1] Ezekiel 1:4a

In the center of the fire, a gleam of metal, like amber sparkled. The form of four living creatures came from it.[1]

"Oh, not them!" Now joln rapidly moved from anger to fright for he knew that depression would be upon him soon.

They had human form, but each of them had four faces and four wings. Their legs were straight and the soles of their feet were like the hooves of a calf, except that their hooves were sparkling like polished bronze. Each of them had human hands under their wings and all four of them had faces and wings. Their wings were touching one another.[2]

"Look at them. Lined up and ready to ..." joln struggled to finish the sentence. He couldn't afford to think this way. The word to finish the sentence, looking at the Spirit moving, would be 'win.' The 'others' were there to win. "It's not fair," thought joln.

The creatures did not turn as they moved; each one went straight ahead and their faces were that of a man, in one direction, and that of a lion on the right, the face of an ox on the left, and the face of an eagle as the final one. Their wings were spread upward; each one had two wings touching that of another and two wings covering its body.[3]

Wherever the Spirit wanted to go, these creatures went without turning as they moved.[4]

All joln could do, since he would not be allowed to cry, would be to hang his head and sigh, for he knew what would soon be coming.

The form of the living creatures appeared like burning coals of fire and torches. Fire moved back and forth between the living

---

[1] Ezekiel 1:4b-5a
[2] Ezekiel 1:5b-9a
[3] Ezekiel 1:9b-11
[4] Ezekiel 1:12b

creatures; incredibly bright, with lightning coming out of it, the creatures darted back and forth like flashes of lightning.[1]

And then, there were wheels, one on the ground beside each creature that had four faces. The appearance of the wheels gleamed like the color of beryl, and all four were exactly the same. When they moved, they went in any of the four directions, without pivoting as they moved.[2]

"Their rims are large and sobering, even frightening,"[3] thought joln.

Although joln would never say this out loud, he thought that the rims were, "not just frightening but awe inspiring too." This of course would be a thought that he could only allow in his crooked brain for a moment. It wouldn't be a good idea to be impressed by the Enemy and His Spirit.

Each of their four rims were full of eyes all around. So when the living creatures moved, the wheels moved beside them, and when the creatures rose from the earth, the wheels also rose. Wherever the Spirit wanted to go, the creatures went in the direction the Spirit moved.[4]

"And when they moved," thought joln, He heard the sound of their wings, like the roar of mighty waters, like the voice of his Enemy, the Almighty. He never liked the record, where it describes what he now saw. The record as found at the beginning of that crazy prophet Ezekiel described this event way too accurately for any good demon to be comfortable. These creatures' sounds were like the commotion that he had heard and loved hearing, for six millennium. He loved the sound when it came because of the sound of an army, and usually a great army.[5]

---

[1] Ezekiel 1:13-14
[2] Ezekiel 1:15-16a, 17
[3] Ezekiel 1:18a
[4] Ezekiel 1:18b-20a
[5] Ezekiel 1:24

Then joln nearly froze, for he knew what would be coming. He had seen it way too often. When these creatures stood still, they lowered their wings, a voice came from above the expanse over their heads,[1] and joln, as his eyes grew larger and larger out of fright, realized that he saw the beginning of the Enemy drawing another soul to Himself.

"Noooo."

He knew that if all things held true, his expectations for Professor Isabela Gonzalez were toast. "Would there ever be an example of their Enemy drawing a soul that did *not* submit to Him?" joln wondered. And he only had to wonder for a split second, for he knew that the Lord never lost. "What can I do to delay the inevitable and cause havoc in her life? That is the game now, Isabela, you loser."

"But what if their peace is real?" reflected Isabela. "What if it isn't an act? What if ..." Isabela trailed off.

"How would I find out if it were an act or not?" she wondered.

---

[1] Ezekiel 1:25

22

Current Era

Two weeks had come and gone since the previous Issachar Men Prayer Group met, and now there were 37 men who showed up at 7:30 am in the chapel. It looked to Dale that Dean seemed right in the middle of his element. He welcomed the men, chit chatting, enjoying their company, and they were enjoying him. As Dale stood at the door watching the men, he couldn't help but be reminded of something he had learned very early on. He had learned that men *really* do enjoy relationship. "How wrong," he thought, "the psycho-babble that says that men are beyond 'intimate' relationships that have nothing to do with sex. It is truly too exciting to watch these men enjoy one another's companionship."

Dale brought the men to order and introduced the study before handing it over to Dean. "I have been working on this book for a few years and it is finally far enough along so that it could become a group study. When you look at the *Wesley Family Prayers Book*," Dale continued, "you see that these men exemplified the idea of praying scripture back to God. Every line in their prayers is from the Word of God, so as we study their prayers, we are actually studying the Word of God. Dean, come on down."

And with that, Dean addressed everyone with the confidence of a man who had been teaching them for a long time. Without an invitation, Dr. Bob merely looked over to Dale and nodded his head, saying in essence, "Dale, good call. Dean will do a good job."

"As we look at the first paragraph of this prayer, remember that this is the Sunday Morning prayer, but it is only the first paragraph of seven in the Sunday Morning Prayer. That means that if we look at one paragraph per two-week period, it will take us three months just to get through this first morning's prayer, and since there are two prayers per day, it will take us nearly two years to get through these prayers that the Wesleys wrote. What I find fascinating about that is that when the Wesleys wrote this, they expected people would go through the entire prayer each day and each week. So please, please, go ahead of this study, and enjoy them on your own, okay? Two years!" Wiping his brow in mock need of wiping sweat from his brow, Dean added, "Whew, I just want you to see the breadth of our study. We will see how quickly we get through this … but that's not our concern for now."

Taking on a caring teacher quality about him, he said, "Before we read our first assignment, let's look at the last question. The last question is the same last question in each paragraph's study. I want us to look at it first, because I think that if answering this is your focus each week, you will be prepared to participate in the discussion of all of the other questions. Notice the question, it says, *'How many verses in the paragraph above are referenced? Do you know which ones they are?'*"

With this he paused, and the men seemed to look at their handout and this question. "Wow," said a few of the men, and low whistles came out of some of the others. "I trust you are seeing the expectation of this question," he offered.

"Do you want us to all use the same Bible version?" someone asked.

"Great question," he responded. "No! I really want you to use whatever version you are used to and are comfortable with. Some of you will have answers, consisting of verses that the others will not. I think our study of Scripture will be much more broad, or 'rich' this way."

"So let's look at and read together the first section:

> *ALMIGHTY and eternal GOD, we desire to praise thy holy name, for so graciously raising us up, in soundness of body and mind, to see the light of this day. We bless thee in behalf of all thy creatures; for "the eyes of all look unto thee, and you givest them their meat in due season." But above all we acknowledge thine inestimable benefits bestowed upon mankind in CHRIST JESUS. We thank thee for his miraculous birth, his most holy life, his bitter agony, his bloody death, his glorious resurrection on this day, his ascension into heaven, his triumph over all the powers of darkness, and his sitting at thy right hand for evermore.*

"Here's the first question guys:"

Which words and phrases give consideration to praising God?

The first answer came from Harry, who sat up front. "Well, it seems pretty obvious, *'praise Thy holy Name,'* right?"

"Okay," responded Dean, "is there anything else in that first sentence that would be considered a praise?"

"A praise?" Harry looked again at the prayer, this time more thoughtfully. "I don't see a praise as much as I see the prayer - a prayer of thanking God for so graciously raising him up, waking him up, I suppose he means."

Stepping in to the conversation, just so that the point wouldn't be missed, Dale asked, "Is there a difference in 'Thanking,' and 'Praising'?" No one answered his question, including a bewildered Dean, and just as Dale started to answer his own question, Jonathan, the worship leader said, "It is sometimes subtle, but yes, I think that there is a very big difference. Put simply, 'Praising God' is Him centered, but 'Thanking God' is me centered." And with that came a collective grunt, "Hmm," as something that seemed to register with all of the men, all at once.

"Go ahead Dean. I just didn't want to miss this opportunity to contrast praising and thanking."

"No, that is great Brother Dale, because it leads us back to the question still on the table. Is there still something else that is considered a praise in the first sentence?"

"Hmm," said Brother Howard in his low African American voice. "Brother Dean, I would not have seen it before, but I believe that if Brother Jonathan is correct, then simply calling God, 'Almighty' and 'Eternal' are aspects of us praising God, I suppose."

And thus began Dean's first Bible study.

Watching from the well illuminated skies above, another of the angelic host, Tephillah, remembered a conversation he had earlier just outside the temple of the Lord with Michael. "I want you to help Dean, okay? He doesn't have much time on earth, and he has found favor in the eyes of our Lord."

Just then the four Seraphim started saying,

"Holy, holy, holy, is the Lord God Almighty,
Who was and who is and who is to come ..." [1]

And as the Seraphim started, the two angels turned to watch and listen. They stopped their conversation and enjoyed the holy proclamation.

"Michael, I've been watching Dean for a while. Thank you for the opportunity to participate in his last days. Can I escort him to the gate of heaven when the time is at hand?"

"I'm sure we can work that out my friend," answered Michael. "Dean truly is one of the special Christians, faithful to God for all that God erased from his life when he became saved."

"I love my job," Dean's guardian angel Tephillah thought as he beamed with a smile.

From another area of the heavenlies, but in the dark underworld of the demon lair katepa observed Tephillah and wondered what this guardian, an angel from the Holy Enemy, would do there. He vowed to make the most of the opportunities that might come his way. "And if they don't come my way, I will make them come my way. This angel of the Enemy is making his presence known a bit more openly than these enemies normally do. I will take you out, you mortal. No one will claim that you have finished well, you ignorant Bible study teacher."

And in another corner of the same area, snorting out a scared whiff of foul breath, joln saw more than made him comfortable seeing. At least he could blame this on katepa but even then he found himself too scared of all of the Enemy's hosts to plan a future offensive, all he could do would be to hope that death would soon be coming ... to katepa.

---

[1] Revelation 4:8b

23

Nineteenth Century

The next morning the air felt muggy as it always did in late September. The birds were out and their singing sounded so lovely. Even the woodpecker's periodic, but rapid, tap-tap-tap into a nearby tree sounded lovely to him. The temperature seemed gently brisk but not cold and Brother Alexander liked that. More and more, as he got older, the cold could be a burden that he didn't enjoy having. And then there were the gnats. "Oh Lord, these gnats have to be a result of the fall. You could not have made them and then said they were good." He loved nearly everything about the location of his calling … except the gnats. Years earlier, when he and Dwight (now known as the great D. L. Moody) had come down here it took them days to get used to the gnats … maybe they never had … and that reminded him of the letter he had just received from Dwight.

After grooming and then tacking up his horse, he mounted Sterling, gave him the reins, and pulled out the letter to read it.

Hello my good friend,
I have just left my home where I have been resting after our campaign to small cities in America. This is the second year I

have conducted this kind of a campaign, and what an amazing experience, Al. But, my friend, it has been too long since we have broken bread and talked face to face. I will be in the Southern States this winter and I want you to join me, if you can. Can you make yourself available?

I have been studying the questions you wrote regarding Wesley Family Prayers Book. Do you remember when we found that old book? Oh my friend, that trip into New York City still causes me to chuckle. Do you remember? We were so excited that we had the newest book in the David Copperfield series, and then we couldn't afford it. I'll never forget mocking you and telling you to, "buy that old book." And you did. And you have used it to bless me and so many others, my friend. I trust that it will be a blessing to you, and maybe your family for many years into the future.

Before going on with the letter, Alex put the letter down and remembered the special visit the evening before from Gretchen. "Gretchen, what a beautiful name," he thought. "Hmm, Lord," he spoke, reverently, "I've been satisfied my whole life being single, and I am content to stay this way. Thank You, Lord, for the intimacy that You bring me. Your will Father is what I prefer."

A few feet away, katepa followed Alexander Rich's horse, and making a shrill laughing sound, that resembled a high pitched snorting pig, "You have no clue what I have started in town preacher. You won't even be able to show your face again. If I know these people preacher, they will skewer you, roast you, and have you for dinner before you even know there is a problem. No preacher, Gretchen will be out of your life for good."

"What else do you want to talk about," cackled a prideful katepa.

Monday morning came early for Ralph Bookman, the Jeffersonville saloon owner. He liked to spend a lot of extra time cleaning on Monday morning, so as to not have to clean so much throughout the week. Sunday night drunks were still sleeping behind the saloon when Harry opened up the back door, begin to put coffee on, and then begin to clean.

Some of the businessmen who wouldn't enter his establishment during the evening because they didn't drink would come by in the morning for coffee on their way to work. This morning Sam entered through the door first.

"Sam," Ralph Bookman said in a hushed tone, "Did you hear about that poor Gretchen McCreedy?"

"Gretchen, the little mercantile shop girl?"

"Little girl?" Ralph responded incredulously. "Why she's a full grown lady, the pertiest Georgia Peach you'd ever seen. Anyway, she and the preacher have been seein' each other out in the woods when he leaves town."

"Brother Rich, our preacher?" Sam asked with a frightful look on his face. "No, I don't believe you. Who told you? That just doesn't sound like our preacher, besides he's old enough to be her father. So who told you? Did someone telling you a tall tale last night?"

"Well that is the surprising part. When I tell you, you'll want to assume like me that he had to be drunk as a hoot owl. But that's the strange part Sam, last night when he told me, he appeared to be stone cold sober. I hadn't seen him that sober in years. That's when I knew that something had to be different and so he must be tellin' the truth."

"Ralph, I wouldn't believe you even if it were a stone cold sober Carrolton Faith you heard it from." And when he saw the raised eyebrows of Ralph Bookman, he knew who told him, and that if Carrol were sober, there might be something to the story, for Carrolton Faith hadn't been sober for a good many years.

Alex put the idea of Gretchen out of his mind to get back to Dwight's letter, only to read:

Speaking of which, has any young maiden caught your fancy yet? I don't think it's good for you to get older with no one to look after you ... who's going to swish away all those gnats?

I love you my friend, and I look forward to seeing you soon. Let me know if you will clear your schedule to spend time with me in January and February, upcoming.

"Hmm, January and February, that could be fun. It would be nice to get out of the weather for two months and sleep in a hotel for a change ... not complaining Lord. You know I love the outdoors.

In the bowels of the satanic lair, looking smugly at one another, joln and katepa smiled. "Moody will be too embarrassed to invite the 'goody-two-shoes' Alexander Rich along with him when you are done with him," remarked a confident joln. And then turning sarcastic and mean he snarled, "unless you mess this up, katepa."

As Brother Alex entered Dry Branch Monday morning to begin work there, Gretchen entered the mercantile shop her family owned. There seemed to be some commotion as she walked downstairs, but she took no notice as her mind focused on the display that her father had asked her to change when they were at breakfast that morning.

"Go upstairs until I come up there to deal with you girl," cried an angry Mr. McCreedy in the direction of Gretchen. "You have shamed our family more than any family has ever been shamed, you harlot. You have corrupted our family. Go-on, go upstairs and I'll deal with you after I have consoled your mother."

Then she noticed the commotion. Her mother, looking at her out of the corner of her eyes, looked at her like she had never seen her mother look at her before. And there were three other ladies, as well as her father, consoling the sobbing Mrs. McCreedy. Confused and dazed, Gretchen retreated up the stairs, completely unaware of the tornado of words that had swept through Jeffersonville.

"Scared and confused," whispered *joln* to Gretchen.

"Angry, ashamed, abused by their daughter, and wishing their daughter had never been born," nearly shouted *katepa* to both Mr. and Mrs. McCreedy.

"We always knew she had to be a tramp. Her former husband didn't die of Yellow Fever, he died of a broken heart. Don't embarrass the McCreedys by telling the whole town, only a few people that really should know, that's all," whispered other demons to the three ladies consoling Mrs. McCreedy.

"How could this have happened to my precious daughter?" wailed Mrs. McCreedy.

"Well, you know," started Mrs. Ellie Squire, the church organist when Brother Rich is in town, "Your daughter is a young and lovely girl. The Bible talks about some widows needing to get remarried, and perhaps poor Gretchen is just one of those ... but don't you worry Geraldine, we will help stop others from thinking badly of Miss Gretchen."

"After all Geraldine," began Billie Carter, whose husband is the church senior deacon. "If that old coot, Brother, oh I can't even call him that anymore, Rich, if that dirty old man were married he wouldn't have his eyes on someone so, somewhat, innocent as your daughter."

"Geraldine," chimed in Victoria Pleasant (who went by Victoria because of how embarrassed she had always been of her real name, Zopha), and whose husband is the church financial officer. "Tonight I'll make Harrold prepare a motion to cut the funding of that, disgusting man who has probably already soiled your daughter. And oh! How many times has he? Oh Geraldine this is such a shame and a blotch on our town. But don't you worry, we will protect you. I don't know what we can do for Gretchen, but we will protect you, Geraldine."

One by one the ladies left the shop leaving Mr. and Mrs. McCreedy there to open the shop late. When they did a face they do not see unless he wants to mooch off of them entered the store.

"Ma'am," Carrolton Faith nodded to Mrs. McCreedy, who still wiped tears away from her face.

"We've got nothin' to give you today Carrol," belted out Mr. McCreedy.

"Oh I'm not here to ask for anything," stammered out a surprisingly soberer Carrolton. This caught the eye and the ear of Mr. McCreedy, who eyed Carrol sharply. "I'm just here to

207

offer my services to you." Sensing no opposition, he felt a little more emboldened and went on, "I had the privilege of protecting your daughter last night …"

And with that Mrs. McCreedy started to sob again, Carrolton got scared, and Mr. McCreedy ran him out of the store.

"Close the store for today, Geraldine. The town will understand," belted out a smiling katepa. "They'll get over it."

"Close the store today, Hatch," sobbed Mrs. McCreedy. "I can't face anyone today."

"Geraldine, don't be crazy. I have the Jacksons coming in this afternoon for their annual supplies … besides, they're from out of town, they won't know about any of this."

"Oh Hatch, I can't bear this shame." She paused for what seemed like ages and Hatch knew he had to let her come up with her own decision about the store. He knew she would because she knew how much money the Jacksons would spend today. "But what about Gretchen? Oh, I want to switch that girl till she is black and blue, and then I want her shipped out to my sister in Savannah."

Gretchen, who had come back down the stairs part way to listen to what could be going on, heard her mom and dad now but it didn't make sense. "What is going on," she wondered, "and what got them so angry? Her father had never spoken to her with those words. Sure he got angry at her at times, but he never used that kind of language."

Searching every part of her brain she pondered, "Had they found out about the New York hat she had 'borrowed' until she could put it back or buy it? That had to have been two weeks ago, that didn't make sense, and besides she knew that they knew she would wear some of the special clothes that came in. She had done this for years, and nearly *always* ended up buying it."

"Gretchen, you really are worthless, that is why your husband left this earth early." whispered joln. "You need to get out of town and leave your family to deal with the shame you have always caused them and has been exacerbated by your wearing a hat that only harlots, and the worse kind of harlots, would wear. You're an embarrassment to your family, and you need to leave."

As a guardian angel watched on, he saw and admitted how amazing it seemed to him, and all of the angelic host, that the demons would change tact, mid-sentence sometimes, if it would add to the mortal's confusion, and eventually their deception.

"Lord," Gretchen began, "I am willing to do and go wherever you want me to … I just want to hear clearly from You."

"Hatch, I am too embarrassed to have anyone come in the store today … and especially, especially … those people. Make them come back. They'll obey you on this. You're … and they're … well, just do it."

"Geraldine, listen to me, I don't care for the way you talk about them just because they are black. Don't let your anger for your daughter cause you to be angry at these sweet people who are soon going to be starting their own church. You can just go upstairs and not be here when they arrive."

"Speaking of which, Hatch," Mrs. McCreedy spoke, matter-of-factly, and clearly enough for Gretchen to hear. "I want you to deal with Gretchen. I want her in Savannah on the next stage."

"Mother and Father," Gretchen came into the room sheepishly, and continued, "Please forgive me. But I've always thought that you knew, and that it would be okay ..."

With her shoulders heaving, Geraldine started to cry again.

"... I'm so sorry that I embarrassed you. Again, please forgive me. I've heard you speaking. If you want me to go to Aunt Ginny's, I'll do whatever you want."

"Gretchen," her father barked, "how could you embarrass us like this? This could cost us our business ..."

"But I," started Gretchen.

"Enough girl." Hatch continued, "The next stage to Savannah is tomorrow morning. Go upstairs now and begin to get your clothes together, *all* of your clothes." he said as he turned back to his wife.

"All of them?" Gretchen asked horrified. Still thinking that this had to do with the hat she said, "Umm, okay. Do you want the hat back too?"

Finally, Geraldine spoke to her daughter, but with a smugness that Geraldine usually used when she talked at the dinner table about others in town. "Hat or hats Gretchen, this is so much bigger than your 'hat' episodes now. Because of what people have seen, now know, and are talking about, I am more ashamed of you than when you ... Oh, never mind you rotten child. Go upstairs and obey your father."

210

24

19th Century

Out of obedience a bewildered Gretchen went back upstairs, into her room and began to fill up her traveling trunk. "This doesn't make any sense," thought Gretchen. "Why would they do this over some foolish hats?"

"Lord, this just doesn't feel right and I don't know why. The only thing I know to do is to honor my parents by obeying them.[1] But I am seeking You, Lord. I need Your help. You have said that You are not the author of confusion,[2] so this confusion cannot be from You. Oh Lord, show me how to seek You with all of my heart. You say that when we do, You will let Yourself be found.[3] I trust You Father, the One who is sovereign over everything.[4] You know the plans that You have for me. I am so grateful Lord, for those plans are not for failure, but for hope and a future,[5] even if it looks bleak right now."

---

[1] Colossians 3:20
[2] 1 Corinthians 14:33
[3] Jeremiah 29:13-14a
[4] Psalm 103:19
[5] Jeremiah 29:11

The store stayed closed for the morning, and when Hatch opened it again, Geraldine had Ellie, Billie and Victoria over for lunch. They had already spent the morning "talking" to a few people. "We are sending Gretchen to my sister in Savannah ..." And with that, the three women "knowingly" looked at each other, raising eyebrows, nodding heads and confirming their thoughts from earlier in the day. Of course poor, pitiful, self-righteous, and just plain selfish Geraldine didn't see a bit of these wordless messages going back and forth between her "friends."

An hour earlier the women had met at Billie's home, around the corner from the McCreedy's store. They decided to get together before they went to Geraldine. This gave the "friends" an opportunity to plan their "support" for Geraldine.

"Gretchen is probably pregnant, bless her heart," whispered two demons simultaneously to the three ladies.

"So poor Geraldine, bless her heart," began Billie. "I couldn't imagine being in her place right now. How embarrassing, and thinking that she could fool us ... poor girl, bless her heart."

"How long has she been widowed?" asked Ellie.

"Long enough for those desires to start up again," answered Victoria.

"And how embarrassing for our church too," cried Billie. "My husband is so angry with this man that we have entrusted with our salvation."

"And that we have paid so much money." added Victoria, the financial officer's wife.

212

"My concern is that she might be pregnant, bless her heart," Ellie began. "After all, God allows difficulties like getting caught to be a warning to others to not fall into the same sins. And you know, with our town growing, we have more and more young people arriving that will learn good lessons from this situation. Oh I hope this isn't the case, although it probably is, but if she is pregnant it will be good for someone to bear the embarrassment of being an unwed mother to teach the younger women to stay away from men completely."

When they were done bandying about all of the potential issues that would come into play for their friend's family they all put on their coats and went to the McCreedy's store. When the ladies finally all sat down together, the three friends watched Geraldine McCreedy wringing her hands nervously. She had become so worked up that she sounded as if she were mumbling and speaking to herself while the three friends were just trying to console her.

Heading downstairs to open the store, Hatch saw the Jacksons looking into the windows. He hustled to the door and opened it.

"Sho-nuff Brother McCreedy, we got afraid we gonna have to return," announced Mr. Jackson.

"Oh, I'm sorry Brother Hubert, we have had some family problems and …" Mr. McCreedy trailed off as Brother Jackson started up again.

"Problems, Brother McCreedy? I's meeting Brother Rich 'morrow, should I 'ave 'im return?"

With an embarrassed laugh Mr. McCreedy quickly stopped that direction, "No," which he said more harshly than he wanted to say it. Continuing he said, "I mean, thank you Brother Jackson, but no." And then leaning toward Hubert, Mr. McCreedy continued, "He is the problem … part of the problem. In fact, you ought not mention his name around here. He's in big trouble with the town folk, okay?"

Stepping back and looking questioningly at his wife, who frowned and tilted her head down, meaning, "Do not ask any more questions honey," Hubert Jackson simply said, "Sho-nuff Brother McCreedy."

As the ladies began to eat muffins Mrs. McCreedy started to cry again. "Is it worse than we imagined dear?" asked Victoria.

"Oh my dear friends, I'm so ashamed. I can't imagine anyone looking at me and not thinking of my daughter … it will just be unbearable."

"Have you talked to Gretchen? Has she told you how far they went?" asked Ellie.

Geraldine shifted funny in her seat, "How far," she wondered, "How far what?" And as soon as she thought it she thought about her business and how embarrassing it will be to see people who knew … something … and from how far away. They would all know, again, something."

The slight movement by Geraldine could not be missed by the other ladies who all looked at each other. "Yes," they all thought in their own way, "Gretchen is pregnant."

"Brother Jackson," asked Hatch McCreedy, "How far along are you in starting this new church?"

"We's got da deacons chosen and dis week Brother Rich will help us writ our articles of incorporation."

And with that Hubert Jackson saw Hatch flinch. "Brother McCreedy, cans I's ask you somethin'?"

"Of course Brother Jackson."

"Call's me Hugh, Brother McCreedy. What's happen' with Brother Alex? He always talks 'bout how he likes dinin' with y'all?"

A darkness fell over Brother McCreedy's countenance and he responded, "It's a long story, a long story."

When the "friends" left Geraldine McCreedy they decided that they would "set their friends straight" so that none of them bothered the McCreedy's by asking them questions. "We'll answer whatever questions they have," all three of the "friends" agreed.

25

First Century

"Why do I find myself thinking about her so often?" Thales wondered.

"Actually," he continued to think, "it isn't that I'm thinking about her that is the problem. It is that I feel, somehow, inappropriate while thinking about her." It seemed very odd for him, almost sensual.

Just then katepa leaned toward Thales, "you are feeling this because you are a young man Thales, and you have the same desires as other men that live in the world. It's natural."

"Father, I acknowledge that these thoughts are from the evil one, or my flesh, I don't know. But I do know that they are not from You. And submitting[1] myself to You, Lord, by faith above all things, I trust You to do something different with my brain.[2]

---

[1] James 4:7a
[2] Ephesians 6:16

Cause me to think differently." And with that the ugliness seemed to be gone, but the thought of Mary remained.

"Father, You say that You give us the desires of our heart when we delight ourselves in You.[1] As I submit my life to You, I trust You to do just that, give me the desires of my heart, and Father where my desires separate from Your will, please change my desires."[2]

It had now been a full three months since Thales had arrived in Colossae, and he liked the city. He got used to it by walking in, around and through it. The way the city seemed to be laid out, Thales would begin where he and his uncle lived which would be called the Artisan District on the western edge of the city. Heading southeast he would come to the old historic section of the city near The Low Gate which is the southernmost entrance into the city. From there he would make his way to the other side of the historic district, all the way around to the northern part of the town, where all of the rich merchants lived. Heading west now through the University District he would enter the Merchant District, and somehow, make his way to the flower stand he enjoyed so much. The city proper didn't take up a lot of space. In fact some would call it small, which he liked because he could take his time and walk all the way around the city in less than two hours.

The first time he walked through the market place when he came to live with his uncle he saw her and remembered what caught his eye first those many months earlier when he merely visited his uncle. He remembered that her chestnut brown hair caught his eye. "And it had a hint of red in it." While she wore

---

[1] Psalm 37:4
[2] Proverbs 21:1

the strict clothing of an orthodox Jewish family, her hair would flip out from one side to another as she rearranged the flowers in her family's flower shop throughout the day.

Not knowing what to do to introduce himself, he went up to her saying that he wanted to buy a flower, which he did. That, he would always remember as their first meeting. As he walked away he turned back a number of times to watch her, and even a couple of the times he thought that she might be looking back at him.

The next day he came back for another flower, and then the next day another. Finally, on this day he introduced himself and during the next two months had begun to get to know her. The more he learned though, the more he wanted to learn, and even though there might be a few details that were potential problems, Thales, ever the optimist began to think that there might be a future for them. But that would be a long way off. He enjoyed the time when he could talk with her, sometimes there at the shop and sometimes by taking a short walk around the Merchant District.

Her father, Benjamin Kuppai, whom he would later learn had been the surname of Caiaphas, the major antagonist of Jesus back in Jerusalem had the rare distinction of being the youngest son of Caiaphas, but because he had a physical defect[1] he could not be allowed into the family business, that of being a priest. And so the day after he reached an age that allowed him to leave, he left home and made his way into the Gentile world.

Benjamin Kuppai, quite correctly, felt like he had always been rejected by his family and his people. So he chose to head in the opposite direction of all of the Jewish history he had to endure and recite during his formative years. When he memorized Moses's book of Leviticus, he nearly left home right

---

[1] Leviticus 21:17

then. Moses had written, "Any of your descendants Aaron, that have a physical defect cannot come near to present the food of his God ... He may eat the food of his God, but because he has a defect, he must not go near the curtain or approach the altar, because he desecrates the sanctuary."[1] And what had been the defect of the son of the great high priest Caiaphas? He simply had a lazy eye, not always, just sometimes.

Nevertheless, after that, whatever anyone said to Benjamin did not matter. He had made up his mind that he would get as far away from his family and their cursed religion as he could. Sure he would make his family follow Jehovah, but he would not. And so when the time came for him to leave, he chose to head *away* from the history of Moses. He headed north into Syria and Cilicia, stopping in Selucia, Tarsus, Derbe, Lystra and Iconium. While in the Derbe, Lystra and Iconium area, he found that he had a green thumb of sorts. He picked up work wherever he went, but he really enjoyed working with the flowers. They had a beauty that no one could fake. He had heard someone compare the lilies of the field with Solomon's robes. And that seemed fitting he thought. There would be no reason for King Solomon to be considered more beautiful than the lilies, or whatever the traveling rabbi had meant.[2] The point that he liked had to do with the irony that the flowers, that were beautiful today and then thrown in the furnace tomorrow, were comparable to their great King Solomon.

He saved money working with the unclean Gentiles, and so being constantly ceremonially unclean, he drifted further and further away from his faith until he met Aikaterine. She would always be the most beautiful Jewish girl he had ever seen, and so

---

[1] Leviticus 21:21-23
[2] Matthew 6:29

dropping the name of Caiaphas, he entered into the good graces of Aikaterine's father, built up a dowry and married Aikaterine.

After they were married, it became obvious that Aikaterine's family did not like Benjamin. Who could blame them, he would come to visit speak with bluster, be very mean, and he always compared where they lived to the richness of Jerusalem. And he complained all of the time. Aikaterine's father said to him, "Then move away Benjamin. Go back to where you are happy. Go back to Jerusalem. Only make my daughter happy, please."

So Benjamin left and took Aikaterine and their little baby Mary. Only Benjamin did not go back to Jerusalem, he went further away from Jerusalem, west toward Philadelphia and Sardis. While in the region of Hierapolis, Laodicea and Colossae, he fell in love with the natural flora there, and decided to try and make a living as his own flower shop owner.

He developed three reputations, two good reputations, and one bad reputation. The bad reputation had to do with him being very difficult to work with for any length for time. If he thought you were wrong, he wanted you to agree with him about it. You didn't argue with him for you would never win, not because you might be wrong, no, but because he argued so well. No one could argue a point, any point better than him. The good reputations had to do with his flowers always being the most beautiful and always lasting the longest. Always! And in seeming contrast to his strong negative reputation, he had another good reputation. And it had to do with fairness. He prided himself in always being fair, in fact more than fair. It seemed as if to the degree to which he could be angry, he made a point to be fair, and even generous.

But when it came to Aikaterine and her arguing ability, she would be completely different than Benjamin. Some said that she had to be nice to keep the customers, but once you got to know her, you would never say that. Her character had always been, and would always be, incurably nice, truly nice. Everyone loved her, and would put up with Benjamin to do business with Aikaterine. She epitomized the truly virtuous wife. Her husband trusted her completely, a complete shock since he didn't seem to trust anyone. She would never talk ill of him, and you just knew she would do him good, and not evil, for her entire life. She always worked with her hands, and seemed to have the ability to bring from afar unique things into both her home and into their business.

If you were up early, before the sun, you would see a lamp on in her home getting the food ready for the day. She would always be very shrewd, buying a field here, renting a piece of land there, selling what needed to be sold, planting crops as appropriate, including flowers for the business and vineyards for themselves. The poor always knew that an extra place setting would be at her dinner table if you were in need, whether you were a Jew or a Gentile. She always seemed to be ready no matter the weather. In fact, her family and her maidservants never seemed to be without, or ill prepared. Her clothing for her and her family never lacked for quality, and if you were lucky enough to buy one of her garments you felt honored. Even her husband, Benjamin distinguished himself as she would dress him in what she had sown.

All in all, she carried herself as a woman of honor and strength, a woman with great wisdom and kindness, always watching over her household. Her children always considered themselves blessed to have her as a mother, and even Benjamin would say to her, as had been overheard once, in what would have been conceived as a rare show of loving emotion. He complimented Aikaterine by telling her, "Woman, all of your father's daughters have done well, in fact, many women, it could be said have done well, but you, wife, you excel them all. Charm can be deceitful, although yours is not, and beauty can be something that passes, although yours has not, but my Aikaterine, because you fear the Lord, you are praised. I am honored to experience the fruit of your hands. You are praised and respected at the city gates."[1]

"Fortunately for some young man," Benjamin thought, "Mary takes after her mother."

He had just been thinking about that, Mary and a young man one day, when he came around the corner from an early lunch and saw Mary talking to a young Gentile boy. "Is this what Aikaterine meant when she said that Mary is falling in love?" Benjamin glowered at this young man, and followed them at a distance. "Aikaterine could not have known that it would be this young man, a Gentile? No, something isn't right here." He knew not to challenge Aikaterine until he knew more about this boy, this young man.

When Mary and Thales arrived back at the flower store, Aikaterine smiled at them, and then she saw Benjamin. She saw the look on his face, both bewilderment and anger. The two kids didn't know he watched them, so she sat there to see how this scene would unfold. "Benjamin is true to form." she thought. He got closer and closer to them so that when they arrived at the shop, he stood directly behind them, startling them, frightening them really. Thales left rapidly, Mary hustled to another part of the flower shop, Benjamin frowned and Aikaterine laughed.

"My good husband Benjamin," she wanted to say to him, "A woman's heart is not under the control of her father. Just ask my father."

---

[1] Proverbs 31:25-31

26

Nineteenth Century
&
First Century

Brother Rich got up early to get to the Marks's home by midday. He enjoyed the time he got to spend at the Mark's home. They had a rooster that would crow about 3:30 in the morning, well before the light had even thought about coming over the horizon. Fortunate for Brother Rich, this rooster could be counted on since this part of Dry Branch had hills nearly as tall as Jeffersonville. Without the rooster, if Brother Alex waited on the sun to awaken him, he would start his day way too late. So he looked forward to "that crazy rooster," as Mrs. Marks would call it.

Just outside of his window tomorrow morning that rooster would start to crow. But this is still Monday afternoon and sitting on the back porch in the back of the Marks's log cabin, Alex turned in his Bible to Colossians, specifically Colossians 4:12, where he read: "and he always prays fervently for you."

"Oh Lord, what would it have been like to learn to pray from Epaphras? He is known as a man who prayed for his congregation, not just faithfully, but passionately. Father, I know that You have blessed me with a desire to pray but Lord, the more

I pray the more I believe that I need to learn about prayer. My day is ill spent when I do not spend six to eight hours in prayer and in Your Word. Forgive me father for ceasing to pray for some of those in my congregations. I confess Lord that some of them are just so difficult. Oh Lord, show me how Epaphras prayed fervently for people in his congregation, even those that he struggled with, including and specifically, those with whom he felt a real sense of disunity."

"You got it, big guy," laughed katepa as he considered all the disunity that he had started working up against Brother Rich just a few short miles away in Jeffersonville.

Speaking to himself, Hael said, "Alexander, I look forward to watching you listen to our Lord, and deal with the upcoming problems the way the Lord would have you and use you as you deal with them."

"Oh Lord, Romans 15:5 tells me that when there is a sense of disunity between me and anyone, I should go back to You and ask You where I have not been following Your Son. Lord, on my heart is my flock in Jeffersonville, Geraldine in particular. Where have I not followed Your Son regarding her? Where do I need to deal with some issues in my life?"

After sitting in silence for a number of minutes, he looked back at Colossians 4:12. "Lord," he began, "do I pray for her maturity, as Epaphras did for his people? Or do I just complain to You about her? Forgive me Father."

"Alexander, you foolish old coot, follower of that Galilean Carpenter, your adventuring has kept you single this long, and your naïveté will keep you single for the rest of your days."

And yet, katepa knew he should be sacared. He had seen a glimmer of something in Alexander Rich that he saw nearly 2000 years ago, in another adventuresome Christian, Thales. It's an attitude that katepa felt sure would cause Alexander's downfall. But instead the Holy Enemy, who claims to use "everything for the better,"[1] used that attitude as a perfect weapon against him, katepa. And it ended up strengthening Thales by turning that adventuresome spirit into a spirit of humility, of all things.

Thales settled into his new routine with his uncle. It consisted of getting up early, usually around six in the morning, according to the Roman clock, spending time in prayer … with a parchment open. And it seemed very odd and strange that every time Thales had a passage opened the words he read would direct the way he would pray. It proved to be very different from the way he had previously started his day "with the Lord."

He would get up in the morning, grab some fruit to eat, and then take his list of things to pray for and talk to God about them. "There is nothing wrong with that," his Uncle Epaphras had said, but then explaining further said, "Let's try something different. Let's let the Holy Spirit direct our prayers based on where we are in the Scriptures."

"Okay," Thales responded hesitantly.

Noticing that his nephew moved forward a bit cautiously Epaphras said, "It will actually be fun Thales, and enlightening. You will see God speak to you in very specific ways. When I

---

[1] Romans 8:28

begin to teach this kind of praying to people I like to start with the Psalm that David wrote that begins:

The Lord is my Shepherd, I shall not want.[1]

"Now meditate on that passage Thales."

"I don't understand 'meditate' uncle."

"Meditating is thinking about the passage, and in a way, rolling it over and over, in your brain. As you roll the words over, you think about what they mean, you think about how they apply to you, and you think about what David may have been going through when he wrote it. Sometimes you are just quiet, sometimes you get a sense of the Holy Spirit prompting your spirit, and sometimes you just go on to the next few words.

"So think about these words, Thales. What are they telling you? If you don't mind, so that I can help you, think out loud Thales. When you're prompted by something, share it out loud, okay?"

After a few moments of quietness Thales said, "The Lord is my Shepherd, I shall not want ... the Lord is my Shepherd, I shall not be in want." And then after a few more moments of silence Thales said, "Oh Uncle, the Lord is my Shepherd, I have all that I need."

"Praise You, Father," chimed in Epaphras. "You see, Thales, when you go to the Lord to pray, you do not always need to take your prayer list to Him. Let His Spirit direct how you pray as you read His Word."

Still sitting on the Marks's back porch, he fought with fewer and fewer gnats as the day drug on. The gnats weren't reducing in number. In fact, it seemed that they were increasing, but Brother Alexander now let them fly in one orifice and another

---

[1] Psalm 23:1

completely engrossed in his time with the Lord. He fought with fewer and fewer gnats because they almost weren't registering on him … almost. They still were, his mind just happened to be elsewhere.

Alexander Rich still wanted the Colossians 4:12 Epaphras to teach him prayer. "Father, what more can I learn from Epaphras?"

Opening his Bible to the 23rd Psalm, and thinking about how he teaches folks in middle Georgia to meditate on scripture, using scripture, and making people keep their prayer lists for another day, he looked at verse one: *The Lord is my Shepherd, I shall not want.* "Did you meditate Epaphras? Did you teach your people how to meditate on God's Word?" As he thought through the ways that God speaks to him about verse one, he realized how grateful he would always be that the Lord made it clear Alexander Rich always has all that he needs.

He started to meditate on verse two: *He makes me lie down in green pastures, He leads me beside still waters.* "Oh Father, thank You for the seasons of rest that You have given me over the years. They have allowed me to experience laying down, as if in lush green pastures. I know that this is Your assurance to me, even in the midst of difficulties. You still allow a rest, sometimes just in my spirit, but the rest is as still waters that Sterling and I need to cross. Thank You Father."

After Epaphras shared with Thales his thoughts on the next sentence, he asked Thales to again share out loud, what the Lord laid on his heart from the following: *He restores my soul. He leads me in the paths of righteousness for His name's sake.*[1]

---

[1] Psalm 23:3

Again, after a few moments, Thales related, "Lord, You have a vested interest in my righteousness. Thank You for looking at me and seeing Your Son's righteousness, because I know that mine is as filthy rags.[1] You restored my soul when I accepted your Son into my heart, I trust You to continue to lead me in the paths of righteousness. I acknowledge Father that as the Lord's half-brother told us that when I am tempted it is on me ... temptations come, not because You bring them, but because I have brought them upon myself.[2] I love that You are interested in me, for Your Name's sake. Praise You, Lord."

As Epaphras listened, his heart warmed and he smiled to the Lord for preparing Thales the way He had, and to himself, because God placed Thales here, in Colossae, where Epaphras's congregation had already fallen in love with his nephew.

Alexander now looked at verse four: *Yea, though I walk through the valley of the shadow of death, I will fear no evil, for You are with me. Your rod and Your staff they comfort me.*

As Brother Alex thought about this passage, meditating on it, turning its words over and over in his mind. He thought about the love and care that God had given him, not the love of *a "young maiden"* as Dwight had cajoled him about earlier in his letter. And then Al remembered Joseph Scriven, a man who had truly known the comfort of the Lord. Alexander read back over the passage in his mind: *Yea, though I walk through the valley of the shadow of death,* and he remembered that this man had two fiancés die just before their weddings.

Alex went on, *I will fear no evil for You are with me.* And he again marveled at Brother Joseph Scriven again, because he took

---

[1] Isaiah 64:6
[2] James 1:14

a vow of poverty, helping others, after his second fiancé's death. *Your rod and your staff they comfort me.*

At this Alexander pulled his handkerchief out of his pocket to wipe the tears from his eyes, for he had read that this dear man had written *What a Friend We Have in Jesus* upon learning of his mother's illness back in Europe, and he did not have the funds to go help her. So he wrote her this poem, which would later be put to music by Charles Converse.

As all of these thoughts ran through his mind, he felt an incredible sense of gladness that he had the opportunity to share this poem and this story with his friend Dwight Moody. And through his friend Dwight this song had become a blessing to so many others.

And as these thoughts calmed him, he found himself singing this great hymn:

What a Friend we have in Jesus, all our sins and griefs to bear!
What a privilege to carry everything to God in prayer!
O what peace we often forfeit, O what needless pain we bear,
All because we do not carry, everything to God in prayer.

Have we trials and temptations? Is there trouble anywhere?
We should never be discouraged; take it to the Lord in prayer.
Can we find a friend so faithful, who will all our sorrows share?
Jesus knows our every weakness; take it to the Lord in prayer.

Are we weak and heavy laden, cumbered with a load of care?

Precious Savior, still our refuge, take it to the Lord in prayer.

Do your friends despise, forsake you? Take it to the Lord in prayer!

In His arms He'll take and shield you; you will find a solace there.

Blessed Savior, Thou hast promised Thou wilt all our burdens bear.

May we ever, Lord, be bringing all to Thee in earnest prayer.

Soon in glory bright unclouded there will be no need for prayer

Rapture, praise and endless worship will be our sweet portion there.

When Thales and Epaphras got to *You prepare a table before me, which is in the presence of my enemies. You anoint my head with oil and my cup runs over …*[1] Epaphras couldn't wait to hear Thales praise the Lord in his meditations.

"Father," Thales began, "Uncle Epaphras has no idea how this part of the Psalm has blessed me for years. Thank You, Father for preparing Hierapolis for my family. For even in the presence of my grandmother's enemies, so many years ago, You were planning for us: Hierapolis and now Colossae for me. Thank You, Lord."

Epaphras opened his mouth, ready to praise the Lord when Thales continued.

"Lord, we are so honored that You anointed us with the Holy Spirit, through my grandmother's faith, and audacity really, to

---

[1] Psalm 23:5

stand before Your loving Son in faith, so that now we are three generations of saved ones, followers of The Way, and eventually a fourth with my children. Oh Father, when the circumcised group realized who my grandmother turned out to be, and demanded that she and her family live under their law, You caused a mighty tribulation. And even in that tribulation, You were working out Your great plan, and in ways Lord, that none of our family (and others, for that matter) could ever had expected, so that truly our cup filled to overflowing. Oh Lord, truly I can thank You for adversity. With all of these persecutions, the Christians were dispersed, us to Hierapolis, and me now to Colossae. Oh thank You Father. I think about all that You did for my family. I do not know why my mother had to die giving birth to me, but my Daddy God, my cup of joy and hope overflows, as a cup running over, I Thank You Father. Thank You Daddy God."

"Whew," thought Epaphras, "What a blessing I nearly missed interrupting that boy's prayers."

Surely goodness and mercy shall follow me all the days of my life, and praise God, I will dwell in Your house for ever and ever.[1] "Father," Alexander started, "I pray for my brethren who believe that they can lose their salvation. Father, every time I talk to them I see a surprising lack of trust in what You have said, and an over exalting of their own abilities. Forgive us Father, all of us, for thinking that we can do something that You have already said will not occur. You say Lord, that nothing can snatch me out of Your hands,[2] no one, and I am a someone, so that means that even I cannot snatch me from Your hands. Father, I trust You to

---

[1] Psalm 23:6
[2] John 10:28b

keep me from ever thinking that this understanding gives me a license to sin. I know that it does not. The truth is, in spite of myself, You allow goodness and mercy to follow me, every single day of my life. Lord, with this promise in mind, I look forward to whatever follows me, tomorrow, next week, and next year. I love You, Lord."

And with that last sentence katepa smiled, another cheshire grin that contorted his face into something grotesque.

Speaking into his ear katepa said, "Something is following you Alexander, 'not too rich' but it ain't goodness and mercy." And then cackling katepa left Dry Branch for Jeffersonville.

27

Current Era

Dean's first Bible study ended at 8:00 am and the men made their way into the cafeteria to have coffee, juice, Chick-fil-A and Krispy Kreme donuts. What a deal, thought Coach Dale. As Dale walked into the cafeteria he had to pass the donuts, they looked disgusting … disgustingly good, and he hadn't decided how many he would opt for today. Then he saw his shot putter, all 365 pounds of him.

"Glad you made it today Clyde," said Dale with eyebrows upraised. Clyde had four donuts on his plate, a Chick-fil-A breakfast sandwich and an eye for more … if any were left.

"I'm pretending like it's the off-season coach."

"Yeah! I am speaking today on Biblical meditation. I may change it to gluttony."

Clyde frowned.

"Point made," Dale thought.

Dale loved this part of his ministry. He would make his way around the tables while the men were eating and fellowshipping. These groups of men often sat at the same tables, and with usually the same men. Again, the relational character of these men interested him. The men developed relationships and so usually, the old guys sat with the old guys, the middle-aged guys with the middle-aged guys, all the way down to college-aged men. Younger than that the youth stayed with their dads, or friends would sit with a friend who sat with his dad.

And then there would be the occasional "older guy" that would spend time with a different group each breakfast. He loved watching them mingle, and well, do relationship.

Dale got to mingle with all of them. They didn't care about his age, and really, they didn't care when a new guy sat down at their table. It always became so exciting to watch, the dynamic of these men's relationships. Dale had learned very early on that these men will come the first few times out of curiosity, but they would stay because of the relationships they built, and that is what he saw, men who were in relationship with one another.

And they weren't just talking about holy things. They were talking about the ballgame, someone's golf game, their work issues, all kinds of things. Another table listened to a new guy Roger talk about how he just lost his job. Dale had just come to that table to hear Mark tell Roger about the day he got laid off.

"Roger," Mark had started, "I remember asking the Lord a number of times if I could leave my employer, but he clearly said 'No' at least three times. So last July when they came to lay me off, I'm not kidding, I remember being so excited, because I knew that the Lord had something up His sleeve."

"You may have been excited Mark, but what did your wife think?"

"That's the best part of the story Roger." A number of men laughed, because they knew the story. Mark continued, "my wife and I share one car so I always pick her up, and I often make dinner …"

Dale went to another table, but he had heard Mark tell the story so many times that he could finish it for Mark.

"… so she is cutting into her chicken, that I had made," Mark continued, "and I needed to tell her I got laid off before she stuck that chicken into her mouth. I didn't want her to choke."

Some of the men around the table chuckled and Mark kept going, "She had just stuck it with the fork and I said, 'Baby, I got laid off today,' and the fork stopped." Mark made a rigid stopping motion with his hand in front of him and everyone laughed so he continued, "And baby, I don't think God wants me to look for work."

Roger's eyes were wide, "You said that to your wife?"

"Yes, and talk about weird, the words were outside of my mouth before I realized what I said. Now you've got to realize Roger, my wife has this wonderful woman's brain where right at the top of her scalp she is concerned about finances and security. But proof positive I heard from the Lord, my wife says, 'I agree Mark.' Now I'm the one whose fork stopped Roger, because that's not my wife."

After the men stopped laughing Mark continued, "What God taught us Roger, is that Matthew 6:33 is still true. When we seek first His kingdom and His righteousness, He promises to take care of all of the details."

As Dale walked to another table he stopped by Bruno, a big good looking muscular man in his mid-forties. He had been a plumber by trade until the day before. Dale could tell by his countenance that the loss of his job devastated him. In fact, his job loss accounted for him being at the Saturday prayer time, for Bruno rarely came. "Bruno, I have to go to the sanctuary to be ready to begin, but you and I can speak later. In the meantime, I will have Don spend some time with you. You'll love him, okay?"

235

Relieved to not be alone, Bruno sighed, "Thanks Doc."

"Don," Dale said, just loud enough for the short, seventy-ish year old man two tables over to hear him. Brother Don, in his late seventies and addressed everyone with, 'A happy good morning to you, my brother.' When Dale described Don he always described him the same way. He said, "My friend Don has more energy than the Energizer Bunny and they're about the same height. The only difference is that the Energizer Bunny is pink, and Don is black."[1] Don came over with as much excitement as Dale had always known Don to give. He immediately got down to the issue with Bruno, and began to be the encourager that he has always been since God had gotten his attention.

As Dale headed for the sanctuary he nodded to Greg who would shortly be announcing to everyone that they should leave the cafeteria and head for the sanctuary. Just before Dale reached the sanctuary Steven, a twenty something single man, stopped him. "Doc, I don't know what to do. I am so struggling with finances. I owe thousands of dollars on my credit card, many thousands, and I no longer have the money to pay the bill. I don't have peace about walking away from the debt, even though there are places out there that can help you do that legally, without filing for bankruptcy. But as much as I want to walk away from the debt, I can't do it. It just doesn't feel right. I used the money, I spent it. It's my responsibility to pay it back … somehow. Will you pray for me?"

"Oh my friend, you know I will. I'm honored to pray for you. Do you trust me Steven?"

---

[1] Don is a real person and my prayer partner. As of the writing of this book he is 82 years old and doesn't act a day over 45. He and I do about 20 prayer conference calls per week. I keep telling the Lord I want Don around for another 20 years.

"Yes, of course I do."

"Come on, go into the sanctuary and sit down. I'll be with you shortly. In fact, sit in the front with me." Relieved, Steven walked into the sanctuary, not sure how he would deal with his debt, but sure that the God of the Bible had the answers.

"No, no, no!" screamed demon after demon who were dogging their assigned men to discourage them because of financial worries. All of these demons turned, saying the same thing, "Don't you have a handle on your man yet, katepa?" Hissing and growling at katepa, these demons were blaming him for their men falling to the Holy Enemy, and now something didn't seem right and they could all feel it.

Demon after demon came by and struck katepa sending him flying up against other demons. Off in the distance they could all hear the rumblings, and they all knew that it would be the sound of the Holy Enemy's angels' wings. They were like the roar of mighty waters, like the voice of their Enemy, the Almighty, and it's commotion sounded like, in this case, what they dreaded, the noise of a great army ...[1]"No!" they all now thought the same thing. "The Spirit of their enemy had already started on the move toward their charges and soon these humans would be filled with peace rather than fear."

In the middle of all of these demons, joln snickered. Sure he could read the handwriting on the wall too, and his other charge would soon experience something, this dreaded peace, that would hurt joln's cause, but it would also be one more thing joln could point out about katepa. Blaming him for his failure, now laughing out loud, coughing out a foul odor and then spittle every

---

[1] Ezekiel 1:24

couple of words, he said looking directly at katepa, "This is actually going to work out well, you loser katepa."

The worship music and announcements were over and Dale stood before the men. He had fifteen minutes to bring them a prayer devotional that he had prepared before the one-hour prayer time started. But feeling moved by the Holy Spirit, and with the memory of the testimonies and concerns of his men from this morning fresh on his mind, he said, "If you are having some anxiety over financial struggles, would you stand up?"

And to his surprise, over half the men stood up. With the men standing, he bowed his head and prayed into the microphone, "Lord, You know that I planned to teach on Biblical Meditation today, but that will have to wait. I trust You to give me the words to say in this hour, blessing these men, because Your Word never returns void, whereunto You send it.[1] Send it to these men now, as I trust You to fill my mouth with Your words. Amen.

"I want you that are sitting to stand up and go to a hurting brother that is standing. If there are two or three in a group, that is okay, I just don't want anyone to stand alone."

After a few moments of gathering around one another Dale said, "Philippians 4:6-7 says that when we come to the Lord about anything that we are anxious about, we can come to Him with prayers and petitions and, what men?"

And they all yelled out, "*Thanksgiving.*"

"Hey, you've been listening." After a few chuckles Dale went on, "But there is another verse about anxiety. It is Psalm 38:18. It says that sometimes anxiety is with us because we have sin in our life. I'm not saying that financial difficulties have come because you have secret sin, No! I'm just wanting to be true to

---

[1] Isaiah 55:11

scripture. So, let us deal with anxiety, but deal with it completely. And to deal with anxiety, I think we need to also consider sin. So before we go any further, each of you pray for forgiveness for any sins that the Lord brings to you. Just you and the Lord. Pray quietly while the men around you are lifting you up. If you want to confess something out loud, do so."

And with this confession of sin, all over the auditorium, the demons were again seething at katepa and those closest to him were striking him. He felt like a punching bag, and knew that it would not be over for a long while, because they would be going to prayer in a few minutes. They would be in prayer for an hour, and then they would go back home to families who would be sickeningly lifted up, because their husband, father, grandfather's spirits would be lifted.

"I'm in for a long day," worried katepa.

Listening to men pray like this all over the room "sounds like thunder going up to heaven," an old preacher friend of his used to say.

Again into the microphone, but quietly, Dale continued, "Now come to the Lord, as you continue to pray, and ask the Lord to show you reasons that you can thank Him for the financial struggles you're going through. Maybe one reason that you can thank Him is because it causes you to turn to Him." Dale paused for a few moments.

All of a sudden, a larger demon, twice the size of *katepa* jumped toward him. And while *katepa* thought this demon would tear him from limb to limb, he saw this other demon lifted up by another demon who punched *katepa*, and then threw him like a rag doll across their entire smelly domain.

Speaking again into the microphone as softly as he could because the men were still praying, and yet he wanted to be heard all over the auditorium, Dale said, "Thank Him that your struggle is *not* a surprise to Him." Again he paused for a few minutes allowing the men to pray. Then he said, "thank Him that He is already in the process of comforting you so that you can comfort others in the same way."[1] After a few more minutes he said, "I want each of you to end with this, repeat after me, Lord, *'Lord,'* I thank You that You have the opportunity, *'I thank You that You have the opportunity,'* To strengthen my faith muscle, *'To strengthen my faith muscle,'* And I get to watch You do it. *'And I get to watch You do it.'* Amen? *'Amen!'*" The roar from the men deafened Dale and continued for a few minutes. Men were hugging and crying, burdens were lifted, and Dale smiled to himself and said, "And you guys still have an hour to pray. Oh Lord, this is too exciting, being in ministry."

Dale's fifteen minutes were up but he continued, "I need to release you to pray for an hour. Remember to pray until you hear the music … some of your guys' watches are fast." A few chuckles. "But before we pray, I have one request to add to your list. It's personal. One of my students got a zero in her psych class because she used this very argument, 'Thanking God for the difficulties,' on her test. This zero for the grade, may result in her not being able to graduate in her major.

"Secondly, and here's my prayer, not just for my athlete, but for each of you: Father, Romans 15:13 is the only passage I can

---

[1] 2 Corinthians 1:4

pray right now, for Julienne and her zero credit, for each of these men that are having financial struggles, for each of us Lord, no matter our current issues, You are the God of Hope, and because of that I trust that You are already in the process of filling these men, their wives and my student Julienne, with great joy and great peace, simply because they are believers, and as you do that Father, these men will go home, Julienne will go home and they will overflow with hope, because that hope comes from You. Praise You, Lord."

Somewhere in the dark caldrons of a stench filled world katepa took blow after blow after blow. He was beaten and pummeled brutally by his brethren.

"And what the evil one tries to use for harm, God the Almighty uses for great good,"[1] smiled Hael, as he followed behind Dale.

---

[1] Genesis 50:20

28

19th Century

A gentle nudge from two demons, assigned to Geraldine McCreedy's three friends, prompted these "friends" to move forward with their "helping Geraldine." "She's your friend after all, she needs your support. The best way for you to support her is to *stop* any talk about poor, poor, Mrs. McCreedy that may come up. You are her friends, so help her." As these demons slinked away, they knew it didn't take much more prompting than that.

It had turned into a most exciting Monday afternoon in the friendly town of Jeffersonville … The three women scattered to all parts of the town, not planning or conspiring with one another, after all they each thought, "We don't want to gossip about any problems our friend has. We know the real story, and that can only help our friend."

And so the women canvassed the town.

"Oh yes, Miss Victoria," said Blanch Bookman, the Jeffersonville saloon owner's wife, "Ralph told me all about it this morning. It seems that dirty old man tried to rape Gretchen. I'm so glad I don't go to church."

"What?" exclaimed the elder sister of Billie Carter, who still lived in her own home in the middle of downtown Jeffersonville, "Do you mean that our preacher and this Gretchen child have been secretly rendezvousing after he leaves town?"

"Pregnant? Is that what Geraldine told you Ellie?" asked a flabbergasted Mrs. Sam Wainright. "My, my, my. What will become of that little baby? Poor Geraldine," and then after a moment added, "and Gretchen too, bless her heart."

"Thank goodness," Ellie Squire told the elder Miss Bessie Bailey, "thank goodness that Gretchen has an aunt in Savannah. She will be heading out there to wait till, well, you know …"

And on and on it went all afternoon.

Ellie Squire, finished up her day of "helping" her intimate friend Mrs. McCreedy by visiting the mill. She had put this visit off, because even though the Borax's were nice people, they were, well, different. She always seemed uncomfortable around them, and at the same time she liked them. "What is it?" Ellie often asked herself as she pointed her buggy to the front door. "I know it feels like they judge me and my friends. That's what it is … but then why do I like them too?"

"You idiot, Ellie." Both demons knew that coming to the mill would be a mistake.

Both Josephine and Bubba were large people. "The size of two people, two people in one," Ellie always thought when she saw them. "They probably needed the extra size and strength because they owned the mill," Ellie now began to be sarcastic in her selfishly narrow little brain. "They probably eat as much as they sell, bless their heart."

"Good afternoon Miss Ellie," Josephine said, bright and cheery as she always greeted everyone. "What brings you out here today? Get down off that buggy and come in here for some sweet tea. I just made some."

After a few pleasantries, Ellie started telling her that, "I need to tell you about my good friend Sister Geraldine, her daughter and our pastor. My friend Sister Geraldine is in a very bad way …" But Josephine startled Ellie by interrupting her.

"Hmm, Sister Ellie, I know you just got started, but before you go on any further, may I ask you a question?"

"Well of course Sister Josephine."

"I'm just curious," Josephine paused, choosing her words carefully, "I know how close you and Sister Geraldine are, but well, why are you telling me this?"

"Well that should be obvious Sister Josephine." "You big cow," she thought to herself, and then went on, "I am trying to protect my friend from any pain. I don't want anyone to see her daughter gone and wonder what has happened and inadvertently ask Geraldine something that would hurt her feelings. We can never be too careful," Ellie went on, "There are a lot of people in our town that would make up stories and gossip." And with that, Ellie paused for a well-deserved moment of self-righteousness.

After a few moments of silence, while Josephine quickly prayed for wisdom to decide how to handle this gossiping sister, and Ellie continued to reflect on her self-righteousness, Josephine broke the silence. "Sister Ellie, I just love the way you played the organ yesterday. Your participation in the service always prepares me for Brother Rich's messages, and it thrills me to hear an organist play on Sunday morning."

Forgetting her intended conversation, Ellie said, "oh, Sister Josephine, thank you so much. You know, I practice and practice and practice, and for someone to compliment my efforts is a great blessing. I get so few of them. And I am grateful for the words of kindness."

Before Ellie could go on, Josephine cut in, "How is your tea? Would you like some more?"

"Oh no, Sister Josephine, I'm fine. That tea is so good."

And without missing the opportunity, Sister Josephine stood up. And Sister Ellie did as well. Gently walking to the door, Sister Josephine reached for the door handle and did not hesitate to open it.

Profusely thanking her, Sister Ellie said, "Oh Sister Josephine, I so enjoy your company. And that tea, Oh so wonderful. You are quite the hostess."

Bubba had just coming to the house while Ellie prepared to mount her buggy, "Let me help you Miss Ellie."

"You are such a gentleman Brother Bubba, thank you."

"God bless you Sister Ellie," said Josephine.

"Thank you, God bless you too," returned Ellie as she drove away.

"Sister Josephine," remarked a slightly sarcastic Bubba, "Do you want to talk about it?"

Over dinner she told him, "Ellie came over to gossip something about the McCreedys and our pastor. I have no idea what because I shut her up. But you could see in her eyes that she wanted to spill all of her gossip, innuendoes, half-truths and probably a fair amount of lies, but honey," she continued, "my spirit tells me something is afoot back in town. Something isn't right."

Putting another slab of steak on his plate Bubba said, "Let me tell you about my day. I meditated on the thirty-first chapter of Proverbs, the wonderful woman of the home, and I thought about you."

Josephine blushed, "I love this man, Lord," she thought to herself.

"And while I spent the morning thanking the Lord for you, I started to think about Brother Alex. Honey, I started to feel sorry for him for not having a wonderful companion like I do." Josephine blushed again, "I started to feel really bad for him, and I stopped working. Literally stopped everything, including the mill …"

"About noon honey?"

"Yes," responded Bubba.

"I thought I heard everything stop. I wanted to ask you about that, if there's a problem I should be aware of."

"There is a problem. It is in my spirit Josie. I just found myself feeling so burdened … No, not just burdened, but troubled, heavily troubled …"

"For Brother Alex?" interjected Josephine for some clarity.

"Yes, for Alex. I love the man, and I think that my concerns for him went way beyond my desire to see him have a companion. So I prayed for him Josie. I prayed for him like I have not prayed for him for a very long time. I went back to my brush arbor clearing that I have made and just started to lift up my friend, and then, and this became really strong on my heart also, I felt the need to pray for some of the men in our church. In fact, do you mind if we just pray for them right now?"

"Oh, of course not," sighed a very proud Josephine Borax, "The food isn't going anywhere Bubba, you pray as long as you need to and that you feel the Lord is wanting you to pray."

And with that, she moved her chair next to his, they held hands and he started, "Father in heaven, hallowed be Your

Name,[1] and all that You are. Josie and I come to You now, not knowing why exactly, but trusting You to lead us as we pray for our town, for our church, and for our pastor ..." Pausing just a moment, Josephine stepped in.

"And Father, we pray also for Ellie and her friends. Your Word says that division is as the sin of witchcraft.[2] Oh Lord, make clear to any, no, Lord open their spiritual eyes and ears, causing them to remember the wonder of Your Word,[3] and how it clearly says that gossip is destructive,[4] and that as they are hearing it they are participating. Father, through Your Holy Spirit prick the hearts[5] of those listening, and let them see the destructiveness of the tongues of gossipers." Josephine then paused and Bubba picked back up.

"Father, we pray as Epaphras did in the fourth chapter of Colossians and verse twelve: laboring fervently for our brothers and sisters that they, and Josie and I, would be able to stand perfect, mature, and complete in Your will, not ours. Father, forgive us as a church for allowing our own emotions to run our lives, our own wills. Lord, You love us enough to allow difficulties so that we can comfort others in ways we are not able to had we not gone through difficulties in our own lives. Father, I thank You for the difficulties in our life ..."

Josephine started to tear up, because she knew exactly what her dear loving Bubba would pray next.

"... Lord, I thank You that Josie and I have not been able to have children, not because we like not having children, we want them, but you have not seen fit to give us any, so we'll just keep on trying ..." And with this slight humor, he felt his wife bump

---

[1] Matthew 6:9
[2] 1 Samuel 15:23a
[3] Psalm 119:18
[4] Psalm 52:2
[5] Acts 2:37m

247

him and her shoulders relaxed so he continued. "Oh Lord, I hurt for our congregation. My heart goes out to these, whom You have honored me with leading as one of their deacons. But Father, there is sin in the camp.[1] And I need Your wisdom Lord. I need the spirit of wisdom and of spiritual understanding.[2] Lord, I feel such a burden for these people. I bow my knees Lord, unto You, that You would grant me to be strengthened by Your Spirit, as I wait on a full and complete manifestation of Your Spirit …"

After pausing a bit Bubba went on, "And Lord, as I think of gossip in our church, I am reminded that James tells us that no human can tame the tongue. He goes on and says that it is restless and is full of deadly poison.[3] I turn over to You Father, the one who would spread gossip. Bring them to the end of themselves, that they would turn to You, recognizing what Josephine has already prayed, that rebellion which gossip surely is, is on the same plain with You as witchcraft is.[4]

At the same time that Bubba prayed, Harrold Pleasant got home to find that Victoria had a nice big dinner on the table waiting for him. "Well," he stammered out the words, more than a little bit excited, "What are we celebrating?"

They had barely sat down to eat when Victoria said, "Harrold, you are the church financial officer, what are you going to do about that disgusting preacher of ours?" And with that, Brother Harrold Pleasant's meal would be far from pleasant.

---

[1] Joshua 7:11a
[2] Colossians 1:9e
[3] James 3:8
[4] 1 Samuel 15:23a

29

First Century

For the next two days Benjamin spoke very little. His countenance troubled, he tried to figure out how serious Mary could be with this Gentile, and then how much he would have to do to deal with it.

"How foolish fathers are," thought Aikaterine, as she would watch her husband. She knew he couldn't stop thinking about their daughter.

Seeing the relationship develop, Aikaterine realized that soon she would have to step in and help "direct traffic." "But for now," she thought, "We'll see what happens."

One of the house churches in Colossae, owned by Anat, a wool merchant traded with Aikaterine. Thales did not know about the connection, but when he prayed for Mary, knowing they needed to be of the same mind spiritually[1] he asked the Lord

---

[1] 2 Corinthians 6:14a

for "wisdom to invite Mary to the right house church, and introduce her to Jesus Christ."

After wrestling with God for days about this, Thales felt like God told him to invite Mary to the house church at Anat's home, and so with the commitment made to the Lord, a scared Thales went to the flower store. He always tried to go there when he would miss Benjamin, and today he would work at doing the same thing. There would be no exceptions. Benjamin looked and acted too scary.

Sitting under the cover of the roof and choosing his words very carefully, Thales told Mary that he, "studies the words of Jehovah very carefully and would like to study them with her one day."

This sounded odd to Mary's ears. In that society, the Jewish men took great efforts to stay away from even remotely discussing anything theological with the women.

Thales went on, "We meet on the first day of the week at 10:00 am (Roman time) in the wool merchant's home, Anat. She is a good Jewish woman that your father would probably approve of and that I believe trades with your mother."

"But you are a Gentile," complained Mary, "Why would you study Jehovah's words?"

"Clever boy," thought Aikaterine, as she did her best to listen in without the two young people knowing.

On the first day of the next week Benjamin had just left the front gate where he sat with the leaders of the city until about noon. Heading back into town he saw Epaphras leaving the wool merchants home. He had seen this off and on in the past, and decided to ask him about it.

"You there, excuse me," a gruff sounding Benjamin called out to Epaphras. With no response, he yelled out a bit louder, "Excuse me there."

At that, the entire group that came out the door with Epaphras turned. There were seven or eight of them including Thales. The moment Thales turned around, he nearly froze. It didn't appear that Benjamin looked at anyone except Epaphras, so Thales slipped to the back of the group away from Benjamin and hid.

"Are you calling me?" Epaphras asked.

"Yes, you. I understand you are a teacher of some kind."

"I prefer to think of myself as a servant, but yes, you can say that I am a teacher," And with that Epaphras stuck out his hand to introduce himself to Benjamin. "I am Epaphras, a teacher of The Way.[1] Some over in Antioch call us Christians."[2] And turning to introduce Thales, he saw with some bewilderment that Thales had disappeared behind their group. So, without missing a beat, Epaphras asked, "Are you Benjamin of Jerusalem?"

"Yes, how did you know that?"

"Well, I have been in town since before you arrived and you," choosing his words carefully, "can make your presence known. I have had the good fortune to be made aware of who you are. I also hear that your flowers are the best in the town."

"Humph," stammered Benjamin, "Well, yes. Be that as it may, I have a question for you."

"Please," an excited Epaphras responded, thinking that Benjamin would be a wonderful "catch" for this fishermen of souls. "I am always available to answer questions for those that are seekers of Jesus ..." The immediate countenance change on Benjamin's face caused Epaphras to hesitate.

---

[1] Acts 9:2m
[2] Acts 11:26e

"Jesus. That Galilean carpenter, so called Rabbi, whom the Romans punished with execution on a cross? I happened to be in Jerusalem when that happened. I may have been young, but I remember it clearly. His followers stole His body so that they could say he rose from the dead. Humph," Benjamin snorted, and then went on. This time he snorted a chuckle, "Is that what The Way is all about, a dead rabbi who grew up as a carpenter?"

Benjamin took a step away from Epaphras, intending to head toward his shop. And with a shallow laugh he said, "You are just another sect of another false religion. When you begin to teach about true religion, you come and see me. I will teach you what is true religion, and it will be teaching that originates with the greatest of all teachings. The teachings from the God who made heaven and earth and will send a Messiah to take away our political chains."

With that Benjamin's turned his back to Epaphras and that would be all that Epaphras could see until he heard someone shouting out to Benjamin, "Jehovah's Messiah is the One we worship." And Benjamin stopped, stiffened, and slowly turned. Laughter gone from his face. Only a hate filled sneer could be seen on Benjamin's face, and he returned to Epaphras, putting his nose merely a few inches from his own.

All Epaphras could imagine is that no one in their right mind would engage this angry man. "Who," he now wondered, "who had said those words to Benjamin?"

"You are that Way?" Benjamin seething out the words, through gritted teeth.

"Why did he look at me when he spit out those words," Epaphras wondered. And then he realized, his words were the words he heard. He had said to Benjamin that they worship the Messiah of Jehovah.

Still seething and speaking through gritted teeth, Benjamin went on, this time threateningly, "Out of Jerusalem, we have been tracking down your kind and killing them. And believe me, Colossae is not too far out of the reach of us. I remember going to the school of Gamaliel with a zealot, whom I last heard captured and tortured your kind."

Becoming more and more comfortable with the control he had over all of these misguided fools, Benjamin cracked a smile and said, "He and I were once friends. I will find where he is and have him come here."

Again, the words were half way out of his mouth when he realized what he said. Somewhat apologetically, Epaphras said, "Are you by any chance talking about Saul of Tarsus?"

Benjamin again stiffened, and Epaphras continued, "His name is now Paul," and slowing down, not for effect, but with a hint of fear, Epaphras said, "He is also a teacher of The Way."

Everyone still waited to see what Benjamin would do. He slowly backed away one step, and then another, and staring at Epaphras alone he realized that this meant war. Somehow, although Jehovah would not allow him in the inner part of the temple, he would serve Jehovah here, in Colossae, standing up for the religion of his youth, the Jewish teachings of the one true God. "Somehow, the Almighty will use me," thought Benjamin.

"You may not be able to control your man katepa," blurted out a proud and arrogant demon, "But I can mine. He will fix your problem in Colossae, and when he does you will owe me." This demon followed Benjamin back to his flower stand and katepa hovered there wondering what to do next.

"I fear that I am in for a beating by these other demons," said katepa to no one in particular.

Heading back to their home, Epaphras and Thales were now alone. "What happened to you when Benjamin confronted me?" Realizing that Thales's hiding caused a huge check in his spirit about Thales ability to lead the Colossae church, Epaphras went on, emboldened now. "You cannot lead these people Thales, if you are going to shy away from fiery ordeals. Fiery ordeals are what we expect.[1] Jesus said it Himself: 'in this life *you will* have trials, but fear not, for I have overcome the world.'[2] And you, my tough future leader, slunk away in fear."

Looking at his uncle out of great respect, and anything but fearfully, he responded, "There is a bit more to my actions than fear Uncle," and then, not wanting to tell his uncle about Mary yet, he said, lightening the atmosphere, "Uncle, I thought he might punch you."

Leaning into Thales, Epaphras whispered, "Me too." And they both laughed guardedly.

---

[1] 1 Peter 4:12a
[2] John 16:33b

30

Current Era

Two Saturdays later, on the third Saturday of the month, the men's prayer ministry that Coach Dale led had returned. The Issachar Men Prayer Group would be meeting today.

Earlier in the week his wife's weekly Thursday Night University Girls Bible Study had broken away from their regular lessons and each girl took a famous old hymn and shared with the group what they had learned about its making. Then they were to tie in what they learned to a passage that had been an inspiration to them.

"Who wants to go first," Margie, Coach Dale's wife asked.

Moving to the edge of her seat so fast that she almost fell off, Julienne responded "Check-out." Everyone loved her and her South-Central Los Angeles flair.

Margie sitting back motioned to Julienne, "Tell us Julienne."

And with that Julienne sped off into an explanation of this poor man whose fiancée had drowned the day before they were to be married. "And then so heartbroken he moved from Ireland to Canada to start all over, where he met and fell in love with another woman. Just weeks before they were to be married …"

Julienne paused for effect. With everyone holding their breath, her eyes began to well up with tears, so she turned her eyes to the floor and said with a cracking voice, "She got sick two weeks before the wedding and never recovered. She died in a matter of weeks."

With a little crack in her voice and a very 'Southern-belle' accent, Sarah-Ann asked, "Well bless your heart, but what did you find inspirational in that?"

"Check-out," Julienne continued, saying this in such a way as to be saying 'be patient, the story continues,' "So he is, of course, heartbroken and believes that God is telling him to be single, but not just be single, to take a vow of poverty.

"Check-out! There is this great little story I found about the way he lived." Looking up into the ceiling, as if to read words written up there, she said, "Check-out, let me see if I can remember the story:

> *Two rich businessmen were on a street corner somewhere in Canada when one of them saw this author I learned about carrying a saw, and watched him. Then one of them said something about wishing he could be him. The other one said he is honest and hard-working, and the first one said, 'then maybe I should run after him and hire him to cut some wood for me.' But the other guy said, 'He won't work for you, he only works for those who cannot work for themselves, and he takes nothing for it."*

"I think your author would flunk Professor Schaaf's business classes," Sarah-Ann interjected, trying to bring the mood a bit more upbeat.

"But check-out," Julienne continues, "He gets a letter from his brother that his mom is ill, and," Julienne begins to tear up again, as do all the ladies in the room, "He doesn't have the money to go home and be with her when she dies. So he does the only thing he can do. He goes to his Bible and writes this poem. Two years later it became a song, and twenty years later became a hit, because of some old preacher named Moody."

Margie smiled to herself, knowing the full story how Moody found out about the song, through her husband's great-great-grandfather, Alexander Rich, but that story would have to wait for now.

Julienne continued on, "So he wrote this beautiful poem." Pausing and then speaking a bit South-Central L.A.-ish, she continued, "I be honest wich-you, I listened to it on Youtube and said, 'Yuk! Too slow and boring,' but after these stories, I went back to it, and jus' love-it." And then beginning with humming it, she started to sing and some of the girls started to sing, the ones who remembered it from their younger days in church:

What a Friend we have in Jesus, all our sins and griefs to bear!
What a privilege to carry everything to God in prayer!
O what peace we often forfeit, O what needless pain we bear,
All because we do not carry, everything to God in prayer.

Have we trials and temptations? Is there trouble anywhere?
We should never be discouraged; take it to the Lord in prayer.
Can we find a friend so faithful, who will all our sorrows share?
Jesus knows our every weakness; take it to the Lord in prayer.

Are we weak and heavy laden, cumbered with a load of care?
  Precious Savior, still our refuge, take it to the Lord in prayer.
  Do your friends despise, forsake you? Take it to the Lord in prayer!
  In His arms He'll take and shield you; you will find a solace there.

Blessed Savior, Thou hast promised Thou wilt all our burdens bear
  May we ever, Lord, be bringing all to Thee in earnest prayer.
  Soon in glory bright unclouded there will be no need for prayer
  Rapture, praise and endless worship will be our sweet portion there.

By the time they were done singing, all of the girls were dabbing their eyes and trying to not smear their mascara.

With her voice cracking as she spoke Sarah-Ann said, "I grew up with that hymn, Julienne, I don't remember that last verse. It's beautiful."

Julienne just rolled her eyes, not ever hearing of the hymn herself, before their recent study.

"Bless your heart, Julienne, but that's not the end of the story," came a weak voiced Sarah-Ann, "I want to know, no, I need to know, why did this inspire you?"

"Oh," A very quiet Julienne went on, "I found myself meditating on the 23rd Psalm. Some of you know the trouble I'm having in my psych class. Anyway this Psalm is always very comforting to me, and so I as I meditated on it I realized that this hymn-writer, Joe Scriven had to have understood the 23rd Psalm like nobody else that I know. Anyway I think that verse four caught and overwhelmed my heart: *Yea, though I walk through the valley of the shadow of death, I will fear no evil, for You are with me. Your rod and Your staff they comfort me.* Oh ladies, I don't care how much crap I have to go through in my psych class, I am comforted, just like this author had been.

"In fact," Julienne continued, "I found myself praying for Professor Gonzalez. I don't know what her problem is, but I suspect it is a spiritual one, so I prayed for God to intervene. Not in my class grade, but in Professor Gonzalez' life.

In the room a silence gripped the girls, and then, one at a time they all began to share what they had learned from their hymns. It turned out to be a long and tearful night.

As they were leaving the house Sarah-Ann asked Julienne, "You're in the same class as me, Professor Gonzalez, right?"

"Yes, but a different time, why?"

"Well what problem are you having? I'm getting good grades in that class, maybe I can help."

"Check-out Sarah-Ann, I'm getting good grades too, I ain't no hick," Turning on the South Georgia sarcasm, and then stopping immediately. "I'm sorry, Sarah-Ann, I know you are only trying to help. There's nothing you can do. Professor Gonzalez gave me a zero and no credit for our mid-term exam."

"How come?"

"Well, it seems she didn't like my use of a Christian answer."

"What?" cried Sarah-Ann, "I did the same thing, bless your heart."

By this time the girls were well away from the door and out to their cars, so Margie had to make a mental note to talk to Dale about this.

In another part of the city, a blurry-eyed, Isabela Gonzalez laid on her sofa putting on a mid-week drunk. She thought about her medical situation when she saw the previous year's university yearbook. Picking it up, she started to look at the faculty pictures, realizing that all, "Yes, all, every one of these people will outlive me." She said out loud to no one in particular. Even though she had started drinking early on Thursday afternoon she still wondered if her splitting headache would be gone by class tomorrow.

"But I don't care." she justified her drinking. "I deserve to be able to do this to myself." And with that she poured herself another drink.

And then she saw Margie Riley's picture. Looking at it closely, albeit through blurring eyes she said, "Hmm, she doesn't look like a mean-spirited, homophobic bigot." Isabela 'knew' that all Christians are both mean-spirited and homophobic. "I know that you are. All of you Christians are narrow-minded."

She poured herself another drink. "But," she thought, "what if she's not a fake?"

Two days later, Margie enjoyed her Saturday morning. She really liked it when Dale left to go to The Issachar Men's Prayer Group. She could spend time with the Lord and let it be long and drawn out. This morning she thought about her Thursday night Bible study with the girls when she thought of Professor Gonzalez.

"Father," Margie confidently but humbly, being careful not to have any arrogance entering the throne room of the Lord. "I know that You have said that You are not willing that any should

260

perish,[1] and so Father I ask You to give me the faith to pray this for Isabela Gonzalez." Praying, still hesitantly and guarded, her faith began to build ... a little, she would admit. "Father, I want to see You work in her life, and if that means You can use me, I'm available. But Father, a woman like her scares me. She seems to me to be a mean atheist. Oh Lord, if there is any other way to save her, please do it, and yet not my will Father, but Yours is what I pray on behalf of her."[2]

"Amen, that's all you need to say. Be a good little Christian and end your prayer there," scolded an ugly demon in the far reaches of his lair.

"And Father," Margie went on, "Let me not sin by ceasing to pray for her."[3]

"Stupid goody-two-shoes," stammered out the very same demon.

---

[1] 1 Timothy 2:4a
[2] Matthew 26:42b
[3] 1 Samuel 12:23a

31

Nineteenth Century

Monday night in the saloon, Carrolton Faith still pretended to be a hero. At least, he sounded like a hero to himself. Men were offering him drinks to tell his story, but to their surprise, he told them his story without accepting the drinks. "Keeping a clear head is now hurting my head," he had thought to himself. But something kept niggling at him while he spoke, "what is it?" he wondered again to himself.

"Those drinks sure looked good," he thought.

"Story? Yeah, well, I had been out in the woods, you see, and something didn't look right. I could see it in Brother Rich's eyes."

"The evil eye!" Someone half-drunk yelled out.

"Yeah, the evil eye. That's what I'm sure I saw. I could see that he had no good on his mind. I had no idea that Gretchen McCreedy would be anywhere near there, until she came strolling up to the campfire. Well, I couldn't just stand there. I knew I had to do something that would keep her safe. And so I got closer and closer …" And with that a waft of someone's whiskey traveled by his nose and he took a deep breath of it.

"Um, you know, maybe I will …" And his attempt at getting a drink trailed off.

"So what'd you do?" yelled someone from the bar.

"Well, of course I didn't want her to get hurt. You never know with a crazy old man like that …"

"Yeah, and a dirty old man," Again others in the bar were helping the story along.

"Well, anyway, I crept closer to the campfire. I got closer and closer, until I knew I could keep her safe, and I, umm, I uh …"

"Were you too drunk to remember Carrol?" yelled someone.

"You couldn't sneak up on a drunk, Carrol," howled someone else.

Feeling embarrassed now, he grabbed one of the drinks in front of him, poured it down his throat and grabbed another one all in one smooth stroke. He swallowed, in one gulp, the next drink and then continued, "So I charged them, see. I charged them to protect Gretchen's reputation. Then Brother Alex sent her back to town, and I stayed with him, sitting there, to make sure that he didn't go after her."

With that the other drunks in the saloon cheered, and Carrol drunk another drink. But somewhere in his mind he remembered something. "What is it that is still bothering me? A prayer? It had something to do with his parents, but what? Oh, I don't know." And with that Carrolton Faith chose to get drunk.

Across the street and down a block Gretchen McCreedy tried to get her clothes ready. While she remained confused still, she refused to be angry. And so she began to talk to the Lord, "Father, I don't understand. Why is all of this happening? Why are my parents so angry? Why won't they even talk to me about this?"

And then she remembered the story of the Syrophoenician woman, who it sounds like, got treated so badly, even by Jesus.

She opened up her Bible to the story in Matthew. It also appeared in Mark she seemed to recall. "Crumbs that fall from the master's table,"[1] rang in her mind. "Father, how is this like me? If anything I have been at that master's table. I have been the one dropping the crumbs. Speak to me Lord," she pleaded with Him.

"Father, as I read this, I see that she had to be determined to make sure that she found You." As she read Matthew 15:21, she saw a note she had made in her Bible. It read: 'Jesus did not want to be found, Mark 7:24.' She turned to it and continued reading. "Oh Lord, You were found because this woman would not give up. Oh Lord, I do not give up either. I seek You. I know that Your Word says that when I seek You, You will let Yourself be found,[2] and so Father, let me find You. What, oh Lord, are you teaching me?" And she read on, this time in the Mark rendering of the story. In verse 28 she read, "… even the dogs eat …"

"Even the dogs eat, Lord." Gretchen McCreedy repeated that part of the verse over and over in her mind and started to tear up, because she realized that there would be no difference in her and those dogs. It didn't matter how little she had, whatever scraps she had from the Lord she would be content with … no matter how little.

"Praise You Lord," a tear streaked Gretchen McCreedy said, smiling and looking forward to the future, whatever it may hold.

She now had a truly bizarre peace that transcended her very soul.[3] And then she thought of Brother Rich. "That's odd," she wondered. "Why would he be on my mind? Lord, as always, I

---

[1] Matthew 15:27b
[2] Jeremiah 29:11-14a
[3] Philippians 4:7

thank You for my pastor, Oh Lord, that I will not see now, for who knows how long," she wiped away another tear, and then resigned to pray for him. "Father, let me not sin by ceasing to pray for Brother Rich.[1] Thank You for the impact that he has on this town and all of the other towns on his circuit. I pray Father, for Alexander Rich, like Epaphras prayed, that my sweet friend would always find himself perfect and complete in all of Your will for his life."[2]

Surprised by her peace and the intimacy in the words she used praying for Brother Rich: "Sweet friend? Where did that come from?" She finished packing and actually looked forward to what lay ahead for her. Then she wondered something that had never crossed her mind before, "I wonder why Brother Rich has never been married?"

---

[1] 1 Samuel 12:23a
[2] Colossians 4:12

32

Current Era

"What a small world," Dale thought as he headed to church for his Saturday prayer meeting. "My great-great-grandfather had a hand in Julienne's story." But the biggest issue would still have to rear its ugly head. The real issue that he would have to deal with seemed to be the discrimination perpetrated by Prof Gonzalez on Julienne.

But it didn't make any sense? Dale could guess her politics, if she were going to discriminate, it would not be against the African-American. It would be against the "Southern-belle Christian, Sarah-Ann." Something didn't make sense, but it would have to wait until next week.

Dale arrived a few minutes early, not as early as he liked to, but today he could blame that on his wife. They had a small falling out, not a big deal, but there were hurt feelings all around, and by the time Dale left he knew that he would be a few minutes late. This further ticked him off, as he wanted to be at Dean's Bible study a few minutes early to watch the men interact before they started. Dean had mentioned something that caught his ear earlier in the week when he previewed Dean's teaching. Dean had said, "Dale, the first time we got together the men were, well, they were sitting in the chapel, and they were talking to each other like, forgive me but, 'Chatty-Cathys.'

"They were kind of cute Dale. I hated to bring them to order so that we could begin."

"I understand Dean. It's the first thing I always notice doing a Bible study with men, the relationships they develop, when they are allowed to build organically."

So here he is, at church, getting ready to walk in, still feeling a little … something … from his wife, not sure what, and then it hit him: 1 Peter 3:7. "Oh, Lord, why did you have to remind me of that verse?" So standing next to his car looking down at the pavement, cell phone in hand, he raised it to his ear. "Call wife," he spoke into the phone, and her phone started to ring.

"Hello," came the soft, loving reply from the other end.

"Baby," Dale said. "I acted like an idiot, please forgive me."

"You were forgiven immediately sweetie."

"I know," came Dale's humble reply. "I know babe, thanks."

"Have a great time. I've already prayed for your message on Biblical meditation."

"Thanks babe. Love you."

"Love you too."

"You're a schmuck and you do not deserve her," came the muffled voice from a still hurting and bandaged katepa, who had been beaten unmercifully two weeks earlier.

Walking into the church Dale thanked the Lord for Margie, "Lord, thank You, thank You. I don't deserve her, but for some reason You have given me a wife that I do not deserve." He thought about his wife, lounging in her nightshirt when he left. She had her knees folded up under her and the shirt stretched over her knees. She had her Bible open and sipped coffee. "I am a schmuck," he said to himself as he went around the hallway into the chapel. "Why did I just give her a peck on the forehead? She sat on the sofa … looking all sexy … and all I could do … oh, only a little peck on the forehead, why? And then the answer came.

He spoke to himself, "Because you were grumpy!

"What an idiot I can be."

He knew he needed to focus on his reason for being at church, but the gratefulness he had for God's gift of a wife that he didn't deserve filled him with a peace that transcended his understanding.[1] Truly, he certainly didn't deserve her.

The men were all talking like 'Chatty-Cathys' when Dean brought them to order. He started in the third paragraph of the *Wesley Family Prayer Book*, followed by the questions and discussion brought out by the men:

> *O that we may begin it this day, in devout meditations, in joy unspeakable, and in blessing and praising thee, who have given us such good hope, and everlasting consolation! Lift up our minds above all these little things below, which are apt to distract our thoughts; and keep them above, till our hearts are fully bent to seek thee every day, in the way wherein JESUS has gone before us, though it should be with the loss of all we here possess.*

- That we may "begin it this day," begin what?

---

[1] Philippians 4:7

- Do your prayers prepare you for "devout meditations," or, your devotions? Or, in the honesty of your own heart, do your prayers seem like a waste of time?
- What is meant by lifting "our minds above all these little things below?"
- How do you handle "these little things, which are apt to distract" you, while you are praying?
- Do you try to remember them? Have you tried writing them down, so that you do not have to remember them … and be further distracted in your praying?
- How do "distractions" impact you seeking God "every day?"
- Have you ever considered that in seeking Jesus, He may ask you to give up all of your possessions, and, in the same thought, all that you desire? If you recognize this, has the possibility of this kept you from fully seeking God's will for your life?
- How many verses in the paragraph above are referenced? Do you know which ones they are?

The men showed up and great interaction occurred over the *Wesley Family Prayer Book*. Most of the men were surprised by the amount of scripture that each line of prayer represented. Dale had to be careful that his ego didn't get into the middle of it, because he heard these men giving Dean answers that represented what Dale had been teaching them. How exciting, the realization of Isaiah 55:11: *that God's Word does not return void whereunto it has been sent.*

One of the men, Greg, took the question about distractions and what to do with them. "Well, for months now, whenever I am praying, I keep a notepad next to me. Anytime some 'noise' or distractions enter my brain, you know, like, 'Greg, take out the garbage' I simply write it down. It's amazing how many times I am in prayer and my 'to-do' list grows. But more importantly, the distractions are gone."

As some of the men chuckled, Brother Don added, "I find that I deal with the 'noise' by practicing verses that I am memorizing. I think the evil one stops putting 'noise' into my brain, because he does not want me to memorize more Scripture which I'll do as long as the distractions are there."

Another man answered the 'distractions' issue by stating that, "… he *loved* the distractions." When everyone finished booing him he added, "Because I take each distraction, and talk to God about it … and they go away, and they have gone away with prayers being ushered up about them."

From a brightness in the sky that one could hardly understand the guardian angel Tephillah, who stood guard over Dean, knew that the Holy Spirit whispered to Dean that he needed to have his abdomen pain checked out.

During the breakfast time, following Dean's Bible study, Dale reminded Brother Don that he would use him as an example today talking about meditation. Don, our "not very pink" Energizer Bunny as usual, had high energy, which all of the men knew as his trademark character. "I'm here and available Brother Dale. I love to tell the story of you and I spending five hours together searching the Word, talking, praying, seeking God, and coming away with those simple words: 'I want to finish spent.'[1] That happened two years ago when the doctors told me I had six months to live."

---

[1] 2 Timothy 4:7

"God is good, Brother Don," said a sincere Dale.

"All the time," came the reply in unison from the men around the table.

As Dale left the cafeteria to head up to the sanctuary he saw Dean. "Dean," he said, "I saw you wincing up there on stage, are you okay?"

"Oh, of course Dale, I'm feeling great."

At twenty-five minutes after eight Greg stood up and announced that the men were to head upstairs, and as dutifully as one hundred and fifty men could do so, they all filed in to the sanctuary.

Brother Jonathan, who led the music, came to the microphone after leading the men in a couple of songs. "I have a new song I want to try on you guys, if you don't mind." The song is Amazing Grace, but with a slightly different twist to it.

"You see," Brother Jonathan explained, "Chris Tomlin found another verse, actually it is the original ending to this great old hymn, Amazing Grace and so he rewrote, actually added to an already existing song and it's called Amazing Grace, with a subtitle My Chains Are Gone." Some of the men clapped acknowledging the song. He started to sing and everyone joined in, and then this chorus came:

My chains are gone, I've been set free ... and the men erupted in song!

Before he got to the "last verse" of this song, Brother Jonathan shared the story. "Apparently the writer of the song, John Newton, worked on a boat as a slave trader early in his life, and later in life he wrote this poem.

Brother Jonathan led them through the last verse and then together the men cried out, *"My chains are gone, I've been set free, my God, my savior has ransomed me, and like a flood, His mercy reigns, unending love, amazing grace."*

"Brother Jonathan," Dale started his message, "You have just found a battle-cry song for us. That is amazing, thank you.

"Men, today I want to talk to you about *Biblical Meditation.*" He introduced them to texts that discussed meditation in Scripture beginning with Joshua 1:8 and a whole host of verses in Psalm 119, but he camped on Philippians 4:8. "Here men," he continued, "is the 'How to,' if you will, of Biblical meditation. Note the difference in this, Biblical meditation, compared to what the world says meditation is. The world says, 'if you are going to meditate empty your mind of everything.' And I believe that Scripture is saying the opposite. Instead of 'emptying' your mind, so that anything can fill it, the Bible says to 'think about these things, the things that are true and noble, right and pure, lovely and admirable, excellent and praiseworthy.' *These* are the things to think on and have fill our mind.

"Let me give you an example. Don, stand up. You guys know that I talk about Don as our Energizer Bunny, except that the Energizer Bunny is pink ..." The men all chuckled, including Don, and then Dale continued in a voice that tried to mimic Paul Harvey. "But now I'll tell you the rest of the story."

And he proceeded to tell them about the five hours Don and he spent on their bellies together, talking to God about the truth of scripture, and the nobility it encouraged in our actions. He shared their discussion about the rightness and purity of their testimony, how lovely and admirable God wanted their testimony to look like in front of others because it would result in others giving glory to God about His excellence and His complete praiseworthiness. Dale told Don to sit down and then looking at all of the men, Dale said, "After five hours of seeking God this is what Don said to me. He said, 'Brother Dale, I want to finish spent.'[1]

---

[1] 2 Timothy 4:7

272

"Men, this is not a testimony about Don, although it could be. This is a testimony about God's faithfulness in the midst of what looks like and feels like problems to us.

"Our meditation," he came to a close, "is more like seeking God. And what does the Lord say in numerous places about us seeking Him? He says that He WILL let Himself be found. Amen?"[1]

A chorus of Amens went up from the men.

"You have your prayer lists. Remember to lift up the men from two weeks ago that were and are having financial struggles. Remember to thank God on their behalf for their struggles, and to give them that peace that transcends every single bit of their understanding[2] even before their circumstances improve, if they do.

"And finally, I asked you to pray for one of my athletes the last time we were together. The issue still isn't resolved but the problem is showing itself more clearly. Pray for wisdom for me and for my wife as well as patience on behalf of my student.

"Remember to pray until the music starts in an hour. Love you guys. Go to prayer."

---

[1] Jeremiah 29:14a
[2] Philippians 4:7

33

First Century

Benjamin entered the flower shop red-faced.

"What is the matter dear?" asked Aikaterine.

"Leave me alone," he grumbled, "you wouldn't understand even if I told you."

Aikaterine raised her eyebrows curiously at her husband, then silently prayed, "Oh great Yeshua HaMashiach, I seek You for wisdom in dealing with Benjamin. You are all Truth, You are the only Way, and You are Life. I only came to salvation through You.[1] Thank You for saving me, save my family also."

"How did that happen?" shouted haodtie. "How did we lose her? And what is she doing praying now?"

And then he heard it, that dreaded rumbling that he knew would be heading his way. He knew that it meant war, but it would be a war that he would not win.

---

[1] John 14:6

"No!" haodtie exclaimed. "No. Noooo." he howled into the foul darkness a cry of agony that every demon knew.

The Spirit moved again. He might still be off in the distance, but His presence could be felt. And the sounds were the sounds of the Holy Enemy's angel's wings, they were like the roar of mighty waters, like the voice of their Holy Enemy, the Almighty, and it sounded like an incredible commotion, like that of the sound or noise of a great army...[1] "No!" again haodtie screamed it out.

"Aikaterine," Benjamin called out a bit more civilly.

Aikaterine went into the home office where Benjamin sat when he called her. He had his old parchments out and made notes with his quill on a new fresh blank parchment. "Aikaterine, can you run the store for me for a while. I'm sorry, of course you can."

"Are you going somewhere Benjamin?"

"Yes, I am returning to Jerusalem for a short time. I need to, well, 're-study,' if you will, my faith ..."

"Why would you not do that here, my husband?"

"Because I once studied under the greatest Rabbi of all time, Gamaliel. He died a couple of years ago, but I need some counsel, so I want to see who has taken over in his place. I expect that I will be gone for a couple of months, perhaps three at the most."

"Alright darling," Aikaterine said a little bewildered, "But can you tell me what brought this on?"

"I just stopped that Gentile teacher Epaphras. I hoped to have some verbal sport with him today and he said something, a number of things, that made me angry." He stopped and

---

[1] Ezekiel 1:24

reflected. Aikaterine saw this and so remained silent. After a few more moments Benjamin picked up his story again, "He called a carpenter I once saw who died as a crucified criminal for being a rebel, the Jewish Yeshua HaMashiach. But that's not all. A very zealous friend I once knew, this Epaphras knew him too, and told me very disturbing things about him." Benjamin paused again, reflecting on Epaphras's words.

"What did he say?" Aikaterine asked.

"He said that my old zealous friend Saul now also believed in this sect called The Way." And with that he put down his quill and started to pack.

Aikaterine didn't know what to do. Should she laugh? "No, that would definitely be inappropriate," she thought. "Should she tell her husband about her trust in the Galilean Carpenter too?" No, for some reason she did not feel this to be the right time. So she asked, "Why don't you just write to Jerusalem, Benjamin?"

"I considered that too, but I realized that if I were going to stop this here and now, I needed to get as much information as I can as fast as I can, return here and do everything to stop his blasphemy." Stopping again, he turned to her, pleading this time for understanding.

"I have always wondered why I could never be a part of the temple workers in Jerusalem," he said slowly, nearly tearfully. Aikaterine came up to him and put her arms around her hurting husband. She pulled his head to her chest as he went on, "I believe, Aikaterine, that the God who created the heavens and the earth has called me to move heaven and earth to stop this sect," pausing now and taking on a hardened bitter tone, "Whatever it costs, I must stop them, here and now."

Holding her husband close to her, Aikaterine lifted her eyes to heaven, and thanked the Lord for using the difficulties to come for her husband's future salvation. She had no idea how it would happen. She didn't even care. She just knew that since this had always been the desire of her heart[1] to see her husband know the real Yeshua HaMashiach as she did, it would happen. And she had a peace about it now. She had prayed for three years for Benjamin. Ever since Anat, the wool merchant, introduced her to Yeshua. And now for the first time she knew that his salvation should be imminent.

"Thank You, Lord, thank You," Aikaterine prayed silently.

Amazingly, the hardened and mean Benjamin Kuppai would melt when in his wife's arms. No one who knew him would ever think that her arms could calm him, but they could and often did. In the quietness of his heart he said, "God Almighty, Maker of heaven and earth, thank You for my wife. I am so blessed to have a woman like her, like King Lemuel's mother spoke of,"[2] a woman of exceptional character. With that he sat there being comforted by his wife without her even saying a word.

As she held her husband in her arms, Aikaterine remembered the day that Anat introduced her to Yeshua. The day turned out to be a dreary day. Anat and she had met a couple of times working out the details of their new trading together. Aikaterine, finally able to spend some good money on cloth, visited Anat to make the final preparations that would protect her family and their servants better.

"Aikaterine," Anat began, "we are both Jewish and so we have a common faith between us …"

Aikaterine nodded a little bewildered, for certainly that had to be obvious. After all they both saw each other every Sabbath day in the temple. "In fact," thought Aikaterine, "their common faith became the reason she chose to reached out to Anat."

---

[1] Psalm 37:4
[2] Proverbs 31:1

Apparently registering this in Aikaterine's face, Anat went on slowly, "Have you ever considered that the Messiah, whom we have been waiting for all of these millenniums, may have come, and we missed Him?"

"No, Anat," Aikaterine responded, actually laughing at her new friend. "You know the teachings, we hear them every Sabbath day. When the Messiah comes he will throw off this yoke of bondage we are under. It is clearly written in the first three Psalms."

"Yes, Aikaterine," Anat smiled and went on, "I agree. And I knew you would know the Scriptures. I am so glad because I can show you the rest of the story."

A bewildered Aikaterine just sat there, and then Anat, by memory starting with Moses and all of the prophets showed Aikaterine that full story of Yeshua.[1] That He came to earth to suffer, and then, enter into His glory. And then she said, "There is a man who fits this description."

Aikaterine remembered that day because she had been unsure in her spirit about something. She did not know what, but when Anat shared those words with her, Aikaterine did not know how, but she knew that it clicked. She knew that it made sense, she knew by faith that what Anat had showed her would forever be the truth, her truth. And then and there Aikaterine gave herself to Yeshua HaMashiach.

Returning in her mind to where she sat, Aikaterine let go of her husband as he got up.

"I will have Anat's husband Ely check in on you. If you need anything, he will help you." Benjamin gave her a hug and set off.

As he walked out of the shop and saw Mary. Coming up to her and hugging her as he left, he said, "What I go to do, I go for

---

[1] Luke 24:27

your benefit my daughter. Your benefit and the benefit of your sisters and your future children."

With that last comment Mary blushed, and letting her father go, she simply said, "Thank you Papa. I love you."

"Where is Papa going?" asked the children.

"To meet Yeshua," Aikaterine thought, but she responded, "Umm, to Jerusalem for a short time. He will return in a few months."

34

19th Century

As usual, on Tuesday morning "that crazy rooster," as Mrs. Marks called it, started crowing at 3:30 in the morning. As had become his custom in this home, Brother Alexander got up with "Crazy Rooster" but not before Elder Ted Marks, who, also as usual, had the coffee boiling for Brother Alex.

"Good morning my friend," started Ted, "Did you sleep well?"

"Always Ted, thank you."

"Coffee just the way you like it Alex, strong and very hot."

"Are you up for spending some time with me this morning while I study God's Word?

"Of course Alex. It's the highlight of your visits with us … besides the Sunday sermon of course."

"I want to do something different today Ted, okay?" Ted nodded his head toward Brother Alex, who he referred to as Alex. They were close friends. And it had been a friendship that spanned at least two decades.

Even though Alexander Rich grew up in Massachusetts he had been in Georgia since his early 20's trying to build a foothold to preach. But the native Georgians didn't trust a Northerner, especially in the 1850's. But Brother Alex hung in there, and Ted Marks noticed that and liked it about this young preacher. So it didn't surprised him when the war started that Brother Alexander Rich, a Northerner, joined on with the Confederates, not carrying a gun but being their chaplain. And even after the war, when some of the people in his part of Georgia would throw out the "possibility" that Alexander Rich acted as a spy during the war, Brother Ted would remind them of the terrible punishment Rich took when his platoon fell captive to the Northerners. They also thought that Rich should spy for them. But he took a great deal of rough treatment because he did not turn against his Southern troops, even though he only recently had let the North.

"So Alex, what are we going to do today?"

"Well Ted, I have been studying the prayers of the Wesley Brothers for our families. Their prayers are all Scripture, and so I think that I want to walk through a couple of the paragraphs with you and ask you the questions I have put together and see if they stimulate your spirit."

"Okay preacher, let me warm up your coffee and then let's go."

They had been sitting together for an hour when they got to the third paragraph. "Whew, preacher, there's a lot to unpack from this isn't there?"

"Yes, and that is what I love about their prayers, in fact, look at what the *Wesley Family Prayers Book* gets into here in this paragraph:

> *O that we may begin it this day, in devout meditations, in joy unspeakable, and in blessing and praising thee, who*

have given us such good hope, and everlasting consolation! Lift up our minds above all these little things below, which are apt to distract our thoughts; and keep them above, till our hearts are fully bent to seek thee every day, in the way wherein JESUS has gone before us, though it should be with the loss of all we here possess.

And Brother Alexander began with his questions again, like he had done for the previous two paragraphs. "Brother Ted, it says: *'O that we may begin it this day'* and I would simply ask you, 'what?' What begins our *day in devout meditations, in joy unspeakable*, and on and on?"

"Well, I reckon Alex that he is talking about our morning prayers. In the third verse of the fifth Psalm, Alex, are those wonderful words that I think the Wesleys are in part referring to in this morning prayer. The passage says: *Come to the Lord in the morning, lay your request before Him, and wait in expectation.*[1] I confess that I've always looked at that as the expectation of my prayers being answered, but this is expanding that expectation to me to mean the expectation of *joy unspeakable, blessing and praises to Him, and hope and everlasting consolation* from Him.

"That's good Ted. I too love Psalm 5:3 and forgive me, but I never saw it bigger than 'answered prayers' either. The next question has to do with the *devout meditations* and what they bring of course, which you already outlined. But my question, not for you but for others would be, do your prayers prepare you for 'devout meditations,' or your devotions? Or in the honesty of your own heart, do your prayers seem like a waste of time? Again, I know you my friend, so let me ask you the question this way. Do you think that those here in Dry Branch really believe

---

[1] Psalm 5:3

that their meditations are a waste of time? In fact, do you think very many men get up in the morning and spend time in *devout meditation*? Now hear me, I don't ask this to judge others or to be gossiping, I truly want to know so that we can help them. This is my job as their shepherd and your job as their elder, and it hurts my heart to sense that they are not beginning the day in devout meditations."

"Oh my friend," Brother Ted began with a twinkle in his eye, "that is why the writer talks about the next issue he is prayin' 'bout, *'distractions.'* I think that the ones that struggle with their prayer life are the ones that let distractions overcome them.

"Let me ask you something my friend, as I see where the Wesleys are going here. Let me ask you, when did you recognize and consider that following Jesus meant giving up all of the possessions you could have had in the North, where your family lived?"

"Oh Brother Ted, what you raise is an excellent question and one that when I am weak I ponder." Alexander chuckled, realizing he would have to handle Ted's question the way Ted handled his. "Because fair play means I should answer your question to me, just as I have asked you questions, let me give you an example that just happened Sunday night.

"When I leave Jeffersonville I always stop at a patch of ground with a square rock that has been a place for me to pray for Jeffersonville ever since I started that church. Well Sunday night someone else happened to be there also and apparently had been there before, I could tell. After some time spent praying the other person showed herself …"And with that, Alex stopped long enough to see Ted raise an eyebrow. "Yep, 'a her,' the very pretty widowed Gretchen, Hatch McCreedy's daughter. And something happened, in me. For the first time I contemplated the possibility of a woman in my life, completely 'accidentally' of course, but the thought has stayed with me for a couple of days. So yes, especially recently have I contemplated the things I have given up being in ministry."

"Alex, there are plenty of pastors that are married. Why would you not think that God would want you to be married?"

Silence hung in the air for a few moments as Brother Rich pondered the question, and then Brother Ted went on, "Let me ask the question differently, why do you think God wants you single?"

"I don't know. I just always have," he paused for a moment, "until two days ago, that is. But do you know what it is that interested me the most about Gretchen, even before she made her presence known? It's the desire to pray regularly with another person, the same person, and have them be a part of this ministry, from a prayer side, and that caught my eye first about Gretchen. She is a woman of prayer. I didn't know that before … and then of course there is her beauty." And with that both men laughed.

"Just be careful my friend," retorted Ted Marks, "I have known the McCreedys since Hatch's father lived. They are more interested in themselves, than even in their kin. They'll throw you, and/or Gretchen, under the stagecoach if it serves their selfish ends."

"I know Ted. The only reason they put me up each Saturday night that I am in town is because they think it gives them more business."

"And you'll need to protect Gretchen. I'm sure they consider her an embarrassment since she is a poor widow. It's sad that some parents are like that, but you know they are, my friend. So protect her by making sure that no one sees you out in the woods with Gretchen. Alex, that is just too scary to say. Just be careful my friend."

"Oh I am. When she made her presence known I sent her right home after praying for her. I'm sure no one saw us, even for those few minutes." Just then a sickening feeling came over Alex. "Actually another person saw us, Carrolton ..."

"... Faith? Carrolton Faith?" Ted finished the sentence incredulously, "And you don't think you have anything to be concerned about? Is he still the town drunk?

"Look at the next paragraph of the *Wesley Family Prayers Book*, Alex. I can tell by your countenance that you are not ashamed of anything you've done relative to Gretchen. Your character is a testimony of your righteousness. The reason you and I have been friends for so long is because you have proved yourself to be a man who trusts God for *all* things, and that every fiber of your spirit, soul, and body is wholly dedicated to what God has called you to do.

"And I'll keep going, Alex. Look, with the brothers Wesley, at what they say next. I know that you desire this Alex, that all of your thoughts and desires and actions *be pure, holy and unreprovable in God's sight.*"

"Ted, how did you know what the Wesleys said in that paragraph?"

And with that Ted opened his own book, of the *Wesley Family Prayers Book*. "Alex, when you were in town, oh I'd say about a year ago, I saw you reading your book and could tell you were studying it. I nonchalantly asked you about it, and then got me my own copy. I've been studying it for a year." And with that a big grin stretched across Ted Marks's face. Leaning over to pour another cup of coffee both men laughed.

"Laugh now you two, for trouble is coming your way, Alexander Rich, that will make the Civil War seem like child's play." And with that katepa laughed out loud, so loud that joln rushed to katepa's side only to wish he could squash him.

"You still have a potential problem in Jeffersonville, my friend," said Ted, and then prayed, "Father, my pastor and I simply come to You trusting You to fill him with the knowledge of Your Will, giving him all wisdom,[1] which Proverbs tells us is better than gold, and spiritual understanding, which the same verse in Proverbs tells us is better than silver.[2] Fill him, that in every way and everywhere, including Jeffersonville, Alex walks worthy of You, is fully pleasing to You, and bears one hundred-fold fruit in every good work, as he grows in the knowledge of You.[3] And Father, because we know that this is Your will, as it is Your Word, we do not pray that You can do it, or even that You will do it, but rather that You are already in the process of working out all of these things,[4] for my friend, in my friend, in Jeffersonville, and in the lives there. And then Father, for some reason, I am prompted to pray about spiritual warfare for my friend. Far from taking him out of it, give him the grace to go through it, with peace as the armor gives us, because of what we already have in Your Son. He is our peace.[5] Let that peace live through my friend, Lord. Also Lord, comfort my friend, comfort him so that he can continue to comfort others in the same way that You comfort our Brother Rich.[6] And in all of these things we pray, completely trusting in You, and thankful for

---

[1] Colossians 1:9b
[2] Proverbs 16:16
[3] Colossians 1:10
[4] Mark 11:24
[5] Ephesians 6:15
[6] 2 Corinthians 1:4

286

everything.[1] We thank You for the McCreedy's, Carrollton, Jeffersonville, and of course here Lord, Dry Branch and Alex's responsibilities. Amen, and Amen."

By now the coffee pot had been empty for a while. The time stretched past 8:30 am. They had been studying and reading and sharpening one another[2] for nearly five hours. And just as they started to talk about the visits that Brother Rich wanted to make here in Dry Branch, Hubert Jackson pulled his buggy up to the front of the Marks's log cabin and got out.

---

[1] Ephesians 5:20
[2] Proverbs 27:17

35

Current Era
&
First Century

"Good morning, is this Margie Riley?" the caller asked, and then paused.

Margie had finished her quiet time about an hour earlier and had just begun to clean the bedrooms. She had already emptied the dishwasher, wiped down the counters in the kitchen, and then vacuumed the living room when the phone rang.

"Yes, this is Margie."

"Hello, this is Isabela Gonzalez." After a moment of silence, she went on, "I don't know if you know me, but I'm ..."

"Yes," Margie interrupted, quite confused, "You are a psych professor at the university. How can I help you?"

"Well, I know that this is kind of, well, weird, and for me, quite outside of my comfort zone, but if you're alone, can I come over and talk to you?"

And with no hesitation at all, Margie said, "As a matter of fact, my husband Dale is gone for the entire morning so right now would be perfect."

"I know, I got on Facebook and realized he'd be gone to some church thing."

"Hmm," said Margie out loud, "I need to rethink all that safety stuff, huh?" Margie laughed and so Isabela laughed too.

"If you don't want me to come over," Isabela started to say.

"No, no, no, I just tried to make a joke. Not a very good one obviously. I'd love for you to come over, let me give you my address."

The children were all in bed, all except Mary the oldest. She watched her mother, clearly deep in thought, and not knowing why, she interrupted her. Mary asked curiously, "Mother, is everything okay?" Continuing on she said, "Don't be concerned about Papa. He will be safe. If a robber knew Papa they would stay away from him, and if they do not know Papa, they will wish they had stayed away from him."

The two laughed, and Aikaterine said, "No, honey, I am not worried about your father. I agree. I pity the person who tries to bother him. I sat here reflecting on a conversation that Anat and I had about three years ago."

After a few pleasantries, very few, because these ladies didn't have much in common, Isabela said, "I have cancer," she paused and Margie saw a tear form behind those beautiful almond shaped, but somewhat bloodshot, brown eyes. Isabela a very Hispanic woman with a touch of Asian blood, which could be seen in the shape of her eyes.

Margie knew that Isabela's ancestry came from Mexico and guessed that her origins were probably near the Guadalajara area because of the influx of Japanese slaves in the mid 1800's. But that conversation would have to wait. She reached over for a box of tissues and handed it to Isabela, who thanked her and wiped away the tear.

"I didn't know I had any more of these left," Isabela gently laughed.

"You've shed a lot of them?" asked Margie.

Blowing a breath of air, as if she had collected it for hours, she responded, "Oh yes, lots."

"How long have you known?" asked Margie, and Isabela seemed relieved to have the conversation carried by someone else.

"A month ago I got the first opinion, and results were bad."

"First?"

"Yes, I immediately went to seek another opinion and that one proved to be far worse."

"I'm sorry Isabela." The two ladies just sat there for a moment. A moment that seemed like it stretched into many moments but in reality only a couple of seconds had elapsed.

Margie continued, "Do you have family near here Isabela?"

Isabela shook her head no.

"Have you been able to talk to others about this?" Margie continued slowly, lovingly.

Again, Isabela shook her head no.

"Isabela, I know that you do not know me, but do you mind if I pray for us before we go further?" And with that question Margie noticed a stiffening of Isabela's shoulders, and a drop in her countenance that made Margie feel like she had just made herself an enemy. "We don't have to if you don't want to Isabela," Margie hurried to say with as much compassion as she could. "No pressure, just whatever you are comfortable with Isabela."

Again silence, and then a crack in the armor. With a smile, a small one, and a resignation in her emotions she said, "Margie, that is, I think, what drove me over here. Every single doctor wanted to pray with me, and frankly, I wanted to tell them where to go."

Margie chuckled, even though she wondered if maybe she should be a little more careful with Isabela.

"I'm sorry Margie, but this prayer stuff is well, it is so far out of my comfort zone that I just don't know what to make of it. I have very specific assumptions about the way you, well, you Christians act, that, well, it has always made me sick to my stomach. And when these doctors wanted to pray with me I found myself being so angry at them." She paused before going on, "and now, for some unknown reason, I find myself wanting to reach out to you. I know that doesn't make any sense, but …"

"Isabela, it makes more sense than you realize."

"I'm not following, Margie."

"What did you and Anat talk about Mama?" asked Mary.

"She asked me if I knew that God loved me," Aikaterine began softly. Mary just sat there listening as her mother went on.

"I remember, Mary, I laughed at Anat and said, 'Of course I do.' But then she said something that made me sit back. She said, 'Aikaterine, He loves you so much that He sent His only Son, as the Messiah, to earth, to die for you.'[1]

I immediately argued with her Mary. I said, "What? Why would He do that? The Messiah would not come for death. He will come for life, for life and for peace."

"No, Aikaterine, that is what our Rabbis have said, but they leave out the most important part. That our works cannot save us. We keep sacrificing animals to atone for our sins, but what if Aikaterine, what if there could be one sacrifice that would suffice for all of us, and then no one would ever again have to sacrifice.

---

[1] John 3:16a

291

That is the Messiah that came to earth, and He came simply asking us to have faith that the one sacrifice of His perfect Lamb reconnected our broken relationship to Jehovah."

"You mean like Jesus, the Galilean carpenter, Mother?" Mary asked, and a very perplexed Aikaterine could only nod her head up and down, so Mary went on. "Do you believe it Mama, that Jesus came to be our once for all time sacrifice?"[1]

With the bewilderment leaving, and a knowing smile slowly coming onto her face, Aikaterine simply said, "Yes honey, yes, I do believe that Jesus is the Christ. I put my faith in Him the day Anat took me through the books of Moses and the prophets and showed me that Jesus, the Galilean carpenter is the Messiah."

"Oh Mama," Mary began to sob. She reached out to her mother hugged her, held on really, for her shoulders were heaving up and down as if a great weight had been lifted off of them.

She continued, "I have put my trust in Him too, mama, but I have been too afraid to tell you and Papa."

And with that the two women hugged for a long time, Mary sobbing and Aikaterine, with tears, thanking the Holy Spirit for moving in the life of her daughter.

Isabela didn't think that she heard Margie correctly, and she certainly didn't understand what Margie had said, if indeed she heard her correctly, so she asked, "What do you mean, 'it makes sense,' Margie?"

"Isabela, I have been asking the Lord for a few weeks now to cause our paths to cross, that I might, well, let's just say, be your friend."

---

[1] Hebrews 10:10

This had Isabela's attention now. "Well, why didn't you just reach out to me Margie?" she said with a hint of anger.

"I wanted to Isabela, but for some reason I felt a, I call it, a 'check in my spirit.' Which is simply the way I word, what I think God does when He impresses upon my heart a 'Yes' or a 'No.' that's the best I can do, for now, in explaining it. You could say, your calling me, is an answer to prayer, my prayer."

Both ladies sat not saying a word, Isabela trying to process and Margie trying to pray for wisdom.

"So tell me about your faith Margie."

"Well, it has nothing to do with feelings. Let me begin there."

Mary coming up for air from her mother's shoulder then said, "Mama, I have been so confused about telling you that I don't feel that excitement and happiness like I did before. I am wondering if I have lost something."

Aikaterine just laughed, "No, darling Mary. What you do not gain by works, you cannot lose by works. Tell me about your coming to the Messiah. How did this happen?"

Margie told Isabela how she came to know Christ as her personal Savior, and how this bore itself out as an act of faith on her part, not an emotional decision. "In fact, Isabela, I have been a lot more like you than you realize. If you'll permit me the frankness, I remember being pretty hard-hearted. The last thing I wanted to do would have anything to do with turning over my life to anyone other than myself, especially a man."

They both laughed a knowing laugh from one ex-feminist to a current feminist.

"Wait a minute," shot back Isabela, "so that means that you did. Eventually, you did turn your life over to a man. How did that happen? When did it happen?"

"In my second year of college I had just had an abortion. At the time I didn't know why I felt so bad. I didn't think that it had anything to do with the abortion. I knew that I had all rights over my own body, I could choose what I wanted to choose. But something kept picking at my brain, actually at my heart, and before I knew it I felt deeply depressed and had no idea why.

"My roommate," Margie continued, "whom I condescendingly considered a goodie two-shoes Christian, could see my hurt and so she asked me about it. I told her that I had an uncontrollable urge to lash out at everyone which I knew. I admitted that I knew how wrong it must seem. So we talked some more, most of the night actually. Well I talked, she just listened. And then she told me about her life, how she too had been upset and couldn't get over it for completely different reasons. I realized that the issue that had been plaguing me had nothing to do with an individual thing she or I had done. Her issues and mine were a lot bigger than that. She told me, Isabela, like I am confessing to you, 'I tried to control all of my circumstances,' and like you Isabela, I came to the conclusion that I had no control over them."

"I've never said, 'Amen' to anything," Isabela said with the hint of a smile, and then letting a larger smile creep onto her beautiful face she said, "but I suspect that is as good a place as any to say it." They both laughed.

"Isabela, do you want the pain to go away? The pain in your heart, I'm talking about, do you want it to go away?"

"I'd like something to go away, that's for sure."

"The God of the universe sent His Son Jesus to earth to die for my sins, all of the bad things that I had done. And here is what caused me to put my trust in Him. I realized, Isabela, that He loved me, in spite of me. He didn't love me because of my goodness. He loved me in spite of me. And He knew that because I couldn't be good enough on my own, He sent His Son. When I realized that, the peace that washed over me caused me to say, 'Yes, I'm all in, whatever that means.' And my mindset, if truth be told Isabella, is still that very same commitment. I try to daily die to myself,[1] trusting Him for what is best for me.

"I don't love Him because I still 'feel' something. No! I love Him because I now know that He loved me first. He, the God of the universe, sent his Son Jesus Christ to die for me, and for you Isabela, even before I knew that I needed Him.[2]

"And my new friend, He is calling out to you also. Isabela, the only question is, are you willing to give yourself over to Him?"

After listening to Mary explain how Thales walked her through a better understanding of her Jewish roots than she had known before. Aikaterine smiled at her daughter. "You too are a Christ follower." She hugged her daughter again, "Praise be to the Lord of Hosts."

"Amen, Mama."

"Mama," Mary said after mother and daughter hugged for a bit, "what are we going to tell Papa?"

And Aikaterine with much more peace than she would have thought possible said, "Mary, it is God's will that all should become saved and that none should perish, do you believe that?"

"Of course I do, Mama."

"And is it the desire of your heart?"

---

[1] Matthew 16:24
[2] Romans 5:8

"Yes Mama, just like that Psalm of David reminds us ..."

"Then quote it with me Mary, as a prayer to Almighty God."

And with mother leading and daughter following, both quoted and prayed, "You, oh God, are the Maker of heaven and earth, and You make it clear to me, that as I delight myself in You, You give me the desires of my heart ..."[1]

"Keep quoting, Mary," and the two went on.

"So I, we, commit our ways to You, trusting in You, and look forward to watching You do it.[2] Bring Papa to know the real Messiah."

Mother and daughter hugged again and turned in for the night.

"I'm not ready to make any kind of a step Margie," confessed Isabela.

"Oh, I disagree," stated Margie a little boldly to a surprised Isabela, "You already made the first step and that first step is the call to reach out to me." Isabela relaxed and Margie went on. "I am honored to be your friend and to walk through this with you."

"Thank you," said a much relieved Isabela. "If you still want to pray, I think that I am okay with that now."

Isabela sat on the sofa with her hands on her knees. Before Margie began praying she rested one of her hands on Isabela's, "Father in heaven," Margie began slowly, wanting her prayer to be very simple for Isabela to follow. "Thank You for answering my prayer, by giving Isabela and me the opportunity to get to know each other. Father, she has some serious medical issues to deal with. I trust You to cause our relationship to grow, and for You to allow me to help her through this cancer, eventually

---

[1] Psalm 37:4
[2] Psalm 37:5

giving her a peace that will transcend every single bit of her understanding.[1] In the name of Your Son, my Savior, Jesus Christ, Amen.

They both sat in silence for a few moments dabbing their faces to deal with tears. They then chit-chatted for a few more minutes and then Isabella decided she needed to leave.

"Hey," Isabela asked as they were walking toward the door, "why did you start praying for me? I don't know, but it sounded like something that you recently started doing ..."

"Julienne George is in my women's Bible study."

"Oh that foolish girl!" responded Isabela with great anger. "She is one of those wacko Christians. I don't have time now, but wait till I tell you. Let me just say this. If I took her advice, I'd be thanking the Lord for my cancer. How stupid is that?"

Margie just smiled at Isabela, "I understand Isabela. I look at Julienne's "foolishness," as you call it, as a great opportunity for the Lord to connect two women, you and I. We'll talk about Julienne another time. If you don't mind perhaps we can email each other our schedules, and let's find a time each week, maybe even twice per week, that we can get together if you're up for that. No pressure but I'd sure like to meet with you."

"So would I, Margie, thank you. I'll email you tonight." She walked out the door and then stopped and turned around, "You know, not all of you Christians are crazy people."

They both laughed, Isabela heading to her car, and Margie to her prayer closet.

---

[1] Philippians 4:7

36

Nineteenth Century

Brothers Rich and Marks came around to the front of the home and saw Hubert Jackson dismounting from his rig.

"Brother Hubert," Ted called out, and then looking at his somber face said, "You look like someone just died. What's wrong my friend?"

Hubert Jackson pressed his lips together, looking down to the ground as he shook hands with Ted and then scooted over to Brother Rich. He looked down to the ground again and said, more to Rich than to Ted, "I don't rightly know, buts I don' think is good."

"Hubert," Brother Rich said, wrapping an arm around his shoulder, "how can I help you?"

"Suh, I think yoose the one needin' hep."

Alexander Rich and Ted Marks looked at each other with dumfounded faces. Hubert, always a very earnest man and not known to worry now looked like a man more than worried, even agitated.

"Brother Rich, ma family visited Jeffesonville yestooday, an while I's talking to Brother McCreedy, he seemed very anxious 'bout you when I mention your name. E'en my wife Elsie noticed, suh."

"Do you know what the problem is Hubert?" asked Ted.

"Well, suh, ah did check roun' a bit an' a stable hand said somethin' bout the town drunk (now sober) savin' the McCreedy girl from bein' 'ravished by the parson,' is what he said."

"Hmm," a thoughtful Alexander Rich lowered his eyes and then continued. "Men," he said, "I think we need to pray."

Ted went back into the house and returned with a big pot of coffee. If he guessed correctly, they were going to be on their knees and their faces for a while.

As the three of them gathered around the garden in the back of the Marks's home, Hubert Jackson already on his belly, Alexander Rich on his knees and the senior Brother Ted Marks sat on a log. From inside the cabin Mrs. Marks observed the group of men. "What a mix-matched group," she thought. "A former slave, a northerner and a former general of the Confederate army. Oh Lord," she started, getting down on her knees too, "only You know these men's hearts. Only You know their desire to see You glorified above all else. Father, see fit to grant their petitions, not because of the goodness in them, but quite the opposite, in spite of them. Father, and for Your glory to be manifested in the midst of great troubles. Oh Lord, as Brother Rich has taught us to do, I now do on his behalf. I thank You for the problems that he is facing.[1] Not because we like it, but because it will be an opportunity for you to be glorified in him, through him and because of him. Thank You Father, and thank You for the peace that I have even now. Oh Lord, I am always amazed how when I just come to You, with what Your Word

---

[1] Ephesians 5:20

says, You give me a peace, Oh Father, a peace that transcends every bit of my understanding, and I sense that my heart and my mind are guarded.[1] And so Lord, thank You for the peace which You are already in the process of giving these men, Your men, Lord. Amen."

Getting off her knees she looked outside to watch what she heard, the groans of men crying out to the God of the universe.

"Righteous, omnipotent, Father," started Ted, "You have brought us here today. It is not an accident that we are all together today ready to lift Your name on high. Thank You Father, as Brother Rich has taught us to pray, thank You for the problems, not because we like them," and with that groans continued to come from the other two men, "but because we know that You are never caught surprised by anything that comes our way."

And like a person gently smoothing the top of a bed sheet Hubert Jackson slid into the prayer, "Oh Fatha, by Your grace and foreknowledge we were there yestooday."

Pausing for Ted to take back up his praying, "Amen Lord, You planned this way in advance and we are grateful, and thankful that we can be a part of it through prayer." Amens from the other two, but with Jackson's strong and Rich's more like a grunt. Ted had opened his Bible to Acts 4:24 and started to read:

And when they heard it, they lifted their voices together to God and said, "Sovereign Lord, who made the heaven and the earth and the sea and everything in them, who through the mouth of our father David, Your servant, said by the Holy Spirit, "'Why did the Gentiles rage, and the peoples plot in vain? The kings of the earth set themselves, and the rulers were gathered together, against the Lord and against His Anointed'—for truly in this city there were

---

[1] Philippians 4:7

gathered together against Your holy servant Jesus, whom You anointed, both Herod and Pontius Pilate, along with the Gentiles and the peoples of Israel, to do whatever Your hand and Your plan had predestined to take place. And now, Lord, look upon their threats and grant to Your servants to continue to speak Your Word with all boldness, while You stretch out Your hand to heal, and signs and wonders are performed through the name of Your holy servant Jesus."[1]

And with this passage being read, Emma Marks smiled, for she knew what would come next. She had heard her husband say it so many times when they prayed in the midst of difficult circumstances, in fact, she started to mouth the words as her husband prayed, "Lord, I am always amazed by the prayer here of these men. If *anyone* had the need to pray for protection, these men did." Emma's smile got bigger, because she spoke in her heart and mind, word for word with Ted, "But they didn't. In fact their words about protection are only four, 'look upon their threats.'" And with that Emma left the kitchen, and the groaning of godly men seeking to touch the throne of their God. "They're gonna have church out there," she thought.

As Ted prayed his way through their Acts 4 prayer, applying it to their situation, the groans of men agreeing in prayer were lifted up. The sounds emanating from these men would even cause the animals in the area to shy away from them as they were wrestling with their Creator and Sustainer. "Father, we do not know why the ungodly even within the church plot, rage, and lie or why others even in the church listen, agree, and pass on the dark things that are said ..."

---

[1] Acts 4:24-30 (ESV)

When Ted neared the end of this passage Alexander spoke up, "Lord, as I have been listening to my brothers pray I am at peace about what I believe You have called me to go through and to do. Father, You want me to continue speaking Your Word in Jeffersonville with all boldness. And Father, I do not know how, but I trust You to do a work of healing in that town. Heal them, Father of their spiritual ailments. This is a spiritual battle. My struggle is not with flesh and blood,[1] which are somehow being used by the evil one. I know that through the prayers of these men, and the working of Your Spirit, this situation will turn out to my deliverance. Father, I eagerly expect and hope, with a sure confident hope, that I will not be put to shame in this problem, but rather with complete assurance and boldness, I trust Your Son to be honored in me, even through me, including if necessary, through my death, for I know that for me to live is Christ, and to die is gain."[2]

There were a few minutes of silence. All three men had experienced this before. And so they patiently waited until one of them felt moved to continue praying. Before long the praying had picked back up.

"Fathuh," Hubert started up again, "heal the McCreedys' of the anger and mistrus' in their hearts for Brother Rich. Fathuh, heal the town of gossip. You have said that da sin of rebellion is as da sin of witchcraft.[3] Oh Fathuh, show these folks that they are guilty of witchcraft in Yo eyes." To this the other men offered up, "Amens," and "Lo'd have mercy," as well as "Fo'give them Fathuh," and "Be glorified Lord."

---

[1] Ephesians 6:12
[2] Philippians 1:19-21
[3] 1 Samuel 15:23a

Brother Jackson, raising the volume of his petitioning, went on, "Open de eyes of their heart[1] to see da hope of Your calling,[2] rather than focus on the dirt of untrue words. And where some Jeffersonville townsfolk are more interested in the trash in their minds, show dem da riches of Your glory, and the inheritance that they have now, 'mong the saints,[3] when they act like godly Christians."

"Brother Ted," Brother Hubert said and relinquished the prayer floor to him, "Would you lead us as we pray the twenty-third Psalm for our brother?"

"Father," began Ted, "We often pray the twenty-third Psalm only at funerals, but Brother Jackson is right, this is a perfect text for our praying right now."

"Oh Lord," interrupted Alex, "Thank You so much. These men have no way of knowing, but thank You so much that You brought this prayer to my heart and mind for me to meditate on yesterday." And with that the grunts and Amens when up in choruses again. They truly sounded like what an old pastor in the future will say, "like the sound of thunder going up into heaven."

When Emma Marks came back into the kitchen the men had been praying for over two hours. She thought she could hear someone humming. And sure enough, Brother Rich hummed "What A Friend We Have in Jesus," while her husband and Hubert Jackson were singing:

Are we weak and heavy laden, cumbered with a load of care?
Precious Savior, still our refuge, take it to the Lord in
prayer.

---

[1] Ephesians 1:18a
[2] Ephesians 1:18m
[3] Ephesians 1:18e

Do your friends despise, forsake you? Take it to the Lord in prayer!
In His arms He'll take and shield you; you will find a solace there.

And then she heard Brother Rich thank the Lord for the ones who were probably spreading rumors about him even now. "Amazing," she thought, "how a man could be so loving and forgiving to be thanking God for them, while they were even now measuring him, figuratively speaking of course, for a pine box."

The morning stage which headed east to Savannah had arrived in Jeffersonville and a bloodshot, puffy-eyed, red-faced Gretchen McCreedy climbed into the coach. Her mother still looking at her with a stony expression stood a few feet from the carriage, just far enough where Gretchen could not reach out to her. "When can I return Momma?" cried Gretchen.

"After the baby is born," whispered a demon into the ear of Billie Carter.

"Not until that baby is born and put in an orphans home," said Billie to Victoria and Ellie.

As the driver cracked his whips over the backs of the horses, Mrs. McCreedy didn't say a word. The eleven o'clock stagecoach took off and Gretchen felt alone in a stage filled with people.

At the east edge of town, just outside of the tiny saloon named O'Sheas, the sober Carrolton Faith walked toward the woods. He carried a bottle of sour mash. He couldn't afford anything else. This hadn't gone the way he had hoped. "She should be mine." he thought to himself. "Now she's headed to Savannah," which to him could have been a whole other world.

As he stood there watching the dust of the stagecoach wheels, he remembered something odd, a verse from Scripture. "A verse about hope and joy and peace, hope and joy and peace," he repeated again. "Why does that ... my parents. Father used to pray that for mother every night."

"Lord God of heaven and earth," Carrolton's father in a low strong voice would say, "You are the God of hope, and because of that I trust You to fill my Minnie with great joy and great peace, simply because she is a believer, and Father, as You do that, I trust You to let little Carrolton see that the hope she has overflowing out of her is from the power of Your Holy Spirit living inside of her.[1] And Father, as Carrol sees that, we trust that he will turn to You at a very young age."

"Thank you Travis," she would always say to her husband, and then turn to Carrol and say, "Are you going to grow up and be a good Christian man like your father?" Thinking about this and seeing this picture in his mind, more clearly than he had seen it for years, he started to tear up.

"His God took your family away from you, remember," yelled a demon into Carrol's heart.

---

[1] Romans 15:13

305

And in one smooth motion and with all the anger he could muster, he raged through gritted teeth and threw the bottle as far as he could. Turning around to head toward the center of town he heard the bottle break far into the distance, but he heard something else. "What is it?" he thought. "What is it? A voice maybe? Yes, a voice, a man's voice." And then his eyes widened, "Alexander Rich, *that* is what you prayed for Gretchen ..." And with that realization an odd sense of peace crept into his soul.

This man, Brother Alexander represented everything that he had drowned in his booze, but it no longer angered him. In fact, he realized that he missed the parson. He missed the parson like he had missed his own father.

And somewhere, up in the brightness of the heavenlies, Tephillah, a guardian angel who had rarely been seen around Carrolton smiled, watching over the new Carrol.

"Thank You my Lord, for the wonderful meals I have had with the McCreedy's. And Lord, as You fix this problem, we trust You to restore what the locusts have taken.[1] The passage we have been praying ends with *Surely goodness and mercy will follow me all the days of my life.*[2] And Father, with all the humbleness that You have given me the grace to have, I trust You to already be preparing goodness and mercy for me ... to Your glory."

"Men," Alex interrupted the praying suddenly, "I believe that I should return to Jeffersonville."

"I believe you're right Alex," agreed Ted.

---

[1] Joel 2:25
[2] Psalm 23:6

306

"Sho' nuff, Brother Rich. Iffins you hadn't said it, Ah would 'ave," agreed Hubert.

"Perfect timing," thought Emma as she brought sandwiches and water to the men. They had been on their knees for nearly four hours.

"Loser," spit joln to katepa, "Isn't this how you lost your other one? Didn't the Holy Enemy serve your charge with a healthy dose of humbleness and you lost him? You are such a waste of my time, katepa."

And for the first time katepa agreed with joln. "Yes," he thought to himself, "this is exactly what happened." And with that thought firmly implanted in katepa's mind, he wrestled with the following three impending scenarios. "The following things are taking place before my eyes: 1) Well laid plans and arguments are being destroyed, 2) God's knowledge is becoming the more lofty, not man's high mindedness, and 3) Rich is taking thoughts captive, thoughts *that instead should bother him.*[1]"

"You are the loser Alexander Rich," cried katepa at the top of his lungs.

"No," whispered joln. "You are the loser, katepa, and I'm going to be rid of you as quickly as you started here."

---

[1] 2 Corinthians 10:5

37

First Century

Two days after their run in with Benjamin, and when they were done with their time of meditating on scripture, Epaphras had in mind to ask Thales to expound some more on his family's move to Colossae. He found it interesting and thought that many of the other saints would want to know also.

"Meditation? huh," said Thales, asking more than telling. "Uncle Epaphras," Thales continued in awe, "that is a powerful way to pray. I want to do that again."

Laughing, Epaphras said, "Not only will you do it again, but you will teach it to the Colossae church my boy. I have two deacons who will help you. They too love praying out of meditating on Scripture.

"Thales, let me change subjects. John Mark's letter, which Paul gave us a copy of, has the story of your mother and grandmother. I must tell you I had heard the stories from my brother and some of it from them a few months ago when I went to ask you to move here, but never expected to read about them. It is still very humbling to have read about them, and so I want to ask you about your family's move to Colossae. Tell me about that if you would. I mean, it's not a surprise to read what she said to Jesus. Every time we are over at her house I see that sharp wit, even now, at nearly seventy years old."

Thales smiled, proud of his grandmother. "I agree, she's one spry old woman. You know Uncle that my mother died giving birth to me on the way over here during the move. But I have listened to my grandmother tell the story many times."

"Thank you Thales," interrupted Epaphras. "There is a reason I am asking. One of Paul's associates has been writing a history of the church's early days and he has asked me to corroborate some of his firsthand accounts."

"Oh, another of Paul's traveling companions, one of which I will never be. Is that who I am helping?" Thales asked jokingly, and then went on without awaiting an answer. "As you know, my mom's name is Euanthe making her the daughter of the woman known as the Syrophoenician woman. My mom died giving birth to me on the trip that they took only a year or two after the Hellenistic Jews were scattered from Jerusalem.[1]

"To hear my grandmother tell it, they were very surprised that they had to leave the Tyre and Sidon area."

"Really?" asked Epaphras, "Why would she be surprised?"

"Well," Thales went on, "because of Peter's vision. You need to hear her tell of it, and have your friend hear her tell it. The detail she remembers is surprising, but that's why she remembered it, I guess."

As Thales began the story, Epaphras could see his seventy-year-old grandmother, an intelligent woman with a strikingly aristocratic look to her. She had a poise that always made him think that Jesus must have seen her coming a long way off ...

---

[1] Acts 8:1m

309

well, since He is God, that's a given … at any rate, this woman has a very humble side too, which Epaphras noted as a unique combination, but an enchanting combination. And that really is who everyone knows her to be, an enchanting older woman, pretty even still, who stands aristocratically erect, and yet is a very humble woman.

As he listened to Thales he saw her, the Syrophoenician woman, not Thales, "Oh that vision," she said with a slightly lower pitch than you would think to look at her, "When we heard about the vision we knew that the Jewish Christians would embrace us too … Oh that vision.

"Peter had been traveling in Joppa when he went up to pray on the housetop about noon. Then he became hungry and wanted to eat, but while they were preparing something he went into a visionary state. He saw heaven opened and an object that resembled a large sheet coming down being lowered by its four corners to the earth. In it were all the four-footed animals and reptiles of the earth and the birds of the sky. Then a voice said to him, 'Get up, Peter; kill and eat!'[1]" In his mind's eye Epaphras saw her laugh and laugh a belly laugh that even he started to snicker at just then.

Thales looked at Epaphras with a baffled look. Thales knew that Epaphras listened to him, but it seemed he looked right through Thales at someone else … Thales went on recounting the story the way his grandmother had told him.

"Did you know that Peter's mother and I were friends? During the persecution when Peter took his mother to safety, he meant to return to Jerusalem, you know, Peter saw me and remembered me. I recognized him too and invited them in. She looked so feeble. As we did so she and I connected both in the Lord and personally. So as Peter's mother told me the story of

---

[1] Acts 10:10-13

the sheets, she scrunches up her face, puts her hands in front of her as if she is pushing someone away and starts to laugh saying, couldn't you just see that big fisherman saying, 'No, Lord for I have never eaten anything common and ritually unclean.' But again, a second time, a voice said to him, 'What God has made clean, you must not call common.' This happened three times, and then the object got taken up into heaven. Well Peter became so deeply perplexed about what the vision he had seen might mean, but what he didn't realize is that men were coming to him from Cornelius, and having asked directions to Simon's house stood at the gate.

"So imagine this," and she pretends to scratch her face as if Peter would, thinking about and contemplating the dream he'd just had. "Peter is setting there trying to understand the dream and what happens? They called out asking if Simon, who is also named Peter, lodged there. Startled, he jumped, and afterwards said that he sensed the Spirit telling him, 'Three men are here looking for you. Get up, go downstairs, and accompany them with no doubts at all, because I have sent them.'' Then Peter went down to the men and said, 'Here I am, the one you're looking for. What is the reason you're here?' They said, 'Cornelius, a centurion, an upright and God-fearing man, who has a good reputation with the whole Jewish nation, has been divinely directed by a holy angel to call you to his house and to hear a message from you.[1]

"Well, after Peter picked up his jaw from surprise, he invited them in and gave them lodging. The next day he got up and set out with them, and some of the brothers from Joppa went with him. The following day he entered Caesarea. And not surprisingly, Cornelius expected them. In fact, he had called together his relatives and close friends, and when Peter entered

---

[1] Acts 10:19-22

Cornelius met him, fell at his feet, and worshiped him. Can you imagine poor Cornelius's excitement?

"But Peter helped him up and said, 'Stand up! I myself am also a man, just a servant.' While talking with him, he went on in and found that many had come together there. Peter's rough spots weren't gone yet, for he said to them, 'You know it's forbidden for a Jewish man to associate with or visit a foreigner. But God has shown me that I must not call any person common or unclean. That's why I came.'"[1]

"Thales, I'm sure that my friend Luke will want to hear your grandmother tell that story since Peter's mother is gone to heaven now. That's such a great story, and I can see her telling it even now. But that makes sense that she would be confused when she realized that she would need to leave also.

"You also said that she seemed 'surprised' but I don't quite see that in your account of Peter's vision? What surprised her?"

"The subject of Peter's dream combined with the attitude of the Christian Jews we now call 'The Circumcised' group. My grandmother thought that finally her kind, Gentiles, would be accepted by the Jewish Christians."

"Not to be huh?"

"No, but not only the Jewish Christians didn't like us, the Orthodox Jews did not like us either, because one of them, old Caiaphas, who I think is the one that happened to be the high priest during Jesus's trial, knew my grandmother. Apparently one of his relatives lived in Tyre and stood by when Jesus healed my mom through my grandmother's pleading.

"So you are saying," asked Epaphras, "that the Orthodox Jews harassed your family because of the healing that Jesus did, which actually proved to so many Jews in Tyre that He really is the Christ?"

---

[1] Acts 10:26-29

"No!" corrected Thales, a bit more forcefully that he wanted to, "I'm saying that the Orthodox Jews harassed us simply because they could not imagine that we, lowly Gentiles, could have *any part* of their Messiah, whether they believed Jesus to be the Messiah or not. Epaphras, this is the sickest sort of racism, and it grew simply because Jesus healed my mother, a Gentile. The idea that a Gentile could experience anything that might possibly be of Jewish origins or for Jews … they couldn't handle that concept."

"I don't get it," said a bewildered Epaphras. "How did they know that?" and then he stopped because it all made sense to him. "I do get it, Thales. Your family faced what Paul faces all of the time when he goes and first speaks to the Jews, only to get persecuted by the Orthodox ones."

"Exactly," exclaimed a concerned Thales. "There is a bit more to the story that I should probably tell you, although this is only for you and no one else, okay?"

"I understand Thales, but you need to let me make a decision after I hear, on whom I can tell what to, since you are being groomed to take over the Colossae church. Do you understand?"

"Yes Uncle, I do, and I trust your judgment. It's more important that I share this with you …"

"No, you fool, don't go there! Don't tell Epaphras about her," wailed katepa into Thales's ear.

And then changing his approach katepa said, "Thales, don't bother your busy uncle with this right now. Later. Tell him later." It would be one of the gentlest pleas katepa would ever make.

When he saw Thales hesitate he thought he had him convinced to keep his Uncle Epaphras in the dark. And then, out of the dark katepa saw a ramrod straight nine-foot angel in a blazing white robe.

"… when we were studying Paul's writing about remaining single, I knew that I needed to share something with you, so that you could pray …"

"Good man, Thales" said the smiling Hael.

"… I need you to pray for me regarding a girl named Mary," continued Thales.

"No," came the cry from the depths of the dark underworld.

"A Jewish girl? Good for you Thales." responded Epaphras with genuine interest. "Does she live near here? How long have you known her? Tell me about her. In fact, Thales, I'd be honored if whenever you want to," Epaphras got up to leave, but turning his head over his shoulder he continued, "share with me anytime Thales. I'm excited for you. Only the Lord can be a true Father to you, but however I can help, I desire to do the best I can."

With Epaphras halfway out of the door, Thales felt like he had just been kicked in the gut, and he stopped Epaphras to tell him all of the story. "Uncle, she is Benjamin's daughter."

As if the air had just been sucked out of the room, everything stopped. As if neither of them breathed, Thales could only think of the love he had for Mary, and Epaphras could only think of the potential problems to the Colossae church that Benjamin would no doubt like to cause.

"Thales, this is a *big* problem, for a couple of reasons, but the biggest one is the spiritual issue that Paul talked about in his second letter to the Corinthians. I had you read and study it last week. Surely you must have had a start when we talked about being unequally yoked …"

Cutting him off as gently as he could, Thales said, "Uncle, that's the problem, she is a believer in Yeshua HaMashiach."

Again, the air left the room, and Thales continued, "Uncle, her father is a very mean, very angry man. He had some flaw physically, somehow and so would never be allowed to be part of the priesthood.[1] He has held onto that with an anger, even bitterness, that pushes him to be the most orthodox person around and, well, that, and the fact that he did not have any sons. His daughter, Mary, works in his flower shop."

"Is that where you two met?"

"Kind of …"

A bit exasperated Epaphras cut him off, "What do you mean 'kind of'?"

"My family would visit Colossae and his lower store. Their family only moved here five years ago. And so I had always noticed her there, but due to her age, I never approached her … never even considered it Uncle … until recently."

To which Epaphras sighed, approvingly.

"So imagine my surprise Uncle, when I started helping in the underground church that meets in Anat's home and Mary's mother, Aikaterine happened to be there. From what I found out she had been there for three years. I knew that Mary did not believe in Jesus as the Messiah, but then I started talking to her about Jesus, and well a few weeks ago she gave her heart to

---

[1] Leviticus 21:17

Yeshua HaMashiach. She now just has to tell her mother, which to my surprise has been difficult for her to do. They are both going to be scared of Benjamin, Uncle."

For the first time in what felt like to Thales, an eternity, his uncle smiled a big smile, in fact he nearly a laughed.

"I don't understand Uncle …"

"Of course you don't, you immature, love sick idiot, Thales," wailed katepa.

"You're in love, she's a Christian, her father is mean and if things keep going like they have been for me, I'm going to be toast."

"… what's to understand Thales, the only thing we can do is pray. I love these kinds of situations. Come here, son." And with that a relieved Thales hit his knees alongside Epaphras. "You begin, Thales."

"Before we pray Uncle, do you now understand why I hid from Benjamin? I suspect that I will need to protect Mary from him, and am willing to but I want it to be when the timing is right. Does that make sense?"

"This is good Thales," began the route that katepa chose to take. "Your uncle wants you to pray for protection, be aware, and be very concerned, in fact, be worried that maybe you should consider stealing her away from her father and moving to another province, where you'll be safe."

"Father," began Thales, "as we begin to pray, I realize that whatever thoughts I may have, I need to by faith trust You to affect my mind.[1] Father, I am reminded of the testimony given by Peter, when he and John were ordered to not preach or teach at all in the name of Jesus. Father, I remember that Peter and John told them that they, the accusers, would have to decide what would be the right thing to do in the sight of God, 'to listen to them rather than to God' or not.[2]

"Oh Lord, that is my desire, that I would see You only, because when they prayed, they were not at all concerned about protection. Father, like them, I recognize that You, Master, are the One who made the heaven, the earth, and the sea, and everything in them. You said through the Holy Spirit, by the mouth of our father David, Your servant: 'Why did the people rage and plot futile things? The kings of the earth took their stand and the rulers assembled together against the Lord and against His Messiah.'[3] Just as they do against us today Father, but Lord simply consider their threats, and grant us that we will speak Your message with complete boldness, while You stretch out Your hand in power, as we minister in the name of Your Son, Jesus."[4]

While the place did not shake,[5] as the early church experienced, Epaphras had been shaken … shaken to his core as he realized the spiritual maturity in the young man next to him.

As the two men ceased to pray, Thales had been finished for nearly five minutes now, and there still remained a silence between them. Their eyes were still closed in reverence and in

---

[1] Ephesians 6:16
[2] Acts 4:19
[3] Psalm 2:1-2
[4] Acts 4:29-30
[5] Acts 4:31a

the silence they both felt the presence of the Holy Spirit. It could not be missed.

"You, you," gasped katepa, "You are destroying me before I have even begun. Oh, you will pay. Thales you will face such persecution from Benjamin. You will wish you were never born. You will wish *you* had died on that trip, rather than your mother."

While the feelings inside of Thales ebbed and flowed, he kept his mind on the spiritual task at hand, remaining in peace. "But how could that happen," he thought, "with all of these thoughts bombarding him? Captive thoughts, captive thoughts, Paul said in the second letter to the Corinthians." And then he remembered, "Paul had said that because we live in the body, we must wage spiritual war through the power of God. Only then would the evil one's strongholds be destroyed in our life, by destroying arguments in our brain, and the 'supposed high-minded things that really raise themselves up against the knowledge of You by taking thoughts captive."[1] Praise You, Lord!

This surprised Thales, because for the very first time he realized that spiritual warfare, from the perspective of what Christ had already accomplished,[2] should never be a "big deal." He remembered that when he expressed this, his uncle had winced, but he assured Epaphras that he absolutely took seriously the demons, for he remembered the passage in the parchments where one angel destroyed 185,000 Assyrians in one

---

[1] 2 Corinthians 10:3-5
[2] John 19:30m

night.[1] And yet, his uncle eventually agreed that from the perspective of what Jesus already did on the cross,[2] Thales did not fight to attain victory, but by faith Thales did battle with the victory already in hand.

"And so even now Father, with all of the silence in the room, your presence is greater than at any time I have sensed it. So by faith, I trust You to keep my emotions in check.[3] I come to You, the Truth,[4] and I come by Your Son's righteousness,[5] not mine, for mine is as filthy rags, as the prophet Isaiah had said.[6] So since I have accepted Your Son and He is my peace,[7] I trust You to give me that peace which always surprises me …" And somewhere in his silent prayer a peace washed over him that delighted him and humbled him at the same time.

As he reflected on the peace that he had, his uncle began to pray, and he prayed from a depth of his gut and with a fervency that humbled Thales all the more.

"Father," began Epaphras, "Paul told the Thessalonians nearly ten years ago, that we are to give thanks for everything,[8] and so today I thank You for Thales. I thank You for Mary. I thank You for her father Benjamin, and for the potential problems that may come our way …"

Epaphras continued on being thankful, thanking God for the deacons in Colossae and the help they would be in this situation. And then he started to just worship God, praising God actually, praising Him for many of the same things he had just thanked

---

[1] 2 Kings 19:35
[2] Colossians 2:15
[3] Ephesians 6:16
[4] Ephesians 6:14a
[5] Ephesians 6:14b
[6] Isaiah 64:6a
[7] Ephesians 6:15
[8] 1 Thessalonians 5:18

God for, although differently. It seemed the thanksgiving prayers were centered upon what God did for them and then the praising prayers had to do with God's attributes. This confused Thales and he planned to ask his uncle about this after they were done because he realized, "Something is different when Epaphras 'praised' God compared to when he 'thanked' God. Oh Lord, open the eyes of my heart that I might understand."

Epaphras prayed for what seemed like an hour, but it could have been more, and when he ended they stayed there on their knees, immersed in the presence of the Lord. No one said anything, they just stayed on their knees.

After a few minutes more enjoying the presence of the Lord, and with his eyes still closed Thales gently quoted again the Psalm they had meditated on earlier in the day:

The LORD is my shepherd; I shall not be in want.
He makes me lie down in green pastures.
He leads me beside still waters.
He restores my soul.
He leads me in paths of righteousness, and always for his name's sake.
Even though I walk through the valley of the shadow of death,
I will fear no evil, for He is with me
His rod and His staff, they comfort me.
He prepares a table before me, even in the presence of my enemies
He anoints my head with oil and my cup overflows.
Surely goodness and mercy shall follow me all the days of my life,

And I, His servant, Thales shall dwell in His house forever and ever[1]

"No, Thales," started katepa gently, "You don't need to ask about the difference. Epaphras is tired, he's spent a lot of time with you already today, ask the question later … on another day."

"Uncle, you thanked God and then you praised God for the same things, but something felt different to me and I do not understand. What is the difference in thanking God and in praising God?"

"Direction Thales, direction."

"Huh?"

"Yes direction. You see, when we thank God those prayers are us centered, but when we praise God, they are him centered. We'll talk more about it later, Son. I have something to do in the marketplace."

Just then katepa yelled to haodtie, "He doesn't need to know all of that, haodtie. Can't you control your rebel?"

---

[1] Psalm 23

38

First Century

Being the end of the day for Agathon he had put away all of his tools. A sandal maker by trade, he did exquisite work because of what he had been originally taught by his father. The family trade for generations had been the carving of idols and his family had been at it for more than three generations, but when Agathon became saved and sensed that what he did for a trade contradicted the Word of God, he and his wife talked about it, sought the Lord together and one day, after hearing clearly from the Lord, Agathon said to his wife, "Hagne, I do not think that God wants me to make idols. I must quit."

She just laughed and said, "Honey, I knew that a very long time ago. You making idols is like the banker who sells money at an exorbitant rate, and that too is contrary to God's will. You see, God has been speaking to me too Agathon. I think what God has been teaching me is that I am to seek Him for His will in everything."

Then she started to blush and added, "And you know how difficult that is for me, my first name is Eve, and it suits my propensity, which you know better than anyone … I desire to rule over everything, including you, my husband."[1]

With age comes wisdom usually, and in this case it had. Agathon merely smiled and said, "I love you too, honey."

That would have been twenty-five or twenty-six years earlier when the Syrophoenician woman moved to the area of Colossae, Hierapolis in particular, with the little baby who now appeared to be his future pastor, Thales. As all of these thoughts were going through his mind something else passed through his mind, his wife's attitude. He felt like her attitude had changed since he became a senior deacon, and just then he heard Epaphras at the door.

"Hello my friend," Agathon said warmly greeting his pastor and close friend. "What brings you here this late in the afternoon. I will see you tonight at prayer meeting, won't I?"

"Yes, but I needed to speak to you."

"Sure Epaphras, I am just closing up shop. Sit down. I'll lock the door and be right with you."

Epaphras looked around. The detail work that Agathon did always showed such talent and brilliance. His training when he grew up had served him well.

"That is just like God," Epaphras thought. "God, You allowed Agathon to grow up in a family that made idols, knowing that he would be saved, and change direction professionally, only to become the best at it, commissioned by the very well-to-do …"

"Say it Epaphras," whispered haodtie, "and because he is commissioned by the 'very well-to-do,' Agathon has become one the Colossian church's biggest tithers. His money is the

---

[1] Genesis 3:16b

reason you can do the things you do, hire your nephew, and go on trips with Paul."

"You are a fraud, Epaphras. You are a fraud and one day you will be found out." From within a cloud of putrid smoke haodtie tried to cause Epaphras to doubt his mission.

"… so that he had the opportunity," continued Epaphras, as he thought about his senior deacon, "to share the gospel of Jesus Christ with those that Epaphras, on his own, could never and would never be able to share with the message of hope."

"I hate you Epaphras," said an angry haodtie. "You are not folding under my influence."

"Agathon, I am concerned about something and need your help."

With Epaphras disappearing so quickly, Thales pulled out his own personal quill and parchment that he used for his journaling.

The poetry of the Old Testament had always been a motivation for him to write poetry himself. So while he spent time in The Psalms, The Proverbs, The Song of Solomon and Job, he desired to write his own poetry.

He loved the five scrolls of the Psalms and all the more since his uncle taught him to pray them back to the Lord. The more he did this, the more he fell in love with these passages. The Proverbs had always been a motivation to him to live righteously and now he also began to understand and marvel at the words of

King Lemuel's mother on the subject of a virtuous wife. Interestingly, he never became interested in the love story of the Song of Solomon. Perhaps it's because he lived in a culture amid too much inappropriate sex. And while he loved the teaching in Job of God's sovereignty, explained through the pen of an unknown writer, he became more and more interested in writing something himself, something that directly honored God but focused upon the Son that he would forever try to understand.

As Thales wrote, he found himself to be a bit of a perfectionist and kept coming back to what he had written thus far. Every time he read it he felt glad that he could honor his Lord in this way.

"But what will I do with it?" he laughed to himself. "This is just my way of praising the Lord."

In a way, he found himself proud of his poetry and for being a student of poetry, a student of words, and most importantly a student of the Word. Carefully he worked through making the point succinctly and honorably. With that running through his mind he picked it up and read it anew. This is what he had come up with thus far.

He called the poem *"Hail, Gladdening Light, of His Pure Glory Poured"*.[1]

> *Hail gladdening Light, of His pure glory poured*
> *who is the Immortal Father, heavenly, blest,*
> *Holiest of Holies, Jesus Christ, our Lord.*

> *Now we are come to the sun's hour of rest,*
> *the lights of evening round us shine,*

---

[1] The poem is a real first-century poem. We do not know the author, but it is found in *Church Hymnary* (4th ed.) #219, edited by John Keble (English Translation)

we hymn the Father, Son, and Holy Spirit divine.

Worthiest art thou at all times to be sung
with undefiled tongue,
Son of our God, Giver of life, alone;
therefore in all the world thy glories, Lord, we own.

He reviewed it again, thinking that it might be completed, when Basileios, nearly out of breath, came for him. Thales could tell immediately that something had to be wrong. "Thales, come with me now. Tell Epaphras, he'll understand. Your grandmother is very ill. She took a bad fall yesterday and is failing fast. I don't know if we'll make it on time."

Grabbing some clothes quickly, and then scratching a short note to Epaphras, Thales and Basileios headed the six miles along the Lycus River from Colossae to Hierapolis, where they lived, and where he had lived until a few months ago.

They were both silent traversing the path as quickly as they could, pacing themselves due to the distance, and because of the uneven surface along the river, they needed to concentrate on what they were doing. So that coupled with them wanting to conserve energy, made for a trip where they spoke little. But Thales' mind worked overtime. What could he do? His uncle is a man of prayer, a man that everyone knew had great 'pull' with God. And so should Thales … right? After all he is Epaphras's understudy. So what had Thales learned? "Oh Lord, I need clear direction from You. I don't know what I'm doing, Lord, and my grandmother is the matriarch of this family. Father," he pleaded, "please heal my sweet grandmother."

Night started to fall upon them, but they could still see the road through the light that still lingered from the setting sun. Soon, thought Basileios, darkness would overtake them and they'd have to slow down even more. "Can you pick up the pace Thales?"

"Of course." Thales said, "I know this route well, try and keep up with me."

And with that Thales took the lead. Approximately twenty-plus years younger than Basileios, it gave Thales the edge and he started to pull away from his surrogate father. And as he took the lead, heading closer and closer to Hierapolis, he started to think about Mary. "Father," Thales said while he walked to his grandmother's home, "Oh Father, I need, no I desire to glorify You, and yet my mind is being pulled into so many directions. Lord, calm my mind so that I am sensitive to Your leading."

Entering his grandmother's home, Thales went quickly to her side. All of her remaining family were already at her bedside. "She kept asking for you, Thales," said Myrrine, his mother's sister, the one who raised him.

"I'm here Grandma," Thales said softly. She opened her eyes slowly, turned her head to the sound of his voice and smiled.

"Pray for me," she whispered.

Gathering all of his courage and every passage on healing he could think of he began. But barely one half a sentence into his prayer his grandmother shook her head gently, saying quietly to him, "Thales, that is your will my son. Pray for me the Father's will. Listen to the Holy Spirit's leading, and pray for me what the Lord wants you to pray, not what you want to pray."

With this gentle reprimand came a peace to Thales and he began to pray, "Father in heaven, the One who created the heaven and the earth, the One who calls Your saints home, in Your timing, I lift up, no, all of us here lift up my grandmother to You. Thank You for the faith that she has taught us all. Give her peace now Lord as she transitions to eternity with You, and …" Thales began to choke up, and Basileios laid his hand on Thales's shoulder to comfort him. Thales continued, "... with You and with my mom, and dad ..."

His grandmother's breathing continued slowing down, and Thales went on, "Father, give us who are remaining, the grace to go through this time. Show us how to transition to a life without my grandmother ..."

Everyone stood at her bed when she opened her eyes wide, smiled like the woman they knew, and then started to talk, quietly, but clearly, "There's Jesus standing and smiling to me," she said. "Oh, and next to him is Euanthe and her husband. I am ready, Lord. Who are all of those other people waiting for me?" And with that she drifted back into a state of unconsciousness that soon departed, as she took her last breath and though absent from her body she entered her new home with Christ.[1]

The home going for a brother or sister of Jesus showed itself to be very different in those days from the pagans, and even from the Jews. It became a celebration really, an opportunity for a reminder of an afterlife, guaranteed by God, and sealed by the Holy Spirit.[2] Just as Jesus lived, raised from the dead, so these Christ followers would be also.

A curious thing would be seen in these early Christians, they were not afraid of death. Truly the sting had been taken out of death.[3] There would be mourning, as one would expect at a funeral, but there would be something more. There would be a hope, not an unsure hope, but a sure hope.[4] The home-going of a Christian would be an event that left all who would participate

---

[1] 2 Corinthians 5:8
[2] Ephesians 1:13
[3] 1 Corinthians 15:55
[4] Hebrews 6:19

encouraged to hold fast to the hope that had been set before them.[1]

There were visitors from all over the region, for everyone who considered himself or herself a Christ follower knew of the story of the Syrophoenician woman. People came from outside of the region, and in the hall where the services were held, in the back of the room, stood Anat, Aikaterine, and Mary.

And further back, beyond where mortal eyes could see, another demon had been beaten by his "friends" for having lost such an influential subject. And now that it's recording included parchments, not just word of mouth, this failure would last as long as the parchments were read ... which all suspected in this demonic abode, could be a very long time.

---

[1] Hebrews 6:18

39

Current Era

While Margie spoke to Isabela, Dale spoke at The Issachar Men Prayer time. He arrived a little early to participate in being one of the "Chatty-Cathys" as Dean had named them. The 7:30 am Bible study started right on time and the men seemed genuinely interested in studying the *Wesleys Family Prayers Book*.

"The insight that these two brothers had for putting passages together to pray is amazing," Greg started off the discussion.

"I've started looking online at other men's prayers," chimed in Don. He continued, "I am amazed at the prayers of Charles Hadden Spurgeon. Did you know that some of them are six and seven pages long? They are sermons in their own right, and from what I can tell this seemed to be how he opened every service, with this kind of a prayer. Amazing!"

Letting the pace of these statements lead his discussion Dean asked, "How has this impacted your prayer life during the week?"

A long silence ensued and just when Dale thought he should jump in to save Dean, Patrick, a nineteen-year-old college sophomore, spoke up. Patrick, a quite good looking young man who, while a full ride athlete on Dale's track team, chose to be at the church whenever the doors were opened. Patrick added, "My Bible reading has actually been reduced, because I am spending more time with each verse."

"I like this kid," thought Dale.

"That is exactly my experience Patrick," Dale just said out loud.

And then others echoed the same thing, with more than one saying, "I felt embarrassed to say that, but I agree. I don't get as much reading done as I used to, but I get a lot deeper with everything that I read."

Standing up there in front of these men, and as proud as anyone could ever be, Dean watched his men. But Dale noticed his posture which, far from standing straight up seemed to have him hunched over to the side, where it seemed he favored his gut.

Walking to the breakfast time Dale asked Dean, "Have you had that checked yet?"

"No, but I will soon Dale, I promise."

Gently grabbing Dean by the arm to stop him, Dale called over to Don. While Don made his way over to Dale, he asked Dean, "If I recall, your wife has insurance, so it isn't a financial reason you're not going to the doctor, right?"

"No," Dean laughed, "She has great insurance. I've just been a little lazy about getting it done."

"I understand Dean, and so I'm making an executive decision, okay?" By this time Don had arrived. "Dean, you're not leading these guys again until you get that checked, okay?"

Dean's jaw dropped.

"I love you man, and it's my responsibility to help you in any way I can." Dale continued, "Don, I have a project for you. Stay onto Dean until he goes to the doctor, okay?"

"You are an arrogant leader, Doctor Dale. Who do you think that you are?" whispered katepa off and on throughout the breakfast time as Dale visited table after table.

Heading up to the sanctuary Dale stopped by the table where Dean sat. "You're not grumpy at me, are you Dean?"

"No, not at all Dale, you're only doing what I will do with these guys as I watch them not deal with health issues. I agree with you Dale, we talk about drugs, smoking, etc. but we leave alone being a good steward of our bodies. I appreciate you holding my feet to the fire."

In the sanctuary, Dale began to speak saying, "I'm going to bring up a subject, that even in our church is controversial, and that is healing. The controversy, I have found comes with the discussion of whether or not God *always* wants to heal you. I contend that it is not always God's will to heal here on earth.

"The first argument is regarding faith. We hear televangelists say, 'If you have enough faith, when I pray for you, you will be healed.' They quote the first half of the passage from James 5:15 which says that, *the prayer of faith will save the one who is sick, and the Lord will raise him up.* But my friends, if you read the passage, you clearly see that James talked about the faith of the person praying. So if the person being prayed for is not healed, it's not on the sick person, like most televangelists want you to think. According to the very verse they quote, if the person being prayed for isn't healed it's really on the pray-er, not the sick person.

"Secondly, we have the famous, *by His stripes we were healed* passage. But look at the context of Peter's quotation, found in 1 Peter 2:24. It is absolutely and completely in the context of spiritual healing, not physical healing. I would argue also that the *'be healed'* passage in Hebrews 12:13 is spiritual healing also.

"Finally, are we saying that God is not in the healing business today? We would never say that. I personally believe that God still does heal and sometimes miraculously. The challenge for us is how should we pray for the ill? And here is where I come down on the subject, and I think that it is the only place that I can land, teaching as I do about praying Scripture, and praying with confidence,[1] no doubting.[2]

"If the Lord lays on my heart to pray for someone's healing, then I do, and I watch them be healed. But when I am not prompted by the Holy Spirit to pray for their healing then I have to pray other Scriptures for them, and I have found Ephesians 1:17-19 as a great passage to pray, but you may find others. Here's how I pray for folks that the Lord does not lay on my heart to pray healing for them.

"Let me use Dean as an example, since I know he's going in to see the doctor this next week, right Dean?"

"Yes, mother," Dean intoned from his seat in the sanctuary.

"Father, I pray for Dean right now Lord, that You, the God of our Lord Jesus Christ, the Father of all glory and majesty and grace, would give Dean the Spirit of wisdom and of revelation in the knowledge of what you have planned for Dean. Enlighten and open the eyes of his heart Lord, that he would know fully and completely, the hope that You have called him to, which right now happens to mean some suffering. And Father, I trust

---

[1] 1 John 5:14
[2] James 1:6a

You to show my friend the riches of Your glory that he has now among the saints, not just when he gets to heaven. Finally, Father, show my friend the immeasurable greatness of Your power in him, simply because he is a believer, knowing that this power is the same power at work in Him, through Your Son. Amen." And with that the men also said Amen.

"Men, pray until you hear the music start." And with that the men separated into their groups to pray.

Getting home to his wife, he found her on her knees in the living room where she likes to pray. Dale walked in quietly, sat next to her and laid his hand on her shoulder. When she finished she got up, gave him a kiss on the cheek and asked, "Guess who came here for coffee this morning?"

"I don't know. The Big Bad Wolf? Maybe Little Red Riding Hood."

"Good guess, a little bit of both, come to find out." Continuing her comments in a genuinely humble attitude, Margie said. "Professor Isabela Gonzalez graced our home today."

And with a long low whistle, Dale said, "I'd sure like to have been a fly on the wall for that."

"Had you been, I'd have squashed you. I think she came over because you were not here."

"So you're not going to tell me what you talked about?" And seeing the tissue box out of place he added, "Never mind babe, you tell me what you want to, when you want to."

"I will lover, thanks for understanding." And with that she gave him a long slow kiss.

40

First Century &
Nineteenth Century &
Current Era

"Agathon my friend," started Epaphras, "thank you for taking care of things while Thales and I were with his grandmother. I am sorry that I could not stay and talk last week."

"You know that you need think nothing of it. I am honored to take care of our house churches, in whatever capacity is needed from teaching to caring for our brethren."

"Thank you Agathon, I know that about you, and am honored to have your confidence, especially today my old friend."

Agathon shifted slightly in his chair, knowing there would be something more serious coming as he watched Epaphras's countenance become even more serious. "It seems to bother Epaphras," thought Agathon, "this impending discussion."

"Epaphras, I want to help. How can I help? No, let me help, and let my help begin by us going before the throne." And with that Agathon did not hesitate, "Father in Heaven, Brother Epaphras and I come before You. We know that You encourage us to come boldly into Your throne room,[1] and so we do that

---

[1] Hebrews 4:16a

Father, not entering in with arrogance, but rather humbly entering with confidence, great confidence, that You incline Your ear to hear our prayers,[1] even though there are thousands of angels worshipping You.[2] Father, You tell us, by Solomon's hand, that the prayers of the upright delight You.[3] Almighty God, maker of heaven and earth, we humbly ask You to hear these prayers, trusting with confidence[4] and not doubting,[5] that You are here where we two are, and so because we pray Your will, we trust You to hear us.[6] Open the eyes and ears of our heart[7] Lord, that we may see You in our discussions. I know that my brother, my co-laborer, my friend, is burdened by this discussion he needs to have. I trust You to give him wisdom, give him clarity, and give him no fear, to share what you lay upon his heart. To You Father we pray, through Your Son, and in the power of Your blessed Holy Spirit. Amen."

"Father," Epaphras picked up, "I am grateful for Agathon's sensitivity to my spirit. We trust You, Lord, to bring Your ultimate will since Your throne is above the heavens and You are sovereign over all,[8] out of our time together right now."

With a relaxed sigh, Epaphras started. "My friend, I have two issues I need to ask your help with, one concerns your wife, and the other, a new convert's discipleship. We need to cover them both, so which shall we begin with?"

---

[1] Psalm 40:1b
[2] Revelation 5:11b
[3] Proverbs 15:8b
[4] 1 John 5:14
[5] James 1:6a
[6] Matthew 18:20
[7] Ephesians 1:18a
[8] Psalm 103:19

"You are entering my trap, Epaphras," chuckled haodtie.

"Oh Father, I want to help Epaphras," a nine-foot tall angel said as he watched the demons hover around his charge.

Carrolton Faith had been having a crisis of his own "faith." After being sober for a few days, getting beyond the shakes, and then thinking about what he had been bothered by, it had become all too clear. First, his own faith, and how he had given it up for the temporary enjoyment of liquor. As he looked back, he realized that he had completely wasted the last twenty-two years of his life. "I climbed into a bottle after the death of my parents," Carrol remembered, "and stayed there. They were killed just before I reached my fifteenth birthday. I found that the liquor dulled the pain of their loss ... twenty-two years ago."

Carrol mumbled to himself, speaking to no one in particular as he sat in the woods alone. After so many years of being drunk, he had a hard time focusing his thoughts for any length of time. "And why do I have this pain in my gut all of a sudden," he thought to himself as he winced from the strong dull pain.

"The Way, the Truth and the Life,[1] is what I remember about, something, about what? About my life? No, I don't think so. About my parent's life? Well, I still don't think so, but I don't know why yet. What is it Lord?"

For a number of minutes Carrolton pondered the only thing he could remember, "the Way, the Truth and the Life." And then he remembered, that's it isn't it Lord? L-O-R-D, Lord. Yes, You, Lord, are the Way, the Truth and the Life. And I remember now, we come to the Father through the Son. He is my Truth!" And Carrolton Faith remembered his Christian faith. He remembered

---

[1] John 14:6a

that he had been a child of God, albeit a long lost prodigal, but a son nonetheless. "Thank You, Lord."

Go back to the Truth.[1] That always needed to be the first thing to do. That is what his father had taught him, about ... about something, about what?" saying to himself now, searchingly. "Go to the truth when ... when what? When in trouble? Going to the Truth when in trouble would be the first step of what? The first step of, of course." He remembered and started to choke up. "When I face spiritual warfare, I begin with the first piece of the armor which is to go to the Truth, because Jesus is my truth. Thank You Father," came the words and the tears.

He heard the birds in the air and in the trees as he laughed and cried with his re-found faith.

"And why do I get to go to the Truth? I remember now, because of His Son's righteousness,[2] not mine. Mine is, oh, what did the prophet say? My righteousness is, is. Yes! Mine is like filthy rags."[3] And with this remembered truth came another set of tears.

"Truth, Righteousness, and what? Oh, Lord, I don't remember, but I don't care. I am just so glad to be back in Your presence. In Your presence," he began to sing, "there is joy and peace. Peace, that's it,[4] that's the third thing that we have in Christ. Yes! That's the first half of the armor. Yes! These are what I already have in Christ. He is my truth, my righteousness and my peace. Oh Father, it has been so long since I have been this close to You. Forgive me, Lord ..."

---

[1] Ephesians 6:14a
[2] Ephesians 6:14b
[3] Isaiah 64:6
[4] Ephesians 6:15

"What a great job I have," a nine-foot tall ramrod straight angel thought to himself. As he smiled he remembered the passages that described faithfulness, the Almighty's faithfulness, and with that he started to quote them ending with, "Oh Lord, You are faithful who called Carrolton into fellowship with Your Son[1] those many years ago. And what You began in him, You will complete.[2] Again, thank You, Lord, for allowing me to participate in Your service, in Carrolton's life."

"Tuesday mornings," Margie had just said to Professor Gonzalez as they met in the faculty lounge. "That's the only time I have free too."

"I love coincidences, don't you?" Isabela said in all sincerity, and really, quite grateful that their schedules would allow this time together.

"Coincidence? After all that you know about me you actually think that I would agree with you that this is a mere coincidence?" Margie mischievously responded.

Laughing with her new friend Isabela Gonzalez said, "I want to ask you seriously on Tuesday, why is 'Giving thanks,' so important to you?"

"You're a great straight person Isabela," Margie responded jokingly.

But before she could go further, Isabela turned on her. Margie saw anger in Isabela's eyes, and then Isabela's lips tightened as if she were getting ready to spew venomous words.

Margie paused, knowing something wasn't right but unable to put her finger on what had just happened.

---

[1] 1 Corinthians 1:9
[2] Philippians 1:6

Just then a demon spoke into Margie's ear, "There is your bigoted homophobic 'friend' or, so called friend."

"Margie, is that a homophobic comment?"

Now understanding Isabela's change in attitude Marie said, "Isabela, how could you say that? What have you seen in me these last few days that would make you think that?"

"Well I thought that I had seen a person who doesn't judge, but ..."

Margie jumped back in, "Of course that is what you have seen, because that is who I am by God's grace. I made the comment, 'you're a great straight person,' in the context of setting yourself up for where I wanted to take the conversation."

Sheepishly Isabela said, "Oh, I get it. I'm sorry. I'm still a bit, well, wary of our relationship. Wait a minute. How did I set myself up? What are you talking about?"

"Just this," Margie continued, "Just this. I'm giving you an assignment. I want you to pretend that there is a sovereign God out there, okay? Pretend that He has a throne that sits above the heavens and He is sovereign over all.[1] And then ask yourself, 'If there really is such a God, what thing, or things can I give thanks for relative to my cancer?' Again, just pretend this is true, and then ask yourself, okay?"

"Forgive me Margie, but you're crazy. Nothing! There is *nothing* that I can give thanks for, N-O-T-H-I-N-G."

"You might be surprised, my new friend." responded Margie.

"Margie, I know that I am joking a lot with you and frankly some of it is out of being a bit scared of our relationship, but please know this, I am thankful for you. In just this short time

---

[1] Psalm 103:19

that we've ... Hey, okay, there is one thing. I have been able to get to know you."

They both laughed and Isabela continued, "I know that my situation isn't any different, but I feel, well, I have a strange peace."

Margie held up two fingers, "Now there are two things that you can give thanks for," and the two women laughed.

"I know Isabela, and understand me when I say to you, I love you."

Isabela let a tear roll down her cheek. "I know you do, Margie. I know you do." And she laughed and held up three fingers.

"Those three things! Okay, there are those three things that I can give thanks for, but I'm sure, nothing else ... I'm sure."

The two ladies parted company and a friendship strengthened that only death would separate.

This time katepa got to see the demon he hated so much, joln, squirm as his upper echelon demon berated him. As joln cowered under the verbal and physical beating katepa heard only a few of the words. He heard how much time had gone into preparing Professor Gonzalez for her work, including the men and women that could have been useful to them, but she had stepped on them, causing them to get out of the psychology business.

"But we put all this effort into her, joln, only for you to lose everything that we have worked so hard to acheive. If you live through this," his overlord, spitting at him now said, right behind his fat rippled face, "I will be surprised, you contemptable loser."

341

41

Current Era

Early in the next week Dale received a call from Don. "Happy Tuesday afternoon to you my brother. How are you today?"

Knowing that this has always been Brother Don's signature 'hello' Dale smiled.

"Good Don, but my day is pretty busy. I took the call because I saw that it is you. Can I call you later?"

"This will only take a moment Dale, Dean is in the hospital."

"What? What's the prognosis Don?"

Don hesitated, but only for a moment. "Not good, maybe a month, perhaps two. But he's already decided he won't have surgery or chemo. Sorry to lay this on you like this, but I thought you'd want to know right away."

Bewildered and shocked, Dale thanked him and went to his athletes' warmups.

Margie and Isabela met and, no surprise to Margie, Isabela had a list of things she could give thanks for. Both women hugged each other and they looked at a couple of items on the list.

"I need to tell you, Margie that I have been surprised by the way you framed my assignment, and then what the assignment led to: 'Assuming that God is sovereign,' made a big difference. Everything I looked at and considered, I tried to fit into that assumption. At first I couldn't do it, but I kept trusting you and although I didn't like it, it eventually became freeing. And in addition to it being freeing it caused me to have hope.

"Margie, if God is sovereign, then my medical condition isn't a surprise to God. If my medical condition isn't a surprise to God, and He is a 'Good God' as you have said, then it stands to reason that He has planned some good to come out of this."

Isabela with questioning in her voice continued, "For the life of me, I have no clue what that could be." Margie simply listened, letting her speak. "But I had a thought, and that had to do with Julienne. What if her direction is appropriate. What if she has the right idea after all?"

"Isabela, pretend for a moment that Julienne is right, what would be the outcome if her patients ask God what they can give thanks for *in* their problems?"

"What do you mean?"

"If Julienne's question to her 'client' is the right one to ask, and her client comes up with items that he or she can give thanks for, then what ends up being the result in the client's life?"

Isabela sat for a long time and then shrugged her shoulders. "I'm sorry, my brain can't get beyond how counter intuitive the question is."

"Good response, that makes sense," Margie encouraged, "So look at yourself, what has happened to your attitude about your cancer." She paused, and when Isabela continued to look dumfounded. Margie continued, "You told me the other day that you had a strange peace about it, right?"

"Yes, well, that's because of our relationship, I think."

Saying each word slowly and deliberately Margie went on, "What has happened to your perspective Isabela?"

Isabela let out a long slow breath. "My perspective has changed from self-destruction to hope," she said with great conviction and certainty.

Three days later, Margie and Dale visited Dean with Isabela in tow. Dale had visited Dean the evening Don called him, only to find out that Dean's smoking that he had given up three years earlier had caught up with him. As Dale expected, Dean had no concern for his own situation, but only everyone else's. He showed an amazing joy to everyone that visited him.

"If he has half the joy you tell me he showed on Saturday Dale, he could be just what Isabela needs to see." So Dale and Margie prayed for Isabela's attitude, that she'd go and visit Dean in the hospital with them. And after they prayed for Isabela, they prayed for Dean that he'd have God's wisdom to say what needed to be said.

And so here they were. Isabela being pretty scared, but she trusted Margie when she said, "You'll meet a guy with only a few weeks or months to live and you'll be surprised by his attitude."

"Hello Dean," Dale said walking into Dean's room, "This is a colleague of mine and Margie's, her name is Isabela."

After some pleasantries Dale and Margie stepped out of the room with Dean's wife, to see how they could support her.

"Dean," Isabela asked, "Why do you have such a positive attitude? That doesn't make any sense to me."

Dean just smiled, and said, "It isn't me, it's God." And seeing Isabel both confused and apparently angry he asked, "Are you in Margie's Bible study?"

"Bible study? No, I've never believed in the Bible or in God. I'm not even exactly sure why I am here."

And with that Dean picked up the electronic box and raised the back of his bed so that he could sit up. He asked Isabela to take a chair so that they could talk.

Heading out of Dean's room nearly two hours later Isabela asked Margie and Dale, "How much do you know about Dean's past?"

"Only a few things Isabela. I hoped to learn more but," and he trailed off.

"He has been really up front and open with me about his lifestyle before becoming 'saved,' as he put it. He seemed to be genuine, quite genuine," she said again and then teared up. She continued, "Why would your God take someone like that? Why?"

Seeing that Isabela needed a few moments to compose herself, Dale gave her one of his handkerchiefs. "Thank you Dale, but knowing we were coming to the hospital room of a terminally ill person, I brought my own tissues." She gave a short smile.

"Isabela," Dale said, "we believe that the Bible is the Word of God, His words to mankind, if you will, and so we choose to believe what He says in His Word, even if it doesn't always make sense. Let me give you an example. You've known Margie long enough to know that she is pretty great right?" Isabela looked at Margie and nodded. "Well she is. In fact, when I talk about her I say this: 'My wife is nearly perfect,' and then I pause and say, 'but she still gets up my nose.'"

Isabela laughed and Dale continued. "So there is this verse that doesn't make sense to me, it says: 'If there is anything between you and your wife your prayers will be hindered.'[1] I have to confess Isabela, I sometimes ask God, 'Why is that in there Lord?' to which He usually replies, because I'm working on your life, meathead."

"Does God actually speak to you? Do you hear him audibly, I mean in your ear, Dale?"

"Great question Isabela. No, I hear him in my heart, like an 'impression upon' my heart.

"So here's the point Isabela, there are some things in Scripture that just confuse, no, more like confound me. And that verse is one of them. But let me bring this back to Dean, okay? 2 Corinthians 1:4 is a verse in the Bible and it talks about God comforting us so that we can comfort others in the same way. You see sometimes God allows us to go through things because the *only* way we can comfort someone else is to go through it ourselves."

Dale looked at her in his rear view mirror when he saw her sit back deep in thought, and so he shut up. Margie started to speak but Dale tapped her on the leg and she said nothing. Isabela sat there, still deep in thought.

A few minutes later Isabela said, "Dean said that I should start reading the book of John. He said that it would be about a love that cannot be compared to anything here on earth. I don't know what he's talking about, but I suspect you do."

Margie smiled, "Yes Isabela, I know what he meant. When we get to our home, I'll give it to you. I have an extra one."

A couple of hours later Dale and Margie were getting into bed. "What an incredible turn of events honey."

---

[1] 1 Peter 3:7

"Oh, I know Dale. I suspect that Isabela is real close to being saved."

"Let's pray for her," Margie turned, cuddling herself into Dale, with his chin above her head, holding onto one another he prayed, "Father, we know that You are not willing that any should perish.[1] We know that You say that if we delight ourselves in You, that You'll give us the desires of our heart.[2] And so Father, we trust You to already be in the process of causing Isabela to come to You."

They were both tired and fell asleep holding on to one another.

Across town Isabela raced through this book of John. "Hmm." She would periodically say, and then turn another page to read on.

Three weeks later, Dale and Margie were still praying nightly for Isabela, and tonight being no exception, they had just prayed for her when Dale felt restless. "Baby," he said. "I think I need to get up and spend some time in the living room."

She grumbled for a few moments because their cuddling had to stop, but then she released him and he gave her a long slow kiss.

As Dale got his robe and slippers on he thought, "It has been awhile since Hael and I have met together."

---

[1] 1 Timothy 2:4a
[2] Psalm 37:4

42

Nineteenth Century

After another bite to eat and knowing that even in the dark Sterling knew his way back to Jeffersonville, as did Alexander, he and Sterling started their return trip. While this seemed highly unusual for him, since he liked to just let things work themselves out, Alex felt a calling to go back there for some reason.

"Lord," he began, "I thank You that Your sovereignty is not in question at all. I thank You, Lord, for the challenges that await me because every single one of them You will use for the better,[1] if You have not already. I thank You Father for Your Word, because I know that it is truth, and because it is truth I trust it no matter what others say.[2] And then Lord, though arrogant people may smear me with lies, I will keep Your Word with all of my heart.[3] Father, that trust actually causes me to look forward to Jeffersonville and what awaits me because You are in control."

---

[1] Romans 8:28
[2] Psalm 119:42
[3] Psalm 119:69

"You *think* everything is okay you big old tub of lard, but no. I am working out the demise of you and your so called 'precious' ministry," cackled katepa. And yet hovering around somewhere is his brain he had a memory … a memory of that angel of his Holy Enemy. "Ah!" He grumbled, "Your parishioners have free will and their free will is where the trouble is coming from. You're toast preacher."

"Why does my gut still hurt," wondered Carrolton? And then just as quickly as it had entered he dismissed it with, "It's just the pain of being sober." So, rubbing his sides to relieve the pain he started to ponder the question he couldn't seem to reconcile, "Does the reminder of Brother Alex really make me think of my mother and father?"

Carrol stood in a dirty old one room building that he made his home, or, where he simply spent the night for the last number of years. The shack sat outside of town and had been deserted for decades. He had been there for what seemed like hours and then staring into the part of his brain that didn't hurt, he looked for verses that he had memorized as a child. A verse started to form in his brain but it didn't seem to him to be a verse he had memorized. "Hope … joy … peace. Hope, joy and peace. What is the verse and when did I memorize it? Hope, joy and … God is our hope, God is our hope, yes! He is our hope and He gives us joy and peace, joy and peace, joy and peace," Carrol lost focus now, but staying with it he remembered, "joy and peace because we are believers ... That's it!"

Carrolton pondered again, "Isn't there more to the verse? It is good enough on its own, 'God, who is our hope, gives us joy and peace simply because we are believers.'"[1] And just then

---

[1] Romans 15:13

Carrol thought of his father. "I don't understand Lord, what is the connection here?" And as soon as he said it he remembered the whole picture. Carrolton Faith never memorized this verse. This is what he heard his dad pray for his mom every day of their life. That Carrol could remember. The verse had sunk deep into his brain because it meant so much to his parents.

"Then why am I," and Carrol froze. His dad prayed that prayer, that verse, for him too every single day, not just his mother. That is the blessing that Alexander Rich gave Gretchen when he prayed for her out in the forest on the other side of town.

He remembered now, the expression of gratefulness that Gretchen had, the same gratefulness that he used to see his mother have and that he had, when his dad would pray this verse.

"But they were taken from you weren't they," snarled a demon from behind his ear. "God punished you and took them."

"But why did you allow them to die Lord?" yelled Carrolton into the forest. "WHY, Why, why," he whimpered, "The war had been over and the hostilities had ended. And yet they were a casualty."

After a few minutes, Carrol's anger wound down and he wiped his tears with his sleeve. "Because My ways are different from your ways,"[1] he said, as if God were doing the talking to Carrolton Faith.

Sitting down exhausted, Carrolton missed his folks, missed his wasted twenty-two years and asked the Lord if He could make them up. "I don't know what to do Lord, but I trust You, the God of hope, who gives joy and peace to believers, simply

_____

[1] Isaiah 55:8

because they are believers, and then causes us to…" Changing direction now, Carrolton asked, "Father, would You allow me to live a life overflowing with hope, and let all of the townspeople see it, but for Your glory Lord, not mine?" Smiling to himself Carrol added, "Romans 15:13," as he remembered where the verse was found ... and then his toothless grin widened.

"Geraldine," Hatch McCreedy said to his wife when they were in bed, "did you talk to Gretchen about how serious things got between her and the preacher?"

"Talk to her about how serious things got? Why no, why would I? Why are you asking?"

With a pause he said, "Well, I heard something today, that, well, never mind honey. It's probably not an issue at all."

"Wait just one doggone minute Hatch McCreedy. You can't say that and then just stop. What did you hear? What are you thinking? If you do not tell me, I will not let you sleep. This girl has embarrassed me enough in this town. What else is going on that I need to be aware of?"

Hatch McCreedy faced away from his wife …

"What had been asked, or said?" she again pleaded.

"Oh nothing …" He wouldn't see her reaction. He wouldn't see her eyes widen and then bulge out with fright. He would hear her short catch in her breathing, but he would never feel the immediate dry throat that would enter her from somewhere in the selfish lobe of her mind.

She could tell he neared full fledged sleep as his breathing had become heavier, so she yelled out, "Hatch McCreedy, you talk to me right now."

351

Being shaken by her now, he awakened and realized she still persisted and he remembered, so he said, "Someone asked me if I knew when Gretchen would give birth to her baby."

"Yes!" roared a demon from somewhere deep in the bowels of the earth. "She believes her daughter is just like a saloon girl."

"Sterling, let's sing some songs okay? Let's begin with that new one that Dwight is pushing everywhere he goes." And with that Sterling whinnied and Alexander Rich began to sing,
"What a friend we have in Jesus ..."

From the recesses of a dirty smelly lair came, "He's not a big enough friend," laughed katepa.

"What do these demons not remember about Christ's victory on the cross," wondered Hael. "The Spirit is moving, Jeffersonville will never be the same." Then with a slight smile, Hael stood alert, being at attention on his post as the guardian angel for Alexander Rich.

43

First Century

"Epaphras, first tell me about Thales grandmother.".

"Agathon, thank you for understanding about the other night. When the runner came to tell me about Thales leaving town and why, I felt like I needed to be there. Even still, I didn't arrive until after she had passed away. It soon became a time of mourning and praising God. As she passed Thales told me, behind tears of course, that his grandmother saw his mother standing at the side of Jesus."

"So she saw Jesus, Epaphras? Like Steven did, when Paul watched him being stoned?"[1]

"It appears so my friend."

"Much is happening Epaphras," said a thoughtful Agathon. "We must be ready and completely prepared when Jesus returns for us. With the persecution from the Jews and from the Romans continuing to escalate, His return cannot be too far off. We must be prepared, fully matured in everything that God wills."[2]

---

[1] Acts 7:56
[2] Colossians 4:12b

"I couldn't agree with you more Agathon, and that is why I am here. We want all of our brothers and sisters to be mature in every way, right?" Being a rhetorical question, Epaphras continued. "When I pray to God for the flock that is exactly what I pray Agathon, and that is why I am here."

"I know you pray that way for us, my friend," responded Agathon gaily. "I hear the way you pray for us."

"My friend, you know that I am grooming Thales to take over here in Colossae, and he will need all of you to carry much …"

Unknown to either man Hagne stood in a side room where the two men's conversation had just drifted. She got ready to leave so that the men could have some privacy when she heard Epaphras say, "It is because of this that I have come to you …" And in an instant the pride-laden thought that ran through her selfish, prideful brain, "Of course you come to my husband Epaphras, you need him."

And her pride that had immediately caused her heart[1] to climb the tallest mountain vaporized by what she heard next. "Agathon, Hagne's praying can't continue the way it is. It's out of line and out of order lately …"

Shocked and hurt, Hagne nearly choked. But resolving herself to now hear every word, she listened more intently.

"What has happened my friend? You and I have always understood her Christian maturity to be a struggle …"

"What?" Hagne no longer simply shocked, she got angry and wanted to take it out on someone.

"… This is difficult for me to say old friend, but your wife's public praying has to stop, and I need you to handle it, or else I will need to, Agathon. And I will have to do it before I leave, because there is too much risk of this becoming a problem if I let

---

[1] Jeremiah 17:9

Thales handle it. He doesn't have the maturity yet, and Hagne is often out of order lately."

If Hagne thought that her husband would stick up for her and throw Epaphras out of their house, she would be in for a rude awakening.

Wringing his hands in nervousness, Agathon responded with, "I know Epaphras, I have noticed it ever since I got elevated to the senior deacon position ..."

Eyes wide open, barely able to contain herself she heard her husband continue.

"... I think that she has let her pride get out of control Epaphras. I will gently speak to her." Pausing for a moment he added. "I don't know how though. A couple of the other brothers and I have talked about it. I will ask them to pray for me before I talk to her."

"Other brothers," she thought so loudly that she became afraid that Agathon and Epaphras would hear her. "Why is my husband too scared to talk to me? And why should he ... No! Why indeed, he has betrayed me. How could he talk about me to anyone?"

"Epaphras," Agathon asked, "You said that there were two things, what is the second?"

"Well, it appears that Thales is in love, and he is in love with Mary, the flower merchant's daughter."

"But is she a Christian?"

"Yes, Agathon. She is saved, her and her mother both are. Apparently they have been keeping it from Benjamin."

"I'd hate to be in their home when he finds out."

"And that's why I wanted you aware of this. Anat is going to be discipling Mary, the daughter. Can you stay abreast of Anat's efforts? Just keep them moving forward, okay? Benjamin has gone back to Jerusalem for a while, and I want Mary to know why she believes what she believes when he returns. She has got to be able to give a reasoned answer, or answers."

"Assuming Benjamin is willing to listen to reason," finished Agathon.

Whispering into Hagne's ear, a demon said, "It isn't right that this be kept from the father, is it Hagne? Somebody ought to tell him, shouldn't someone?"

With that encouragement, a plan hatched in Hagne's head. "Hmm," she thought, "I wonder how difficult it would be to reach Benjamin, the flower merchant, in Jerusalem."

44

Current Era

Ready to leave their room Dale went back to the bed and kissed Margie gently on her forehead and made his way to the living room. He opened up his Bible to Hebrews and Dale began to read again what the Word said about angels. He had just read in Hebrews 1:6, where the passage says of Jesus, "Let all the angels worship Him."

And just then Hael began to materialize, but not just Hael, another angel also seemed to be with him, and they were deep in conversation. It seemed that they did not even notice that Dale sat there and just then, Hael nodded his head to the other angel and in an instant Tephillah disappeared.

"A friend?" Dale inquired, feeling a little bit of confidence in this unique, to say the least, relationship. He added, "You guys were deep in conversation, did someone just die?"

Hael stared at Dale, wondering what he should tell him and wondering only for an instant, when he said, "That is a fellow guardian angel. He is preparing me for an impending, um, job that I get to participate in with him."

"Well forgive me for saying this," Dale felt a bit cocky now. "But I didn't see a name tag, and, well, you guys do look alike. Does it ever get confusing?"

Giving it right back to Dale, Hael said, "for your information mister, to our eyes we do not look alike. So why am I here? Oh yes, to let you see into the lives of a couple of men of prayer … although I wonder if this isn't a good night after all, Mr. Sarcasm." And seeing the pained look in Dale's eyes he stopped.

After a few moments Dale said, "I don't know what got into me back there. I am honored that you are taking the time to give me insights into your world."

"Why don't you give me a rundown on what is happening in your life Dale, okay? I know that I already know it, but it is helpful for you humans to 'get it off your chest,' which is what I hear you saying you need to do."

"Well," Dale started, "My new good friend Dean has been in and out of the hospital for the last six weeks and he just got readmitted two days ago. My wife is mentoring a very liberal professor from the university here who is letting one of my athletes fail to graduate, and you know I think that's good enough for now." He said this, raising his voice. The longer he spoke, he realized he got angrier and angrier.

Hael just sat there, watching Dale process and think. After a couple of minutes, Dale said, "Thanks Hael, I didn't realize that I had been so angry about all of this stuff."

"I know Dale, I understand … as best I can," and they both laughed.

"But Dale, is there something else that is bothering you? Is there something that you keep underneath the surface and it rarely comes up?"

Dale started to fidget, and then that silence returned. He looked down at his hands and a lump started to form in his throat.

"Hael," Dale stopped and had to wipe a tear away. He tried to start again, but couldn't get any words out. Looking up at Hael, Dale pursed his trembling lips, and then lifted a finger as if to say, "Give me just a moment."

Hael, every bit the patient gentleman, knew that Dale realized he would wait for him.

And so in silence they waited, but far from Dale regaining his composure, his shoulders started to raise and then lower. And then he started to convulse in silent sobs.

Hael reached over and put his massive hand on Dale's shoulder. After a few more minutes Dale lifted his head and tried to speak, but again his words were drowned out by sobs.

Finally, Dale said, "Many years ago Hael, Margie and I made a very big mistake, and the way we handled it, well, it's just as bad, or worse than the mistake itself. Many years ago, Margie had an abortion." And the floodgates of tears came again to track coach Dr. Dale Riley.

Waiting for Dale with his hand on his shoulder, Hael started to hum or something. It wouldn't just be simple humming, it seemed like an orchestra of notes coming together and being "hummed" out of Hael's mouth. Dale noticed how soothing it became to him and soon he looked up at Hael and tried to speak again.

"Hael, what can you tell me about my child? Is he, or she, angry with us?" And Dale's lower lip started to tremble again.

Hael slipped his hand from Dale's shoulder to underneath his chin and gently lifted his friend's head to look into his eyes. Hael leaned down so that they could be on the same level and he said, "Dale, there is a lot that I cannot tell you, but I think that it is safe to say that when you cross over Jordan and see Jesus standing there, beckoning you into heaven, there will be another person, tall and good looking, that you will know immediately, and I can tell you, he will be very proud of you my friend."

With that there were more sobs from Dale and more silence from these two good friends. And then Hael continued, "let me tell you about a couple of men, men who faced very serious issues. The problems are completely different Dale, but the handling of them and the expectation upon God is exactly the same."

Continuing, Hael said, "Let me tell you about Thales. You know that He's the nephew of Epaphras, and he fell in love with the daughter of an obnoxious orthodox Jew, who is Caiaphas's son."

"What?" Dale nearly came out of his chair, clearly getting his composure back. His attention remained on Hael now.

"Yes," continued Hael, "can you imagine being on friendly terms with that in-law?"

"Whoa, did his prayer life all of a sudden surge Hael?

"Actually Dale, come to think of it, no. He already had a strong prayer life, so the problems that were getting ready to occur in his life that he has no clue about were not going to affect him nearly as much as they would have otherwise.

"It is much like Dean. You encouraged him to be a man of prayer, Dale, and you saw the way he has handled folks that come to visit him."

"Yes," Dale laughed, thoughtfully, "He is completely, no, he is only interested in praying for people that visit him. They come in to encourage Dean, and they leave encouraged."

Dale observed Hael's attention being diverted to something else, and then he said, "Dale, I am getting ready to be called, so let me tell you one thing quickly about your great-great-grandfather."

Dale came to attention, and moved to the edge of the sofa.

"You know that he fell in love late in his life. Well, their courtship is not anything to wish upon your friends, or even your enemy. It seems that the townsfolk thought he took advantage of the girl and then," Hael, distracted again continued, "And then there were accusations of rape."

"Whoa, whoa, whoa, do I really want to hear this, Hael?"

"The accusations were not true, Dale." The distraction returned and this time kept Hael's attention for a bit longer. "The point, Dale, is how your great-great-grandfather Rich handled it, okay?"

"And how did he handle it Hael?"

"He and his closest friends were pray-ers, Dale. How do you think?" Hael had another distraction and moved to stand up. "How do you think they handled it?"

And without waiting for an answer Hael stood up, and then the look-a-like angel appeared, and Hael said, "I need to go, Dale. I'm sorry. We will continue this as soon as I can."

Dale, both dumbfounded and more than a little angry, actually a lot angry. He knew that he could do nothing about it. Hael had started an incredibly important insight into his great-great-grandfather and couldn't finish it? "The reason for his departure had better be important," thought Dale, and then speaking to the empty place where Hael had just been he said, "This isn't fair, Hael."

As the other angel whispered into Hael's ear, Dale thought he heard him say, " Hael, it's time to be Dean's escort."

45

Epilogue

Hael never got bored escorting a saint to heaven. There is something about bringing a child of the King to the throne of Almighty God and watching the awe on the face of the one he just escorted. Actually, that isn't correct. The angels didn't merely escort a Christ follower to heaven, they carried him.[1]

And then Hael thought of his current charge, Dr. Dale Riley, and the unique understanding that Dale would have with other Christians in the past, because the Almighty had given Hael the great and awesome project of reaching out to and then contacting Dale personally.

"Would Dale ever know the full story of Thales and his challenges with Caiaphas's son Benjamin, or how he resolved the situation as it related to his growing love for Caiaphas's granddaughter Mary?" As Hael thought about poor Thales he remembered the painful spiritual warfare that Thales had to endure. "Lord," Hael continued to think out loud, "Paul told these humans that their struggle isn't with flesh and blood,[2]

---

[1] Luke 16:22
[2] Ephesians 6:12

which of course I understand and completely believe, but poor Thales."

"What about Alexander Rich?" Hael then wondered, "Would Dale be able to know of the many adventures, and the incredible spiritual warfare Gretchen and Pastor Rich worked through even though they were separated by half the state of Georgia?" Hale paused and then smiled large thinking of the mill owners, Bubba and Josephine. He always laughed when he thought of them. They were always a great deal of fun. And they were incredible supporters for Brother Rich during this difficult period of time."

"Oh, Lord," Hael then thought, "When will Professor Gonzalez be converted, and how will she deal with her atheist and agnostic friends? And Lord, what of the pastor's prayer group that You are placing on Dale's heart. What will happen there? Thank you for the opportunity to guard Dale.[1] I look forward to doing Your bidding[2] with him as his ministering angel.[3] Thank You, Lord!"

While Hael would never admit this, there could be one more thing he privately thought about, "I wonder if I will be able to sit in Dale's car with the top down, my wings spread out and Dale driving? Ahhh, one can only hope."

---

[1] Psalm 91:11
[2] Psalm 103:20
[3] Hebrews 1:14

Book Two

There is much Spiritual Warfare that our prayer heroes will need to deal with, and therefore numerous facets of Spiritual Warfare will be dealt with in book two. As with this book, our desire is that through the fun of a novel you have learned prayer. During book two you will learn what Spiritual Warfare is, what it is not, and enjoy the same fun read.

Expect it out by Christmas 2016.

The Pray-ers

Novel 2

Spiritual
Warfare

WESLEY FAMILY PRAYERS BOOK

You will note that the nineteenth-century era and the modern-day era use a unique Bible study. The Bible study book is real, and the author wrote its questions. The author's copy of the original book of prayers dates back to 1790, and the characters in the novel are actually using it, along with the questions. It will be available through CTM Publishing Inc. at www.ThePray-ers.com in 2016.

REFERENCES

I want to bring up another issue regarding the Bible references. In other works, when verses are broken down, they are at best broken down into a or b, meaning the first half of the verse or the second half of the verse. In this book you will find that I use a, b, m, and e, with the following definitions.

a	Beginning of verse or first half of verse
b	Second half of verse
m	Middle of verse
e	End of verse

THE THREE ERAS

This book takes place using three different eras in church history. There will be a story from the first century. My thought here started with "Who better to learn prayer from than Epaphras?" so I took license to write about Epaphras, through the eyes of his nephew, a made-up character named Thales.

The second era included in this book is one of an itinerant preacher. One of my great joys is to read old forgotten books about these itinerant preachers. Their love for truth and for teaching their people is inspiring to me.

Finally, the current era needed a character to round out the book. He has been fascinating to write about. I hope you enjoy him too.

Admittedly, the book has become autobiographical to some extent—not completely of course, but in some areas of many of the characters—but I won't tell you where.

Lastly, regarding the time frames, it became apparent that to read the book and enjoy its variety, a little help might be needed to maintain some understanding of the lengths of time each story is taking, and so here goes:

ERA	TIME FRAME
First Century	Takes place over a period of 3 months
Nineteenth Century	Takes place over a period of 3 days
Current Era	Takes place over a period of 4 months

P.S.: Each chapter is titled in the era it depicts. Where more than one era is referred to in a chapter, the titles are listed in the order that the eras are revealed.

CHARACTERS
(Alpha order, according to era)

NAME	DESCRIPTION (Angels and demons)
djaod	(Pronounced jay-odd) He is a senior demon over joln and haodtie.
haodtie	(Pronounced hode-tie or HĀ-Tee) This is katepa's overlord when katepa is in Colossae.

NAME	DESCRIPTION
	(Angels and demons … cont.)
Hael	(Pronounced HAY-EL) A guardian angel assigned to Dr. Dale with special instructions to make contact with the mortal. He also guarded our first-century prayer hero and our nineteenth-century prayer hero.
joln	(Pronounced joe-Ln) This demon is katepa's overlord in The New World and has become an overlord by politics.
Katepa	(Pronounced kuh-teepa) This demon is assigned to our three heroes, in each era where they are placed. You will find him at odds with his demon overlord joln.
Tephillah	(Pronounced tef-ee-luh) Another guardian angel.

NAME	DESCRIPTION
	(First Century Era)
Aikaterine	(Pronounced ī-kat-er-een) Mary's mother, wife of Benjamin Kuppai, and a loving sweet woman.
Agathon	(Pronounced A, as in apple, A-guh-thon) Senior deacon in the Colossae church. A solid, godly man, whose wife is Hagne.
Anat	(Pronounced An-at) Wool Merchant in Colossae who has a house church in her home.

NAME	DESCRIPTION
	(First Century Era … cont.)
Basileios	(Pronounced Bass-ill-Ēos) Thales's uncle, married to Euanthe's sister and raised Thales as his son.
Benjamin Kuppai	(Pronounced coo-pī) Owner of the flower store, father of Mary, and the youngest son of Caiaphas from the New Testament.
Epaphras	(Pronounced Ee-pafras) Thales's mentor and uncle is also the current leader of the Colossae church.
Euanthe	(Pronounced U-aŃ-thee) Thales's mother, who died giving birth to Thales. To tell you more about her would give away too much.
Hagne	(Pronounced Hag-nee). Prideful wife of the godly deacon Agathon.
Mary	Daughter of Benjamin Kuppai, the flower merchant in Colossae.
Myrrine	(Pronounced Meer-In) Thales's aunt, who raised him as her son.
Thales	(Pronounced Thī-Lees) The first-century hero in his mid-twenties and with the great opportunity to learn prayer from none other than Epaphras[1], whom even Paul applauds. Thales is also the grandson of that great woman of faith, the Syrophoenician woman[2].

---

[1] Colossians 1:7; 4:12
[2] Matthew 15:21-28; Mark 7:24-30

NAME	DESCRIPTION (19ᵗʰ Century Era)
Alexander Rich	Nineteenth-century hero in his early fifties and an itinerant preacher in central Georgia, who grew up in Massachusetts with D. L. Moody[1], making them childhood friends.
Billie Carter	Geraldine McCreedy's friend whose husband is the church senior deacon.
Bubba	Deacon at the Jeffersonville church and solidly devoted to righteousness.
Carrolton Faith	The Jeffersonville town drunk (also called Carrol) whose parents were God-fearing folks when they were alive.
Ellie Squire	Geraldine McCreedy's friend and the church organist.
Hubert Jackson	The African-American brother and soon-to-be pastor in Dry Branch that Alexander Rich is mentoring. They are also prayer partners.
Josephine	Wife to Bubba and a solid Christian woman. The couple own the Mill in Jeffersonville
McCreedy Family	A nineteenth-century family that owns the mercantile store in Jeffersonville. Hatch and Geraldine are the father and mother. Their daughter is Gretchen, a thirty-one-year-old widow.

---

[1] Moody grew up in Northfield, Massachusetts, being born in 1837

370